in the Pursuit of Eden

a novel
by
Stephanie Fowers

Hopeless Romantics

TWISTED TALES SERIES (Young Adult Fantasy)
With a Kiss
At Midnight
As the Sun sets

HOPELESS ROMANTICS BOOKS (Sweet Romance)
Jane and Austen
Out of the Mouth of Babes
In the Pursuit of Eden

ROMANTIC COMEDIES (LatterDaySaint/Inspirational)
Prank wars
Meet Your Match
Rules of Engagement

FILMS
8Stories

in the Pursuit of Eden

a novel
by
Stephanie Fowers

In the Pursuit of Eden
Stephanie Fowers
©2019 Stephanie Fowers

Published by Triad Media and Entertainment

Published by Triad Media and Entertainment, Salt Lake City, UT
Triad.film.productions@gmail.com

1. Fiction. 2. Romance. 3. Suspense. 4. Inspirational.
ISBN: 9781090491138

LINE EDITOR: Shannon Cooley

CONTENT EDITOR: Lucinda Lahn

COVER DESIGNER: Jacqueline Fowers
AUTHOR BIO PHOTOGRAPHER: Ashley Elliott

Dedication

Dedicated to my hiking buddies: Jacqueline, Tanya, Becky, Carily, Cindy, who encouraged me to write a "hiking" book. Now they know where my mind goes while on our adventures!

Chapter one

vy, meet me at Karaoke Jams tonight at 7. Bring the journal."

I reread the message my twin brother Brekker had left on my phone. He'd left me lots of kissy face emojis— as if that would make me feel better about it. It didn't. Sighing, I slid into the front seat of my rusty orange Ford Escort, lifting the red skirts of my party dress to get inside, my high heels scraping against the pavement. I threw the journal on the side seat next to my purse.

My brother didn't have to tell me that he meant Eden's journal. It was the unspoken rule in the Payne family that we stay away from it because of that curse. We came from a family of treasure hunters… failed ones. Our father had left his pregnant wife behind in '89 and lost his life on a disastrous expedition before Brekker and I had been born. We'd promised our mom we'd never go after that treasure. I'd thought Brek meant it. Until recently. What was his problem? Brek's request had reduced my stomach into a pit of nervousness.

I started my car and the engine light went on. That wasn't too unusual. There was always something wrong with it. I was glad it was a cool summer night because then I could use my air conditioner without overheating my car and stalling it. Always a plus, since none of the windows on the driver's side rolled down either.

The restaurant was down the steep street, and my brakes squealed in protest as I fought through the San Francisco traffic. It came to a standstill after two blocks, and I looked over at my phone again while my best friend Caitlyn sent me a slew of messages: *"Ivy? Did you get Russell to come? Send him a picture of your dress! That'll do it!"*

I smirked at that.

I'd done everything I could to get my boyfriend to come to Karaoke Jams that night, but lately Russell had gotten bored of "us." He never said it, but I could tell. Now that I was in a traffic jam, I texted him again. "Russ! You'll never guess where I'm at right now!"

I shot that off and waited for a reply that I didn't get. The problem was that we saw each other all day long at work and so I had to do what I could to bring more mystery into our relationship. Of course, that wasn't why I hadn't told him about my poor background or that I was drowning in debt. No, being interesting meant buying dresses I couldn't afford and sending pics of how much fun I was having in them.

Lifting my phone, I fluffed my blonde hair, put on a canned smile, and took a picture of myself from above, and then another… and then another… and then another until I found one that didn't make my nose look too big or my eyes too droopy. And then I uploaded it to Instagram with a perky message, "Going out to Karaoke Jams tonight! Going to party, party, party!"

Maybe that would get Russell to come.

If I could get there myself. Looking to the side at the rough neighborhoods, I peered into the alleys, seeing them disappear behind dilapidated buildings. I'd grown up in that area. Spying an opening on the street, I took the shortcut, glad of the protection of steel around me as my car crawled through alleyways. Passing the broken-down tenements brought back bad memories. While growing up, we'd spent our nights and some of our days at our grandparents' while our mom worked swing shifts at the local bar. We'd watched our father's relatives lean over maps of hidden treasures and waste away in a cloud of cigarette smoke and botched dreams. Our grandfather had even dragged us on a few failed road trips. That had pretty much deterred me from the practice, but Brekker was different; it had only encouraged him. It was in his blood.

And what was in mine? Mine was to leave all of this far behind. I wanted success, love, to be respectable… and I wanted my car to stop smoking. What was wrong with it? The whole front of it shuddered, shaking my hands almost off the steering wheel. There was a loud popping sound and then it started hissing and—I gulped—slowing down. There was nothing I could do. I was now officially broken down in a dark alley in the absolutely worst part of town. One I knew too well.

My hands tightened on the steering wheel. "Nooooo!" I wailed. "Not today! Not here!" It was Eden's curse! I sprang from my dying car, hitching down my red skirt as I shoved open the hood, the whole thing smoking in my face so I couldn't see a thing. I couldn't afford something like this!

"Ivy, is it?" a rough voice called from behind me. My shoulders hunched and I turned, seeing a couple of men drift out from the side building. It was just my luck to break down in front of the local pub where mom had worked back in the day. It was where every lowlife in the city came through.

"Look at you! I would've known you from anywhere." Swiveling, I looked into the leering eyes of a tall, wide-shouldered older man. I knew him and wished I didn't. "You've grown," he said with an appreciative whistle. "You're as pretty as your mama."

I tried to ignore that and put on a casual air, even though I was scared stiff. "Thanks Gary—I think my car might be dying."

He snorted. "Nah, it's dead. You're in luck."

"I'm in luck?"

"Big Engines Repair is just down the block… if you can get it there."

I gestured ineffectually at the smoking car and I got dozens of offers for rides from the men milling around staring down at me, but no offers to help push the Ford down the street. "C'mon," Gary said. "Paul will come take a look at it."

I scraped my purse from the seat, throwing Eden's journal into it, while clutching at my cell phone. I shot off a few texts to my best friend. *"Caitlyn, if I die, Gary killed me. Also, can you come get me at Big*

Engine Repairs?"

I didn't even attempt to contact Russ. Adjusting my purse over my shoulder, I declined all offers of rides. "I can walk!" I reassured them. Gary's eyes trailed down my dress to my heels and I pretended not to notice while I sped away to the mechanics. One moment of bad luck— okay, *a lot* of moments of bad luck—and my past came to greet me like the nasty uncle of an old friend. It felt especially eerie since I was living far above my means and by all rights belonged here. A few catcalls were aimed my direction and I nodded, acting like it was completely normal to travel down this alley dressed up for a night on the town.

Gary fell into step beside me. "You know, it's not safe in this neighborhood."

"Oh really?" I put on my brightest smile and kept going.

"You moving back here?"

I shook my head. Very vigorously. I was suspicious that Gary thought I belonged here. I felt like if I didn't leave soon, I could very well prove him right—but my mom and I had worked too hard to get me through college to see that happen. If only I'd studied something that made more money.

The bright neon sign for Big Engine Repairs was in sight, and I breathed a sigh of relief. The frames of the doors were slathered in greasy fingerprints. As I neared, I thanked Gary for his help, though the man had no intention of abandoning his fun. Instead, he pulled out a cigarette to smoke outside while I went into the building. He shouldn't have bothered. It was like walking into an ashtray. The memories of heavy smoking from my father's relatives came to me like the stink of this building clinging to my dress. Apparently nobody had heard of health inspection codes, but that was how they did things here.

The mechanic wasn't at the front and I had to root him out from the back, calling the name that Gary had given me. "Paul?"

As soon as he rolled out from under a car and stared at me under heavy, curling brows, I knew who he was, too. He was a regular at the pub, and he was one of my mother's many admirers. I hoped he didn't remember me. "You here to pick up a car?" he asked.

"No, drop one off… hopefully." And never come back to claim it if things turned for the worse. "It broke down in front of the pub."

He stood, looking thin as a rod with a mat of fuzzy gray hair. His cigarette smoked in a nearby ashtray, and he set it in his mouth like an accessory.

"I was hoping that you could take a look at it," I said, feeling awkward.

Scratching his neck, he stared at me like I'd grown two heads until Gary found us back there. He laughed, his manner still off when he watched me too long. "You remember Laura's girl," he said. "Ivy? She's come to grace us with her presence."

"You work at the pub?" Paul asked hopefully.

I denied it vehemently and he sighed and suddenly understood that I broke down when Gary repeated everything I'd said. Paul stuck his hand out to me. I stared at it. "The keys," he said. "You can sit in the lobby over there."

His lobby was near the front glass windows. Paul and Gary took off, leaving me the run of the place, and so I sat down gingerly on one of the plastic chairs. A hairline crack in the plastic widened under me and tried to catch at my dress. I squirmed to find a more comfortable position. On a side table, I saw magazines that were more than twenty years old. Kevin Costner was up for an award. Meryl Streep still looked like Meryl Streep.

To calm myself down, I played with the charm bracelet that my twin brother had given me. Brek had laden it with little trinkets that he had collected from all the exotic locations he'd explored. It made me feel like I always had a piece of him whenever we were apart, which was often. I'd wondered what he'd bring now that he was safely back from his deep lake explorations at Shipwreck Alley in Lake Huron.

My life was so drab compared to his. Sometimes social media was the only thing that made me feel like I was doing something with myself. And I wasn't. Not at all, though I half suspected Brekker was doing the same thing with his adrenaline rushed expeditions. We were twenty-nine, hovering on the edge of thirty and we had nothing to show for it.

Almost nothing.

I worked at a dead end job at the Gasket Sweat Shop. What I'd thought was a cute name had turned horrifyingly real during the seven years that I'd worked there. My salary position somehow translated to seventy to eighty hours, and I didn't have the title or get paid for the job that I did. I'd thought things couldn't get any worse, but that was before the big merger a month ago. Now I had to deal with *Micromanager Mike*. The nickname I'd given him was horribly fitting.

I felt cursed. It was Eden's curse actually. Somehow our bad luck had turned into the family joke. Some people called it Murphy's Law, or that the worst thing that could happen, would, but we said, "Oh, it's Eden's curse." I knew it was crazy, but I secretly believed there was some truth to it, though it had just taken a little longer for it to catch up to me.

The crowded buildings snuffed out what light was left of the summer evening, and my mind went back to the journal that Brek had asked me to bring. I slid it from my purse. The last time I had read it was in high school back when I was still a dreamer. I read the first entry and was immediately drawn in, almost smiling. Eden certainly had a flair for the dramatic:

Eden's Journal: January 5th, 1855 — Flint Saloon, San Francisco

Will Pratt was a mean old skunk with a quick hand and quick eyes. He held his cards tight like they was going to run off. And they might could. Times was hard and we was fixin to be smarter than the devil and twice as sly if we was going to pull a fast one over Old Pratt. I hitched up my skirt and leaned real close at the poker table, watching as Lucius took a seat on the other side of us.

I loved the very sight of that gambler, from his lantern jaw to his heavy, black brows. Lucius Payne was uncommon handsome, a mountain of a man from the

6

French borders—as calm as they came and clever to boot. Whilst other men worked out their days to chisel their gold out of them cold mountains, he slept the day away in a warm bed and won the gold off them silly prospectors at the tables at night.

To the other men in this town, I was worth only a flake of gold for an evening, but I saw the way Lucius looked at me from time to time, like I was something more. A voice inside me always knowed he didn't see me as a ruined woman. He rarely raised a hand to me, and when we was away from the other girls, he stroked my hair and called it gold. He told me, "Eden—you're my clever and good girl!" Never you mind he told me I warn't the kind for marrying. I reckoned he loved me.

I worked myself into a sweat finding ways to prove my love back to Lucius, maybe so'd he know I was worth marrying. He fretted about them prospectors running out of gold in them mountains. Word was they'd all shove off to the frontier and then where would we be? That was how things were when Will Pratt swaggered into the Flint Saloon that morning, flashing his gold piece and weaving some yarn how he swiped the coin from Shoshones up in bear country.

"Centuries ago in a rougher time," said he, "some old Spanish monk hid up a treasure of gold in them Deseret mountains where them Mormons live on that yonder side. I tell ya, there be bags of gold stashed away in Shoshone country, just waiting for someone to stumble on it all and drag it away."

Ain't none of us believed any word of his tales until I seen him take out that gold piece! It had a cross carved on the outside and mighty strange patterns on the other. He claimed it was the key to that there treasure. Grabbing up my skirts, I tore up them saloon stairs to tell Lucius what I'd seen. He hustled Martha out of his room—who warn't near as smart as me—and as soon as he got the whole of my tale, he throwed on his shirt.

We set on a scheme to cheat Pratt out of his gold. I'd eye his cards like I did with them other prospectors and Lucius would keep a lookout for my sign like he always done and we'd take all the winnings. But Pratt was a tricky old coot. He wouldn't let me anear the poker table and kept refusing my attentions, which was in no way common. He musta suspicioned us and so I tucked next to Lucius and fed him cards on the sly. The old prospector gabbed on about that gold coin and how the Shoshones said he shoulda stuck around them Deseret Mountains until spring because that was the only time the treasure was to be found. Once you laid for it, you

7

wouldn't have long to git at it. And no man must do it on their own—there must be a helpmeet or other for it ain't possible otherwise. He talked all sorts of nonsense of ghosts and he polished up with tales of curses and lake serpents, and we let him do it since it made for all manner of distractions.

Lucius won hand after hand until by and by, Pratt had nothing but that gold coin left. The old prospector ran his thumb down the edge of it before he throwed it on the table. He said if the coin won him the game, it was good luck, but if he losed it then it must be bad luck and he'd want no part in it. And should we win it, we'd best beware ourselves. That kind of talk put the fear of God in me, but Lucius didn't let it bother him any. Cool as a cucumber, he laid down his winning hand. Pratt nodded like he knew whatever come was his due and accepted the fates until Lucius stood and—if it warn't the strangest thing—he tripped... and just like that, Lucius's extra cards went falling from his sleeve.

He was never one to git catched like that, and I was in a sweat when I judged the coin was bad luck after all! I was most ready to give up our winnings right then, especially that cursed coin, but Lucius was pulling at his gun the same time old Pratt was. I raised a howl and feared for Lucius' life since I was certain sure that coin meant the death of us all, but Pratt had been the first to lug that coin straight from the mountains before we ever laid a hand on it so when the guns went off and the smoke cleared, he was the fool falling to the wooden boards of the saloon, flat as a washboard.

The law wouldn't take kindly to our miserable business, so I done put up a powerful fuss, hollering that Pratt was sore at losing, but some of the girls screamed out all hot that Lucius was a cheat. We knowed we was in for it. Lucius tugged at my arm and swiped up the gold coin too. I wanted no part in it, but it didn't matter because the bad luck was on us now. We cleared out of town at a ripping rate, running off with horses on our way out. Course, it was one thing killing a man, but stealing a horse would git us strung up. The moment I pinched the reins, I knowed we was never coming back. That treasure was a'calling us and it had a hold of us good."

I pushed Eden's journal to the side of my lap and sighed. Poor Eden. Poor, stupid Eden. All she had found was trouble with that

in the *Pursuit* of Eden

treasure. The fact that her journal ended up in the hands of the descendants of my great, great, great, *great* Grandpa Lucius and not hers proved it. But she got her revenge on us all, I supposed, with that curse. Here I was in a bright red clubbing dress, leaning back in the hard chair at Big Engines Repair Shop at six o'clock at night, cooling my heels—or rather swinging my heels in my impatience—in the worst side of town while I waited for the final diagnosis of my car. It was Eden's curse.

The buzz of my phone showed I had gotten a text from Caitlyn. *"I'm coming, my friend! If Gary killed you, I will avenge you!"*

I smiled. Caitlyn had taken no convincing. Plus, it gave her a good excuse to see Brekker at Karaoke Jams that night. I knew that she liked my brother, though she'd never admit it to me.

The hefty metal door at the front of the building squeaked open on its hinges and Paul stalked to the front desk. I stood up and hurried over to where he wiped his greasy fingers on the invoices. "What's the problem with it?" I asked.

He shrugged. "The engine fell out. It fell out!" He added a few swears in there. "How did that happen? Supposing we can fix this thing, it'll cost you about $2,000."

I was already shaking my head. There was no way I could handle that kind of expense, even if I charged it. "Just tow it. Just tow it!" I tried to imagine my life without a car—and it wasn't too hard since I'd imagined it plenty of times since nothing worked in it. "Wait," I said, "can I get some money out of it?"

He gave me a disbelieving look and ground his cigarette butt into the cement floor. "Towing costs you, little girl."

I reddened, but I knew how these businesses worked downtown. "How about I give it to you for parts and we'll call it good."

"Is there anything that works in it?"

Was that a trick question? "The scrap metal has to be worth something—the seats maybe. C'mon."

He sighed and tapped his dirty counter before fixing me with a considering look. "How's your mom?"

I tried not to gag. So he wanted to work that angle, did he? Mom was a lot nicer to her fans than I was. "She's alive," I said. And still living in that cramped apartment where we'd grown up, but I made up a crazy backstory so he wouldn't try to hunt her down. "She met some Swedish guy and they're skiing the Alpine slopes. She's so busy she can't even make time to pick up the phone."

I hoped that convinced him not to pursue her, until he transferred his interest to me instead. "That's a pretty dress you got there—you got some company tonight?"

"I'm just going to pay," I said. "How much does it cost to tow a car to the junkyard?"

"Well, you got the towing fee, plus my fee. That'll come to about $300."

I didn't want to argue with him about it. This place gave me the heebie jeebies, like it could magically suck me into it again, so I pulled out my Visa card. "I think there's a little bit on this one."

He tried it with no luck. "Nope."

I gave him a MasterCard. "How about that one?"

"Nope."

"Okay." By now I knew the Discover card wouldn't have anything on it. I could try my Bath and Body Works card, but that would be ridiculous.

"You know what," he said. "Just forget it. I'll sell it for parts." I relaxed in relief while he muttered, "I'll search your seats for change." I'd already done that, but I nodded and would've been super embarrassed if I'd been anyone else, but I was used to this.

Before I could get too depressed by the thought, Caitlyn drove past the window outside, honking and catcalling from her Ford Mustang convertible. "Ivy!" she shouted.

I swiveled with relief. My best friend was a cute button of a girl with big brown eyes and big, curly red hair. We'd taken a lot of the same classes at San Francisco State, and after graduation we'd been

10

roommates for about six months before realizing we made better friends. Somehow we'd passed that first test of friendship and now we couldn't get enough of each other. I headed for the door like it was my sanctuary.

"Hey!" Paul shouted after me. "Being a pretty face won't always get you out of paying. Next time save your money instead of buying party dresses—unless you plan on putting them to good use!"

Now *that* embarrassed me. I felt the heat infuse my cheeks. "Oh, I plan on it," I said. If this night had taught me anything, it was that I was going to fight Eden's curse and make something of myself. But first, I'd talk some sense into my brother and sing a few killer karaoke tunes while I was at it. I escaped to my freedom outside.

Chapter two

The door of Caitlyn's silver convertible slid open like melted butter as she reached across the passenger side to shove the door open for me. "Get in!" she said. "Frankie's hungry!"

I smiled. Frankie was what she'd named her Mustang. I got in, and she squealed over my dress while I made a big deal over hers. It was tradition, even though hers likely cost about five times more than mine. Caitlyn came from a rich family in the bay area. And even if she occasionally forgot I didn't have as much money, she was never a snob about it. I didn't begrudge her good fortune, either. She wore a red and aqua green number that made her red hair look amazing.

"So?" she said with an insinuating look. "Your brother agreed to do karaoke? He isn't going to drop some bad news, is he?"

My hand tightened on my purse where I'd stuffed Eden's journal. I was sure he would, but why did he think he had to butter me up first? The journal belonged as much to him as it did to me. There was something more to this and I was afraid of what it was. I shrugged. "You haven't seen him karaoke."

She giggled under her breath, and I knew she was looking forward to it. After a few cars honked at us for stalling traffic, she waved brightly at them and joined their ranks, weaving around the streets and leaning on her horn with the best of them.

I watched the buildings speed by. They were built close together, and the further we traveled into the tourist traps, the prettier they became, painted in bright, stylish colors. The bay glistened in the distance under the setting sun, though the peace was ripped up by the traffic flowing through the city. The convertible top was down and the sea wind blew our hair all over the place, making mine bigger than before. I hadn't bothered to straighten all the curls out of it today. The humidity wouldn't allow for that. We were only a few blocks away from the waterfront on Pier 39, and it felt nice to be out of the grime of my old neighborhood. We reached the parking garage, and Caitlyn took the meter ticket without a flinch.

I felt a little guilty. "First hour is free," I said.

Biting down a smile, she nodded. "Thanks. I'll keep that in mind." She went straight to the third level and parked the closest she could to the elevator that would take us down to Karaoke Jams. We both got out. Now that we were standing, the difference of our heights was more pronounced. I was five foot nine, and a veritable Amazon compared to Caitlyn. She was tiny. Even with her four-inch heels, her head barely reached my shoulder.

Taking the elevator, she gabbed on about the massage she'd had that day. She still felt tense and she blamed it on her family's latest drama. They were fighting over where to spend their spring break—but definitely it would not be in Hawaii again!

"You need to come on vacation with me," Caitlyn started to say before she stopped herself and then, twisting her lips, decided to go with it. She wasn't always perfect at not inviting me to things that cost me money. "But you should. It's just not as fun without you."

"I don't have the vacation," I said hurriedly before she could offer to pay for it again. "And if I did, now wouldn't be a good time, not with Micromanager Mike trying to take over the office."

She made a face. "I hate that place!"

"I hate it more," I said with a wry smile. "But good news: I've applied for the purchasing position so hopefully I can start getting paid for what I've been doing all along."

"And you think Micromanager Mike will give the job to you?" she asked.

"Why wouldn't he? I'm already trained. This would save him money."

The doors to the elevator opened and we stepped out onto the pier. "Don't be so sure about that," she said. "Nothing at the Gasket Sweat Shop makes sense."

I should've taken that into consideration when I applied for a job with the name "sweat shop" in it, but they weren't that bad. And there were a few benefits I got there that I wouldn't get anywhere else—like my boyfriend Russell from accounting. I just had to figure out a way to get him here tonight.

Karaoke Jams was a cute, kitschy little restaurant tucked behind the wharf with a great view of the bay and the ships sailing past. It had a red roof and brown planked siding like it was an old fisherman's hut. Water lapped against the pier and barking sea lions fought for a spot on the wharf as we passed the huge bronze crab in the middle of the square and found our way inside. The wails of people singing loudly in a microphone carried through the restaurant. Brekker was waiting for us at a booth with a sour expression on his face. Despite his unusually dark mood, I let out a giddy shriek at seeing him. Caitlyn grinned broadly and covered her ears. I was gratified to see Brek's eyes light up with his smile.

He pushed away from the table and I ran into my twin's arms. We hugged like we had in the womb. Of course, Brekker was a lot bigger now. His arms were bulked with muscle. They wrapped around me like I was nothing. He lifted me off the ground and I screamed some more. It felt so nice to see him after everything that had happened. The people at the surrounding tables perked up with interest, some with annoyance. Our reunions were often like this. Our family often joked that I displayed my different moods through my screaming. Now that I was older, it was still partly true.

Caitlyn couldn't wait for her turn anymore and so she wriggled under our arms and hugged us both together. "Ah, my beautiful Gemini Twins are back together again!" she cried.

Probably not, since those were boys; maybe we were more Apollo and Artemis, but no matter. Useless facts we learned from our majors at school were only good for moments like these. She only meant that we were like Greek gods because we were blonde and taller than she was.

"You just keep getting more and more beautiful!" she shouted up at Brekker.

I cracked a smile. Caitlyn knew that would embarrass him, and it did. His face got red. He was one of those guys who liked to grow an ugly beard to cover up how attractive he was, though he was clean shaven tonight and looked a little leaner since the last I'd seen him. He had gotten plenty of sun in Michigan, and I could hardly wait to ask him all about it.

"Picture! Picture!" Caitlyn implored me. Old habits were hard to break and so I raised my phone to snap a selfie of all of us hugging— and sent it out to Instagram for good measure. Just like I had planned, not tagging my twin brother in it at all so that Russell would have no idea who he was and come running. *Totally genius.* I tried to think of an appropriate tagline that my favorite online dating guru would encourage me to say and I finally settled on, "Guess who I found at Karaoke Jams tonight?"

Caitlyn giggled as soon as she got it on her phone because she knew exactly what I was doing. "That'll get Russell over here," she said.

"Russell?" Brek asked.

I gave Caitlyn a warning look—she wasn't supposed to talk about my boyfriends in front of my brother. He never understood why they couldn't put me above everything else in their lives. Pretending an air of indifference, I shrugged at him. "Oh, just some guy I'm dating. He didn't want to come tonight. He's probably doing that guy thing you all do."

Brek's head tilted and he looked protective. "And what's that?"

I inwardly cursed Caitlyn's big mouth. "You know, he just wants alone time; he's retreating into his proverbial man cave so he can stand to be around me again. All guys do it."

"He doesn't want to spend time with you?"

He made it sound awful. In a way, it was, because I couldn't seem to keep Russell's interest unless I resorted to tricks, but what else was I supposed to do? Be alone? If I didn't try, I wouldn't find anybody.

Brekker looked disapproving, and I shifted uncomfortably, searching desperately for a way to get him in the hot seat instead. "Where's Angel?" I asked, putting my own challenge in my voice. Angel was his annoying, pretentious girlfriend. She was a Lara Croft wannabe who liked to show up other girls because she was supposedly tougher and sexier than all of us lower beings. I probably hated her as much as Brek hated my boyfriends, so maybe this was just a protective twin thing. I wasn't sure.

Instead of answering me, he sat down at our booth and indicated for us to sit with him. I did so gratefully, hoping that he had dropped the Russell topic, but the fact that he didn't want to discuss Angel set off alarms in my head. He usually liked to talk about his precious girlfriend, even if I grilled him about everything she did wrong. That only meant one thing—the two had broken up.

"Eden's curse is working overtime on the Payne family," I muttered. "She's made losers of us all." He glanced up distractedly and chuckled low, but I was dead serious.

A scuffle broke out on the karaoke stage as a few giggling girls fought over which song to choose until they agreed on singing something from Taylor Swift. Brekker waved over a server and ordered pizza, making clear that it was on him. Once again, I was glad that I didn't have to pay and felt a little ashamed. I really needed to be a better friend and sister and get my finances in order. Clearly, he didn't want to talk about Angel, and so he asked me about work. *Another forbidden subject.* I tensed, my eyes narrowing meaningfully at her. However, Caitlyn didn't get the memo and started to gossip about everything I had told her in confidence. "Her new boss is a total micromanager," she said.

I tried to make her stop talking with a swish across my throat, but Caitlyn wasn't catching on. She blabbed on about my miserable life while I sank under the table. "He made a list of everything he wants her to do in the office and one of them is reading his mind."

"What do you mean?" Brek asked.

"Well." She brightened. "If he looks at a file, he wants her to go fetch it. He shouldn't even tell her that he needs it. She should just know he wants it by his eyes."

"Are you kidding me?" My brother turned to me with an angry look.

"Don't worry," I said. "I applied for a different position. And I already know how to do it so…"

"Yeah, she's been doing it without the title or pay for a while now," Caitlyn tattled.

Brekker's eyes were going hard and I squirmed. "It's fine!" I said.

"And her new boss doesn't get technology either and so when he slips up, he throws her under the bus to upper management like she was the one who did something wrong, but he can't read an online calendar." Caitlyn giggled like it was a huge joke. I felt like kicking her under the table, but I knew she still wouldn't get it. "They keep changing what they have to do to qualify for their bonuses," she continued. "And guess what? HR put them all on diets so they could qualify for the worst insurance plan in the state."

Brek looked over at me. "I passed my physical the first time around!" I defended myself.

"Barely… her blood pressure was off… and they read her results wrong so they thought she had diabetes for a day." Caitlyn laughed loudly. "And they keep moving her around because everyone wants her desk. She just makes it look so good." She tsked. "I told her to quit. How long have you been at that pit of despair, anyway? Six years?"

"Seven," I muttered.

"Just quit and fall back on your savings," Caitlyn said. "I mean, it's not like you're one of those people who live paycheck to paycheck."

I flinched since I most certainly was one of those, but I wasn't about to volunteer that information to the table. Brekker met my eyes and I knew he was on to me, but he was the same way so he couldn't lecture me, either. He was good at what he did, but he never made money on his excavations. If he did, he only lost it in the next scheme. It didn't make sense since he was the talented one in the family. He had a knack for finding things that were lost. It had started out with that missing dog in the neighborhood when we were eight. Brekker conducted his own search and rescue and brought him back to the crying little girl. The finds got bigger over the years. He went from lost keys and coins under the couch to arrowheads in the mountains to rare rocks and bones and lost civilizations in Mexico. School didn't teach him that; it was in his blood. Yet after all my schooling, what did I do? I worked at a dead-end job and took pictures of things. He lived life and I recorded it. We'd been this way since high school. I was happy for him but annoyed at myself.

The server set the pizza in front of us with our own personal plates. Mine was a cute little setup with parsley on the side, much too cute for pizza, and I was so struck by the hilarity of it that I had to take a picture and send it to Instagram to cheer myself up.

"What was that?" he asked.

"If you don't take a picture, it didn't happen," I said with an uneven laugh, then took a quick bite of the pizza. It didn't taste as good as my Instagram filter made it look, and I tried to choke it down with Brek's eyes on me.

"Is that to get Russ to come or are you trying to make someone else jealous?" he asked.

"Knock it off," I said. "Tell me why you want Eden's journal."

He leaned back and then after giving me a searching look, he launched into his explanation. "I've found a rich backer who will fund me to get that treasure in the Uinta Mountains."

Though I'd suspected it, my heart sank at the revelation. We had long since figured out that the Uinta Mountains were Eden's Deseret Mountains. And going after it there was what had killed our dad—I couldn't let him do this. "Who is this backer?"

18

"He goes by Walker, but I don't think that's his name. He doesn't want to be identified." At my incredulous look, he waved his hand dismissively. "He's rich, so he's a little eccentric. You should meet these benefactors I work with—they're all a little odd like that. It's not a big deal."

"Brek!" I slapped the table. "We're fatherless because of that treasure. You told mom that you wouldn't even look into—"

"It's a lot of money, and I really need the money, especially now. The backer is paying me part of it up front and then the rest when we uncover the treasure." He hesitated before saying, "The deal is that whatever we find, we give to him."

"You promised that?" I couldn't believe it. "What if you actually find Eden's treasure?"

"Of course I'll find it. Look, I don't think dad died in some freak accident looking for that treasure. He's not that much of a moron. I think something else happened."

I was offended by the moron statement and felt myself turn prickly. "What do you think happened?"

He went silent then shrugged. "They never found his body. Don't you think that they would've at least found his body?"

So, he had no evidence, just a hunch. Most of the time Brek was right, but I didn't want to think about that.

"Anyway, I'm not dad," he said, "and I'm not as stupid as that ancestor of ours who got himself cursed by a ghost." He laughed low at the thought, because Lucius had turned into a joke in our eyes. "I'm not going to fail. I've done far more dangerous things than this."

"That doesn't make me feel better," I said.

"Then come with me." He said it so offhandedly that I almost thought that he hadn't said it.

"Wait, what?"

He straightened and got into his negotiating stance—the one that he had perfected when we had haggled with our Halloween candy back in the day. "I want you to dig up that old camera of yours and document this," he said. "If we don't find Eden's treasure then at least we'll have something to show for it this time."

There was no way I was doing this. Sure, documenting life had once been my passion—my death grip on social media was just a shadow of what it used to be—but that was high school. I laughed in his face. "That was a long time ago."

Caitlyn made a sound of disappointment.

"C'mon," he said. "We can bring in Eden's story. Her story needs to be told—you can give a voice to the voiceless."

At that exact moment, someone chose to croon a song from *High School Musical* into the microphone. It was startling… and strangely appropriate for the moment.

Brekker smiled. "You of all people should know what that means, to get your voice out there."

"Splashing something all over social media doesn't exactly make it more meaningful," I said, deciding to be truthful—especially when the singer onstage was proving to us that not all voices were created equal. Besides, I was torn about Eden. A part of me looked down on her for being so clueless about life and letting herself get dragged through the mud because she liked some guy. Another part of me wondered what it would be like to let everything go and be stupid like that.

"Why do you want to bring attention to yourself anyway?" I asked. "They won't give you a permit for this. A documentary's not a good idea if you have to sneak around."

"That's the best part," he said. "The treasure's on private land. 400,000 acres of resorts and logging towns. Legends of treasure in the Uintas are their main tourist attractions—we don't need permits. They encourage people to take a go at it. We're good."

By now Caitlyn looked intrigued. "This is the vacation that we've been wanting to take, Ivy!"

"No, no, no! The whole thing is dangerous!" I said. Those other people going after gold would be amateurs. Brek wouldn't be toying around—he'd take risks no one else would. "I'm not going to walk into

Eden's curse."

Brekker scoffed. "You know what our family's problem is? We keep playing into a self-fulfilling prophecy. Maybe if we didn't always set our hearts on things that didn't matter?" He looked meaningfully at my cell phone and I knew that he was referring to my Instagram posts. "At least go out and live a real life."

"Okay, okay!" Caitlyn stood to get our attention, putting both hands on the table, still managing to be shorter than us when she was standing. "You'd better tell me right now what Eden's curse is all about!"

We looked over at her, absentmindedly. I'd mentioned Eden's curse to her before, but just like every inside joke and phrase I used so often with my twin, I'd forgotten that not everyone knew what we really meant. Brekker gestured at me to tell the story, and so, shrugging, I did my best. "Eden is this girl who was in love with one of our great, great, great—a million greats—grandfathers. His name was Lucius, and he was kind of a jerk actually. She worked at a saloon in San Francisco…"

"So, a prostitute?" Caitlyn asked. "Wait, wait." She dug into her purse and pulled out her phone and started to film me.

"What are you doing?" I asked.

"I'm starting the documentation!"

"I said I'm not doing this!" I glanced over at Brek and he smiled and relaxed. I was sure he recognized her as an ally now. Everyone was turning against me.

"Yes, yes, I know," Caitlyn said with a dismissive wave. "Oh!" She turned her phone on herself and summed up the story up to the point where she had interrupted me then flipped the phone back on me. "So, she's a saloon girl," she said.

I gulped, trying to ignore that I was now on camera. I really hoped it wasn't on Facebook Live. "Yeah, it was kind of a horrible time back then," I said, "during the gold rush era. Anyway, she ran off to the Uinta mountains with this guy Lucius to find this *stupid treasure*…" that slur, along with a pointed look, was aimed at Brek, "and they finally found these caves where they thought the treasure was hidden, and.... uh... the rest is kind of lost in Payne family legend because we're only going by Lucius's account of what happened. He went in there with Eden and the caves started filling with water from the lake. The guy got scared and he left her behind to die."

"But... but... why didn't she run out herself?" Caitlyn was so distraught she briefly lowered her phone. "Was she stuck?"

"I have no idea," I said. "But she pleaded for his help and he ran. She drowned in there, alone."

"That's horrible."

"I know. She loved that guy—I'm not sure what was worse, getting betrayed like that or drowning."

"Drowning," Brek answered for me.

I glared at him before continuing, "So, Lucius dragged himself to shore and since she hadn't survived, he stole all her stuff, including her journal, and ran off with it. Now we have it." I pulled it out from my purse and set it on the table. It was a leather-bound book, the pages yellowed by time. "It has all the clues in there on how to find the treasure; you know, if anyone wants to die a horrible, watery death."

Brek heaved a heavy sigh, his eyes rising to the ceiling.

Caitlyn gave a little gasp and picked it up with her free hand. "So, this is real! This really happened."

"Yeah, except the last part she hasn't told you yet," Brekker said with a wry expression. It was all part of the family legend, even the most absurd parts. "Lucius was on his way out of the forest and he heard this moaning noise and turned and there was Eden, standing there, sopping wet, just staring at him."

"You said she drowned?" Caitlyn's eyes were huge now.

I tried not to laugh at her fear. "Look," I said, "this came from a guy who was probably a drunk... um, but, whatever. He said Eden pointed at him and told him that as long as he and his descendants set their hearts on treasure, they would never find it."

"And she's right," Brekker said with a steady look at me, "because we're all losers."

"No!" Caitlyn let out a wail. "That is so not true!"

I was stuck in a job that I hated and I was up to my neck in debt because I couldn't tell myself "no." We were always looking for the next big thing and never really getting it. Brek was successful at what he did, but he never got ahead because he couldn't call it quits. So yeah, "loser" was a pretty fair assessment. Curse or self-fulfilling prophecy, it didn't matter. Eden called it. Lucius' vanity and greed had seeped through the generations to us.

"Either way," Brek said. "What gives Eden the moral superiority to go throwing curses around? She would've pulled the rug out from under Lucius if given the chance. I read what she wrote about Adam."

I held up my finger, having no choice but to defend Eden on this point. "Lucius didn't love her. Adam did—he'd never leave her."

"Stop romanticizing it," he said with an easy laugh. "These were outlaws fighting over more money than any of them had ever seen, more than anything we've seen."

"I need to read Eden's journal," Caitlyn said.

She was still filming, and she turned her phone to Brek when he said flatly, "Go for it. It's all gushy and romantic and stuff—it's really hard to stomach. You'll love it."

I felt a hand on my shoulder and I glanced up to see Russell. His dark eyes trained on mine and he planted a kiss on my lips, and I felt my stomach explode into a million butterflies. My grimace that had been aimed at my twin turned into a cheesy grin, and the fight seeped out of me, turning me into a soft wad of jelly. "Russ!" I cried. "You came!"

Chapter three

I patted the seat next to me and Russell took it. He was tall and muscular in his lanky way, his Italian ancestry showing in his dark, curly hair and black eyes. He put a proprietary arm around me as he turned to Brek. Curiosity and a little suspicion stretched across his handsome face. "What did I miss?" he asked.

"Everything." Caitlyn put her phone away, smiling secretly.

I cleared my throat. "I was just telling my brother that I won't set my heart on things I can't have." *Like Treasure.* I snuggled into Russell for Brek's benefit. "I have plenty of reasons to stay in San Francisco."

"This is your brother?" Russell looked miffed, like he had just wasted his time in coming. He pulled his arm away from me and inched back, glancing down at his phone. The karaoke singers hit a particularly nasty note and he flinched. Brek raised an eyebrow at me, and I knew he was starting to seethe on my behalf.

"Russell." I scooted closer to him. "You haven't met my twin yet. This is Brekker. He just got back from Michigan."

Russ glanced up, appearing bored. "That's right—he's the treasure hunter."

"Archeologist and marine biologist," Brekker corrected him. *Without any schooling*, I amended in my head, though I supposed my brother ran with the top experts of the field, so that was something.

I brushed Russ's hand with mine to get him to act more like a boyfriend, but the guy was oblivious to the importance of this moment. I was going to get an earful of "I told you so!" from my brother if Russ didn't start acting more affectionate and fast.

Caitlyn cleared her throat and rubbed meaningfully under her eye.

I tilted my head at her, trying to figure out what she was saying until she finally reached out for me over the table. "You've got mascara under your eyes, Ivy." She rubbed it out from under my eyes while I tried not to struggle. Oh great! The worst time for that to happen—I needed to look beautiful and in charge of the situation and I had raccoon eyes the whole time? Caitlyn must have read that in my expression because she hurried to defend herself. "Friends tell!"

Normally, we did—when there was food in our teeth or a zipper unzipped—though we tried to keep it on the down low, and not in front of an audience we were trying to impress. Seeing Brek's sour expression, I forced a smile at him, trying to figure out a way to get him to lighten up. "Cheer up! I'll let you know when your mascara runs, okay?"

Russell stopped mid-texting and glanced over at me like I had grown two heads. Breathing out in disgust, he stood up. "I'm going to get some drinks."

At least Brek waited for him to step away from the table before laying into me. "What is that thing? Is that supposed to be your boyfriend?"

"Shhh."

Brekker was enraged so there was no keeping him quiet. "And you're working at some joke of a place?"

"You never cared before! Besides, there's nothing wrong with working for a living."

"No, there isn't, but you're only supporting yourself so you might as well find a job that won't suck out your soul." I tried to shush him again. "What?" he asked.

"Russell works there too."

"Of course he does. I'm not even surprised. Three things, Ivy—quit your job, dump your boyfriend, join me. I'll pay you."

"That's four things."

"We're wasting valuable time. We've got to go now. The best time to search for Eden's treasure is in the spring when the snow's melted, not too early, not too late. The end of June is perfect."

"Yeah, I also got that from Eden's journal. I can read too, smarty pants!"

Caitlyn watched the two of us argue in fascination, her head whipping from me to Brek. She dug in her purse for her phone and started to record us again. I tried to ignore that.

"Then you also know that it takes at least two people to find it," Brekker said, "and according to what she wrote in her journal, I think that second person has to be someone smaller and more agile." I couldn't believe he was even suggesting this to me. I couldn't even run a mile on a track. He leaned over the table and picked up Eden's journal. "If some saloon chick can pull it off, you can."

"She died!" I sputtered. "Wait, this isn't about documenting anymore!" I accused. And then another suspicion—Brekker usually traveled with a team of archaeologists, geologists, and biologists. "What happened to your real team, Brek? Where *is* Angel?" I hated his girlfriend—however, the sight of her would be welcome if she could take my place.

"She's a backstabber and a thief, and I dumped her," he said. Caitlyn gasped in delight then reddened and tried to hide it while Brekker leaned back, giving me a challenging look. "I thought you'd agree that was a good move?"

"Yeah, but…"

"You should do the same with your boy toy and come with me." He momentarily stunned me with the declaration and he took advantage of my silence to plead his case. "I wouldn't put you in danger. You won't be diving and rappelling. I'd do all the hard stuff. Ivy… you're not happy here."

"Don't make this about me. This is about you! I'm probably the last person you asked to come with you. What happened in Michigan, Brek?"

"You got it wrong, Ivy. I just want to see you live your life!"

"Oh you do, do you? I'll show you living life… and it's not

throwing it away on some horrible treasure." I stood up and marched over to the karaoke stage. A part of me realized that this wasn't exactly proving my point, but I couldn't back down now. Caitlyn recorded it all and somewhere in the back, I noticed Russell had gotten his drinks and had stumbled to a stop to watch in horror.

I yanked the microphone from the stand. This would be better if I put everything I had into it. Making a quick decision for my song, I punched it into the machine and found "I love it; I Don't Care," by my favorite British pop singers. I hated seeing my brother put himself in danger all the time and I hated how my life was turning out and I hated everyone rubbing it in. I half shouted the song, half sang it, still managing to keep it somewhat on key. The song was definitely in Brekker's face, and despite himself, he started to grin. Caitlyn shook with laughter, intermittently recording me and clapping her hands together.

When I finished, I curtseyed and bowed low. I waved like a beauty queen on a float and found my seat, glaring defiantly at my amused brother. "I don't have to be like you to be happy, okay? Stop trying to sell me your dreams. I enjoy being a normal person."

"Ivy?" Caitlyn cried out. She was still chuckling at my performance. "Really? In what world are you normal?"

Russell came back to the table with our drinks, looking shocked. "That was… loud."

I wanted to throw my hands up in surrender. Why couldn't Russ act like a normal boyfriend when it counted? He looked embarrassed on my behalf—it wasn't as if he was the one performing in front of the whole restaurant. Brekker noticed and went back to fuming. He sat up and pulled something from his pocket. It was another charm for my bracelet. This time it was a camera, and the meaning of it hit me like a hammer.

"I'm happy," I repeated moodily. "I'm not going after some dream—some ridiculous thing that we won't ever reach, something that will burn me out like it did to everyone in our family. The things our mom had to endure because of it? It's intolerable. It's an obsession." I raised my hands. "Don't get me wrong, I have my vices; I have plenty of them, but dreams like that will burn you to a crisp."

Finally, Russell had the sense to look concerned. I guessed he hadn't noticed I was fighting with my brother before this. "Honey?" he asked. "You okay?"

I nodded.

"Do you want to go?"

It was obvious Russell only offered because he had wanted to leave since the moment he'd gotten here, but I didn't want to desert Brek. I was worried what he'd do without me. He wouldn't listen to me either. There was nothing I could do. I nodded and Russ rewarded me with a kiss. I suddenly felt unsettled by how mechanical I felt lately when we kissed. But that was silly. I mean, it probably just meant that I was getting comfortable with him, right? Except that I wasn't.

"Oh, hey!" Russ tweaked my nose. "Give me a smile." He picked up his phone and kissed me for the camera, snapping a shot of us for our friends on Snapchat.

Nope, I felt nothing. Again. It was even worse than before. I blushed hard under my twin's knowing gaze as he crossed his arms over his chest to watch my train wreck. Brek's words were already getting to me.

I slid Eden's journal across the table to him, determined to fight this. "I'm fine. I have a secure job and a secure relationship and a secure life." *And I was deeply in debt. I wasn't going anywhere.* I wasn't sure where that thought came from, and I straightened in confusion.

Brek picked up the journal and I got nervous seeing it in his hands. He could get killed in this venture. Caitlyn seemed to read my look and she spread her hands across the table. "Let me talk to him," she said. "I'll text you."

Maybe she could perform miracles. Meanwhile I had to work one on myself. I squeezed her hand and walked out of the restaurant with Russell into the dark night, trying to convince myself that my life wasn't as bad as Brek made it out to be. Things were getting better. I already knew how to do the purchasing job. I was good at it—Micromanager Mike would be crazy not to give it to me. Russell and I took the elevator to the top floor of the parking garage while I found myself debating aloud every argument my brother had made against me. "Brek doesn't know what he's talking about," I complained to Russ. "I feel really good about that job. I'm getting it!"

The elevator doors opened and we stepped into the lot where he had parked his light blue BMW on the third level. The lot was uncovered, though the stars over us were blocked out by the harsh neon lamps over the parking garage. Russ's hand found my back. "Maybe you should concentrate on being an admin two instead?"

That derailed my train of thought and I burst into a laugh. "Why? I'm doing the work of a purchaser. I might as well get paid for it." And I would be happy doing it. My life was fine—I kept repeating it. I was going to be fine, but that was before we got stopped by a beautiful brunette with blue catlike eyes. She had jumped out of a cherry-red SUV and ran to us from across the parking lot, waving way too excitedly for my taste "Russ!" she shouted. He looked startled.

"Who's that?" I asked.

He reluctantly released the information. "Anna from the IT department."

Our company was far too big to keep track of everyone. "Is she new?"

Russ nodded and got the door open to his BMW before tucking me inside. He shut the door on me before Anna reached him. It gave me the perfect view of her sliding her arms behind his back to embrace him. "I heard the good news!" she screeched. "You got the job!" The car doors didn't muffle her voice at all.

Job? I was stunned, but I couldn't push open the door to ask about it since Russ was standing in front of it, and I couldn't roll down the windows since the car wasn't on. He'd trapped me in here. I briefly considered going over the console to get out of the car on the other side so I could join in this conversation, but that would make me look like an idiot. Still, I didn't know Russ was leaving the Gasket Sweat Shop. And why did this girl know about this new job before I did? I felt a little jealous, and then another thought hit me—I'd be so bored without him at work.

"I start tomorrow," he said, shoving his hands deep into his pockets. "So yeah, yeah, I'm pretty excited."

"Well, I heard they made the right decision," she said, pressing his arm. "The other applicants were terrible." Eventually Anna noticed me through the glass of the car window. "Who's this?" I waved ineffectually and when Russ didn't move from the door, I had to take matters into my own hands. It was getting a little ridiculous, so I pushed at the door and he had no choice but to step aside.

As soon as my high heels met the ground, I got straight to business. "You're leaving us, Russ?"

He looked confused for a moment, before Anna caught my meaning. "No—the job's in-house," she said. Her eyes narrowed at me and she lifted a finger, shaking it in recognition. "Wait, do you work at the Gasket Sweat Shop too?"

"Yes, my desk is kind of tucked away in the corner."

"Behind Larry?"

"No farther."

"Next to Stuart?"

Did she know everyone at this company, except me? "Further, I'm like hidden in the back room. They always play musical chairs with me—the least favored desk of the month is the one they give me." I chuckled, but she didn't. It actually wasn't that funny.

Russ reluctantly introduced us. "This is Ivy. She's the admin in purchasing. She works for Mike."

Her mouth made an "Oh," and then she clapped with excitement. "So you'll be working with *our* Russ then?"

"Wait, what?" Nothing she said was making sense... though it was starting to come together, and I wasn't liking it.

"She doesn't know yet," Russ said, confirming my suspicions. He didn't even need to say it, especially when he turned to me with a tight smile that I knew was fake the moment I saw it. "I got the job in purchasing, Ivy."

The one that I was applying for? My heart plummeted while a million accusations ran through me—I thought I had it! Russ didn't warn me that he was applying for it too. He let me go on about it? And how was he more qualified? My gaze slid to this girl whose hand was sliding down his back. "You're kidding?" I asked.

"No!" She beamed.

I readjusted the strap of my purse and without another word, headed back to the elevator to find my brother and Caitlyn at the karaoke joint. I knew that Russ had been distant lately, but no way had this slipped his mind. When had he planned on telling me? Russ tried to stop me, but not before reassuring Anna that everything was fine. "Wait up!" he shouted at me.

"But I thought you were leaving?" she asked in some confusion.

"No, no," he denied it. "She forgot something in the car. We were going right back in—I'll talk to you later!"

Who was this girl? Anna was not just some girl from IT. Russ ran to me, talking fast and taking my hands before I could get into the elevator. "I'm sorry I didn't say anything sooner."

Yeah, he'd be sorry. Here I was trying to resurrect whatever thing was dying between us and he was living this whole other life behind my back. "What did you want to say?" I asked. "Something about taking my job or that you have another girlfriend? Are you hiding some lizard children I don't know about?"

"No, no, it's just…" looking over at Anna, he lowered his voice, "Don't take this personally. No one from work can know you and I are dating."

It was all over social media. Didn't Anna use social media? Of course she did; she was in IT. How else did she know he was here? Anyway, I didn't care. Brek was right about Russ and I was done. "So you and Anna, huh?"

"Oh come on, it's not like that. I'm not hiding you. We're going to be working in the same department now, and HR wouldn't like that."

I tugged my hands from his. "You shouldn't have gone for the job behind my back."

His face reddened. "What did you want me to say? You're not the only one who has to pay the bills. And your boss wasn't going to give you the promotion anyway. He said you're a better fit for the admin position and... he said a few other things."

I couldn't believe it. "He actually told you why I didn't get it? What else did he say?"

His breathing hitched. "You're really going to make me say it?" Before I could decide if that was a good idea, he spilled the beans. "He said... you were a slow learner."

"I'm slow...?" I gasped at the shock of it. "I'm doing the purchasing job already and I pick up everybody's work. How's that slow?"

"Yeah, but he expects an admin to bring him coffee and get him files—and you haven't been doing any of that. He plans on moving your desk next to his tomorrow."

"I'm getting moved again? That's rich."

"And you can't follow anything on his list." Micromanager Mike was putting so many restrictions on me that I felt like I couldn't breathe without him making up a new rule. "Besides that," he said. "No one was supposed to know about the list and you told everyone."

Because it made him look very, very bad. He couldn't earn my respect; he had to order me to it. But how did Micromanager Mike know I had told anyone? My eyes narrowed on Russ. Apparently there was a spy in our midst. Had he done it to get the job?

"Is everything okay?" Anna appeared before us, biting her lip. No sane person would approach us arguing... unless it really was her business somehow? These two had to be a thing.

"Welcome to the team, Russ," I sneered at him. "Just wait until

Micromanager Mike turns on you. That will take exactly twelve hours."

Anna looked offended at my words. "Micromanager Mike?"

Great! It seemed she was best friends with my boss. I couldn't think clearly. I just had to get out of here before I got myself into more trouble.

"What's going on Russ?" I heard her asking. "Are you two dating?"

I wanted to know that too. Anna seemed mighty cozy with my boyfriend. "Yeah, Russ, are you two dating?" I asked.

"We've been on some dates together," he hedged, "—that doesn't mean we're dating."

That was very vague. "Who are you talking about?" I asked. "Anna or me? Or both of us?" He looked between us, frozen to the spot. "Tell me, Russell!" It came out a strangled scream.

He gave in immediately. "Anna is very special to me." That was all I needed to hear—I had been a fool. No wonder he had been so AWOL lately. He was playing us both—well, me especially. I pushed inside the elevator. As I did so, I heard him trying to explain to Anna again, "I'm sorry, I'll be right back. I've got to take care of this."

No, he didn't. I faced my palms at him and shook my head. "No," I said. "No." The elevator doors closed between us and I lost no time rushing into Karaoke Jams. I headed for the booth where I'd left Caitlyn and Brek, but I saw they were gone. I felt trapped and frustrated. Everything was closing in on me and here I was trapped in a stupid restaurant with nobody. Nobody. The thought made me want to break down in tears. *But not here.* I needed somewhere private where I could cry. I tore blindly toward the exit, but a thought stopped me dead in my tracks. What if Russell was still out in the parking lot with Anna? A pit settled into my stomach. I would still have to go to work in the morning. Knowing about them, and how Mike talked about me and— everything! I really was trapped. How could I have let myself become such a slave to my job?

I called Caitlyn and when she didn't answer, I left a text and got nothing. And so, I tried my last lifeline—Brekker. I left a message, whining the whole time. I knew what kind of answer I'd get. I told you so. But he wasn't responding either. I was starting to feel a little suspicious, but I didn't have time to think about what it meant. I was too busy freaking out.

"Ivy!"

Turning, I saw Russell had spotted me and was coming for me. My eyes were brimming with tears and he nudged me into a booth, trying to calm me down. He handed me a drink and sat down beside me. I noticed it was water and started downing it, hoping it would get me to stop crying.

"Shh shh." He put his arm around me. "It's okay, baby." *Baby?*

Now he suddenly cares about me? He handed me another glass, talking the whole time. "Mike is Anna's dad."

Micromanager Mike had a daughter? Russ had shocked me into silence. My gaze lifted to Russ as everything started to come together. Was this why he got the job? Had he sweetened her up on purpose? "Maybe I should just find a new job," I whispered.

"Oh c'mon, Ivy," he lectured me. "What are you going to do with a history degree?" I huffed at that. Was this his way of trying to smooth things over between us? He tried a different tactic. "Look, just... you weren't supposed to know about the job until tomorrow and... and you're training me when you come into the office. We need to find a way to put this behind us. We're going to be spending a lot of time together."

I took a steadying breath and studied the charms on my bracelet. The camera stood out from them all—it was made of a polished blue shell—the detail was amazing with tiny white jewels making up the buttons. I'd love to be taking pictures, maybe at a beach or a meadow or... the forest. I'd do anything to be free of that office now. "Why?" I asked. "Why do they want me to train you if I'm not even qualified for the job? I'm slow. I can't follow lists."

I was clearly being sarcastic, but he didn't catch that. "I'll help you

with all that," he said. "It's not like we have to stop seeing each other."
He slid his fingers down my arm. It was ironic. Now that he was afraid
of losing me, Russ had never been so attentive. "You're my little lost
lamb," he said. I gaped. Did he really just call me that? "You've never
had anyone show you how to work your way around office politics.
You need someone like me to guide you."

"Baaaah," I said, giving him my best impression of a baby lamb.

He stiffened. "What?"

That's when I threw my water at him. It dripped down his face
before I registered that I had done it. "I'm nobody's lost lamb," I said.

Anna gasped behind us. She had come in time to witness what I'd
done to her fake boyfriend. "What did he ever do to you?" she cried.
"You know what? You can try going in tomorrow, but *Micro-
Management Mike* might have something to say about that after I talk to
him. I think it's best you found a new job!"

Eden's curse was alive in me, and at the moment I didn't care. I
pushed past Russ in the booth and put some distance between us,
feeling shaky. "Sounds good to me," I said. "Why don't you tell that
micromanager what to do with his lists while you're at it? On second
thought, give those lists to Russell. He's going to need help doing his
job when I'm not there to train him, especially when Mike figures out
he's cheating on his daughter."

"Unbelievable!" Russ shouted at my back. "You're putting this on
me? Don't pretend this is my fault. You did this. You hated it there so
much. And before you try to blame this on some curse from a crazy girl
named Eden, I'm gonna break it to you: You've made your own luck.
You never wanted to be here with the rest of us normal people and
everybody knows it."

My shoulders tensed. He was right—but I'd been desperate for
the money, and I'd never really wanted to try anything else, always
afraid that I'd be a failure at that too, and I felt more trapped as he kept
going at me. "You pushed us all into this," he said. "You're overrated!
Yeah!"

"Overrated?" He'd shocked me with that and I turned on him. "What's that supposed to mean?"

Even he didn't know how to answer. I wondered if he might have had some sort of inferiority complex with me. How? I was so low on the totem pole. Sure, I wanted something better for myself than serving coffee. Was that what he meant? "You push everyone away," he said finally. "No one wants to work with you." Was he talking about Mike or himself? Or everybody at work? Before I could argue, he blabbed everything Mike had told him, "You weren't second choice for the job; you weren't even third or fourth!"

Oh! So now Russ had gone full Team Mike, had he? Not surprising since he'd done everything he could to steal that job. My head was spinning. I needed to get out of here. How had I been so wrong about this guy? Had Russell *ever* cared about me? He'd probably gone for me because I was so *overrated* then found out I was human and tossed me for the next big thing. The tears that I had tried to keep back came in a tumult as I made a beeline for the exit. "What are you doing?" Russ asked, his tone faltering. "You're just going to walk home?"

Russ no longer had a say on what I did, and so I stormed out without answering. I was so upset that I couldn't even formulate the perfect Facebook post about it in my mind... well, I mean, I kinda knew what it would say already, and it would get hundreds of angry and shocked-face emojis, but no, the fight had been taken out of me.

Inhaling the warm summer air, I tried to not let the consequences of this night hit me all at once. Was I fired or had I quit? Technically this was me quitting, but that meant no unemployment, no severance. I had one more payday. That bought me one month with my housing, but what about food? What about the basics? And then if I didn't have a job by the end of the month? I had to say goodbye to my freedom and move in with my mother in her cramped apartment downtown. The thought sent a fresh wave of sobs wracking through my body.

I made it as far as the gas station a block away, with my feet sliding around in my heels, before Brek tracked me down in his orange Jeep. The doors in the front were off in the style of a true adventurer. Taking one look at me, he slid from his Jeep and I couldn't help it, I let out a sad little scream and ran into his arms. This one was kind of a wail, but he knew what it meant, and he wrapped his arms around me and held me. "It's going to be okay," he said. "It's going to be okay."

"It was horrible, Brek! I lost everything! It's all gone! You were right about Russ, but it's not a good thing. It's…"

His eyes took on an angry glint. "Wait, you lost your boyfriend too?"

"He took my job! And he cheated on me." I guess my message had been pretty vague. "Why are you mad?" I complained. "You didn't even like him!"

"So? No one does that to my sister!"

I hugged him for that. "He said that I pushed him to it and I push everyone away. I don't!"

"What an idiot. I'll kill him."

I knew that he didn't literally mean he was going to kill him, but it felt good that someone felt protective of me, for once. "I'm way over my head—I don't have savings or… or… a plan!"

"I know. I know."

He rubbed my back, trying to calm me down. He was still in comforting mode and I let myself cry into his shoulder.

"And I hated it there, and was it a good thing? Was it a good thing that I can't go back? Maybe this is a good thing!" I felt a little hysterical at this point, and he pulled away to look at me, half laughing, half-furious on my behalf.

"Maybe I can take a telemarketing job," I said, "but that would kill me. I'll end up waiting tables where mom worked."

That took the laughter out of his expression. "I won't let either of you wait tables there," he said with an edge of steel in his voice.

"It's not that bad," I cried. "I'm strong. I can do it. Oh! But I'm going to be poor forever, aren't I? My cards are all maxed out, and,

and… I want to be responsible, but I don't know how. I'm such a loser!"

"Hey!" He pushed my hair away from my eyes and gave me a serious look. "This isn't the way I wanted it to happen, but I think this is your chance. Ivy, don't you see? Nothing is holding you back anymore. No job. No stupid guy, maybe not even housing." He made a sound of disbelief at my bad luck. "It's okay. We'll solve the mystery behind Eden's treasure once and for all."

I pulled away. My scowl felt like it was etched in a face made of stone. It was just like him to not take any of this seriously. "Brek!" I wailed. He was doing a lousy job of pretending not to be overjoyed that I had hit rock bottom and was now free to join him.

"Also, you have black mascara running all over your face." He grinned. "You look like an emo clown." I swatted at him and he laughed, easily defending himself with a muscular forearm. "Friends tell, Ivy!"

I sniffed, wondering if the answer to all my problems actually stood in front of me. "How much money is this eccentric backer offering?" I asked.

"A lot…" Brek said. "He's crazy, but I'm doing it because I want this find, Ivy. We've lived with this shadow our entire lives… and…" Brekker hesitated, on the verge of a confession, "I want to find out what happened to Dad. Don't you?"

"I do," I sobbed. For some reason it meant the world to me when I'd thought I didn't care only a few hours earlier. "I'll start an online campaign," I said. "I'll put a spin on this story that will bring in a huge audience; that way we'll make tons of money whether we're successful or not… *most likely not*, but we'll be so rich that we won't know what to do with ourselves. We'll help mom. We'll get her out of that apartment downtown. And I'll show Russell that I'm not slow!"

"He's not going to care either way," Brek said with another hug.

"I know." I wiped at my eyes, letting the last reservoir of my tears run free. I wasn't sure why I was crying now—out of exhaustion or relief that I was free.

I heard a car drive up and recognized the low hum of Caitlyn's convertible. She had brought Frankie. She hopped out of the side door. "I came as soon as I heard!" she said. Taking one look at me, she let out a cry. "Oh, Ivy, what did Russ do to you?"

"We're going to the Uintas," I said. Now that I had cried out all my tears, I felt as emotionless as a sleepwalker, like this wasn't really happening. "I'm tired of this curse."

"Oh baby, I know," Caitlyn said. "I'm already packed."

"What?"

"My bags are in my trunk." At my incredulous look, she had the grace to blush. "After you left, Brek and I got to planning and… well, we were going to find a way to convince you when you got home tonight." I glared at her for betraying me to my brother. She was so in love with him! And with Angel out of the picture, she probably thought she had a chance. Chuckling, she read my look and rubbed my hands. "Don't look at me like that! You need this vacation! Just think about it, an exotic hiking trip! It'll be fun? Yeah?"

"But…" I had gone through the worst night of my life. "I wish you'd convinced me earlier."

Chapter four

*I*t had taken us two days to make the fifteen hour drive from San Francisco to Grizzly Lake Resort. Somehow I'd ended up in the back seat for the majority of the time, scrunched between Caitlyn's luggage and my brother's treasure hunting gear. We didn't know how long the expedition would take us, so Caitlyn and I packed almost all the hiking and workout clothes we owned, which was a lot for Caitlyn and not so much for me.

My best friend talked louder and faster when she was giddy. She planned this out like we were vacationing at a resort while my brother mapped out treacherous hikes. And I was caught in the middle with my camera that I hadn't used in any serious, official capacity since high school.

Going with my brother was possibly the stupidest thing that I had ever done, besides all those Pinterest fails—attempting to build my name out of aluminum blocks from old store signs (there are absolutely no "V's" for Ivy), attempting Destroy the Dress photos in the ocean and getting thrashed by waves. And of course, there was dating Russell and getting stuck in a mind-numbing job for the last seven years with lousy pay... but this was definitely the fifth or sixth stupidest thing I'd ever done. Luckily, Eden's curse didn't include car sickness, so I passed the time reading Eden's journal. I peeled open the page to the second entry:

Eden's Journal: February 26th, 1855 – Flint Saloon, San Francisco

We lived off the land, robbing stagecoaches and mail carriers for a piece until Lucius found a warrant for our deaths off the body of a gun for hire.

When Lucius brung me the warrant, he got quiet and jittery like he always done when he asked me to read for him, like he was afeared I'd swell up and put on airs. He was always laying into me for fooling around and writing in this here journal at night. My ma had been a fine woman and learned me at her knee, though she upped and died of consumption after Pa left us like any good, proper woman should. I'd have died too if the good folks at the saloon warn't kind enough to take me in. I supposed surviving was a bad habit with me.

I studied our faces on the paper. I sure liked seeing Lucius next to me. We looked mean and ornery and not quite ourselves, but sure enough there were our names and a reward for our capture at $50. Dead or alive. It got me to thinking what I'd do with $50, but Lucius would hear none of it. He said it was past time to ride out of these parts and find ourselves a fortune. I was so shook with joy he wanted me to tag along, I judged he meant across Lake Erie from whence he come, but he shook his head and waved around that cursed coin. Pratt said there was more where this come from and we'd find it. Spring was a'coming and warn't that the time to hunt the mountain over for this treasure?

I let out a scream and spit out such fire at the notion, but Lucius kept charming me. "Eden! Don't you want something more than being a whore?" I told Lucius I did, but he ignored all talk of marriage and started going on about what we'd do with all that money. It didn't matter what we were before or what crimes we done. If we come back to town with bags full of gold, all'd be forgiven. We'd be pillars of San Francisco like the McConnell's and the Jackson's. Everyone knowed their fortune came from powerful shady dealings. Should I dig me up some gold, maybe I might could open up a school or a saloon or something respectable like that. Ma would fancy me being a proper woman and smile down from heaven.

It got me to thinking. Folks looked down on me now and said I was no kind of woman. If'n I was rich, ain't no one would thrash me around. I'd never feel the arms of them smelly prospectors 'round me again. Should someone give out orders, I'd be the one to do it. My mind was half made up when I saw Lucius looking at me the way he did and smiling like I liked.

He kissed me so's all thoughts of bad luck fled me. And by and by, we set off for the fine state of Deseret to find us some Shoshones to point us out the gold in them mountains."

I felt like I'd been similarly tricked, although I could've used a few kisses from a cute guy to make me feel better about it. The wheels beneath us crunched against the gravel of the resort as we reached Dry Gulch. Brek put on the brake and I couldn't get out of his Jeep fast enough. My legs felt numb and my back threatened to cramp up as I forced my way out of the bulk of Caitlyn's luggage and trip snacks. "Coming through!" I warned.

Caitlyn didn't move fast enough from the front. In fact, she didn't seem to hear me as she chatted amicably to my brother about how beautiful the colors in the sky were turning, or how massive the lake was against the horizon, and "Just look at this quaint little town—it's absolutely adorable. Was this a logging town? Can they cut down the trees here?"

I couldn't see what she was talking about, and so, feeling claustrophobic, I began snapping open the plastic canopy at the back of the Jeep to make my escape.

Brekker glanced back at me. "What are you doing?"

"I... have... to breathe!"

Feeling like the undead pulling from my grave, I tumbled from the back seat, my sandals flopping between my feet and the rocky ground covered in dirt. It was cold. The sun was setting behind a forest of pines and aspens in the mountains. Goose bumps sprang over my bare arms and legs under a chilly breeze. During our last rest stop in a cute little place called Heber, it had been 80 degrees, and I had been sweating in my shorts and slouchy tee. Checking the app on my phone, I saw that it was 39 degrees in this small logging town. Cold for San Francisco standards.

Brek had parked in front of the Grizzly Bear House. It was as big as a warehouse and looked like it had been remodeled from a high pitched gable barn with timber siding. The store was kitschy and gothic all at once. On a flush wall on one side of the lodge, the name of the store was painted in bold red letters as if someone had vandalized it. Under that was a bigger-than-life mural of a grizzly bear strangling a fish near a waterfall.

It must be the social hub of the resort. The Grizzly had a wrap-around porch near the entrance, and a steady flow of people walked over it, past life-sized statues carved from black walnut into bears and moose and squirrels. The store was where we'd check in to get the keys to our cabins.

Behind the barn-like building, past a beach of rocks and trees, the Grizzly Lake stretched out, glistening orange under the setting sun. The whole mountainside of thick forest surrounding us was pockmarked with sparkling pockets of water. The Uintas was the place for lakes—400,000 acres of private land made up of hunting preserves, resorts, and logging towns, and somewhere in that was hiding Eden's treasure. Our treasure.

My sweaty clothes from the hot car ride down were turning into something like an icy sponge bath against my skin, and I plunged back through the plastic canopy on Brek's Jeep to dig around my seat for a coat. Luckily, Brek had told me to pack layers.

"Ivy, get your camera too!" Caitlyn said. "Catch this beautiful sunset!"

My camera was packed under the seat where it wouldn't get crushed, and with my body hanging halfway into the Jeep and half out, I slid the Canon 5d Mark II from the bottom of the seat along with my coat. It was all I could reach for now. The Jeep doors opened and I felt the vibration of it against my stomach as Brekker slid out of his seat for a stretch. Caitlyn followed.

"Hey!" I held my hand out to her. I was getting stuck. "Could you help me out...?" It came out muffled behind all of Brekker's equipment and the doors slammed shut, blocking out their murmurs of conversation. Neither of them thought anything of my acrobatics in here. "Hey! Help me!" But they didn't hear me. With a grunt of frustration, I writhed, complaining under my breath, the charms of my bracelet jingling as I tried to fight my way out until I felt two strong hands clamp onto my bare legs and pull me out.

Sliding down, I twisted and came face to face with a man I'd never seen before. A handsome man with hazel eyes, a week's growth of beard, and a gray stocking cap over his dark, untidy hair. A mountain man? He set me on the ground like I weighed no more than Caitlyn and I held my camera between us, mesmerized. He wore a black down parka, and he looked warm. His eyes searched mine, his dark brows drawn and serious, like maybe I had something to say. My brain had turned into mush at the sight of him, but the sparking neurons were starting to connect enough for me to whisper, "Thank you."

And like he couldn't help it, his sober lips split into a grin and he said, "My pleasure." I was stunned by his southern accent. It flavored his deep voice like smoked hickory, and hearing it come out of that mouth, that sensitive, expressive mouth, I felt my knees go weak. "Next time, you can save me," he said with a wink.

He let me go to retrieve a backpack from the planks of the steps. It looked like it belonged to the Special Forces. *So did he!* Heaving it onto his back, he made his way over the wraparound porch, not looking back, like he was used to rescuing damsels in distress on a daily basis. He wasn't dressed like a cowboy; he wore worn-but-stylish jeans, tan hiking boots. Maybe a logger? Pushing past a bench swing piled high with merchandise from the store, he disappeared into the café. I felt like I'd just sighted Big Foot. Guys like that weren't real in my world.

But this world smelled of campfire and pine, made stronger by the curls of smoke escaping the chimneys in the town. I circled to find Brekker and Caitlyn, dying to ask my best friend what she thought of this guy, but they'd already deserted me. I searched around me in shock. It hadn't taken them long to seek the warmth of the Grizzly Bear House. Before I could join them—and the beautiful mountain man—inside, my attention was caught by the other end of this town behind Brekker's Jeep.

The town of Dry Gulch was a logging town where real people lived—it wasn't just a resort. Judging by the cramped trailer parks and the luxurious, renovated cabins, the town demographics ranged from the filthy rich to the dirt poor. Tangled up in the weeds in the nearest trailer park were rusting pickups and Datsuns that hadn't moved since the 70's.

Lifting up my camera, I snapped shots of the vintage cars under the reds and oranges of this magnificent sunset. The rusted-out automobiles made a stark contrast to the Super Deluxe Monster trucks and SUVs parked on the cabin lawns for weekend-long parties. Remembering myself enough to pull on my coat, I zipped it up then captured the image of those along with the streaks of clouds dragging over the shining lake behind them. The color melted from the sky like candy cane ice cream.

This place was… indescribable. And even though my camera was better than a cell phone, it still couldn't capture the beauty of this evening. Nothing ever could—not that I didn't try. I was the kind of person who couldn't go out into the sunset without taking a shot of it, but then I'd put it on Instagram and retreat from it to watch the *Kardashians*. There was no retreat here. For the first time I realized that this was going to be different from anything I knew.

"Ivy!" Caitlyn pulled from the store to find me. "What are you doing?"

I put down my camera. My hands were numb from the cold, and I wondered if our eccentric backer's money could also be used for gloves and hats, too. I wasn't used to these kinds of temperatures in June—especially late June.

"C'mon," Caitlyn said. "Let's get something to eat."

That was enough to get me up the stairs. I pushed past the same swing bench that my nameless rescuer had. The door went off with bells and chimes that hung over the entrance when I walked inside, and hot air blew into my face, but I still couldn't bring myself to take off my coat as I followed Caitlyn inside. The place was huge. Anyone could get lost in here. It was an impressive-sized establishment with dimmed lights and timber mazes for walls. There was a café to the side of the store, and I made my way to a booth where my brother waited for us. "What took you?" he asked.

"Getting stuck!" I said, giving him an annoyed look during Caitlyn's sounds of sympathy. "Thanks for your help, by the way. I shouted for you to come get me."

He looked blank and snickered a little. "You were stuck in my Jeep? How?"

I made a face. "Don't worry; someone helped me."

"Who?" Caitlyn asked. It didn't take much to intrigue her.

I turned, searching the store for the man in question, but I couldn't find him. A group of three elderly gentlemen sat at a table on the other side of the café. They jostled each other, laughing and chatting. One of them wore a deputy uniform. The others I assumed were loggers—retired probably. Looking from them, I saw that there were three levels to this store, and I could see onto each floor since they were only blocked off with railings and a circular staircase shooting up the middle.

It would be the perfect place for townspeople and visitors alike to congregate, eat, swap stories, and socialize. Upstairs on the third floor had a sign that said, "Bear Den," and it looked the part with a bar and a pool table. The second floor was called, "Animal House." And it carried more of those carved wooden animals that were displayed on the balcony outside. We sat in the café on the ground floor. It was part bakery, part soup house, and named simply, "The Grizzly Café." On the far side, partitioned off from us near a cash register, was an area designated as a convenience store, more or less, with plenty of tacky merchandise stuffed in the display windows.

Seeing the racks of winter gear, I rose halfway out of my seat in excitement. "They have gloves. And hats. Brekker!" I turned to him.

"Please tell me that some of that money for this expedition can go towards keeping us warm."

"Shh." Pulling forward, he whispered so only I could hear him. "Before you start talking about our expedition, let's lay down a few ground rules for this documentary. If we're uploading episodes, don't give away clues that no one else knows. We don't want anyone finding this treasure before we do."

I didn't let the speech faze me. "So is that a yes or a no for buying warm clothes?"

He looked exasperated. "A yes!"

"Thank you!" I stood then hesitated and sat back down. "Brekker, how am I supposed to put anything on YouTube if we can't talk about..." I lowered my voice, "the clues?"

His eyes narrowed, but I was a lost cause. "We'll show our adventures and talk about the legends that are common knowledge around here, and we'll leave our best footage for after we find it."

Caitlyn was eager to be helpful. "We should ask the people in the Grizzly about the legends. We can film their interviews for our 'documentary,'" she added finger quotes here. "And that way, we can find more clues on how to find the treasure. No one will be the wiser."

I nodded and pointed to her. "See, now that's a good idea." Pulling out my cell phone to celebrate the moment, I took a picture of the two of us. Then, ignoring my brother's mocking comments, I opened up Instagram and added a filter. "Finally a vacation with my best friend," I wrote in the caption. I'd even throw in a few pics of those gorgeous mountains. It wasn't my usual shtick, but Russell loved anything to do with the outdoors so this was solely to get back at him... and if I could get a picture with that cute guy, I'd do it, too. Lately my whole life was lived as revenge against those who'd wronged me.

After adding the right hashtags, I pushed the button to send the pic out to the world, and it wouldn't send. My mouth flopped open. "We don't have cell service," I breathed out.

Caitlyn echoed my distress with a horrified sound. Brekker laughed and stood. "Welcome to the big, bad outdoors, girls."

I couldn't believe it. Caitlyn left us to try to get cell phone service at various places in the building, holding up her phone to the heavens as if some higher power might take pity on her. My brother went to order us food, and I followed behind him, making my way past the table of older gentlemen. They were a jovial group and made themselves comfortable, teasing the old man standing behind the cash register with the familiarity of old friends. "You're not my doctor, Bill!" the stouter of the plaid-fleeced dressers called out. "I'll order the extra bacon if I like."

Bill, as they called the man behind the counter, had thinning, white hair, and a tan, weathered face. He cracked a smile that sent his face into a mass of cheerful wrinkles. He dressed warmly in a gray sweater with a shawl collar, and as he came out from behind the counter, I saw he wore comfortable bedroom slippers. He set a plate of bacon next to his portly friend with hands that had grown pale and soft with age. "We'll see what your wife says when you come home smelling of bacon."

"As long as it isn't your perfume, she'll be fine."

The others at the table laughed. As we neared the counter, they shushed each other and turned their backs like they were attempting to give us privacy. Bill came around the other side, wiping off his greasy hands with a pristine towel. "What can I help you kids with?"

I wasn't used to being referred to as a kid. It pulled a smile out of me. Brekker didn't seem to like it as much; he was all business. "We'd like dinner and keys to our cabin."

Bill nodded and checked his books, tracing a shaky finger along the inscriptions. "Under what name?"

"Payne," my brother said. "Brekker Payne."

A couple of the old timers from the table snickered. I looked over at them and caught one of them spying on us. He turned away with a grunt and then sipped his soup and broke into a chortle. It was echoed by his other contemporaries around the table.

"Never mind those knuckleheads," Bill said. "They're taking exception to your name."

"My name?" Brekker asked, with a suspicious glance at them.

"It's a famous name in these parts. You ever have an afternoon free, I'll tell you about Lucius Payne. He's probably an ancestor of yours."

I met Brek's wary eyes. I wasn't aware anyone knew the story of our ancestor besides us. It didn't bode well when going for the treasure. He was the bad guy in that story. We should've gone by aliases. "Is that so?" Brekker managed to get out.

"And this is?" Bill turned to me.

"Ivy," I said. "Ivy Payne."

That set off the old men into laughter again until they elbowed each other to silence. Even the aging deputy had no sense of dignity.

Clenching his teeth, Bill shuffled over the creaking wooden floor in his slippers to a stack of keys hanging on a wall. No key cards. It seemed an archaic way to do it, like we were at the Bates Motel. After finding the correct set, he placed them firmly on the counter, asking for Brekker's information and ID. All of which he laboriously recorded in his book. "Can I get your wife's ID?" He pointed at me.

We both held our hands up in denial. "No, no, no."

"He's my twin," I was saying the same time Brek said; "She's my sister."

"Who's older?"

We hesitated. Why did that matter? "I am," Brekker said finally.

"Well, that wasn't very gentlemanly. You should've let her come first." And then without skipping a beat, he asked, "Are you here for the Raspberry Festival?" We didn't know what that was and so he pointed at the poster taped to his cash register. It was definitely handmade with raspberries colored laboriously around the edges. The festival was on July second, a week from now. "We like to bring the Fourth of July weekend in with a bang," he said with a wink.

"We'll likely be here," Brek said, then, tapping the counter, finally decided we'd be staying for a month. If we needed to extend our stay, it would be easy enough, Bill assured us. Brekker also fessed up to a third lodger, though we couldn't find my friend at the moment, seeing as she was looking for cell phone service. That sent the old men laughing again. They were a regular peanut gallery.

As my brother impatiently waited for Bill to get all the required information, my ears caught the sound of snores and labored breathing coming from the floor, and peering around the counter, I caught sight of a gargantuan white dog sleeping near a fireplace. A Dogo Argentino, judging by the mastiff's broad muscular shoulders and short white fur. My heart warmed at the sight of him. I loved dogs.

Bill noticed my interest and tilted his head at the dog while he copied down Brekker's ID number. "That there's Skip," he said. "All he does is sleep nowadays. He got old."

That got a laugh from the table of hecklers to the side of us. "We all did!"

Glancing over at them, I smiled. *I wasn't sure if I was supposed to hear that.* These old timers seemed tight-knit. I wondered if they had grown up here together, worked and played side by side for who-knew-how-many years. *At least 70.*

"You got any ATV's?" Bill asked us. "Or any other motorized vehicles you plan on taking up the mountain—there are designated trails for that." Brekker had his Jeep, but he was shaking his head. "We have some rentals," Bill said, "if you change your mind, though most of 'em are being rented out by Unit #3."

A movement drew my eye to the stairs, and I saw the mountain man who had rescued me earlier. He came from the game room, taking two steps at a time down the squeaking stairs and checking his watch like he was waiting on someone. If Caitlyn hadn't disappeared, I'd have elbowed her and she would've immediately understood. He was a beautiful man. Judging by his accent, he certainly wasn't born here, but I wondered if he was now a permanent resident of Dry Gulch; a logger or an experienced hiker. Maybe both. He wasn't as aware of me as I was of him, which probably meant he was used to gawking females.

Once he reached the main floor, he found a table across from the hecklers, and before they could turn on him too, Caitlyn wandered back to us, stealing the limelight. She held her cell phone stiffly at her side. "Excuse me!" She pushed her way to the counter, getting on her tiptoes to be seen. "Where can we get cellphone service here?"

"Here and there." Bill muttered into his book. "People don't have much luck around here."

Caitlyn was flabbergasted. "How do you communicate?"

"The Pony Express," one of the old men muttered into his soup. The expected laughter followed.

Bill gestured at a phone attached to the wall. "We got these set up in the nicer cabins if you really need to phone out."

Caitlyn turned to Brek, tossing her curly red hair over her shoulder, imploring him with her eyes. "Which do we have? A nicer cabin or a… a…?"

"A rotten hillbilly cabin," Brek said with a smile, "with one room and a mattress full of bedbugs and ticks."

Bill chuckled low and I felt sorry for him. He was surrounded by comics. "Now, now, that would cost extra. We only save those for people who want the full experience."

I thought of our online documentary and wondered how we could upload our teasers to build up our online audience. "What about internet?" I asked.

Bill glanced up from his careful writing, giving me more deferential treatment than he gave Caitlyn and my brother. "Well, you've got to set that up. I reckon you need some sort of cord and to contact a phone company."

Caitlyn listened intently, her hands clasping the edge of the counter to keep herself as tall as she was. "Which one?"

That stumped him. "Well, I don't rightly know."

The old men from the table guffawed loudly. "You'd be better off asking Sasquatch, girl. Bill might know how to hitch a horse and buggy. Try that!"

"I'll tell you what," the old deputy said. "As soon as you figure out how to get the internet, you tell me. I've been meaning to write back that Nigerian king. He's got some money for me."

"Now shush," Bill lectured them. "Nobody wants to hear from you, Frank."

"You can't live without internet?" asked the man who had lobbied Bill for extra bacon. "In my day we talked to people face to face..."

Bill sighed and handed my brother the key. "You're in Unit #4," he said. "Try to enjoy the quiet life while you're out here. Things are different in Dry Gulch; they're slower. You might find you like it, or you might hate it."

His speech seemed to go into one ear and out the other when Brekker, looking exhausted, asked, "Can we have our dinner sent up to our cabin?"

The older gentlemen at the table seemed to disapprove of the request, likely because it didn't seem sociable, more likely because they were bored and wanted to play with us. But Bill took it in stride. He nodded, looking eager to be a good host.

I scanned the menu, past the sandwiches and comfort foods. They served breakfast all day, but right now, I was freezing. I needed something to warm me up. "What soup do you have?"

"We've got the tomato, the beef and vegetable, the chowder, the cream of basil."

"Why don't you try the basil soup," one of the old men suggested. He was the one Bill had called Frank—the deputy, and the tallest of the group, with a handlebar mustache and a crown of baldness on an otherwise full head of hair. Brek glanced at them distractedly, like he didn't know what to make of them.

The shorter, stout one bristled on my behalf. "She'll get what she wants. She has her own mind."

I interrupted them. "Is the basil soup good?"

All three of the men at the table turned as if given permission to speak. "It's fine. It's plenty fine Be sure to order the large. You'll need more than a small to keep your strength up."

"I wouldn't let her starve," Bill argued with them.

There was nothing for it but to make our introductions at that point. Frank's hand shot out and I shook it firmly. "He keeps the peace in Dry Gulch," Bill explained. "If you don't mind, he'd be grateful if you caused him a bit of trouble. He's hardly got anything to do besides jailing drunks."

Harlan, the bacon lover, had an eye for good food and proceeded to order our whole meal. Pat looked to have twenty years on them. He was Bill's accountant, and he bent over his cane, though his hand trembled from the exertion of it. Who knew how long it took him to do the accounts. He whispered in a shaky voice, "I'm so old, ain't nobody knows I'm alive or dead half the time."

Frank pointed brutally at my shorts. "It's cold out there," he informed me. "You mightn't not wear those shorts either."

"I think she's figured that out," Harlan said in my defense. Standing, he tottered over to the glass case at the deli bar and pointed out his favorite desserts. "You have a sweet tooth, of course? You'd like the cinnamon sugar rolls, and the butter bread."

Bill was out of patience with them. "She'll be here for a month or more. She'll have a chance to try the food!"

"A month?" They looked intrigued. That even caught the attention of the beautiful southern man at the far table.

"I see." Frank's perceptive eyes crinkled up at the sides. "You're after Eden's treasure, are you? I figured with the family name Payne that you'd stay away from it…"

He had shocked me into silence. It really was true—people who weren't us knew more about Eden than we thought they did. Apparently she was a legend around these parts. I struggled to find a response. *We weren't supposed to give away too much.* I glanced over at Brekker and looking impatient, he gave me the go ahead. "It's just a…"

How much did these old men know? "We're doing a documentary."

"A documentary, you say?" Harlan leaned against the display case. "You've come to the right place. A lot of people come through asking about the Eden treasure, and we're the ones who know something about it."

"You do?"

"Yes ma'am, we grew up in these parts. That treasure is part of our heritage."

I couldn't get over what Brek had told me about this place. "This town just allows people to go looking for it?"

"We're on private land here," Bill said. "We can do what we want."

Pat grumbled something about taxes that got Bill worked up. "The government puts their hands in everything," Bill said. "Until we turn over ARPA, we're going to keep fighting 'em and if that means opening up these lands to treasure hunters and game hunters and tree hunters and whatnot, we'll do it and tell the government to take a hike." Brekker loved that kind of talk, and a slow smile crept over his face.

"Of course, no one's found Eden's treasure," Frank said, wandering over. "We hope they don't. It's our main tourist attraction."

Caitlyn dug out her phone to start recording. "How would you like to bring more tourists to this town?" Now we sounded like reporters, though we still looked the part of inexperienced hikers. Brekker was now grinning broadly. Caitlyn's oversized coat was longer than her shorts, the sleeves longer than her arms too, but that was partly by design since she had tugged on them to keep her fingers warm. Her legs were covered in goose bumps.

"You heard of the lake monster?" Frank asked. He stroked his mustache in thought. "It's a big serpent that swallows up boats. Maybe an occasional lone swimmer."

"Too cold," Pat wheezed out his response. The exertion was too much and he coughed into his hand. "Too cold... to swim." He managed.

"Oh." Harlan took it upon himself to translate for the grizzled man. "He means it's too cold to swim in that lake." Putting one hand on my back and the other on Caitlyn's, he herded us over to their table to tell us everything that they knew. "That it might be. That it might be. The bottom of Moonlight Lake has never been found, I've heard."

"How about the tale of a long lost gold mine buried underneath it?" Frank asked. That drew Brekker from the counter and he stole a chair from the table that belonged to my handsome rescuer and dragged it to where we sat. I cast my mountain man an apologetic look in case he'd been saving it for someone, but his furrowed brows were already knit with dark foreboding. His attention wasn't on me, but on Frank as he tried to tell his story. "Word is that there's a treasure down there, so far below that no one can reach it," the old man said.

"If not that lake, one of those round about it," Harlan added. "Maybe Sinkhole Lake or the Merry, Reflection, or Adam's Lake." He laughed. "Any number of those lakes in these parts."

Bill scoffed. He had deserted his station to join us, but not before he changed our orders from takeout to stay. We didn't debate it as he set our bowls and spoons in front of us with a cute little napkin shaped like a grizzly bear. Caitlyn and I both ooh-ed and ah-ed over our food and took pictures of it as the old men warmed up to their stories. We had them. *Or they had us.* It probably wasn't normal for them to have such enthusiastic listeners for their stories.

"That's nothing," Bill said. "I've seen things around here that would make your skin crawl, unspeakable things."

"So unspeakable he won't stop talking about it," Frank said.

The other men laughed. They had the air of men who had nowhere to go, and so I decided to play that to our advantage. "You think those things have to do with the treasure?" I asked.

"Everything here has to do with that treasure," he said with a stern look. He settled into a chair and poked his finger into the table to emphasize his point. "There are things out there in those mountains that guard it. I've felt it. They're unseen things. They know when you've come for it and they watch. They call. It's what brought you here, I reckon—that treasure!"

Before I could deny it, I felt my skin prickling at his words as a chill ran through me.

"Wait!" Caitlyn elbowed me and pointed to my camera, and at her insistence, I took out my Cannon Mark to film. It seemed a little overkill with Caitlyn's cell phone trained on them too, but none of the men complained, only preened under the attention.

Caitlyn recapped the story for my camera like she had somehow become the narrator of this story. "These men have explored these mountains and have seen odd things." Putting her hand on Bill's shoulder, she said, "This man, Bill." She hesitated when she didn't know his last name.

"Bill Strong," he said.

"Bill Strong," she repeated, "has seen unspeakable things in these mountains, things that watch him, call to him… to anyone who wants that treasure hidden in the Uintas. Eden's treasure."

Very good, Caitlyn. She had missed her calling in life.

"Go ahead, Bill," she told him. *Or maybe she hadn't missed her calling—because here we were.*

I turned the camera back on him. "I can't explain it," he said, "but it knows who you are and it figures out your name soon enough. It attaches itself to certain people, almost like it wants you."

"Who does? Who is it?"

"We call it the Bone Man."

Well, that was creepy. "Aren't you going to eat?" Bill interrupted his story to ask me in a suddenly cheery voice, like he hadn't just scared me silly. "You can't listen to these tales on an empty stomach."

"Ah come now," Harlan said, giving us a sympathetic look. "These girls don't want to hear this."

"Yes, we do!" Caitlyn and I said at once. I took a mouthful of soup to encourage Bill to continue.

"It uh… it sort of attached itself to me when I was hiking Lake

Adam once."

His friends jeered, and he shook his head, still sticking stubbornly to his story. "There are plenty of moose and bear and cougars in these mountains, I know! I know. But an old adventurer like me knows the difference between them and… something else. This was different. It was almost human. It kept on trailing after me, hiding behind pines and just watching. It got to be that I grew used to this… hollow feeling. It found me every time I went to Lake Adam. Mostly it left me alone, until years later… well, it had its fun with me, let's say. I was trekking through those mountains with my buddies, and ol' Skip," he pointed to the hearth where the dog lifted his head at his name then dropped lazily back to his pillow, "he was rooting around, having a grand ol' time catching quail and squirrels. Then he stopped. I reckon he heard it before I did. I don't know why, because when the noise reached my ears, it was an unholy screech, the most unnatural sound I'd ever heard, like something mourning and raging all at once. Ol' Skip, he didn't like it; he made all sorts of whining noises like he wanted out, but I had to find out what it was. I had to see what thing had been following me all these years I'd come to Lake Adam. Skip tried to keep me back. I should've known something wasn't right. When I wouldn't leave, he took off running, and that terrified me more than anything. I took off after him. Before I knew it, I was wandering through the forest by myself, calling after Skip and shaking like a greenhorn on a half-broke horse."

"It separated you from your friends," Pat rasped out under his breath. The hand on his cane shook at the exertion his words cost him.

"What?" I was terrified.

Bill nodded in affirmation. "And what do you know, I saw Bone Man, after all those years. It stood on top of the rock mine, on top of those cliffs above me, like Sasquatch, almost with the form of a man but not quite; it was all sharp and bony. It had two legs, sure, and it stood there for a tick, watching me with eyes I couldn't see. Then it hunched over and climbed down the side of the mountain, too fast, too

57

unnatural, too wrong using all the wrong joints. It was surrounded by these black dogs… I think they was dogs. Maybe just shadows, but they growled all the same. And as Bone Man came at me, closer and closer. I couldn't make out a face. I don't think it had one. The closer it got, the more afraid I was that it didn't… but it had a mouth. It sure did, because it let out a mournful cry, like something out of horror flick, and it carried through the wind, very odd sounding, and it said something that shook me to the core. As sure as I am sitting here next to you, it said my name. 'Bill,' it said. 'Bill!' And nothing else, like it didn't know how to say anything else."

Caitlyn was frozen to the spot. My soup was long forgotten. Looking from the lens of my camera over to Brek, I saw he sat very still, like he was trying to figure out this guy's game.

"Then what?" I asked in a whisper.

Bill shrugged. "I ran. I ran and ran until Skip found me. His tail was between his legs and we barely stopped running to greet each other. We took stock that the other was alive and kept going until we caught up to the rest of these knuckleheads. Of course none of 'em believed me."

Frank guzzled his soda through his straw. "He was drunker than a skunk."

"A sight like that is enough to sober up anybody," Bill said in his defense. "How do you explain Skip, Frank? He'll chase after anything, squirrels, moose, bear… but Bone Man? He leaves it alone. It spooked him good. Ain't no one will get me near Lake Adam. When I'm trekking those mountains alone, I stay far away from the cries and the shouts. And if the wind even tries to whisper my name? Why, I keep on walking."

"What…?" Caitlyn cleared her throat, since her voice came out strangled. "What do you think it is?"

"Like I said, something is protecting that treasure." Bill sat back, looking satisfied now that he'd related his tale, especially since he'd terrified most of his audience.

Frank wasn't about to be outdone. "You sure you aren't being chased by Eden's ghost? That drowned girl Eden," he turned to explain as if we didn't know. "She was the first who came looking for that treasure, back in the old west days. Some say she wants revenge for what her beau did to her; others say she found that treasure and she wants no one to have it."

"What do you not understand about the name Bone Man?" Bill asked. "It was in no way female."

"How long did Eden wait under those waters?" Frank argued. "Ain't nothing gonna look female or male after that. No matter." He turned grimmer, most likely trying to steal the spotlight from Bill. "I think that's what happened to them brothers," he said. "Them missing brothers."

"Shh, they don't want to hear about that." Harlan's face was blotched red. I would be surprised if he wasn't as horrified as the rest of us. "What happened to them shook us all."

"This place is a Bermuda triangle when it comes to people looking for that treasure," Bill mused. I was super uncomfortable now, especially since this could be our destiny.

"When did they come? Was it the late 70's?" Frank asked.

"The 80's," Harlan corrected. "But don't mind these boys. These are just scary campfire stories."

"70's are creepier," I inserted.

"The early 90's," Frank said with a snap of his fingers.

"The 90's are creepy too," Caitlyn said. "Have you seen the *Blair Witch Project?*"

Her query brought blank stares. *Clearly not.*

"Either way." Bill pulled forward in his seat. "The brothers came poking around here, asking lots of questions."

"They came with a team, as I recall," Frank said. "There was a nice lad with them—tall fellow, dark haired. Pleasant. I liked him well enough. He seemed to know his way around the mountains."

Brek stiffened, and I realized the significance of this. Our father went looking for this treasure in '89. He fit that description—we'd inherited our mom's blondeness, but we had his height. "What was his name?" my brother asked.

"Not rightly sure… can't remember," Frank said, "but they were looking for that treasure. They were the real thing too; they had all this fancy equipment and fancy education."

"They were clever boys, those brothers," Bill said. "One of them was an archaeologist, geologist, linguist—he studied all them Spanish symbols in the area, and he came round here asking about the legends we heard. The youngest brother, wasn't it?" Frank nodded, and so did Pat, leaning heavily on his cane. Bill squinted to the side, as if he was looking into the past to pull out his memories. "He had a special interest in the Spanish Priest who came here in the 1500's. He looked for Spanish symbols in the rocks and trees. I thought it a hoax myself."

This was sounding more like Eden's journal; though she had only briefly mentioned the monk, they had searched for the Spanish symbols too. "And then they disappeared?" I asked.

"Yeah, yeah. I remember that night. One by one, they vanished in that group, like they was getting picked off. It was spooky. I remember the first one we couldn't find—the tall, pleasant one."

"David?" Brekker asked. "Was his name David?" My ears rang at our father's name.

I was afraid Brek had blown our cover when Bill's eyes narrowed at him. "Have you heard this story before?"

Brekker shook his head and I did too. Caitlyn also denied ever hearing it, but we had broken the storyteller's train of thought. We might not have gotten to hear the rest, but after a thoughtful look at us, Bill continued the story as if he were too caught up in his memories to stop. "Maybe it was David." He shrugged. "It was a long time ago. The others went looking for him, asking around, especially that oldest brother. He was beside himself. The younger one, not so much. He got tense and silent. I don't think he was going to let anything get in the way of finding that treasure. Their father was some rich bigwig in the city. That kid was trying to impress him, I think."

I didn't care about that. What had happened to my father? "Did they ever find the guy who was missing?" I asked.

"No. One day he was there, the next not… and then the brothers went looking for him. And like I said, they disappeared too, along with their team. A search party from the city came poking around here. As far as I heard, they never found a one of them."

Harlan accurately read our expressions and attempted to calm us down. "Honestly I think those men just got embarrassed and ran off. They didn't find anything after all that bragging and didn't want to show up back here with egg on their faces."

"No." Bill shook his head. "Believe what you want, but there is something unsettled in that wilderness. I think those boys woke up what was sleeping out there, something bad and it's hungry for more."

The handsome man made a sound of disgust behind us. I'd forgotten he was there, especially after hearing about my father. He stood up to leave, his heavy hiking boots tromping over the planks of the floor.

I stood up, training my camera at him. I didn't want him to leave like that. "You got something you'd like to add?" I asked after him.

He turned, the fibers of his nylon coat squeaking. "Yeah, you bet I do." There was that sensuous southern accent again. It was a deep one, like he was from Tennessee or South Carolina. "None of that is real."

The old men threw their heads back, laughing and elbowing a disgruntled Bill who seemed surprisingly good-natured now that he'd told his tale. "Oh, Aiden, now?" Bill asked in a friendly tone. "You're not telling me you're a disbeliever?"

Aiden? Aiden. The old men knew his name. Maybe that meant he'd settled in Dry Gulch. Did he work the logging industry? Aiden looked torn, like he hadn't meant to get involved in our talk and he hesitated between blowing us off or telling us off. Caitlyn's attention was trained on him. I knew she was mesmerized for the same reason I was.

"You've been in these mountains?" I asked. He nodded once, and my reporter instincts took over. I didn't know they'd be so strong, but for some reason it felt like he knew more about this story. "What have you seen?"

Caitlyn turned her cell phone camera on him too, which made us seem more paparazzi than I wanted, but I wasn't about to tell her not to do the same thing I was doing. Aiden's lips twisted, his eyes angry. I wasn't sure why I was pushing this, except now this had to do with my father. "The only thing happening up there is…" he began and then, as if he thought better of what he was going to say, shrugged. "Well, it's a warning to stay away, if anything. It's dangerous up there."

The old men hooted and hollered their amusement. I lowered my camera in the noise. I'd read him wrong. He wasn't a disbeliever; he was upset that we were poking the bear.

Bill called out to him in a challenge. "Sounds like you have a story to tell. Let's hear it, boy."

Aiden looked over at me with a hard glint in his eye. "You want something to film?"

"You bet I do." I read the challenge in his sexy southern voice and so I met his sarcasm with some of my own. He wasn't going to intimidate me.

He talked into the camera. "There is only one thing that I know… Bone Man isn't the worst thing in those mountains."

He had Caitlyn's attention. She pulled closer to film. "What is?"

His dark expression would've scared away a less oblivious person, but she was too caught up in her reporter role to notice, or care, and so he gave in. "It's that thing that calls out in the darkness," he said with a lift of a brow. "Just when you think that you are nestled safely in your sleeping bag at night, it comes slowly creeping, pulling at the zipper of your tent… with the face of pure evil… We call him Crazy, Evil Squirrel in these parts."

Frank and Harlan had a good chuckle at Bill's expense, who proclaimed he told the truth. I shut off my camera. What a dork! I was irritated and slightly amused. Caitlyn was still recording us, but now I was a part of her show. She went between me and this new guy, giggling. Maybe this added in an element of human interest, but it was annoying.

I crossed my arms. "Oh really?" I asked. "So you're above all this then? Let me guess—you're one of those guys who runs off to the mountains because you can't connect to people?"

"And you're one of those girls who fakes smiles with people you hate and takes pictures of food you didn't make because you want to feel special. Come find me when you really want to live." He gave me a cocky grin.

Jerk!

Brekker straightened with anger. I defended myself before he could do it. "I'll pass. I'm a little busy pursuing Eden to bother with lowlifes like you."

"The treasure doesn't exist. Go home before you hurt yourself… or someone else." He glanced meaningfully over at the old men and for a moment, I felt ashamed. "Your film will bring all sorts of trouble to this town. You put something like that out there and this place will be teeming with all sorts of riffraff." He could be right, and I felt ready to apologize, but then he said, "Dry Gulch is better off without you."

I grunted out my displeasure, but he gave me no time to defend myself. He left the store through the front. The bells on the door swung wildly. I should've let him go without a fight the first time— before he'd ruined the image of my perfect rescuer. Caitlyn watched him stalk past the full glass windows, the porch light illuminating his exit. He kind of had a swagger to his walk. She turned to me with a broad smile and clicked off her phone. I knew she loved him. Me? Not so much. His words still stung. What did some good 'ol boy from a small town know about me anyway? We weren't going to change his beloved mountains.

The old men at the table were eating it up. Their expressions ranged from astonishment to full-blown delight. "Where can we find this documentary?" Frank asked in all eagerness.

Caitlyn tore her attention from the departing bad boy and smiled cheerfully. "We're putting it up on YouTube."

"The YouTube, huh?" Bill asked. "I've heard of the YouTube."

Harlan pointed to the door where Aiden had left us. "Will that go into the documentary?" he asked. "The love interest?"

"Love?" I turned to them. "No, no, that was not love. None of us are in love with him."

Harlan chuckled. "That's what they all say."

Bill was nodding too, along with Frank and Pat, who had practically slept through the whole conversation. Brekker stood up, impatient to get out. We had the keys and so we headed out the door, promising to give them links to YouTube as they heckled us on our way out. The men had given us some interesting stories for our documentary, but as for clues, there wasn't much to go on. I wasn't sure who'd gotten hustled more—them or us.

"Let us know when to tune in!" Frank called out.

"I'd set up the internet for that," Bill added.

Well, now he'd do it. I set my shoulders against the laughter as we left the same way our belligerent mountain man had gone.

Chapter five

*C*aitlyn dug through the back of the Jeep to pull out her luggage in the dark. She had packed more than Brekker and I combined, and she tried to find her warmer clothes. I hadn't imagined that it would still be so cold in the spring, but Brek must've since he was already bundled up in a puffy red coat and warm gray gloves.

"Thanks for the head's up," I said.

He gave me an ironic smile. "It's not like you've never been to the mountains before."

"That was more than half a lifetime ago! I'm a city girl now," I said. "That's what I've been trying to tell you!" I pulled out my pillow and blankets from the back seat. Slinging my backpack of clothes onto my back, I headed for our cabin. Not only was it colder in the wilderness, but it seemed darker out here. The lights streaming from the cabins on either side of us weren't enough to light my way, and I stumbled.

"Hold on a second." Brekker flipped on his headlights like a big spotlight on me. I wasn't sure whether to be irritated or grateful, but at least I could see where I was going. Unit #4 was a cute, two-story log cabin with a balcony at the front that leaned against a pine tree so that the forest surrounding it looked like a part of the architecture. A barbecue and a picnic table were set into an alcove next to a large screen door. The rest was in shadow, which was creepy, especially after Bill's tall tales. I had overestimated my courage in this remote place. The lofty pines creaked above us.

Brekker set down four of Caitlyn's bags by the door and struggled with the lock until he got the front door open. Reaching inside, he flipped on a light that flooded through the door and windows. I followed him inside. The furniture looked like it came straight from a 70's slasher. The tweed upholstery on the couches and chairs was bright orange. The lamps were those boxed kind only found in cheap motel rooms. There was a television set straight from the early nineties.

"Oh wow!" Caitlyn peered around me. "Did they do this on purpose?" She caught sight of the TV and did a little dance. "No one will believe we stayed here, Ivy! It's so, so retro!"

"Don't get used to it," Brek said. "We'll be camping outdoors most of the time."

"In this cold?" I was more shocked than I had been before at the prospect.

"It gets warmer during the day," he promised. "And we'll just have to get you some warmer things at the Grizzly tomorrow. You're going to need... uh... everything."

At least he got that.

Caitlyn made a face. "We can't sleep outside! What if Bone Man gets us?"

Brekker groaned. "I should never have let you talk to those old guys. They were just having fun with you, girls, anyway."

I wasn't so sure about that. The story wasn't true, but it sounded like Bill believed it.

Caitlyn wanted to believe, too—she wouldn't let it go without a fight. "Not only do we have to sleep outside, but now we have to deal with ghosts." She grabbed my hand and squeezed it in her excitement. "Let's watch a scary movie tonight!"

She could always get a laugh out of me. Strangely the idea sounded appealing. I just wasn't sure what movies we could get on this old box. Flipping it on, I saw most of the stations looked like a big blizzard with static white noise. If we left it on one of those channels, we could pretend we were in the movie *Poltergeist*. Brekker couldn't take it anymore and flipped the switch off. We went back to unpacking. As soon as we saw the exposed rafters in the loft upstairs, Caitlyn and I claimed the room on the ground floor. It was old school, but it didn't look like a torture chamber. Plus, we'd have our own twin bed... made for really tiny twins.

I tested out my mattress. It was flat and stiff, and when I tried to stretch out, my feet hung over the edge. I wondered what Brekker had to deal with upstairs, but decided he deserved what he got, not that he'd care. He was used to roughing it far worse than this.

Throwing my pillow and bedding on top of the brighter, stiffer bedding, I returned to the Jeep and noticed that the cabin next to us was alive with activity. They had about a dozen ATVs parked on the grass. *Great. We were next to the party house.* Not that I cared about the noise keeping me up all night, but I had a "fear of missing out," known as FOMO in other circles. I knew it would get bad when we weren't invited to play, and if we were, then Brek might have to kiss his best helpers goodbye... at least one of them. Caitlyn had FOMO worse than I did. She came outside and made a wistful sound. "Let's go over to Unit #3 and introduce ourselves."

"No, no, no," I said, knowing she was serious and resisting her as much as I could. "We're here to work."

"And part of that means making connections to other professionals."

"I doubt that's what they are," I said with a laugh.

"Good."

But before she could make her case, Brekker came outside and Caitlyn straightened, wanting to make a good impression on him. She busied herself with the rest of her luggage. Brek barely noticed her efforts, tucking his equipment under his arm and taking it back to the cabin. He'd lap us soon. It was getting cold and I didn't want to be out here a minute longer. Party house or no. I hurried to gather the rest of my things, including a cute, red midi dress that Caitlyn insisted I bring because, "You never know!"

With my hands full of things that were in no way appropriate for camping, I heard the door open at the party house and the volume from it rose dramatically. I looked over the bundle of clothes in my arms and my knees went weak. My mountain man had walked outside onto the balcony. From the light escaping the still-open door, I saw his breath leaving his lips.

"Caitlyn," I squeaked. Aiden had somehow joined the party house.

She knew immediately, probably before I did. She let out a giggle and I shot her a warning look that she wouldn't see in the darkness. Luckily the night hid me from him too. He had shed the thick black coat and was wearing exactly what I'd imagined he'd been wearing beneath it—a red plaid button up that accentuated his muscular frame and broad shoulders. Just like a man of the land should.

He leaned on the railing of the balcony and stared over it, straight at our cabin. Of course he didn't know I was staying there. How could he know? And if he did, he wouldn't care. Despite how we'd first met, he thought of me as a spoiled city girl. But that didn't add up. If he was so angry at meddling outsiders, why was he hanging out at the party house? He sure had a lot of friends. I was trying to figure out who he was when he turned and went back inside with that signature swagger of his. I loved that swagger, and I hated it!

Caitlyn's hands went to my arm. "Let's go talk to him!"

"No!" I shook her away. I'd be keeping my distance from Unit #3 now. Nothing would change my mind.

Brekker came back and snorted when he found us still outside. He rubbed it in. "I told you not to pack so much."

"I didn't!"

He was halfway to our cabin when he stopped abruptly and gaped at Unit #3. "Wait," he said. I glanced over to see what he saw. Through the open window, a steady stream of people walked past. Most of them male. His whole body went rigid. "It is!" he growled. I guessed that didn't mean a good thing. He set his equipment on the porch, not able to get the straps off his shoulder fast enough.

"What are you doing?" I asked.

"Angel," he said under his breath. "It's Angel!"

His Angel? Ex-girlfriend Angel? Why would she be here? "What are you going to…?" He left me mid-speech and tore after the party house.

All I could think of was Aiden. He was in there too. I didn't want to see him again. "Brekker?" I chased after him, but he wasn't listening. He was stiff with anger. "Wait until morning. Don't talk to her now."

But Brek had always been a man of action. Caitlyn had stopped laughing. One mention of Angel made her see the danger of the situation. The way my brother acted meant he wasn't over her. My best friend trailed after us, more reluctantly than she normally would while I tried to talk sense into my brother. "Please, Brekker! I don't want to go in there."

"Don't! I've got this." He barged into the cabin and I felt like I had no choice but to follow him. It was warm inside. Stuffy actually. It was no wonder Aiden had gone outside. The cabin was packed with men. Tough ones. Caitlyn stumbled to a stop behind me and her urgent hands clasped my arm again; this time she wasn't playing.

We were wrong. This was not a party house. There was a difference between pretty boys partying it up and trying to impress the girls and rough men who acted worse when a girl was in the room. These were the kind of ruffians that I'd thought Aiden was afraid we'd bring to his town with our documentary… except they were already here. The men were going over maps and arguing until Brek found his ex-girlfriend in their ranks.

"Angel!"

She stood near the fridge, talking low with Aiden. He held a copper cylinder device the size of a cell phone and she ran her slender fingers down the length of it, looking curious. At her name, she circled in surprise, her full lips making an O, her raven black hair swinging becomingly over her shoulder. Angel couldn't have planned her seductive turn better if she had been in a movie. She was the smoldering Tomb Raider type, and she knew how to get a man's blood pumping in her skimpy black tank tops.

And Brekker was a man, wasn't he? Though his eyes blazed with the intensity of his emotions as he came face to face with her, his rage won out. "What are you doing here?"

She bit her lip, her surprise at seeing him melting away with a smile. *She already knew he was here!* No woman would regain her composure like this. Angel couldn't hide it from me. Exchanging glances with an amused Aiden, who I steadfastly ignored, she placed her hand provocatively over Brek's. "You're traveling light, Brekker. Where's your usual team?"

He was silent, refusing to react to her goads.

Her gaze trailed over to me. "Aww, you've brought your other half. I was beginning to think you were hiding your twin from me." She scolded Brek like they were still on the best of terms. "It's been too long, Ivy." That was only because I refused to be around Brek when she was with him. Her eyes found the diminutive Caitlyn next. "Or are you here for pleasure, Brek?" Angel giggled like that was a ridiculous notion and faced her ex again. "Surely, you're not planning on using these two as your team? They're so cute."

Laughter followed that. Angel's cohorts had gathered around us. She had brought her own team of treasure hunters. They kept their distance for now. I was grateful. They were all so big, even Aiden towered over me. But Brekker was a formidable force, and he crossed his arms. His biceps from his countless adventures were bigger than his weight lifting days in high school, and I was relieved to see he could take any of them on, though maybe not all of them at once.

"Oh, Brekker," Angel still hadn't released his hand, and she stuck her lip out in a show of pity. "You're so unprepared. What happened to you?"

I wanted to catch both ends of her hair in a catfight. How dare she act so superior? Everything she knew about Eden's treasure she would have heard from Brekker. It basically belonged to our family. She'd know nothing about hunting treasure if it wasn't for him. Why, of all times, would she come now? There was more to their breakup than

Brek was telling me. He wrenched his hand from hers. "You didn't answer my question," he said.

"I imagine I'm here for the same reason you are." She wouldn't say what that was, but I doubted she was filming a documentary.

I glanced nervously at the group of men. They were built for action, fighting, for anything she needed. Where did she get the money to fund so much manpower? My gaze caught with Aiden's... who I'd thought of as my rescuer. A slow smile crossed his face and he made a kissy face my way.

I stiffened.

"You're still here?" His voice was deep and soft like black velvet as he tucked the shiny cylinder he held into his back pocket. "How's documenting life?"

He was on that again. I was so annoyed. "Great, as long as it's not yours. How's pretending to be someone you're not?"

"It's all right. Got any tips?"

"Yeah," I said. "Stick closer to the truth next time. Pretending to care about some sweet old men was a little unbelievable coming from you."

Caitlyn made a sound of approval.

"How about I say my concern was for you?" he asked.

That surprised me, until I remembered we were talking about how to lie here. "Then I'd say stop wasting your time. I'm not interested."

I heard Caitlyn's cheers, mingled with his men's jeers. Our fight was going public. I was surprised that Caitlyn wasn't recording this.

"Hunter." Angel touched his arm, distracting him from our argument.

"Hunter?" Caitlyn mouthed, nudging me. She made a face. Exactly my thoughts. Why was Angel calling Aiden by the name Hunter? Had he faked that too?

"Tell me what you want to do about that problem we were talking about," Angel said.

Aiden... or Hunter rather, blew out and thought a moment before saying, "If they join us, they only get 15% of the cut and I'm not offering more."

15%? That was insulting. It looked like he was calling the shots here, not Angel. That's where she got the money. Aiden was in charge here. All that talk about saving the town from riffraff seemed even more ludicrous now. He wanted Eden's treasure, whatever that was, and he'd tried to get rid of the competition.

Angel turned to Brekker. "What do you think? 15%? You're here anyway, and you can't seriously be thinking you can hack it on your own, dragging your sister along and her... best friend. Join us."

"Join you?" Brekker repeated incredulously.

Who did they think they were? Darth Vader? I crossed my arms, glaring at Hunter. The name fit better than Aiden anyway. It belonged to a meathead. I was a tall girl, and my head still didn't reach his shoulders. I tried not to notice they were knotted with muscle, and his arms were even worse.

"Sorry, we don't have any slots open on the team," Brekker said. I nodded beside him. Maybe a little too vigorously.

"Brekker." Angel sighed, drawing closer to him. She put all her seductive skills into that move. I knew that was how she got her way with him before, and I braced myself. "You don't want to put your sister in danger. She isn't as experienced as you or me. Don't you care about her at all?"

I pushed between them and gave her a knowing smile. "We're trekking out tomorrow. So if you don't mind, we've got a lot of work to do."

"We'll see how long you last." That was from Hunter this time and his gaze swept over me in disapproval. "I've heard all I need to know about you."

"From Angel, right? See you around, *Hunter.*" I turned to leave, catching sight of Brekker's angry face behind me before realizing the danger. If we didn't get out soon, he'd start a fight. These men were too giant—they barely fit in this cabin. "Brek, let's go."

"If you need anything, just scream," Angel called gaily after us. "I've got a lot of manpower, but it's really cool you've slimmed down your team so much, Brekker. I could never do that."

Feeling the insult like a punch to the gut, I grabbed a hold of Brek's arm and tried to ease him away. Caitlyn clung to his other side when one of the rough men blocked us from leaving. This man had shaved his head, with a nick in it that seeped a little, and a jagged scar across his pale eyebrows. He got in my face, staring at me with watery, ice blue eyes.

"Let us through," I said. He wouldn't let me slide past him. Brekker wasn't going to take it. He shook my grip from his arm and pushed the bully away with his shoulder. This started a shoving match that knocked Caitlyn and me back. The next thing I knew Brekker and his assailant were swinging punches.

"Stop!" I shouted. Without thinking, I tried to run into the mass of fighting men to save my brother, but two hands clamped onto my shoulders and ripped me back from them. I twisted and saw that Hunter had me. My back ran into his hard chest. "Let me go!"

He was too busy for that. He shielded me and Caitlyn from the worst of the fight, knocking away one of his men, then he shouted down the one going at it with my brother. "Rosco! That's enough!"

Rosco pulled back, rubbing the blood from a face that looked like it had been sculpted from chalk. Brekker lowered his fists. Even Angel looked shocked, but what did she expect? She couldn't just waltz into town and steal everything my brother had ever cared about. She had gone too far.

Caitlyn pulled from us to fix her tumultuous red hair now that streamed over her face. Brekker saw Hunter still had me in his arms, and he stiffened and ran the back of his hand under his bruised lip. "Let Ivy go."

Looking up into Hunter's hazel eyes, I felt myself melt, then tried not to melt. He had rescued me again. "Yeah, it's best you leave," Hunter said with an accent made thicker under his duress. The breath of it tickled my ear as his hand loosened over me, but he must've thought better of letting me go completely because he took another look at his men—especially the widely grinning Rosco—then forcibly walked Caitlyn and me to the door, essentially herding us through the pack of wolves. Brek easily caught up, growling insults under his breath, as he took back his role as our protector.

As soon as we were outside, Hunter leaned against the doorframe, his hand swinging casually. "Have fun wandering the mountains," he said.

I glared. He took every opportunity to rile me. I got that. I was used to that with my brother, but with this guy it infuriated me. "We'll tell you when *we* find what *you* came for," I said.

In lieu of a reply, he shut the door between us. Hunter was done talking to us. The way back to our cabin through the darkness was silent and tense. The pines stretched out like a skeletal fan over our heads before we reached the streaming lights from our porch.

Looking over at Brek, I saw that it illuminated in stark relief his tormented expression, but he didn't look surprised, and that made me suspicious. "Why did we come when Angel did?" I asked. "Is there something you're not telling us?"

"It's just as much a shock to me as it is to you."

I didn't believe him for a second. Brekker had some explaining to do, but he was in no mood to talk about it. As soon as we got back inside, he tore through the outdated living room and stormed up the stairs to the loft. The sound of him setting up equipment drifted through the planks of the ceiling and I knew he wouldn't be coming down any time soon.

Caitlyn bit her lip worriedly. "He isn't over her, is he?" I couldn't answer, but I suspected she was right. "I hope she runs off with one of those beefy men and never comes back…" she said, then her eyes darted to mine, "just not with Hunter."

I collapsed onto the stiff, orange couch then gave out a pained grunt. Nothing about that piece of furniture was comfortable. Caitlyn

74

sat down beside me, but—learning from me—more carefully. Her expression lit up with sudden mischief. "Hunter? Can you believe it? His name is Hunter? That's just *too* manly."

Despite everything that had happened, I broke into a smile.

"And his arms are corded with muscle. I'm not usually into men who are rocks, but when he stopped that guy from ramming into me, his biceps bulged like that." She made a wide gap with her hands to demonstrate.

It felt like betraying Brekker to appreciate it. "Stop it!"

"You like him," she accused. "You like him and you like his sexy southern accent. All I can say is, goodbye, Russ!" Of course she was playing matchmaker now that her sights were set on my brother. I hated to break it to her, but neither of us were going to get anywhere with these men. But it was fun to dream, although in my case, Hunter was my nightmare. He was too good at pushing my buttons.

"No," I said. "He's not my type. Imagine every time I tried to introduce him. This is my boyfriend, Hunter." I said it with all the manliness I could muster and went cross eyed at the attempt.

Brekker shouted down the stairs at that. "That will never happen! If you try to hook up with that idiot, I'll officially disown you!"

Caitlyn and I met eyes and broke into giggles. She found the remote to turn on the TV. We got static on the screen and she mindlessly flipped through the channels. "I wish we had the internet," she said. "Could you imagine the Facebook post we could write up on this?"

I still wasn't over Hunter's stinging comments about how I should live my life, not document it, so I shrugged. That was the world we lived in. Maybe not right now since we were stuck in a backwards cabin in the middle of nowhere with no cell phone reception and nothing to watch.

After endlessly searching for something on the tube, Caitlyn found *Law and Order*. That was playing everywhere all the time as far as I was concerned. I went into my room to try to drown it out and gathered my blankets around me. I could hear the noise from the party house in the back, and I rolled my eyes now that I knew what was really happening there.

We were no different than the saloon girl and the rascal card shark. I dug through my backpack and pulled out Eden's journal. I'd loved these stories as a kid, but over time I'd realized how messed up poor Eden was. She followed Lucius Payne around like a puppy, and my ancestor would betray her. I wished that she had gone for that other guy—his name was Adam Black and he was a trapper. He had a thing for her, but Eden did what a lot of us did, she went for the guy she had worked the hardest to get because it was a habit. It didn't matter if Lucius was good for her or not—she felt the greatest connection to him and the rest she imagined. Every good thing she made him out to be wasn't real. In the end, her eyes had been brutally opened to it.

But Adam? Adam, I felt, would've been different. I opened the journal to the part where she met him and smiled a little to myself at the romance of it.

Eden's Journal: June 12th, 1855 – Mountains of the Deseret

We shoved out of the Gold Fields of San Francisco and scrabbled through the California Trail. Three long months it took us, and we might never have made it had we not thieved and stoled along the way. We passed plenty of men hankering on making their fortunes where we'd left and they was plenty disheartened to see us fleeing it. But we told 'em we'd found religion. Lucius said it was more humane that way, and I was inclined to agree. It made us seem more honest folk and none of them came riding after us when things turned out missing.

Lucius was bent on finding Adam Black on account that him and Mr. Black was such good friends. They'd come over from Canada and partnered up on the Mormon Trail way back when. Mr. Black cooled his heels in Salt Lake City while Lucius went on to San Francisco. Lucius heard a while back Mr. Black had turned to scouting and fur trapping. Mr. Black was awful good friends with an old Shoshone Chief and Lucius knowed the man could help us find that treasure. Mr. Black had lived with the Shoshones for some time and the legend came from them so he might know something about it. He was a good sort of man. Lucius made it a point of saying it when I got to fretting. "No, Eden, he's a good sort of man, you hear?"

It was a mean and miserable journey through the Forty Mile Desert and the Humboldt River Valley Passage to the City of Rocks, and from there we hove to Salt Lake City where we employed the use of an old Mormon travel guide to find them Deseret Mountains. Lucius took to moaning and complaining, and I was in a sweat to fetch this and that to make him more comfortable, but it warn't no use. Our horses insisted on dying and my shoes wore through. My toes pestered me something awful with blisters and frostbite. I thank Providence we didn't git brain fever or yaller janders. The camps a piece from here had plenty of them outbreaks.

We struck up to the town of Dry Gulch first and told anyone we come acrossed we was Mormon and newlyweds and looking to homestead, and they dropped housewarming gifts on us like it was Christmas—blankets and salt and pork and all manner of supplies; plus two horses if'n we promised we'd return 'em. Promising faithfully and hoping I was in no way fibbing about them pack animals, I felt sick with shame and I'd half a mind to make our wedding vows real, but Lucius would none of it, not when we had a job of work ahead of us.

The good folk from Dry Gulch told us we'd find Mr. Black's cabin up a ways in the mountains. It was cold going, as there was plenty of snow and so's we'd had to make good use of them blankets. It warn't too long before we stumbled acrossed Mr. Black's place tucked away in a sweet meadow with a backdrop of mountains. It took my breath clean away and I raised up a query, "Whyn't we civilize ourselves here?"

Well, Lucius didn't like that! He tore into me with the hottest kind of language, "We warn't here to homestead! Stop thinking above yerself and git yer head on that gold!"

Problem was that Mr. Black was nowhere whereabouts, no matter how we hollered after him. And there warn't none of his horses in the barn neither. Lucius told me to cook up some vittles the homesteaders gave us, whilst he left to fetch us his friend. I stowed away in that lean-to just laying for Lucius so'd we eat, but it got dark and there warn't no Lucius. I got to worrying and shivering. We was all alone up there with wild dogs and bears and who knowed what else? I slid out my shotgun and loaded it, and when there was still no hide nor tail of Lucius, I buried myself in the hay and waited there for any manner of wild animal or beast to come upon me.

The night's uncommon cold in these parts and I felt my fingers freeze on the trigger of my gun. My whole body shook and trembled like a rattle on a snake, and I got to imagining all sorts of fears. What if someone brung out the warrant on us? Suppose'n the law catched up to Lucius and them bounty hunters shot him dead? Suppose'n they was coming for me next? I was most ready to cry so's when I heard the steps in the barn and took a peek through the hay, my heart dropped to the bottom of my boots when I saw a man slinking around.

This warn't Lucius. This were an intruder if I'd seen one. He held a lantern high to his face and that's when I knowed he warn't Mr. Black neither. He was a younger man, in my estimation, not the elderly gent I'd come to expect—strong too, like a lawman should be. He'd seen plenty of sun, but he warn't red and burnt like we'd been out in that desert. His hair and beard warn't near as dark as Lucius' and he kept it trimmed like the men in these parts done.

When he turned to me, my heart felt like it would escape my chest and I came a tumbling out of the hay with my gun frozen to my hand. I think I might have shot the man straight through except my fingers were so cold I couldn't git the trigger down. He took one look at me and hit the ground.

When I didn't shoot, he set down his lantern and raised his hands. "Now settle down," said he, and he moved slowly on me, ducking and dodging as he come, trying to talk me down so's I put down my gun. And I would've if I hadn't been so afeared. His hands found mine and they warmed me right up while he pointed the barrel away. Then he slid the gun from me, his eyes on me the whole time, talking low like I was a wild animal. As soon as he got the piece from me, he asked me for my name and I told him, but it didn't register anything with him. Of that I was mighty grateful. That meant he weren't no lawman. That's when I asked if he knowed Mr. Black, and he told me he went by that name. He was Adam Black!

I coulda fell down weeping in my relief, but then I told him Lucius was missing. He straight up said, "Never mind that, Miss. You're as cold as a kitten lost in the pantry."

And he wouldn't hear another word. He took me in his strong arms and tried to git me warm. That got my heart leaping in my chest but soon enough I stopped my shaking, and he brought me inside his one room cabin and got a fire going, still working on my extremities and giving me hot drinks until I was all snug. He was mighty sorry to see such blisters on my feet and he worked on those next. It was then that Lucius pushed his way in. I felt sore about it, on the account Mr. Black and I were getting along so fine, but then I scolded myself. What would it be if something had happened to Lucius? Would I just go on as if he were nothing? I was a more faithful woman than Lucius reckoned, though he accused me of taking a liking to Mr. Black, and all sorts of impolite talk when he saw us so cozy at the hearth.

Mr. Black wouldn't hear none of it and said all sorts of things that warmed my heart so that I thought I'd never be cold again. He said to quit bullragging and treat me like a lady or he warn't helping Lucius for nothing. Lucius lost no time telling him I worked the saloon before this and I stoled this and that and I warn't to be trusted, but as I was the only female in these parts wearing a dress and petticoats, I judged Mr. Black couldn't help but treat me like a fine lady during the days we was snowed up there in those mountains. He was a different one, and I suspicioned Lucius had it right. Adam Black was a good sort of man.

I touched those words on that part of the journal, reading them again. Adam Black was a good sort of man. For not the first time, I wished Eden had gone for him. If she had, Lucius might've gone his own way after failing to find that stupid treasure, and he wouldn't have taken off with her journal and kept it for clues. His descendants would've forgotten all about this nonsense. I listened to Brekker pace the floor above me. He was still in a rage. Angel represented what he couldn't have—money, professionalism, success. My life was built around things I couldn't afford and had no business going after because I lived beyond my means—now I was paying dearly. None of us were happy.

Listening to the police sirens and the low murmur coming from *Law and Order* in the living room, I carefully shut Eden's journal and wrapped myself in a blanket to join Caitlyn there. She looked up as I walked in. "Thank goodness you didn't fall asleep!" she said. "I didn't know how much *Law and Order* I could take. Let's have a real party."

At the sound of us relaxing, Brek called down from the loft. "Ivy! I need Eden's journal."

I'd wondered when he was going to ask for that, and for a moment I thought of refusing him. If there was the possibility of talking him into giving up this idea and coming home with us, I'd do it, but my debt kept me trapped and Brek's insatiable passion for the hunt had been made stronger with Angel's interference. We'd already used up a lot of our backer's money on gas, food, rentals and supplies; there was no going back now.

Brekker got tired of waiting for my reply and made an appearance at the bottom of the stairs. The Roman cut of his blond hair was messed up in the back where he must've laid on the bed. I noticed his bruising lip and didn't comment, knowing he wasn't in the mood for my sympathy. "Where is it?"

I marched into my room to retrieve it. "Brekker," I said when I came out with it, "there's not much in there." He plucked it from my hands and was halfway up the stairs before I could shout up to him, "Give it back when you're done!"

He made some unintelligible reply, but I knew he would. It was my only reminder of dad. Somehow it made me feel like I knew him a little better, knowing he'd kept it with him like I had.

Caitlyn turned the heat up in the fake hearth near the boxy TV set. "Look!" She pointed to the VCR in the shelf under the TV. "How old school is that? When is the last time you've seen one of those? I saw the video cassettes on the shelf behind that huge white dog at the café. Let's check one out from the office."

I smiled and decided to forget my troubles. "And order some chocolate too," I said.

"And pizza!"

"Yes!" *If they had it in this town.* Noticing that the curtains were wide open, I looked through the window at the "party house" next door. Their lights were still on. They hadn't bothered to close their curtains either. I could see everything: Hunter at the table tinkering with that copper device again, Angel leaning close to him, his team of ruffians making themselves at home in the fridge and on the couch. Rosco manning the remote. Shuffling out of my blankets, I left my nest on the couch so I could close the curtains. I didn't want Hunter to see me lounging around and eating out of pizza boxes or the next time he saw me he'd use that against me too.

Caitlyn found the old rotary phone and laughed while she tried to get in all the numbers to call the front desk. "This is roughing it, Ivy."

Not quite roughing it.

I thought of Eden and how she'd come through here half frozen in mid-June to find a treasure she hardly wanted, and how she'd lied and cheated her way into coming to Dry Gulch because she'd do almost anything to survive, and for the first time, I felt very close to her.

Chapter six

*T*he next morning, we wandered through the supplies at the Grizzly Bear House. We'd woken up before it was light, and it was still freezing outside. I could see my breath all the way to the main office, and I felt desperate as I picked out gloves and warm stocking caps, socks, a blue puffy coat, windbreaker pants, anything on sale that I could layer over my exercise clothes to keep me warm. Luckily, I had some hiking shoes I'd used when I'd dated Russ, or I'd be dealing with breaking those in too.

Caitlyn already had all those things—in bright pink and orange— so she was there for emotional support and trinket shopping. She found a magnet that said Dry Gulch on it and another with the Grizzly Bear House that she simply had to have.

I knew that I was over-packing, but I was terrified I was going to miss something. Bug spray, first aid kit, cleats for the snow if we found any, a rattlesnake bite kit, ankle braces, knee braces. I had to be prepared for every horrible eventuality, though I was sure I was missing something. Turning the corner of the store, I came upon the bear spray and picked it up.

"Bear spray?" Brekker lifted his head from the compass he was considering. "Are you going to fit all that in your backpack?"

"I'll make it fit!"

He laughed a little, though his mood was sober after last night. I could see his heart in his eyes and it was broken. Angel had done a number on him. He'd never had patience for my sympathy, so instead I tried to muster up excitement for tromping through the cold mountains, facing wild animals and who knew what else? I put the bear spray in my basket.

Brek had been up most of the night looking at maps and making notes from Eden's journal. Her scribblings gave us an edge: the treasure was located in caves hidden by a lake near a cold-water geyser, but what lake? What geyser? All the searching in the maps hadn't identified one. The Shoshone Indians had helped Eden find the lake before. According to them, it was sacred and must be returned to its original form. She had described the layout of the land, but that was the geography of the time. It could be any of these lakes in the Uintas.

My brother decided that the first lake we'd explore would be Moonlight Lake up the mountain about seven miles. It was the most obvious choice. According to the people in town, it was surrounded in urban legend—the serpent monsters, the hidden treasure, the bottomless pit. I doubted it would be that easy to find Eden's treasure, since anyone would look for it up there, but we had to start somewhere. The plan was to spend the day there and come back for more supplies that evening. We wouldn't start camping until we got further out in the Uintas—much to my relief, since the days and nights would only grow warmer from here. *I hoped.*

"Smile!" Caitlyn said across the way.

Out of habit, I posed and said, "Day!" which was what we said instead of "cheese" because that made our mouths go into a grimace. Caitlyn snapped the picture and cooed over it. She was taking pictures of everything. Normally I'd join her in the fun, but I was cold, and besides, I didn't want to get caught and ridiculed for not living life.

The sound of ATVs outside told me that Hunter's cabin was awake. Nothing they did was subtle, which was probably a good thing since I wanted to keep my distance from them. A few of his men drove past the windows in the predawn light, and I hoped that meant we wouldn't see them for the rest of the day.

I took my basket of hiking supplies to the cash register. Bill wasn't behind the counter this morning; only a tired-looking lady with messy hair and a thick sweater under a boxy coat. The heater was cranked up behind her and it was so hot that I pulled at my own jacket, forgetting how cold I'd been seconds earlier. She wordlessly scanned my things and tossed them in bags. I turned to find Brekker, since he had the money, and noticed Hunter standing behind me in his hiking gear.

I jumped and he smiled. "Relax," he drawled. "I'm just here for food." He had a water bottle and some jerky. His eyes roamed to my mass of purchases. The cashier was still scanning them. "Are you buying the whole store?"

I didn't answer, since I was a little sensitive about overbuying right now. "Why do they call you Hunter?" I asked instead. "I thought your name was Aiden." It was practically an accusation.

"That's the name I checked in with, yeah."

"So is that your real name?"

"Yes."

"Hunter or Aiden?"

"Both." He was trying not to smile now, which irritated me. "Why do you care?"

I didn't know. One name screamed knuckle dragger, the other sounded like an intellectual British guy. "Aiden Hunter?" I asked. That was something in between.

He watched me suspiciously now, and I wondered why. When I refused to back off, he nodded once, and I turned back to the register, deciding to ignore him until I left.

Caitlyn came prancing over and slid the debit card my way. "Brekker is going back for the maps," she said by way of explanation, and she added more supplies to my pile, only making Hunter wait longer to buy his measly breakfast. I was secretly glad. She turned to him with a smile. "Thanks for saving us last night. Ivy won't say it, but I think she likes you."

My eyes widened at her, and I glanced over to see him grinning. He only did that when he was making a fool of me, which was a lot. "I don't know what she's talking about," I said.

I shouldn't have bothered because Caitlyn danced her eyebrows suggestively and whispered conspiringly to him, "See?"

84

"Yeah," he said. "It's obvious now."

I straightened in outrage. "You're the one who brought those guys you rescued us from, so you know what? I'm not grateful because it wouldn't have happened if you hadn't been here."

He was silent in the face of that and I thought that ended it, but then he said, "I did rescue you from the Jeep." It sounded extra cheeky with his accent. "And if I hadn't been here, you'd still be hanging upside down with your lovely legs swinging in the air."

"What?" Caitlyn asked in absolute delight. My face went hot. "Why didn't you tell me about that?" she shrieked. I had nothing, except it was super embarrassing when I thought of how ridiculous I had looked. Swiveling to him, she asked, "So you just keep rescuing Ivy over and over again?"

He nodded, clearly enjoying my discomfort.

"It was twice!" I defended myself. "And I'm only counting the one time!"

"So you do count it?" he asked. His eyes searched mine and I couldn't read what was in them, but it felt suspiciously like flirting, and I couldn't have that. Maybe I'd liked the idea of Hunter rescuing me before, but I didn't when I was angry at him.

"Why are we even talking about this?" I willed the cashier lady to go faster, but I think she was going slower, probably listening in, but who wouldn't? If it wasn't me, I'd do it too.

"Don't worry," he said. "The first rescue was on me."

"The second one wasn't?" Caitlyn was relentless. "Oh, Ivy, you know what that means. You owe him."

"I don't count the second one," I reminded her.

"Maybe she'll count the next time," Hunter said, as if I was a walking accident waiting to happen.

I couldn't help it—he knew how to get to me—and I twisted around. "You're not rescuing me again. I'll be fine."

He smirked. I passed the debit card at the lady and she ran it through the reader while I clenched the side of the counter, trying to keep myself in check.

"Oh! Please don't judge the team by us," Caitlyn reassured him, probably realizing that we were coming off bad. "Brekker is actually really good at what he does. He's a professional." I tried to give her the signal to stop blabbing, but she was in a chatty mood. This was how she was when we went dancing, and normally it won us lots of guys, but I didn't appreciate it here. "We're new at this," she said.

"Where's his old team?" he asked. "Nothing against you ladies, but if he's so good, why can't he work with professionals? He's not hiding something from you, is he?"

"All right, game is over," I said. "He's trying to get into our heads, Caitlyn."

Caitlyn look intrigued. "Is that so? Why? I thought you were more of a southern gentleman?"

And nothing would stop her flirting! "Does it matter?" I asked. I collected the receipt and our bags. Caitlyn took the hint and helped me out, shrugging at Hunter like she couldn't control my rudeness.

"Watch out for Evil, Crazy Squirrel," he said at our backs. He set his paltry water bottle and jerky on the counter. "If your heart isn't set on the treasure, it'll leave you alone, but it has a special vendetta against anyone related to Lucius Payne."

That made me stumble over my feet. Had he overheard that from the old men last night? Or had Angel told him about our family history? I decided to play it off. "I've got my bear spray!" I called over my shoulder. "Nothing coming after me stands a chance—not Bone Man, Not Evil, Crazy Squirrel. Oh? And neither do you." I twisted my lips to make a kissy face at him like he'd done to me and I left, not waiting for his reaction.

I joined Brekker outside as he came back to the Grizzly wearing his heavy duty frame pack. He had packed it with his scuba gear and geological instruments. Caitlyn giggled at the sight of him. "My, you're a rock of a man!"

No matter how I tried, I couldn't see him through her eyes, but I admitted he was looking especially tall and athletic this morning in his tactical pants with zippers all around the leg. He could tear them off at any length. Honestly, I was more jealous than anything. I wanted those and his coat. It was another one of those layering creations that I had to duplicate with windbreakers, fleeces and my workout clothes. Caitlyn made a big deal over him while he ran an experienced hand through my purchases. "That's the best they've got?"

"What did you expect?" I asked. "It's from the Grizzly Bear House."

"I guess it'll do."

"Brek! You knew that I'd never done this before. You should've warned me before we reached the sticks!"

The bells and wind chimes clashed over the front door of the Grizzly. Brekker peered over my shoulder and straightened in a threatening stance. I didn't have to look behind me to know that Hunter was coming through that door. My brother's gaze shifted from him to me, and I turned, seeing Hunter watching me. Hunter nodded in greeting, took a nonchalant sip from his water bottle, and almost ran straight into a telephone pole, totally ruining his bad boy image.

I snickered. "Hey careful! You don't want *me* to have to save *you*!"

Brek groaned like I shouldn't talk to the enemy, but this was trash talk, and I hoped it stung, but unfortunately it didn't faze Hunter like I wanted. Smirking in return, he climbed his four-wheeler like it was a horse and raised two fingers in a salute. He gunned the engine and sped past us to join his team in the backwoods somewhere. What a hick! I couldn't think of enough insults for him.

Caitlyn nudged me, laughing. "He's perfect for you."

I made a face at her. Brekker was not deaf! And he was shaking his head, embarrassing me further. "No, no, no. I hope you're not thinking he's cute, Ivy. You can do much better than that."

"I know!"

"You know?" He looked worried. "You've never listened to me about guys before."

"Well, I'm not an idiot. You think I'm an idiot?"

A smile touched his lips. "No."

I started putting on my layers and stuffing my purchases in my backpack. I'd bought too much. Brekker was right; it would be a tight fit, and I refused to let him be right about another thing, so I got it all in. The hard part was getting the overburdened backpack on, and I struggled to get my arms into the straps. Caitlyn and Brekker helped me out with that until I felt myself tipping. We had to start moving or I'd fall over. "Let's go!"

And so we set off for the trail to Moonlight Lake. I was armed with Eden's journal and my Mark II, and Caitlyn with her camera phone. The morning was still cold, but it got warmer the more we went up the mountain until we were taking off layers. Brek was faster than us, and after yet another wheezing cry for rest, we voted that he couldn't be the leader anymore. Caitlyn led us for half a mile after that, stopping to take so many pictures that Brekker made a new rule that we were only allowed to take three pictures until we reached the lake, but after she got so caught up in her bad date story that she forgot to walk forward, he made the final rule that she also could never lead. That left me as the remaining leader, who was neither too fast nor too slow, which made me the baby bear in this scenario.

Taking the front, I soon got caught up in the scenery. The mountains were lush and green with pines and aspens. Ahead of us in the distance they looked blue, the tallest of them capped in snow. Even in spring. It was the perfect time to come, though, because everything seemed brighter and greener. Tiny wildflowers popped up through the budding grass next to our trail, which wasn't too bad. I'd expected patches of ice, but it was getting too hot for that, and we mostly found mud that turned into patches of dirt the farther we went. In fact, the temperature had risen about fifteen degrees from the morning and it was only getting hotter from there.

I took off another layer until I was down to my last one and I was still too hot, so I made a mental note to layer shorts under my clothes next time. The trail branched off from the ATV trail into a foot trail, which meant we wouldn't have to deal with the loud motors and whirring engines from the thrill seekers partying it up for the weekend. It also meant we wouldn't run into Hunter—thankfully! I didn't want him to see me like this. My relief was short-lived, as the trail got narrower from there with jutting rocks and tree roots. I could see why the ATVs couldn't go through it.

After another half mile, we sat down at Caitlyn's insistence and took a granola bar and water break. A squirrel chattered at us through the trees, and I laughed and tapped Caitlyn. "Hey! Evil, Crazy Squirrel."

She caught sight of the little guy and dimpled, throwing her hair behind her shoulder to look provocatively up at Brekker. "Save us! It's a monster."

He looked confused, and I tried to stop her from explaining, but no, she went right on ahead, reminding him about Hunter's Evil, Crazy Squirrel story and how he'd warned us about it this morning, and then she blabbed that Hunter had pulled me out of the Jeep to rescue me before we even knew who he was and how I was in love, though I didn't know it. I rolled my eyes.

By now, Brek had figured out that I didn't like being teased about Hunter, and so he was caught between taking advantage of the moment and growling under his breath about what he'd do if this guy looked at his sister again. Meanwhile, Evil, Crazy Squirrel was barking like a mad dog at me, and I threw a piece of my granola bar at it.

"Don't do that!" Brekker lectured. "It will chase all the hikers for their food."

"I thought you were going to say he wouldn't know how to forage for food if you fed him," Caitlyn said.

"Not these guys," Brekker said. "They'll never starve. They're ornery, little thieves." Looking at his watch, he stood up.

I knew it wouldn't be too long before he started going into drill sergeant mode. Sighing, I packed up again. My back was starting to hurt, but I knew if I complained about it I'd look like I'd brought too much… which I had. Stretching to my feet, I almost toppled over again, and Brekker had to steady me. He knew better than to give me a hard time. For some reason he needed us. Hunter's words came back to me, and I tried to ignore them. But why had Brek taken us when he could've gotten a much better team?

Soon, the sights of the wilderness began to blend into each other. My feet kept getting caught on the rocks and tree roots so that I had to watch my steps more carefully. The green that had seemed like emeralds earlier became background to my heavy breathing. The trail got steeper, and even though Caitlyn and I did yoga and Zumba at the gym, we weren't used to this kind of workout. My legs were killing me. I desperately tried to find topics to keep everyone talking so I could distract myself from the pain. I'd even welcome taunts about Hunter to do this. Caitlyn began to go over her plans for our documentary, and I was surprised at the thought she'd put into it. She wanted to make it into a web series and edit and upload webisodes on our channel after every expedition. Brekker seemed indifferent to the idea, so I took his silence as permission, though I wondered what had taken hold of his mind. Was it the treasure or something else?

After too many false peaks where Caitlyn was positive that the lake was just around the bend, Brekker played a game with us—who could hike without complaining? He won, of course, and so he upped the stakes and said that he would carry the pack of the second place winner on the way back. That shut both Caitlyn and I up, even though the last stretch was excruciating. I felt it in my shins and my back and my lungs. But I knew we were close. I felt it, and as we passed through a final grove of pines we reached the meadow with Moonlight Lake glistening at its center. A few ATV trails reached it from the back like dripping ribbons in the distance, but so far we had the place to ourselves.

Caitlyn and I collapsed on a flat boulder, leaning heavily on each other. I didn't have the strength to take off my backpack, but eventually I edged the straps off my shoulders and lay flat on my back, staring up at the sky. "How many of these do we have to do?"

Brekker made a buzzer sound with his lips and Caitlyn pumped her fist and shouted, "I won!"

I groaned. How did that count as a complaint? My backpack was ten times heavier than hers! I decided to pretend that I was undergoing an intense arm and back workout to feel better about it. Now that we were no longer forbidden to take pictures, Caitlyn made good use of her camera phone. Not to be outdone, I pulled out my camera while Brekker shuffled through his pack to get his supplies.

The photographs looked like they were hardly real, like paintings in my camera. And before I was tempted to admire the images more than the real thing, I set the camera aside and made myself sit and be present while the miracle of nature enfolded before me. The lake was still and reflected the sky so that it looked almost aquamarine. It was about the size of five football fields with steep, pale gray crags dividing the pools into romantic lagoons. A line of trees on the other side of us blocked a part of the beach from us. Next to us, Brekker was unwinding a line from a spool.

"What are you doing?" I asked.

He chuckled. "I'm going to see how bottomless this lake is… and then I'm looking for underwater caves."

Caitlyn's eyes got huge. "What are we supposed to do?"

"I'm going to carry a line with me, and so I want you to make sure that I don't lose the other end. Can you do that?"

She eagerly drew herself up. "Of course." She'd also film the whole thing. She narrated while she caught footage of Brekker getting into his scuba gear, including the face he made at her when she cat-called him before he put on his face mask. At this rate, she'd have too much material. The water was freezing, and when he got in it splashed over us and I grimaced. It felt like the lake was made up of glacier water, which was probably right since it was spring and everything was melting.

It was nerve-wracking when he went under. He hadn't told us

what to do if the line did get lost, but there was also the danger of getting caught up in it, and he took a knife with him just in case. The whole thing seemed dangerous to me.

He came up after about fifteen minutes, pulling off his mask and gasping from the cold.

"Did you find the bottom?" I asked.

"Besides some shallow shelves, no, it's too deep—I think it tunnels into underground aquifers. But I swam along these mountains of rocks—there are walls of limestone down there." He wiped the water from his face. "No caves yet."

"Don't go into any if you find them," I said. "At least tell us first."

He nodded wordlessly, but I wasn't sure what he would really do when it came down to it. The second time he went under the water, I pulled out Eden's journal so I could concentrate on something besides my worrying.

"That's the journal?" Caitlyn asked. Still keeping an eye on the line, she pulled closer to peer down at the book. I turned it to the first page to find the illustration that Eden had made of the coin they'd cheated off the prospector, Bill Pratt. It had a cross on one side with two holes on either side of it, and she had sketched the other side to show a nondescript sort of design. Caitlyn made impressed noises. "Not bad."

"Maybe," I said. "Who knows how it really looked."

We giggled.

"Is that the treasure we're trying to find?" she asked.

"Probably. I mean, this is the coin she stole off some guy in the saloon, and he said there were more." I flipped through the entries until I found the one she wrote after she had first met Adam Black. I read it aloud while Caitlyn watched the line.

Eden's Journal: June 26th, 1855 – Mountains of the Deseret

Mr. Black sure knowed how to make friends. As the days grew warmer and the snow melted from the trees, the two of us got to be thick as thieves. Lucius got hot and ornery when he saw it, and he grumbled out plenty of complaints on how I put on airs, though nothing that he'd let Mr. Black hear since the man had threatened to leave us high and dry if Lucius didn't treat me like a lady. It was sure nice to see Lucius care enough to think anything of me one way or the other.

But there warn't no reason for Lucius to fear, and I let him know it. My heart was as much his as it was from the start. I'd come all the way from San Francisco for him. I'd left my business and all I had in the world for him. And I'd do it again if he asked it of me. Still the man needed something to chew on to wile the time, and so I let him carry on about me and Mr. Black until the snow melted and we was free to come out of doors and worry our minds on something else.

Mr. Black left a message for the Shoshone Indians in the woods so that sure enough, they came a calling. Mr. Black shaked hands with their chief. They was good friends. Lucius promised them a turn of good luck should they git us this treasure. Them Indians warn't too keen to help until Mr. Black promised them a cut. Lucius made all sorts of grunts and disapproving sounds behind us, but Mr. Black done it all the same.

The chief figured that was a good enough deal and him and Mr. Black shaked hands on it. A few days later, the Shoshones come back to the cabin and brung us to a lake. We hacked around brush and trees to git there and it was thick around us so's I had to shake ticks from my dress. The lake was a sight to see, but much too cold for swimming. It was the prettiest blue, like the blue of Lucius' eyes, I reckon. I told him that and he turned as red as a tomato, which made me laugh and kiss him on his red tomato face.

The chief hunted around a bit in the trees next to the lake until he found some water a bubbling from a tiny stream. He told tale it shot out from the ground every so often like a fountain when it rained hard and the snows melted, but the land must return to what it once was, and that the treasure would be found somewheres roundabouts. We poked around it, but how that weak gurgle of cold water could hide a treasure was beyond me. Lucius got to panning, but soon grew bored and fidgety and begun to think we was on a fool's errand, especially on account that he didn't believe the chief deserved such a hefty cut of the find. He said if'n the Indians knowed where it was then why didn't they just git it themselves and not share any of the loot with the lot of us? I was inclined to agree.

None of us rightly knowed if we got the right place or the right lake, but Mr. Black said we gots to be patient in order to shake this blasted treasure out. His words sounded right to me and so we kept on until the chief told us the treasure was more'n likely to be in the lake than anywheres. That set Lucius off again, but Mr. Black kept calm as a priest.

Brek came out of the water and climbed up onto the bank, but not before chucking some cell phones a few feet away from us and then a piece of equipment that looked like it came from the 70's. "Someone else has been in this lake," he said.

"Um, yeah." The cell phones were long gone. One of them was a flip phone. I picked up the long pole-like thing with a box of wires stuck to the end of it. "What is it?"

"A metal detector. I can't figure out why someone would bring it underwater, but...." He cracked a grin. "I've seen weirder things."

Brekker peeled off his wetsuit, leaving a bare chest that would be much too muscular for Caitlyn's peace of mind. Before she could go into cardiac arrest, I tried to distract her. "Lucius is a piece of work, isn't he?"

She laughed. "He's adorable, always complaining and grumbling."

Obviously she was being sarcastic. "I wonder if Eden ever read her journal back to herself and thought, 'why do I even like this guy?'"

"Now you know my pain," Brekker said, overhearing our conversation. He struggled to tug his shirt over his wet hair.

"Don't get me started on your girlfriends," I said. His eyes went stormy at the reminder, and I regretted bringing it up. I changed the subject, "So you know anything about this geyser in Eden's journal?"

It was enough to launch him into his scientific analyses. "Geysers come and go—the one in Eden's journal sounds like it's a cold water geyser, so that means there could be some pockets of CO2 built up around the banks of the lake where this treasure is hidden. So we should watch out for bubbles—that would be CO2 escaping into the water." He shrugged. Brekker might not have had any formal education on this subject, but he had spent enough time with professionals to be well versed in it.

"Where do you think we'll find this geyser?" I asked him.

"No idea. Things have changed a lot since 1850. I doubt it exists anymore."

Still, it would be a better clue than the ones we currently had. "What if it dried up? What would we look for?"

His face scrunched up in thought. "Deposits of orange or white travertine, just a thick layer of rock that's orange or brown or yellow, sometimes green."

That could be anything around here, but it might give Caitlyn and me something to do while we waited for Brek to explore in the water. "Maybe we should look for it in the woods," I said. "Eden said they found something near the lake."

Brekker looked uncertain. "Even if you found a deposit buildup, it might not mean anything." He picked up his GPS to study the map. "There is a lake up the mountain a little ways from here. How about you go up there and check up on the rock formations for me?"

Was he suggesting we go up another steep incline? "No, no," I said quickly. "I'm not hiking uphill again." At his surprised face, I amended, "Today! Besides, I think this is important. Don't you, Caitlyn?"

Seeing the danger of too much strenuous exercise, she adamantly agreed. "That's fine by me. Let's go, Ivy!" She took me by the hand and we left our backpacks to sun on the rocks and headed into the woods.

"Hey!" Brekker called after us. "At least take your packs!"

I shook my head. "They're heavy!"

"A whistle, then." He dug one out and ran over to slap it into my hand. "There could be a bear in there."

"You told me they were hibernating," I said. "Were you lying?"

Probably. He flushed. "Okay, then you could come across a lion."

"Lions?" I scoffed. "We're not in Africa."

"Mountain lions," he amended. "But probably a lot more moose than anything."

Waving behind me, I sauntered away from him. Rocky and Bullwinkle didn't exactly put the fear of God in me. "Like I'm really scared of moose."

"Why not? They'll stomp on your head."

I drew up in a panic. "Then why'd you even take us here, Brek?" I heard my voice take on a hysterical note.

He sighed. "Stay within screaming distance. I'm not kidding. Even those meatheads with Angel won't go exploring in there alone."

That wasn't very reassuring, but Caitlyn was tugging on my hand, and so we went into the foliage of trees while Brekker went back to taking samples and who knew what else. After his stern warnings he didn't seem too concerned, and I tried to take comfort in that. He was probably trying to freak us out so we'd stay nearby to help him.

We hadn't gone too far into the forest before it felt like it had swallowed us up. It was dark and cold. There was frost on some of the branches still, and what had looked like a trail quickly disappeared. Maybe this wasn't such a good idea, but the thought of proving Brek right and rushing out just as quickly as we'd gone in made me push forward. I'd still be within screaming distance like he'd said.

Caitlyn looked up into the branches that strangled out the sky above us. "This is like every scary movie that takes place in the woods."

It was just like her to make this worse. Now my mind was conjuring up every scary movie imaginable—complete with cannibal rednecks. I didn't know what I was looking for exactly. Eden's journal made me think that I might find a babbling brook that squirted out a geyser of water every half hour, but I didn't hear any water, just dead silence. The Evil, Crazy Squirrels had also hot-tailed it out of here. It wasn't very reassuring.

"I wonder if this is by Lake Adam," Caitlyn said.

My heart lurched at the reminder of Bill's story. I forced my voice to stay casual. "Bill was just trying to scare us. There is no Bone Man."

"Shh," she said. "Don't say his name."

"It's not like he's Voldemort."

She giggled and shushed me again. I was trying to pay attention to the landmarks so that we could find our way back out again, but the trees were beginning to look the same, and so were the rocks. Finally I stopped and built up a stack of rocks. "What's that?" Caitlyn asked.

"Cairns." I had learned that trick from my grandfather. "That way we can find our way back again. They're our trail of breadcrumbs." I straightened and we trailed deeper into the forest. I grew more confident with a way out and marked off spots on the map. This made us more vital to the cause. Brek might think that we were wasting our time, but if we could find the geyser—even a dried up spout—then this lake would have to be the one that Eden described. We wouldn't have to hike anywhere else. We could haul out the treasure in one day and wave to Hunter on our way out. I imagined the look on his face. A twig snapped in the forest, interrupting my happy little fantasy.

Caitlyn froze. "What's that?"

"I'm sure it's just…"

"Bone Man," she answered for me.

"Must you?" I laughed a little. "I don't care if he's not real—don't talk about Bone Man when we are in the middle of the forest!"

Another snapping twig followed the first until it sounded like a stack of snapping spaghetti noodles. My whole back tingled at the danger and I put the whistle to my lips, still hesitant about blowing it to bring in Brek to rescue us. Before I could make my decision, the sound abruptly stopped.

I met Caitlyn's eyes and broke into another nervous laugh. "I'm not sure what's worse?" I asked. "Whistling to bring Brek running or dying out here? I think I'd rather die."

She wasn't smiling. "What if Bone Man takes you?"

"Or Evil Crazy Squirrel?" I added to show how ridiculous she was being.

"Or Hunter?" she asked mischievously.

She got me there. He'd be worse than Brek—my pride would kill me. No matter; I was beginning to lose hope that we'd ever find a dried up geyser in this tangled forest. Clearly this had been a failed mission from the start. I admitted defeat to a grateful Caitlyn, and we backtracked, following my little rock cairns on the way back. As we neared a grove of trees, the bushes shook ahead of us. My knees buckled in response, and I didn't know where to run as a herd of deer bounded out directly in front of us. They were big, powerful creatures, nothing like the diminutive Bambi I had pictured, but with brawny shoulders and long, legs that rippled with muscle. They landed hard on their hooves on the other side of us. Caitlyn screamed and the whistle dangling from my lips dropped to the dirt. They scrambled past us and up the hill, running sideways as they circled us like spinning coins in a roulette wheel. They escaped some unseen terror where we were now headed, which also happened to be our only way out. I picked up my whistle, my fingers shaking.

"That's fine," I said with more bravado than I felt. "I'm sure they were just spooked because we were coming."

I stepped closer to the spot that they had just cleared for us and noticed that Caitlyn wasn't following. "Caitlyn, you can't just stay behind."

"I can't move. I'm terrified."

"You're... really?" I took her hand and helped her take a few steps forward, until she dug her cute little hiking boots into the ground.

"I'm not kidding!" Her face had lost all its playfulness, and her lips jutted out stubbornly. She looked like she might cry. "We have to go a different way."

"But we'll get lost..."

"I have a very bad feeling about this. We cannot go in there!" I couldn't fight her when she was talking that way. She was terrified.

"Okay, okay, how about you stay here and I'll check it out."

She moaned out in warning, but didn't stop me. I wasn't sure why I was volunteering to be the sacrificial virgin but it seemed like a bad idea not to go the way we had come, especially with Brekker's warnings not to get lost echoing in my ears. I just wanted to be out of this forest and in the sun again. The closer I walked to the thicket of trees, the more I wished I'd never heard about Bone Man. A soft breeze made a low whistle through the branches, and I willed my ears to not take anything it said out of context, like my name. It was silly, but in irrational moments like these, I had a special reason to be afraid: I was the descendant of Lucius Payne. If anything malicious was out here, then it would be after me to get its revenge. After all, hadn't it been Lucius who left Eden there to die by herself?

Poor Eden. As I walked closer, my whole body shaking with fear, I realized how bad her last moments had been. It was scary enough to be by yourself, but to know that you were going to die alone? And knowing how stupid you had been to trust in that grumbling, complaining bumbling idiot of a man she had described as Lucius in her journal? He must've been very good-looking for her to fall for that. Catching my breath, I hesitated outside the dark abyss of the trees ahead and steadied myself before I went in... and almost ran straight into the backside of a moose.

I stopped just short of its haunches. Its fur was thick and it towered over me, not sensing me near. It was much taller than the deer that had scared the living daylights out of us. I knew nothing about moose, but if it was like a horse, I was within kicking distance. *Or it could stomp on my head!* Keeping my eyes trained on it, I placed one foot behind the other to back slowly out of the trees, creeping as quietly as I could. As soon as I was far enough away, I fled back to Caitlyn, not able to control my expression of horror any longer. "A moose!" I mouthed.

She gasped and ran. "Caitlyn!" I rasped. I dashed after her, knowing that we'd still have to find our way out to Brek, but we couldn't let the moose catch us either. We tripped through the foliage, scrambling over rocks and fighting our way through branches and weeds. I thought of ticks and of Eden having to shake her skirt free of them, but I didn't remind Caitlyn as we trampled through the forest. We splashed through water seepage, but I couldn't see through the weeds well enough to see if it was a long dead geyser with deposits of travertine or anything because I was too scared the moose was after us. The whole idea of finding the geyser seemed ludicrous anyway. As soon as we broke through the worst of the brush, I smelled something off, like a hermit was out there cooking onions or something. "Ugh," I said. "What is that smell?"

Caitlyn sniffed, shaking her head, and groaned. "I don't know. It's awful!"

"Campers?" I asked. "Maybe someone's cooking fish?" Whatever it was, it was strong and it wasn't fading. At least that meant we were closer to civilization, but I felt sorry for whoever had to eat whatever that was.

Tearing around the bend, we saw the lake on the other side of the meadow, and just like that, we slowed down, laughing hysterically at our near escape, though Caitlyn was crying too. Brekker was in the distance, and I lifted my whistle to let him know that we were coming. It probably wasn't necessary, but I wasn't taking any chances. He turned and I still blew on it.

He came running, but as he neared his expression fell into confusion, and then his nose wrinkled in disgust. I guessed he smelled the camper's food too. "What happened?" he asked.

"Moose!" I said as soon as he could hear. "I almost ran into a moose, right into the back of it. It was huge, but it didn't see me. I don't think!"

Caitlyn snorted in annoyance. Her red hair hung in strings around her face and she looked exhausted. "I thought you said it was a bear!"

"Well, moose are just as bad," I explained. "They stomp on your head!"

"No, they wouldn't! Brek was being dumb." She sullenly lowered herself to the ground and pulled off her shoes, dumping out the rocks. Her usual happy spirits had taken a vacation. "And it stinks out here! Why does the great outdoors stink so bad?"

Brekker's nose was still wrinkled and he tried to wave the odor away. "That's a skunk. Did you get sprayed?"

Caitlyn shrieked. It was just too much. "That's what it is! Ivy!" I took a step closer and she held up her hand. "No, stay back! The smell gets stronger the closer you get. It's you! You got sprayed by a skunk. You can't smell that?"

"Well, yeah," my hands went up in my defense, "but I thought someone was cooking eggs or something." It smelled nothing like dead skunk on the road, but it was still awful. Maybe this was why no beef head from Hunter's team would go into the woods by themselves. "How do I get this off me?"

"Those are some stinky eggs!" My brother was trying not to laugh now. "You don't happen to have any skunk remover in that backpack of yours?"

I shook my head and Caitlyn groaned. She should look on the bright side. After this, Brekker couldn't possibly take us hiking anymore today. "All right, all right!" He seemed resigned to our incompetence. "Let's get you girls home!"

Chapter seven

The wilderness wasn't that fun. Tired, and frustrated, we headed back down the trail. The shin splints were worse coming down the steep mountains. It felt like Caitlyn was moonwalking backwards she was going so slow, and no amount of games would get her to hurry, even with Brekker carrying her backpack. The trail forked into the ATV road, which was a relief because it was less rocky. I wasn't sure how many rocks the bottom of my feet could take anymore, though Caitlyn was worse off because she was breaking in new shoes.

Brek stopped us to put moleskin on her feet. Not even my brother's administrations cheered her up. The four-wheelers were getting louder in the distance. "Why can't we go on an ATV?" Caitlyn asked my brother. "What are you, some sort of purist?"

"We can't reach all these lakes with them, and I'm thinking you need to work up to the harder hikes anyway or you'll never be able to do those."

"That wasn't one of the harder hikes?" Caitlyn was beside herself. Brek's mouth tightened, and I was sure that he was thinking very fondly of Angel and her team of professionals about now.

My face felt hot, and looking down at my red arms, I realized that I'd forgotten to put on my sunscreen. I wrestled with my pack and found it, knowing that it didn't work retroactively. Brek caught sight of me, and I knew by his grimace that I was as red as I felt. "Why did you buy sunscreen if you weren't going to put it on?" he asked. "It doesn't work if you leave it in the bottle."

I wasn't in the mood to banter. "Yeah, who knew?"

Brekker, of course, wasn't done lecturing, though he hadn't used it either; he was just so tan that he didn't have to worry about it.

"I get it!" I snapped back, feeling testy. That skunk smell was making me sick. Luckily, the skunk had grazed my leg and so I had changed out my workout pants for one of my windbreaker layers then thrown my old clothes in plastic. The scent of it still lingered and made us all want to throw up. Me most of all—since it had soaked into my skin.

While hiking down the trail, I'd tried to roll up my windbreaker pants so I wouldn't be so hot, but after too many complaints from the others, I rolled them back down, and now I was stuck with sweaty pants, a stinking leg, and red lobster skin. All my purchases at the Grizzly hadn't saved me today.

Trying to forget my worries, I stretched to my feet and pulled out my phone to take video, hoping to cheer up Caitlyn and my brother. "We've had a few unlucky breaks on our first day in our pursuit of Eden," I said. "And one can't help wonder if this is the curse on the treasure or something else? Caitlyn is breaking in her shoes and Brek is trying to patch her up. Thank you, Brek, you're the hero of the hour!"

Caitlyn picked up her cell phone with a tired grimace and recorded me in return. "And here we have Ivy, who braved the forest with her friend, Caitlyn, where we found a herd of deer, a monstrous moose, and a skunk. Ivy got sprayed." She turned the camera on herself. "Fortunately, audience, you can't smell it, but let me tell you it is awful."

I laughed. "Don't forget the sunburn! How red is my face?" I turned the camera to myself and knew I'd caught myself at a bad angle, but I didn't care anymore. We were in the wilderness now where anything could happen. And it did.

The ATVs sped over the hill. They were a lot closer than I'd thought, and I scrambled from the trail to get out of the way and tripped, ramming my cell phone into my leg so that it popped out of my grip and fell right onto the pathway. I fell flat on my backside, looking from it to the oncoming vehicle, and before I could warn the driver about my phone, the wheels crunched over it. The driver put on the brakes when he saw me and stopped just in time for the back wheels to take out the rest of it. I turned to Caitlyn who still held up her phone. "Did you get that?"

She nodded in horror. I looked up to the driver and wasn't the least bit surprised to see Hunter staring down at me under the broad brim of his green John Deere ball cap. He had stripped down to a white tee, wearing relaxed jeans that looked great on him. And I was a sunburnt, smelly mess. He grinned at me.

"My cell phone," I said, pointing under his wheels.

He had the grace to look apologetic as he backed up his four-wheeler. Not bothering to get up from where I sat, I crawled over the dirt to scrape my phone from the trail. The whole front of it was crushed in, the cracks spreading over the glass like spider webs.

"Oh, I am so sorry about that," his voice dripped with regret and southern accent, but I couldn't appreciate it as I tried to hold my phone together. It seemed appropriate that I had nothing now. He sniffed loudly, and my head lifted in dread as I realized what he was smelling—me! His eyes widened on me as the rest of his team came riding up behind him.

A few of them stopped to trash talk. Rosco was one of them. I noticed his fists were scraped up like he'd gotten into another scuffle. He looked me up and down like the creepy guy he was. "What do we have here?"

My brother moved to stand before Rosco could pull a Weinstein, but then the guy sniffed and made a face. Shaking his head, Rosco thought better of sticking around my stench and revved his engine and rode up the sides of the trail to get away. Likewise, the others also opted for clean air rather than giving us a hard time. They were lazy troublemakers. They drove loudly past, hooting and hollering.

Hunter chose to stay and brave the smell. "So…" he said. "You didn't run into the Evil, Crazy Squirrel today?"

I lifted my shoulders. "Just the Evil, Crazy Skunk… and the Evil,

Crazy Four-Wheeler."

"I am so sorry," he began, laughing a little so it ruined the apology. "Let me make it up to you."

How? Would he buy me a new phone? I pushed out of the dirt to stand and he leaped off his four-wheeler to help me up and dust me off, his nose wrinkling the whole time. "Wow, that skunk got you good!"

"You got me good!" I wasn't sure what that meant, but he looked more ashamed and muttered more apologies so even I felt bad. Brek watched the whole thing with suspicion; and desperate to stop my brother from whatever he was thinking, I laid a hand on Hunter's stomach to hold him off and then wished I hadn't because it made me very aware of him as a man. Again. He was all muscle. His eyes met with mine. They were touched with green, and I got lost in those hazel depths like I'd never seen that color before. His breathing hitched, and I knew the attraction between us wasn't one-sided.

Somewhere behind us, Caitlyn giggled.

"Ivy?" Brek shouted at me as one last ATV came up behind us. I didn't have to look to see that it was Angel. Hunter stepped back from me, and now he and Brek had come to uneasy attention at the sight of this magnificent creature of the forest. She was in another tank top. Her skin glistened under the sun. Her hair had blown into a tumultuous black wave behind her.

"You really should be wearing a helmet," I muttered, "...and lots of padding."

Glancing down at me, Hunter looked amused and tapped the brim of his ball cap. "You're so right," he said in a voice that I couldn't take seriously. "That's what my nana always said."

I knew what he was getting at. I was a molly-coddling schoolmarm clutching my pearls, as my brother liked to say. I crossed my arms, supposing that Hunter and I were back to being archenemies, and I didn't mind a bit. This was something I was more comfortable with.

Angel's lip curled up in disgust. "What is that stench?"

Brekker couldn't help it. He threw me under the bus with a laugh. "Ivy."

Normally, Caitlyn would join in the fun, but she seemed annoyed with the appearance of Angel and the fact that Brek had softened towards her overnight. Angel must've sensed it too because she threw him a flirtatious look. As soon as Brek saw it, he stiffened as if remembering himself. "No one's forcing you to stick around," he said.

That pulled a denial from Angel's lips. "I'm concerned, that's all. Today must've been such a trying day for you. Your sister and her… friend are real troopers, but there's no need to drag them into all of this."

"They're doing great, Angel," he said. "Besides, fifteen percent of the cut? That's a horrible deal and you know it."

"Twenty," Hunter returned.

"Eighty," I said without another thought.

"Eighty?" Hunter asked. "You're not worth more than fifty."

"Be careful," I said. "We might take you up on that."

"Ivy!" Brek said between clenched teeth. "You're not calling the shots around here."

I shrugged. I knew that our mysterious backer wanted the whole treasure—whether it was worth it or not—and supposedly the reward we'd get from him would pay off my debts, set me up for a few years, fund Brek's next expedition, and maybe get our mom some better housing; but could we get to it before Hunter's team did? "Something is better than nothing," I said, and then, since I knew Brekker would never agree to it, I nudged Hunter and said, "Throw in some skunk repellent and I'll take it down to forty-nine."

He breathed out in frustration while Angel tried to appeal to my brother. "We could do this a lot faster if we worked together."

"We're never working together again," he said.

I hid my smile. Good for him. "I guess that settles it," I said. It was time to pack out before it got too dark. Aloe Vera and a bath in tomato sauce called seductively out to me. Forget Hunter's eyes—that was just me being stupid anyway. We all had our weak moments. I went to my backpack while Brek went at it with his ex-girlfriend. It was just the normal bad breakup. Nothing special. *He never understood her. She never supported him.* Hunter's hints that this was something more seemed unlikely.

Caitlyn held her phone protectively against her while I dug through my backpack. I tried to figure out how to get my broken cell phone in there or if it was even worth it. Rearranging my things, I slid out Eden's journal and at the sudden silence, looked up to see that both Hunter and Angel had caught sight of it. The argument had all been snuffed out. Brek watched on warily.

How much did they know about Eden's journal? I stuffed it back in, pretending not to notice their interest, but it was too late to hide it from them. If they were aware of its existence then now they knew I carried it with me. Normally, that wouldn't seem like a big deal, but I had a feeling that Angel would stoop to anything.

She cleared her throat. "We're going to be seeing a lot of each other during the next few weeks; the least we could do is get along. Maybe we can go out tonight?"

Caitlyn snickered knowingly. Brekker's eyes narrowed in suspicion. As they should.

"All of us," Angel amended. "Not just you and me, but your friend, and your sister... and Hunter."

That was the wrong thing to say. Brekker picked up his backpack one-handed and slid it on like the confident, newly independent man that he was. "Absolutely not."

Angel wisely said nothing, merely inclined her head like she was used to these little emotional outbursts before she got her way with him. I knew that look too well. "Let's go, Hunter," she said before lifting herself delicately up onto her four-wheeler with all the charisma of a model in a car commercial. In this case, the product was herself.

Hunter looked deep in thought. He didn't immediately follow after her, instead, pushing down his cap, he glanced over at me. "You look really hot," he said.

Wait. Hot? Brek's lips tightened.

"Your face is all red," he interpreted like I was slow, but I knew he meant the pun because of the mischief dancing in his eyes. "You need to take better care of yourself."

I shook my head to deny it and he whipped off his ball cap and stuffed it over my head. I was too surprised to fight him. "That's for the sun. You'll thank me later."

He got back on his ATV. With his brown hair freed from the cap, he looked more carefree. His hair was longer than what I was used to seeing on the business men I'd dated, but it was wavy in all the right places and a stray strand hung over his eye.

That's when I realized he was doing the same thing to me that Angel had tried on my brother. It wasn't going to work. I shouted over his engine. "That doesn't count!"

He looked surprised. "What?"

"That *wasn't* a rescue." In an instant, I felt stupid for bringing it up.

He smiled slowly.

My fists clenched. "Actually, it's the opposite of a rescue, so we're even."

"Not quite," he said. "I still owe you a phone. Then you'll be in the red." He inched a few feet forward in the four-wheeler so that he was even with me. "My hat looks good on you." And then he took off. Angel cast Brek a sullen expression over a bare shoulder before following Hunter down the trail, her back straight.

"Can you believe that?" I asked. Brek didn't hear me. He was too busy drilling a hole in Angel's back with his glare, so I turned to Caitlyn instead and jumped when I saw her phone was up like she had been recording the whole thing. "You caught that?" I asked.

"Yeah." She nodded. "That was good stuff."

108

"It was not! None of that was good stuff!" I knew I sounded like a petulant child, but this whole crazy episode had reduced me to one. I readjusted my backpack and began the long trek to our cabins. I didn't take off Hunter's hat either.

Chapter eight

We trudged to the front of the Grizzly Bear House before going to our cabin. Something had to be done about that stench of skunk, and we all agreed we didn't want to track it into the place we would call home for the next few weeks. Bill would know what to do, if anyone. I'd have googled it, but I didn't have a phone... or service or anything. It was the weirdest feeling. It was like all ties from my old life were cut from me, and strangely, I liked it. I'd had no idea how trapped I had felt before.

"Wait out here," Brekker said.

I smirked, feeling like the smelly dog. "Hurry then!" They nodded, and I fully expected them to come out within minutes. When they didn't, I hopped from foot to foot. Standing still made me cold. The sun was setting and it brought the chill.

Dropping my backpack to the dirt, I tugged out my coat. "Ew! Ew!" I cried when I discovered that my workout pants had smelled up everything else in there too. I should've burned them when I'd had the chance. I tossed the pants in the garbage, but then cringed when the stench overpowered the can and made the whole front of the store stink.

A flush crept up my neck as a few vacationers passed me by and gagged visibly at the odor. I was sure they knew it came from me. How could they not? I half expected the good ol' bullies from Hunter's group were more than happy to spread the story around.

Blowing on my fingers, I would've waited outside a few minutes longer but then I heard the familiar whirring of ATVs coming closer and my stomach sank. I wasn't about to wait around to see if those were Hunter's men. I leaped up the wooden stairs to escape. I couldn't face those guys like this again. I plunged into the store, the bells crashing at my entrance.

Wandering through the store and trying not to touch anything, I caught sight of Bill first. Frank and Harlan had gathered around a computer behind the counter. Pat hunched over a table next to it, clutching his cane and peering intently at all the excitement. I found Caitlyn contorting behind a computer desk to plug something into the wall. Brek was lifting the desk up so she could fit through.

I didn't have to come too close before Brek looked over at me with a contorted face. "Ah, it's worse in here. You weren't supposed to come inside."

My hands flew to my sides. "How long was I supposed to wait while you moved around all the furniture? It's cold out there!"

The Dogo Argentino lifted his head from the pillow near the hearth and made a strangled yelp before escaping into the back. "Skip, where are you going?" Bill called. The old timer turned to me with a smile. "Now, now, what's the problem?" Bill patted my back, like I wasn't a leper. "I can't smell a thing."

"Thank you, Bill!" I was tempted to hug him for his kindness, but I supposed that would be cruel.

Frank and Harlan nodded. Pat was a different story. He lifted his head and carefully said, "She stinks!"

"Oh hush," Harlan said. "You can't smell a thing. He never can," he explained to me. Pat made some sort of inarticulate sound that Harlan thought was hilarious. It made me wonder if I was somehow the butt of a joke.

"I've got just the thing, Ivy." Bill shuffled over to one of the shelves in the store and pulled out a bottled container. "I put this on ol' Skip all the time when he wrestles with those varmints." It was official. I was as bad as the dog.

He handed it to me, and I read the label. "Skunk Off."

"Just a bit of hydrogen peroxide and baking soda," Bill explained, like I cared what was in the ingredients at this point. I just wanted to be free of this smell.

"Can I put it on clothes?"

"Yes, yes, it will take it right off. Just throw it all in the wash." I was relieved. I didn't want to have to buy new winter gear. Brek's backer might be rich, but it would be a waste of our resources. "I've got a machine back here you can use. You can go ahead and throw what you have in it."

"Do it!" Brek said. He turned to me and the table shifted, making Caitlyn cry out from underneath it.

"What are you doing?" I asked.

"We're going to follow your adventures on the YouTube," Frank said. "We're connecting to the internet. The company came and set us up this morning."

My heart warmed at that. Caitlyn pulled out from the table, looking disheveled. "Now, you need to click on this button on the right side of the computer and put in your password."

"Password?"

Her expression fell. "You don't know your password?"

I let her sort that out with Bill while I left to fetch my workout pants from the garbage. As soon as I brought them inside, it sent a visceral tide of horror rippling through the store. "Bring them here!" Bill called out. "Bring them!"

I stuffed them into his hands and he threw them in the fire to let the flames extinguish them. "I thought we could put those in the wash?" I cried.

"Not those. Do you have anything else?"

I was almost afraid to give them to him, but at Brek's nod, I relinquished the rest of my clothes, including my coat. With the courage of an experienced veteran, he smelled them each then nodded. "These we'll put in the wash."

Meanwhile, Caitlyn was busy putting in the new password. "So then you make sure you're always signed into it, so you won't have to remember it," she explained.

"So we'll have the internet from now on? As long as we don't bump the cord?"

"Yeah, as long as you pay the bill."

The old men were grateful, but incompetent. "And how do we get to your show on the YouTube?"

"Yes, well, then you open up this tab…"

"Isn't that a drink?" one asked.

"What?" she sounded confused. The generation gap was too wide for her to understand.

"A Tab," Frank said with a nudge. "It's a drink." She gave him an obligatory giggle as they plied her with dad jokes. She was trying so hard to be patient. Bless her soul.

I followed Bill into the back room and stuffed my clothes into the wash, including my coat. "Be careful with that," Bill said. "You'll have to let that air dry." He glanced up at Brek with a wink. "I learned that the hard way after my wife passed." He poured half the bottle of Skunk Away into the wash, leaving the last of it for me.

My hands went to my windbreaker pants. They hadn't been sprayed by the skunk, but they'd been resting against my leg all day. "I need something to wear out of here!"

"Oh!" Bill disappeared like I was going to strip at a moment's notice. I wasn't that free-spirited! He returned with a jean skirt and an ugly sweater with a bear crocheted on the front of it. "Consider it a housewarming gift," he said. My heart swelled with gratitude. Bill was the best resort manager in the world. The outfit was a little big, but it would get me out of here. The males left the small room so I could dress, and I hurried to change before tossing my pants and shirt into the wash.

Coming from the laundry room, I heard Caitlyn asking for permission to use their computer sometimes, mainly tomorrow. I should've known she had an ulterior motive for helping. "We want to upload some new episodes," she said.

"How?" I asked. "We haven't done anything yet."

"Oh, I got some good footage today," she said with a giggle.

Was she talking about me and Hunter? "Absolutely not! That's not going in."

Caitlyn gave a secret smile, and I silently wished her luck, since she knew nothing about editing. Thankfully.

"You going to put Aiden in your show?" Bill asked, as if the two were the best of pals.

"Oh yes." Caitlyn said.

"You know they call him Hunter," I said. "He goes by his last name."

"Does he?" Bill looked thoughtful. It was enough to silence Harlan and Frank too. Pat was sleeping over his cane. But they didn't care to explain their sudden navel-gazing. Maybe Hunter had a reputation in these parts. Was that why he hadn't used his full name on the register? "Come back tonight to get your clothes," Bill said, abruptly changing the conversation. "I'll throw them in the dryer, except..." he held up a finger, "not the coat."

Brekker clapped his hand over Bill's in a true expression of gratitude. "We appreciate your help! I've never seen anything like it."

Bill glowed under the praise. "Anything for you, youngsters. You know that!"

I didn't understand why Bill and his friends were being so nice, but it felt comforting to have someone look out for us. Our own grandfather had been a gruff fellow who drank the nights away on those camping trips. He smoked over his maps and grumbled out curses when we got too close to what he was writing. None of us had been particularly close to him, but had he been anything like Bill— things might've been different.

We set off for our cabin, and Caitlyn and Brek insisted I take my shower first. It was a purely selfish offer, but I took it anyway. It felt so good stepping under the warm spray. The water and Skunk Off took away more than the stench; it washed away the cares of the day, so that when I stepped out of the shower I felt like a new woman, a nice smelling woman… one who could sleep for a full week. I got into my own clothes—skinny jeans and a floral, lightweight blouse—and felt like I was stepping into my own body again.

Pushing out of the bathroom, I leaned against the frame of the door. "How do I smell?"

Brekker sniffed the air. "Like Ivy. Next!"

Holding a pink, soft, Egyptian cotton towel, Caitlyn pushed her way into the bathroom with an apologetic look at Brek. "You won't be sorry you let me go first," she said.

"I'd better not." As soon as she closed the door, Brek turned to me. "How long do her showers take?"

"Pretty long," I admitted. It had been one of our points of contention when living together. I stretched, feeling stiff. Now that I was free of that clinging odor, I could think clearly, and the first thing I noticed was how much I ached.

"I'm going to take a twenty minute nap," Brek announced.

"You'd better make that an hour," I said, tilting my head at the shower.

"Are you kidding me? I'm going to starve to death." He hesitated on the stairs and watched me pleadingly. "Ivy, can you get us some food at the Grizzly?"

I sighed. I had to pick up my clothes over there eventually, so I put out my hand. "Give me the card."

He pressed it into my palm, like he'd been expecting me to say yes. "Thank you! Thank you! Caitlyn wants lemonade and a chicken salad with a squeeze of lime. I'll take a steak, medium rare, with a side of fries," he said before disappearing into the loft upstairs.

That was specific. And planned out. They had decided my fate while I was taking my shower. I wasn't sure if the café had that stuff—but there was the Bear Den upstairs on the third floor. I wasn't looking forward to bumping into Hunter or any of his team again. Either way, I had to be on top of my game if I did. Going to the mirror, I took special care in my appearance, dabbing on a bit of makeup to cover up the redness of my face, and putting a no-frizz solution in my hair. Being the smelliest person in the vicinity had done a number on my self-confidence, and I wasn't about to be seen at such a disadvantage again.

My hair blower was in the bathroom with Caitlyn. My brush was missing, and I hunted for it and found it on the floor. My sweater wasn't where I had put it either. My mind clouded with suspicion, and I swiveled to study the room. What else was out of place? Was it me or had someone gone through our things? But why? There was only one thing we had of value. Eden's journal. Angel knew we had it, and it was the only reason Hunter really wanted to work with us. Had they searched our place for it while we were away?

"Brekker?" I called for him. He didn't answer. How could he possibly fall asleep that fast? If he was, I didn't want to leave the journal here, not with Caitlyn in the shower. I stuffed it in my purse. My bear spray went in next. I also packed my loaner clothes from Bill in a bag to return them. Taking a deep breath, I fluffed my wet hair and put on the warmest sweater I could find along with some boots. It would be a cold walk between here and the Grizzly now that night had fallen.

Closing the door to our cabin, I locked it—not that it had done any good before—and hurried down the wooded pathway to the store. One look at #3 and I knew they weren't there. Their lights were off and their ATVs were gone. Could they not walk anywhere? The quiet out here was almost creepy. The air was frigid, and I broke into a run to escape it. When I neared the Grizzly, I saw that it was hopping with customers. The lot was crowded with vehicles. The wait for food would be excruciating.

Pushing my way through the doorway that announced my entrance, I noticed that Bill wasn't running his café tonight. He hadn't turned in, either, because Skip slept lazily next to the hearth. The action was all upstairs in the Bear Den where I could see the pool table through the railings. It was a rough crowd. They held drinks and laughed uproariously. Most of them I didn't know—a lot of loggers maybe—but I recognized a few of Hunter's men. I couldn't expect not to see them. They'd be a permanent fixture here for the next month or so, like we'd be.

Brushing past the racks of clothes in the darkened store, I passed Bill's dinosaur computer and slipped into his laundry room to throw my clothes in the dryer and set my wet coat on a hook. I marveled at Bill's trust. Leaving his stuff in an unlocked section of the main office would not fly where I was from. My clothes would be gone the moment I turned my back on them.

Coming out, I set the bag of Bill's loaner clothes next to his computer. He had put a screensaver on it that made my heart melt—it was him and his grandkids. They all wore jean shirts, and he had his cowboy hat. They surrounded him and were laughing. It made me feel a sense of loss for my own family. We were all too far apart to pose for pictures like these.

Loud laughter from the Bear Den broke through my thoughts, and I squared my shoulders to face people again. Holding my purse tightly to my stomach, I hiked up the two flights of stairs, feeling like I was hiking to the top of the mountains again. As soon as I reached the landing, I was out of breath.

A few rough-looking men leered my way. I straightened my shoulders. This was as much my place as theirs. Still, I hurried past them. There were two lines—one to order food and the other to be seated. Mine was slightly shorter, but not by much. I scanned the menu. Sure enough, there was Brekker's steak and fries, and Caitlyn's chicken salad and lemonade. I didn't know what I wanted yet, but I had plenty of time to decide. I tried to relax as I peered through the crowd, not realizing that I was scanning the room for Hunter until I found him at a table with Angel.

My heart gave a little skip at seeing him and I gave myself a stern lecture as soon as I noticed it. He must've barely come in because he was still wearing his coat and steel-toed hiking boots with his faded jeans. Angel, on the other hand, had lost no time divesting herself of her bulky coat. She was in one of her signature slinkydink outfits.

The two of them tinkered with that odd little cylinder device that Hunter had been holding in the cabin the night before—they twisted it from side to side, but couldn't seem to figure it out. I'd thought it was some piece of equipment used for geological extracts, but if so, it must have malfunctioned for them to pay so much attention to it. Well, Hunter's eyes were on it. Angel's were on him. Her hand kept resting on his arm. I gave a snort of disgust. She looked real broken up about losing Brek.

A commotion broke out to the side of me and I turned. Two men from Hunter's team were playing a loud drinking game that wouldn't end well. Rosco was one of them, and he slammed his glass on the table, the muscles on his shoulders rippling down his arms. It drew a crowd that pounded the tables in a countdown.

The sooner I could escape this place the better, but the line was horribly slow. A few people had cut in line while I wasn't paying attention. I growled a complaint under my breath.

"Heard you got sprayed by a skunk?" A man with putrid smelling breath leaned over me. He laughed drunkenly.

I stepped back, wishing I still smelled like a skunk so he'd keep his distance. "Yep, yep, that was me." I attempted to brave this one out, but the guy kept getting in my space. "You mind?" I told him. "I'm trying to get food."

"Don't let me stop you. I'm just giving you a little company."

Before I could respond, I felt two hands rest on my shoulders behind me, and I twisted around, then relaxed when I saw Hunter. I was more grateful than I should be to see him. "Here, let me get you away from these fools," he said. "Your brother will thank me." He tried to guide me away from the line.

"No!" It came out halfhearted, since I was relieved to have Hunter with me. "I've got to order."

"You can at the table." He motioned at a server who mouthed

that he'd be with us soon. That convinced me, and I let him take me to his quieter table in the corner. Angel waited there and didn't look surprised to see me. Still, I'd take her over drunk guy any day. Maybe.

"Your brother sent you here all alone?" she asked.

I hated how she acted all superior, like she was the only woman who could handle herself, although maybe in this case she was right. That made me angrier. I shrugged. "I had to pick up some stuff in the wash." Then I winced at the reminder of the skunk.

She let it go, more intent on getting out her prepared insults. "He should be more careful with the women in his life." She rose abruptly from her seat to join some of Hunter's men at the pool table. Rosco was there too. He'd left his drinking game, a little shaky on his feet. She wrapped her arms around him to steady him then whispered something in his ear that made him grin wickedly.

I made a face. "She doesn't really want Brek. She's just mad he dumped her." I said it before I realized my audience.

Hunter broke into a smile. He gathered up that cylinder piece of equipment before I could take a good look at it and stuck it in his coat before he sat across from me. "Find anything at Skunk Pond?"

"Oh? Is that what we're calling it now?" I relaxed. Part of me had wondered if this had been a setup to make me spill my guts, but if he wanted to get in good with me, he wouldn't have mentioned the skunk. Maybe this was a normal conversation. "We didn't find anything, but that isn't too surprising. I mean, how many lakes are there in these mountains?"

"Thousands."

"Thousands," I repeated. And we would have to hike to them all if we didn't find this treasure soon. The thought deflated me. The server came, but before I could order, he asked for our drinks. "Water," I said quickly. Hunter searched my face and ordered it too. The server rushed off before I could give him any more details about my order.

Hunter leaned back in his seat like we had all the time in the world. Judging by how busy this place was, he was probably right. "I hope you like hiking," he said.

I broke into a smile. "Not even a little bit."

"But your brother knows what he's doing. He must have an idea of where to start?"

And Hunter was at it again; he couldn't help but dig for information even in a social setting. I tossed my hair behind my shoulder, deciding to call him on it. "You won't get anything out of me."

He laughed. "Let's just talk about you then." His gaze was unwavering on me. "You're not wearing my hat?"

Really? I couldn't help warming up to him when he was being so ridiculous. "It didn't go with my outfit," I said. "Besides, it doesn't make up for crashing into my phone."

"No, it doesn't." He sat up straighter and leaned over to me. "Let's get you a new one in town."

That was embarrassing. I couldn't afford it and I'd never let him spend a cent on me. "No, no…"

"You have insurance on it?"

"No."

"You're a trust fund baby? You don't care about money?"

"No. I'm here, aren't I? I just lost my job so I'm not going to buy a phone anytime soon."

"Way to make me feel worse," he said. "What happened?"

I grimaced. I hadn't meant to say that. I didn't want to get personal with him, and now he felt sorry for me. "It's not a big deal. I was at this place for seven years, and it was awful. I mean, it was doing the same thing over and over again, and I was long overdue for a change. I can find something better. I got a degree."

"In what?"

"History," I admitted.

"Oh, so you're a socialist."

"No!" I laughed. "How about we talk about you now? You're an archaeologist?"

120

"And geologist and linguist."

"What?" But he had a drippy southern accent and his name was Hunter! I'd expected community college. Maximum. Maybe that made me a horrible, judgy person.

"My grandfather was a little crazy about my education," he explained. "It's kind of a family thing. Everyone goes into archaeology."

"So, people call you Hunter? Was that the name of the dog?" I asked. He looked confused. "Like *Indiana Jones*?" I laughed but he wasn't getting it so then I felt like a jerk. "It's just a reference to a movie."

"It's my last name." He lifted a shoulder. "And considering my line of work, it stuck. Normally I can find anything. Of course here, no one knows what they're doing."

"I know the feeling." It slipped out before I could take it back.

"What about that journal?" he asked.

That was enough to put me on high alert. "Journal?"

"You know, the one from that dead girl everyone keeps talking about in these parts. Angel told me you had it."

I was already prepped with my answer, but now the lie sounded ridiculous since he knew so much. I reminded myself that they had likely searched our cabin for it. "I have no idea what Brek told Angel, but we don't have a journal." And I was very disturbed that I had brought it with me. I tightened my purse next to my stomach, and his eyes drew to it. I was also a horrible liar.

The server came back with our waters and I gulped it down while he took our orders. I was sure he wasn't expecting mine, but I went through the whole list, adding a sandwich and fries for my own dinner. "And also, that's for take out," I said. The server nodded.

"Put it on my bill," Hunter said.

"No, no," I said. "Do not put it on his bill. That's too much."

He tilted his head at me. "I thought we were friends now."

That confused me. *We were?* "Yeah, yeah, of course," I agreed, though I wasn't feeling it.

"Put it on my bill," he told the server, who nodded and hurried away.

I decided since Hunter was probably footing the bill for his whole team, too, then it wasn't that much more, but I still felt guilty for taking it. "So are you a trust fund baby?" I asked.

He laughed. "Touché."

That didn't answer my question. I was sure he'd done it on purpose. We were sitting by the railing, and the cold air drifted over me from below. Feeling the goosebumps prickle over my arms, I rubbed them down. The sweater wasn't enough. I wished my coat would dry faster, but who knew how long that would take?

"Cold?" he asked.

Hunter was paying close attention. I tried to deny it, then, with his eyes on me, I babbled, "My coat's in the wash, but I'm fine. It's just a little colder here than San Francisco. I'll get used to it."

He shimmied out of his coat and insisted I put it on, then when I shook my head and demurred out of politeness, he stood and held it out so I could put my arms in, and I had no idea what to do. Was this a Southern thing? A guy had never put his coat on me before. Hunter looked so cute behind me that it was hard to resist. Finally, I laughed and put my arms in. It felt ridiculous, like he was dressing a baby, but at the same time I liked it. He was such a gentleman.

Of course it was too big for me. The coat swallowed me up so I had to push the sleeves as far as they would go to find my hands, but it still held his warmth. Looking pleased with himself, he sat down, and I saw he wore another plaid shirt. This one was green and accentuated the broadness of his shoulders. It would've gone great with his John Deere ball cap.

"Soon, you'll give me all your clothes," I said, then blushed when he feigned a scandalized look.

"What else would you like?" he asked.

"I didn't mean it!" I said, then shrieked when he made to take off his shirt next. "Stop!"

I must've said it too loud because his men at the pool table looked over at us. Angel's eyes narrowed at us and she picked up a pool stick and sauntered around one side to sink her ball into the pocket. Could she be any cooler? I rolled my eyes.

"You're not a fan of Angel?" he asked perceptively.

"What made you figure that one out?"

"Just a hunch." His forehead wrinkled as he remembered something. "Wait. You've got something of mine." He lurched over the table and reached around me to dig into his coat pocket.

I jumped back, putting my hand over his. "What are you doing?"

"Sorry, I forgot." His mouth clenched, and he glanced up at me, his face a breath away from mine. I liked the way he smelled, like a woody floral. This guy had no problem getting close to me. "Hope you don't mind." He retrieved what he wanted from his coat and pulled away. I saw he held that cylinder device. It looked a bit like a kaleidoscope with copper siding. Was it a metal detector?

"You could've asked!" I smiled, trying not to show how flustered he'd made me.

"Sorry." He set it to the side. "Just some toy a kid gave us." I knew he was lying, like I was lying about Eden's journal. Maybe it was some high-tech GPS tracker. We didn't have any of those fancy things, though I knew Brekker did when he worked with companies backed by a lot of money.

Hunter tried to gather the thread of the conversation, but I knew his mind was still on the tech that had almost ended up with me. He snapped his fingers when he finally settled on what he wanted to say. "Tomorrow we should go out to the lake. See if we like working together."

I broke into a laugh. Nothing served as a better reminder that this whole thing was to soften me up for a business transaction. To his credit, he tried to work through the barrier between us. "C'mon, I'm not so bad. Admit it—you like me."

"You should have given my brother the coat, not me," I said. "Like Brekker said, I don't call the shots. You're wasting your time."

He stilled and his eyes lingered too long on me. "I wouldn't say that. There's nothing wrong with mixing business with pleasure."

That was doubtful. I had a sneaking suspicion that Angel had come up with this plan. She cracked another ball over the pool table and two of hers went in. Rosco rolled his eyes and straightened, beating his pool stick against his palm and shouting at the other player through the din. They must have some high stakes. She yelled at them to quiet down and repositioned her aim.

Looking over at Hunter, I saw he wasn't watching the game. He was waiting for me to respond, and so I laid my hand over the table next to his. "This is not mixing business with pleasure because I'm not doing business with you."

He looked intrigued. "So this is all pleasure?"

Wait, no! I flushed. "Forget I said anything." I laughed into my hand and desperately changed the subject. "How did you get into all this anyway, Hunter? What's your story?"

He floundered, likely because it was off script. "I... was raised by my grandfather. Let's just say he's a collector. Expeditions are his thing—not to say that I wasn't into it for a time, but um, I found out a few things about this place, some personal things, and he was keeping things from me, and so I think, well, this is the only way to know the truth."

I had no idea what he was talking about. "That was very descriptive."

He ducked his head in a chuckle, and I admired the contours of his face. Though he had a strong jawline, there was a vulnerable curve to his cheek. He was kind of pretty—Brek would mock me if I ever said that aloud, no man wanted to be pretty—but in Hunter's defense, it was in a manly way. "That's all I've got," he said. He wasn't ready to tell me everything, and I wondered what he was hiding. "What about you?" he asked.

He knew everything about me already, but I played along. "My great, great, great, great grandfather left a lady to die and we can't get over it, I guess. Our hearts are always on treasure until we find it."

"Is that why you're doing this?"

I thought about it. Not really. I just wanted a different life than the one that I had. I shook my head. "No, I mean, I need the money, but... no."

The server set the oversized sacks of takeout on the table between us, and my eyes rested on them, almost reluctant to go. Hunter seemed disappointed too. But I had to remember what this really was about. He was just trying to get Eden's journal from us. Biting my lip, I shuffled out of his coat and tried to return it with a light laugh. "I hope it doesn't smell too much like a skunk."

"You can keep it until you see me again."

I imagined Brek's reaction if he saw me wearing Hunter's coat and I shook my head. "That wouldn't go over well."

"Your brother hates me that much?"

"Maybe if you hadn't been hanging out with Angel, he might've given you a chance. Actually, no, he doesn't like any of my boyfriends, so..." I gave him the coat, blushing wildly.

He accepted it with a wry look and slid his arms back into it before returning the device back into the side pocket. We both had our secrets.

Angel yelled at the men at the pool table. She had won, obviously, but that didn't seem to be the problem. Rosco's pale face had gone red and wrinkled with his rough movements. They were getting louder, but at least I wasn't at the center of it, though it terrified me. Hunter seemed used to the commotion, just studied me under hooded eyes. Then turning mischievous, he sniffed the shoulder of his coat. "It smells like you now."

I wasn't going to let him be flirtatious. "Like a skunk?"

"Nope." He reached out and surprised me by taking a strand of my hair and rubbing it through his fingers before letting it go. "Like your hair. What's that I smell? Lavender?"

He was good. He was really good! He knew what I wanted to hear—especially after smelling so awful today. I was probably beaming when I stood up, but I knew I had to get away before I fell for anymore of his sweet talking in that adorable southern accent. Readjusting the strap of my purse over my shoulder, I gathered the handles of my bags. "Thank you for the food. I'd tell Brek you were the founder of the feast, but he might not be too happy about it."

"I didn't do it for him."

Hunter paying attention to me would only make his case worse. Maybe he didn't get it. I gave Hunter an enigmatic smile and turned, running straight into the jostling pair of men. Rosco was at the center of it. An elbow knocked into my hand and my bags went falling, along with my purse. Realizing the danger, I dove for the purse, seeing the contents stream out like the pieces of a jigsaw puzzle over the crowded floor, along with Eden's journal. Angel shouted over them, but I couldn't get to it fast enough when a foot almost trampled my hand. And just like that the journal was swept away under scrambling feet. I pushed through the men, and saw it was in Rosco's hand—the bloody knuckles were a dead giveaway.

My fear of losing the journal made me lose all inhibitions, and I grabbed his arm and caught sight of it again before Rosco shoved me away and hid it behind his back. "Give it to me!" I shouted.

"What are you talking about?" Rosco leered down at me, showing me his overly large teeth.

"I will scream." I opened my mouth to do it, and Hunter came out of nowhere. He nudged Rosco so that the man was handing the journal back.

"It fell out," Rosco said with a glare. "I was just giving it to you."

Hunter exchanged glances with Angel and I caught it. He hadn't been quick enough, but it made me immediately suspicious. Had this been the backup plan if Hunter failed to get the journal from me? He was touching me all night, but my purse was just too far from his hands. I couldn't believe that I'd fallen for it! The only reason that he had returned it was to avoid getting caught.

I stuffed the journal back into my purse, wondering how to get out of here with it still in my possession. I found my wallet and my bear spray on the floor, and stuffed those into my purse, clasping it firmly to me. "Hey, hey. Are you okay?" Hunter's hands were on me again. "I'm sure they didn't mean it."

They did! Gaslighting 101. I glared at him. "You set me up."

"What? I wouldn't do that to you," he said. "Hey, look at me. Don't be mad. Don't be mad. It was a misunderstanding." He was talking to me like I was a fuse ready to go off. And I was.

He handed me one of my takeout bags from off the ground while the crowd jostled me from behind. When he did so, I saw the cylinder device he'd kept from me in his pocket, within reaching distance. He had already tried to steal from me, and my attention homed in on it, feeling the fury course through my blood at his trick. I wanted to take whatever I could from him. He handed me my other takeout bag and without another thought, I threw myself against him like someone had pushed me from behind, then I slid the device out of his pocket without him being any wiser. "Watch it!" I said and dropped the cylinder object into my takeout bag, untangling myself from his arms. "What's your problem anyway?"

He put his hands up to show he was innocent. He was this time. I was the guilty one now, and I felt fully justified. Hunter watched me like he didn't know what to do with me. "Let me walk you home."

Getting back to the cabin would be a problem. I didn't know who to trust. My bear spray might not cut it. So far Hunter had resorted to tricks, and I didn't think that he'd outright mug me for the journal, but there was the issue of him discovering what I had taken from him before he got me home. I could come clean, but I was too mad. My thoughts went to Bill, and looking through the shafts of the railing, I saw the light on his computer was on.

"Someone's waiting for me downstairs," I said and rushed away from Hunter and Angel and their oversized minion Rosco, taking two steps at a time to the ground floor.

My intuition was right. Bill sat behind his computer, laboriously looking up YouTube videos of laughing babies. "Hey there!" he called out when he saw me. "This YouTube is quite the invention. You can find anything on here, can't you?"

"Pretty much." Turning, I saw Hunter still watching me at the top of the stairs and so I asked Bill to walk me home.

His whole face changed at the honor of it. "Why, of course. Of course." He got his coat on while I gathered my clothes from the laundry room.

"It's just so dark out there," I said as way of explanation.

The last thing Hunter saw of me that night was Bill taking my side and leading Skip through the door on a leash. Even he wouldn't mess with a fierce Dogo Argentino. They were worse than skunks, I'd heard.

Chapter nine

aitlyn lay in the twin bed next to mine, her blankets twisted around her head. The only sign she was alive was that she kept pressing snooze. I flipped on the light to wake her up and got ready to leave for our hike, but even that wasn't enough to make her stir.

My backpack was much lighter this time. I didn't pack as much, though I'd snuck in a little Skunk-Off just in case. I slid on shorts and put fewer layers over that than before, trusting I would get hot about fifteen minutes into the trail anyway.

That weird tech that I had stolen from Hunter went into my coat pocket. It felt like it was burning a hole through it. The guilt was getting to me. Stealing wasn't exactly my style, but for all I knew it was only a cell phone charger and I was beating myself up for nothing. I'd show Brekker, but then I'd have to explain that I stole it. He'd ask why and then I'd have to tell him about last night. Then he'd confront Hunter. Angel would get involved, throwing herself seductively at him, and then he'd fall more in love with her.

So the answer was, "no," I shouldn't show Brekker. But I didn't have my phone to look up what it was either. Bill's internet was the only answer, but it was too early for him to be awake, so I'd have to wait until we got back from our hike that night to figure out what I had.

I came out of my bedroom to find my brother eating a bowl of oatmeal on the stiff, ugly couch. My coat hung over the fireplace in the living room and I checked to see if it was dry. It was. Mostly.

"Where's Caitlyn?" Brek asked.

Still asleep. Her alarm went off again and I winced at the sound. "Let me go check on her real quick."

He twisted around to pin me with a stern look. "We need to leave in fifteen minutes."

I wasn't sure if Caitlyn was capable of getting ready that fast, but I stuck my thumb up to avoid the fight. We'd try! I came inside our bedroom, closing the door behind me. "Caitlyn," I whispered. "We've got to go."

She groaned.

"Caitlyn." I leaned over her bed. "You there, little buddy?"

She groaned again. I wasn't sure what to do. She shoved her blankets to the floor and stared up at me, her hair a red fuzz curling around her pillows. "I've been thinking. You need someone to stay behind and do the technical side of things. I can upload the videos."

"What?" I sat on the edge of the bed. "You don't want to go!" I accused.

"No, no, no. I do… but my feet don't want to go."

"If you don't come with me then there will be no one to tell Brek to slow down."

"Are you coming?" my brother shouted from the other room.

He already sounded like a drill sergeant, and I desperately tried to talk her into coming. "What about this thing you've got for Brek?" I knew it was low, but romance was the only thing that worked with her. "You're going to let Angel swoop in and steal him?"

She snorted in disgust. "There's only so much I'm willing to do to get a guy, okay? Besides, he's still not over Angel. And honestly, I don't want to see her stupid face anymore. If she drives by all done up and beautiful one more time, I'm gonna pull her hair out. I hate to say it, Ivy, because you're my friend, but I am way over Brekster."

I'd argue it, but I didn't think they'd make a good couple anyway. But something else was worrying me. "You can't stay behind. It won't be safe." I explained how I believed that someone had broken into our cabin. "There were things out of place."

"Oh please." Now that she had almost successfully gotten out of the hike, she nestled into her pillow. "You're not exactly clean."

"I think that those guys with Angel want Eden's journal."

"I'll lock the doors. I'm not afraid of them."

"We did lock the doors!' I said. "And... you don't even know what they did last night. They tripped me and tried to steal the journal. That guy Rosco, you know him?"

"That big ugly jerk?"

"Yeah, he had it in his hand and I was going to scream down the house before he agreed to give it back to me. I think Angel and Hunter planned the whole thing! He tried to sweeten me up—let me use his coat, even bought our dinner!"

She had turned from her pillow and sat up, her face twisting with all the redheaded temper she had in her. "You didn't tell me!"

"I didn't want Brekker to know because..."

"Angel," she finished. She threw her pillow to the floor with her blankets in another rage. It made me believe that she wasn't entirely over Brek.

"I had to get Bill to take me home," I said. "So, it isn't safe for you to stay here by yourself."

"Listen!" She put up a finger and waggled it at me. "We're not letting bullies win here. We're going to fight. I'll call in Bill and those other old men and have them fix stuff around the house for me when I'm in here and then I'll spend the rest of my time hanging out with them at the café while I put together our footage for our web series."

She really didn't want to go hiking.

"Are you sure?"

She nodded. "Angel and her trashy friends won't ruin my vacation."

Brekker called for us again and I got up from her creaking bed then turned on my way out the door when I remembered. "One last complication... I might've stolen something from Hunter after they tried to take Eden's journal from me."

Her eyes widened at me, and then her lips flattened into a thin line. "Good," she said. "Good." Her freckles were more pronounced now.

"They might come back for it."

"I'm ready for them. You know what? You go out and get Eden's treasure. I'm not slowing you down anymore, but I can help you over here—after I get a good breakfast and maybe get some sun—but after that, I'm going to make your footage into something beautiful. Leave the SD card in your camera by the TV and take a new one today. I've got some ideas of what I want to do."

Editing wasn't my forte, and for a moment I considered her offer. Even if she didn't get around to learning the film editing program all by herself, it wasn't a big deal if she stayed home. And if she did master it? That would be a load off my mind. I stuck my hand out. "Deal."

She placed her little hand into mine and we shook on it. Then she retrieved her blankets. "Turn the light out when you leave."

I almost laughed. She had never worked so hard to get out of going with me before. Brekker peered at me curiously when I came out of the room without Caitlyn. I unloaded the SD card and shrugged. "She wants to help us edit the web series here." I watched him closely for any sign of disappointment. Brek blinked a couple of times, but that was the extent of it. I was a horrible matchmaker. Did I want him to get over Angel or didn't I? "She's such a good, dear friend."

He laughed. "Keep telling yourself that. She wanted out of hiking."

I didn't have a defense for that, so I'd try again later. I wanted Angel out of my brother's life for good. We marched out the door, and for a moment I envied Caitlyn as the chill of the outdoors sunk into my bones. After what Angel and Hunter had done, I had something to prove. It was time that I embraced who I was. I was a Payne, whether I liked it or not, and treasure hunting was in the blood.

Hunter's team was already gathering on their lawn, walking in and out of the cabin with supplies and casting curious looks our way. Rosco put his mauled hand over his mouth to shout over at us, "Where's the short little one? Did she fall into a crack somewhere?"

My hands balled into fists. I wasn't sure what would keep them out of the cabin more—knowing she was in there or not, so I ignored him.

Hunter came out of the cabin wearing the coat that we had shared last night. He had a new ball cap. This one was red. Apparently he hadn't taken my advice on the helmet. Moron. He looked over at me, and I steadfastly avoided his gaze. Did he suspect I'd stolen from him or did he feel guilty about what he'd done?

The door to our cabin opened and Caitlyn shuffled out in her blanket. "Brekker!" she called.

We both swiveled. Crooking her finger at him, she beckoned him towards her. My jaw dropped when he came without a fuss. I was proud of her. Caitlyn was fighting for her man. He bent over her so she could whisper in his ear.

"You didn't tell your brother about last night?"

I jumped. Angel startled me. She had slunk over like a snake and I hadn't seen her coming. With some difficulty, I pulled myself together. "What's there to tell?" I chanced a look at her face as she watched Brek with Caitlyn. Angel acted like she knew him so well. And maybe she did—if Brek had any idea about last night, he'd be fighting Rosco right now. "I took care of it," I said.

"What's your reason for not telling him?" she asked.

What was that supposed to mean? Did she think I didn't want Hunter to get in trouble? Or was she talking about what I stole? "I don't want to be involved with any of you," I said, "so from now on, let's just stay out of each other's way."

She inclined her head, and I moved away from her before she tried to mess with my mind more. Brek was pulling away from Caitlyn and he looked much more entranced with her than he had since Angel had come into the picture. He reached my side. "What did she say?" I asked.

"You've got a lot of explaining to do."

My head jerked up to meet Caitlyn's eyes and she dimpled and waved. Had she thrown me under the bus? She closed the door, and I nudged Brekker. "Tell me."

"Nope," he said through clenched teeth, "not here."

That made me worried. We passed the men outside their cabin, but he didn't tackle any of them, namely Rosco. Hunter came back out of the cabin with a net full of mountain climbing equipment swinging against his back, and I froze, watching Brek from the corner of my eye, but still nothing. Angel likewise got the same treatment. What had Caitlyn told him?

We were back on the motorized vehicle trail, heading for the footpath. Brek wanted to explore the area above Moonlight Lake. It was called Sinkhole Lake, and apparently we would've gotten it over with yesterday if I hadn't gotten sprayed by a skunk. The morning was brighter than the one before it, and I peeled off layer after layer until I was in my shorts. It was a relief to be free. I'd have taken the ball cap that Hunter gave me, but I still couldn't get over last night and so I made sure to apply sunscreen instead.

The path finally split from the motorized vehicle to the footpath, and we weren't too far up the trail before Brekker broke his silence. "Why are you keeping things from me, Ivy?"

Inwardly I chewed out Caitlyn, outwardly I shrugged. "Just come out and say it, Brekker. I can't take the suspense anymore."

"You got Hunter to pay for our meal?"

"Well, I…"

"I mean, that's priceless. What did Angel say? Let me guess, he didn't tell her. Why do you keep all the good things from me?"

"I don't know—you seemed pretty mad whenever he talked to me."

"I was. I am! But you've got a special power over the bad boys, so maybe I should just let you go for it. Caitlyn pointed out how that could be a good thing for us."

"How?" I sputtered. "I don't want anything to do with him."

"Good, if you did then I'd be against it. Maybe you can mess with his head and chase him out of town."

Caitlyn was not helping the situation with her little schemes. "I'm not a robot, Brek, and I can't compartmentalize like you men can. I'm this close to falling for the guy—bad boy or not—so don't push me. He's too cute!" He looked startled at the revelation, and I decided to come clean. "I stole something from him last night. Hunter was trying to take Eden's journal from me last night, and so he had this high tech thing and I stole it, okay!" I pulled the device out of my coat and showed him. "I'm sorry, I was really mad."

"They tried to ambush you?" His voice was low with anger. I nodded quickly. "You should've told me," he said.

"I didn't know what you would do to those guys." I still didn't. "You're a little protective," I said. "A lot protective."

"Of course I am. You're a part of me—I can't explain it."

"Well, I was protecting you too by not saying anything. I can't stand Angel, Brek. The more we deal with her, the worse it gets, so I didn't want you going after her and falling for her all over again."

He let that digest with a little smile before his eyes veered to the device in my hand. "Let me see it." I gave it to him and he turned the cylinder over in his hand, moving the copper siding around with no results. "I don't know what it is. A phone charger?"

"You don't know?" I was disappointed, but then hopeful that it really wasn't something important because I felt guilty. "It could be completely useless."

He laughed and handed it back. "Just throw it in the lake."

No, I felt too bad about it. I'd try to find a way to sneak it back to Hunter. Slipping it into my backpack, I followed Brek up the incline and we trekked the rest of the way in an uneasy truce. I listened to my hiking boots crunch against the rocks and the soft dirt. It was a lot faster without Caitlyn and more boring, but at least my backpack wasn't stuffed full of useless items like last time. We passed Moonlight Lake, and I paid silent homage to the passage of the woods where I had been sprayed by the skunk as we made our way up to the second lake.

Sinkhole Lake was up a steep slide of rocks and boulders, and we resorted to boulder hopping to scramble to the top. Caitlyn would've hated the heights. It felt like a Donkey Kong game going from level to level.

Remembering that I was supposed to document this, I took out my camera from time to time to record the adventure, trying my best to imitate Caitlyn's style of narration. "Yes," I said. "We are actually scrambling over boulders to get to this lake. It had better be worth it."

I turned the camera to Brek. This was what he lived for. He perched on a rock ahead of me like a mountain lion, his shoulder blades jutting out from his broad shoulders, the muscles on his arms rippling. I was sure I looked more like a newborn fawn learning to walk in comparison. He was much faster than I was, but he slowed down when he remembered himself, or when I shouted out my complaints. "There's my brother," I said. "He's in his element... and then there's me. As you can see, I'm a little behind."

"Put away the camera," Brek called. "Maybe you'll catch up."

"He's got a lot of faith in me." I shut it off and lodged it safely in my bag between the layers of my discarded clothes. Then I followed after him again, only to take the camera back out to capture the moment when we entered the basin where the lake was. The light glistened off the water and it took my breath away. The far bank was held up by a wall of rock towering above us in dips and peaks like the top of an ice cream cone. And where Moonlight Lake below was an aquamarine color, this lake was tinged with green. It teemed with Sago pondweed just below the surface, especially near the banks where it was shallower. Brekker explained that while Moonlight got all the groundwater, this lake got most of the water from the glacier and so it just kept expanding throughout the years.

The bottom of this lake wasn't formerly a crater like Moonlight Lake, but it was still hard to find because of the amount of silt in the water. Once Brek left the banks, he couldn't get close to the bottom with all that mud while he still attempted the impossible of finding anything resembling a cavern. This meant it was all the more crucial to hold the line to guide Brek's way. I recorded the moment he came up from the surface in his scuba gear. We were missing Caitlyn to "ooh" and "ahh" over him, but I tried my best to make it exciting for our online audience. "Just think, ladies," I said. "He's single."

He hadn't found too much of interest down there this time around. A few cans, and a fishing pole caught in the pondweed. No treasure. He threw them out on the bank, and my brow knit at the garbage. "And he's environmentally conscious, girls."

Brekker acted like that was a bad word. "I'm not hauling *that* out of here."

"And that's going to be edited out in post," I said.

"Leave it in." Brek peeled his wetsuit down to his waist and sat down on the sandy bank.

"That one's for the ladies," I said.

He gave me a look seething with irritation. "I can't see anything down there! Not the least bit. No rocks! No caverns—that I can tell. This is a dangerous dive. I don't even want to think about why they call this Sinkhole Lake." I didn't know why they did either. At my confused face, he sighed. "Teaching moment—sinkholes are holes in the ground when water dissolves surface rock, like this limestone here. It might happen because of the presence of underground caves. Mud or other debris can plug them up, and that's how you can get a lake on top of it, but... if there is a cavern underneath here? I can't even think how we'd find it. No way could we stumble on it on our own, unless we figured out a way to unplug the debris... or if the mud sucked us in and pulled us out into this cavern on the other side."

My heart lurched. "Are you kidding me?"

He nodded slowly. "Sinkholes are creepy, but no, it's not usually like that... unless that Spanish priest stumbled on something freaky. Let's just say I am really hoping that those caves are not here, but I'm worried because... is that camera on?" No, I'd turned it off during his tirade. He straightened. "Get it on."

He pulled out a book from his pack while I did so and he got down to business. "This lake is known for the Spanish symbols on the rocks and trees. X marks the spot!" He pointed to the X in his book on a list of symbols with their meanings. There were pages of them. "The Spanish marked their treasure maps up with these. In the 1500's, they used them to mark their mines too, and in this case, the markings might even point to buried treasure." His eyes shifted from the book to me. "You can keep recording, Ivy. We're not the first to find these symbols near Sinkhole Lake so it doesn't matter if we tell the world about them."

He pulled out a paper that showed a rough sketch of the basin with illustrations of trees and rocks with symbols drawn on each one. "This is a crude map showing where the symbols are around the lake. This says there are seven, but no GPS coordinates, so they'll be hard to find." He set the maps down and pulled a granola bar from his pack.

"Is that it?" I asked.

He gave me a double take. "Yeah, shut off the camera and eat!"

Grumbling about giving me a head's up, I put it away and gathered my lunch from my pack. Without Caitlyn's instance on taking breaks, I'd let too many slip away from me, and I was starving. I devoured my sandwich in minutes and started on my apple next. There was still something that I didn't understand. "If other people have these maps with the symbols and what they mean, Brek, then why haven't they found the treasure yet?"

His nose squinched up with his cocky grin. "They aren't as good as I am."

I laughed—if only it were so simple. These Spanish symbols were mentioned in Eden's journal, which Brek already knew. Were they the same ones?

While we ate lunch, I tugged out the cylinder device I'd taken from Hunter. The closer I looked at it, the more I wondered if it was a camera or a scope. The glass on one side could be a lens, but where were the controls? Peering through it, I saw the lake in front of me, but in no way magnified, plus a display of Roman numerals randomly set around the screen in no particular order. What did it represent? GPS? Altitude? Speed? What I'd do for an instruction manual. Considering how much Hunter and Angel had been tinkering with it, they couldn't figure it out either.

"Have you seen anything like this?" I asked Brek. He appeared mildly curious as I pressed around the copper siding, searching for buttons and plugins or an opening that concealed them. I only found some labels that looked to be written in Arabic etched into the side of the cylinder. It was so odd. When I twisted the copper siding, it clicked at the movement, but nothing happened. It would be hilarious if Hunter had been telling the truth and this came from a kid.

Brekker stuffed the wrappers of his lunch back into his pack. "You ready for this?"

I tucked the cylinder back into my pocket. After yesterday, I wasn't eager to go tromping through the woods again. "I had better not get sprayed by another skunk!"

"Don't worry. They only stick around marshy areas. The woods are far enough away from the lake."

"Just like yesterday," I muttered, "and I still managed to find a skunk."

"There must've been a marsh in there, or a pond."

"Yeah, I splashed through it," I reminded him. Probably when I got sprayed. My brother had assured me of all sorts of things before we'd started this trip, and it was annoying to realize that he didn't know this terrain at all, even though he acted like he did. "The bears probably aren't hibernating either."

"No, they aren't," he admitted.

I glared at him. I couldn't believe anything he said anymore. I wondered what had happened to his team, and I knew he wouldn't tell me. Putting away my lunch, I gestured for him to lead. "After you!"

Brekker did his best to find the seven symbols on the makeshift map, but after wandering aimlessly through the trees, fighting through the brush and weeds, it got hot and the hornets came out. It forced us out of the cover of the trees into the heat. I really wished that I had brought Hunter's ball cap with me, and remembering my sunscreen, I reapplied it. Then I brought out my camera and turned it on. "Are you sure they're really here?" I asked.

"No, I'm not." Brekker was getting testy, and unwilling to play it up for the camera.

"Who made your map? Can you contact them?"

"I tried and got nothing. It's not a hoax if that's what you're thinking. There were other accounts online of hikers finding the symbols. Turn off the camera. Let me think."

I did.

He went back to his phone, and I peered over at the screenshots that he'd taken from an online conversation. My eyes widened when I read the theories from the contributors of the website. "Did you get that map from a treasure hunting blog?"

"Don't judge. These guys have dedicated their lives to this treasure. They've made all these claims about Spanish mines, and they've tried to back it up with the things they've found. Smelters, Spanish symbols. They have pictures."

I looked through them on Brek's phone, trying to match the photos of symbols carved into trees and rocks with what we'd seen so far, but everything was too close up with not enough of the background to get a better idea of where those landmarks were. "We should try to target these treasure hunters as our audience for our webisodes," I said.

He snorted. "There are probably like ten of them."

Brekker always had to dismantle my ideas, and I waited for him to read through the thirty or so posts on the topic before he said, "This guy says it's by the Old Spanish Trail, wherever that is, past cleared land where he found old Spanish armor..." He looked up. "Nothing is cleared land over here. When was this written?"

"2002," I read over his shoulder.

He groaned. "How about this one from 2005? It says the symbols are between the two lakes when he found it off the trail a ways off."

"Between this one and Moonlight?" I asked.

"I'm not sure. Lake Adam is just east of here."

Was it so close? I remembered Bill's story and didn't want to go anywhere near there. Of course, in the middle of the day it was less terrifying. "That's where Bone Man followed Bill," I said.

He looked thoughtful. "Makes me wonder what Bone Man really is... I mean, if Bill wasn't lying about the whole thing... or was drunk."

All I knew was that I wanted to keep my distance from Lake Adam. "How about we check between here and Moonlight Lake, instead?"

Brek made a chicken "bak bak" sound, but I didn't care. He'd have a fight getting me to Lake Adam. "All right." He took a deep breath and pushed back into the woods where we headed the opposite way that we'd gone earlier. The bank of this lake pushed deep into the mountains behind us, and it took us the better part of the afternoon to comb through the woods and into backwoods country. We scaled a few more rockslides before the bottoms of my feet began to ache. Brek was relentless. He entered another grove of trees and stopped, abruptly. I skidded to a halt behind him, afraid that he'd stumbled over a moose... or worse, a skunk.

"What? What?" I asked.

"Get out your camera." His voice was low and breathless.

I did, excitement rushing through me at the prospect of finally finding something. As soon as I began to record, he gave me a dark look. "Do you know how long aspens live?" I shook my head. "Forty to a hundred-and-fifty years. None of these can possibly have survived from the 1500's."

He stepped aside so that I could get a shot of the aspens. These were the seven trees from Brek's map. "Whoever put this together knew what they were doing," he said and pointed down the line of trees. "This symbol on this first tree means gold, and this is silver on the next one. This is copper, lead, zinc, saltpeter, and this last one? Well, that's the best one of all. It says, 'It's not here.' They should've added 'Loser,' to it—that would've made it complete." He looked frustrated, though his eyes also danced at the humor of it.

I grunted out in displeasure. "Well, that explains why no one has found Eden's treasure yet."

He pushed the map into my hands and brushed past me, putting as much distance between himself and the twenty-year-old gag as he could. "Besides Eden."

"And she died," I reminded him. He didn't answer, and I wondered if Brek would go to such lengths. He strode away from me, and I put the camera away. "Where are we going?"

"Home to our cabin… and then to our neighbor's cabin. Maybe Angel has some better leads."

I was astounded he'd reached such lows. "You can't! You're giving up?"

"Never, but Angel talks when she tries not to." That sounded dangerous. I wondered how he had figured that one out. "You can work the Hunter angle," he added.

He must be desperate! "You can't be serious!" I didn't want to talk to him again, and if Hunter asked me about that device, I'd give myself away. Of course, I could just give it back to him. What would he do after that? Whatever it was, it wouldn't be confiding in me.

"C'mon, Ivy," Brek said. "It's all part of the adventure. You don't like him; you're fine."

"Did you hear anything I said on our way up here?"

"So he's a pretty face? Here's your chance to follow in Eden's footsteps… and maybe we might stumble onto something she did right."

"She died!" How many times had I pounded that into my brother's skull? Not enough. So caught up in my worry, I barely noticed that we were taking a different trail going back. I thought Brek was trying to avoid the rock slides, but there wasn't an easy way to get down to Moonlight Lake from here. It glittered from the cliff's edge below us. It was stunning. I dropped my pack on a flat rock, deciding to take some pictures, not caring if Brek got ahead of me anymore. I hadn't spotted any wild animals so far, and I figured that we were making so much noise arguing that we'd scared them all off.

My camera couldn't possibly pick up what the lens of my eye could, but I tried to capture the depth of the valley below, using the shadow cast by the clouds to get the deep green of the forest with the lights shining off the aquamarine lake. Turning to the rockslide at my back, I gasped and fumbled with my camera. I'd almost missed this natural wonder in a wall of glaciated red limestone behind me. The surface of it was smooth and polished where a glacier had scraped across it leaving striations on the face of it.

Sinkhole Lake was behind it, and this limestone held it in like a natural dam. It was glorious, in a word, and I snapped pictures of that too. The bottom half of this towering wall was covered in moss and shrubbery. Here and there, oversized boulders called erratics had been dumped by this same glacier and rested to the side of me like big Easter Island heads. The years of trailing after my grandfather to the locations of his next get-rich schemes had embedded this useless geological knowledge into my memory. I'd gotten out of those expeditions as soon as I was old enough to make my own decisions, but I was surprised at how much I loved it now. I felt like I was standing in the middle of Stonehenge.

By now Brek was so far ahead of me that I'd have to run to catch up, and so I reached down for my pack to put my camera away and noticed that the flat rock where it rested had something scratched on the surface of it. Peering closer, I saw an X. Not an ordinary one—the edges were curled.

"Brek!" I shouted. "Brek, get back here!"

He didn't turn at first and so I kept shouting at him. I was so excited that I was between crying and laughing. It was just a stupid thing that I did, and he knew it meant something. When he caught it in my voice, he stopped in his tracks and came running to me. "What is it?"

"There's an 'X' over here!" I cried. Well, it looked like an X with two circles on either side of it, and then a triangle. I pointed, and he took a deep breath and knelt to inspect it.

His lips curved up. "The cross here means treasure belonging to the church," he said. "And that triangle points to where it is." It pointed the direction of the rock wall that held in Sinkhole Lake. His eyes veered to that, and he looked nervous since he had expressed earlier how much he did not want the treasure to be in that lake. "Who knows if that's exactly what it's saying, but it's a clue. And..." his hands trailed to the circles on either side of the cross. "I don't know what those are," he finally admitted.

I did. "Brek, Eden drew that in her journal." Dragging it out from my backpack, I opened it to show my brother. There was the cross on the coin with the two circles on both sides of it. "It was on old Pratt's coin she stole."

"What did she say about it?" he asked. "She talked about the symbols, but there wasn't much there..."

I knew her journal well at this point and I flipped it to the page where she wrote about the Spanish symbols and skimmed through it.

Eden's Journal: June 30th, 1855 — Mountains of the Deseret

Mr. Black's a funny rascal. He don't know what to make of me. As the days warmed up and we'd git out to hunt for treasure, me and Lucius had ourselves a row now and then. I'd git all fired up about this or that, and Mr. Black just laughed and tipped his hat, and told Lucius it was best to defer to a lady. Lucius thought that was hogwash, but I rather liked that kind of thinking. Nows I git to making up any excuse to talk to Mr. Black—I couldn't rightly remember any gent treating me like that in all my years. It feels real nice, like a relaxing dip in the lake on a warm day.

He hadn't no objections to setting himself down to talk to me. Mr.

Black learned himself a thing or two in school like reading and writing. And he knowed figures and whatnot. And he was right fascinated with them Spanish symbols. Those Shoshone Indians pointed them out in the rocks roundabouts. They was the way to git the treasure. They found him a shiny stick and said it would point him where to go. When's I saw what they done gave him, I got real jittery about such devil tricks because I knowed it was one of them wands used to find treasure. When Mr. Black seen me shaking at the sight of it, he talked real low and comforting and said them Spanish priests were religious folk and wouldn't have nothing to do with no witching sticks. Their makings was a thing to return the land to what it once was. That was all he got in his hand, not anything wicked, but a tool, like a compass, and so I calmed down considerable after that. Mr. Black wouldn't fib; Lucius was real stern about that when I asked him.

We had always assumed that Eden was a little gullible here, that the "shiny stick" she was talking about *was* a "shinny stick," commonly known as a diviner's rod, that the superstitious used to find underground water, and in earlier cultures, treasure. Witching sticks were absolutely useless, and it had been a low point for Mr. Black to trick her into thinking that wasn't what he was doing, but now I wondered if it didn't mean something else completely.

What if...? What if? I pulled the cylinder device from my pocket and saw it through different eyes. This wasn't some tech from the Far East. What if that shiny stick was a lot smaller than I thought it was. What if... as Mr. Black said, it was a tool to find this treasure, not some superstitious thing at all.

"Brek?" I felt horrible and excited all at once. "I think I stole something important."

Chapter ten

*C*aitlyn was nowhere to be seen. I tromped through the cabin in my hiking boots, calling her name. We never should've left her alone. I had suspected that Hunter's men had searched the place while we were gone; why hadn't I listened to my gut? "Caitlyn!" I shouted then turned to Brek. He didn't look quite as concerned as I felt, but he read my look.

"She's fine," he said. "She'll show eventually."

I ground my teeth. He was hardly the worried suitor, which made me doubt Caitlyn would ever get Brek to forget about his conniving, dark haired Angel. Men were so dumb right now. "Hey, let's just get some dinner at the Grizzly," he suggested. "Maybe we can get Hunter to pay again."

That was not funny! I threw my backpack on the floor of my room and dug out the thing that I had stolen from him. I wasn't sure what I was going to do with it, but I wasn't leaving it behind to get snatched like Caitlyn had been. I pushed the journal into my purse for good measure, grabbed my coat, and marched out of the cabin without Brek. It was evening, though the sunlight hours had a way of holding on in the summer months and it wouldn't be dark for a few hours yet.

"Wait up!" He easily caught up to me and stuffed his hands deep into the pockets of his coat. "I'm sure she's doing better than we are. She's probably curled up in a blanket reading somewhere."

"In the middle of the forest? It's freezing."

"Well, no…" He had nothing for me, but his mind was clearly on other things. After spending the afternoon searching for more Spanish symbols and not finding any, we had decided to brainstorm at the cabin. Despite the arrow pointing the direction of Sinkhole Lake, it

146

wasn't as clear cut as we wanted it to be. There was still the matter of the circles on either side of the X, which could drastically change the message of the symbol. Besides that, Eden had said that the shiny stick would point the way. The Spanish symbols might hold a message for us, but we didn't know what. Brek had leads at other lakes and other clues to explore, and I had a "shiny stick" to figure out.

We neared the Grizzly and took the stairs two at a time—that was the advantage of having the long legs of our giant Viking ancestors, which only made me worry about the poor diminutive Caitlyn we'd left behind to fend for herself. As soon as we pushed open the loudly clanging door, I heard the karaoke music drift down to us. Both Brekker and I stared up the three flights to spy Caitlyn singing her heart out in the Bear Den. The old men cheered and applauded; the other patrons in the pub soberly drank from their pints, not knowing where to look in their discomfort.

I grinned. Trust Caitlyn to set up karaoke wherever she went. Brek was rolling his eyes, but he loved it. He followed me up the stairs just as Caitlyn finished up singing "It's Raining Men." The old timers, minus Pat who smiled serenely at his chair, stood up for a standing ovation. They were the only ones clapping in the whole establishment and so I joined in. After nudging Brek, he did too.

Caitlyn saw us and bounded off the makeshift stage that had somehow been built while we were off for the day. She was like Snow White with the seven dwarves, or Pollyanna to the town, or Heidi with her grandfather… basically, she managed to take over the place in a matter of hours with her sweet charm. She took my hands and swung them in her excitement.

I laughed. "What have you been doing while we've been away?"

"Well, I learned how to edit footage," she said. "I've put a few things together that I want you to see. Oh, and Bill and Frank and Harlan stuck around to talk." My gaze went to them at the other side of the room. They had found their seats again, feasting on fries and macaroni and cheese. Caitlyn dimpled. "I told them that you and I were pretty good at karaoke. And one thing led to another..."

And now we had a karaoke stage. I was impressed, and my hand itched to take the microphone. If it weren't for Hunter's men scattered through the crowd, I'd totally go for it. Rosco took a deep pull from a brewski and I tried to ignore his stares as I scanned the group of stunned patrons—who were only now trying to regain their manly dignity after Caitlyn's serenading. Hunter wasn't among them. I spied Angel coming from the balcony area, her cheeks red from the cold outside.

Seeing Brek, she came straight for him. I could only guess that meant she suspected we had taken the cylinder device. I knew she'd see straight through Brek's lies and I steeled myself for the confrontation. Her eyes wandered lazily to Caitlyn and dismissed her with a glare before she returned her attention to my twin. "You missed an interesting afternoon," she said.

Brek's careful eyes were on her. "I've a feeling there will be more entertainment to come."

"There is," she said and closed the gap between them. Caitlyn met my eyes in horror—Angel was directing all her charm on Brek and he was too weak to resist—and I tried to get between them before we lost him altogether, but it was too late; he was already following her as she led him away from us. "I need to speak to you," she said in a low voice. "It was a misunderstanding. I want to explain."

"Brek!" I hissed, taking his other arm. "Don't leave us here."

He lifted a brow to shoot me a skeptical glance. "Yeah, watch out for the old men."

"I'm not kidding!"

His grin flattened into a line and he turned serious. "You've got this." He shook my grip from his arm and chucked my chin. "Remember what I said. Go get us dinner."

I'd rather not, actually. Was this what Brek thought he was doing with Angel—sacrificing for the cause to get her to talk? Nothing she'd say would be work related. But there was nothing that I could do short of dragging him away, and I knew I'd lose that fight. I let him go, turning to a fuming Caitlyn. "Did you *see* what she did?" she asked.

Brekker allowed Angel to lead him outside onto the balcony. He was not blameless in that encounter. "Did you see what *he* did?"

Caitlyn looked miffed, and I didn't blame her. All of her earlier happiness from the karaoke was ruined. "This is a new kind of low."

I sighed. "He's being stupid… but for a different reason than you think. He wants us to infiltrate the other side and get information out of them." She looked shocked, and I slanted her a look of accusation. "I blame you."

"Oh." Her face got red. Her plan to gain Brek's confidence had backfired on her in a big way.

There was no reason to dwell on it now. I shifted away from the balcony and leaned against the bar, lowering my voice, "I have something to tell you."

Before I could let her know about the cylinder and what it meant, Caitlyn's eyes rounded and focused on something behind me. I stopped talking immediately and glanced over to see Hunter closing in on us. It took all my willpower not to clutch my purse where I had stashed the stolen thing next to Eden's journal.

His attention was on my face as he approached, and I tried to read his expression to see if it was full of accusation or regret from last night. There was neither. He only watched me with interest, like a cat with a mouse. He brushed past my arm and reached behind me to get some napkins. "Where's your brother?" he asked. I couldn't get over that southern twang, and I forced myself to remain indifferent to him, even though his arm was still behind me. "Why isn't he guarding you from me?" he asked.

"Angel has him," Caitlyn said with a sullen twist to her lips.

She wasn't her usual talkative self with Hunter, but he didn't seem to notice. He smiled slowly. "He's fraternizing with the enemy?"

I didn't appreciate him acting like we were overdramatizing this. I whipped my hair behind my shoulder—perhaps a little sassier than I had intended—and whipped him in the face with it. He laughed in response, and I turned to face him. "Is that what we are?" I asked. "The enemy?"

"I hope not." Then he tapped the countertop of the bar between us and pressed my arm with his fingers, looking deeply into my eyes with a smirk playing on his sensuous lips before he left for a table next to the old men.

"That was so hot," Caitlyn muttered.

It was, and I tried to slow my breathing. He would use me, like Angel was using Brekker. It would not be the other way around. There was no way I could ask him about the shiny stick without him suspecting I had it.

"I wish Brek looked at me the way *he* does with you."

"Stop it! It's all a game to him… but I think I might've won this time." My voice turned into a whisper. "Remember that thing I stole from him? That tech?" She nodded. "It wasn't what I thought it was—it's more important. Eden wrote about it in her journal. I think it's a compass—a special one that might show us how to find the treasure."

Her face brightened for the first time since Angel had taken off with my brother. "Do you have it with you? Let me see."

"Not here."

"It's in your purse?"

"Yes, but…"

Her face turned pleading, and, still feeling bad about Brek's rejection, I took her hand and pulled her the direction of the restrooms, then thought better of that when I remembered Angel and instead led her into the hallway between the busy pub and the kitchen so that we were free from any curious eyes. I opened my purse so she could look inside, but before I could stop her she reached in and plucked out the cylinder. "Not so fast!" I said. "No one can see that I have it."

"They won't." She turned it over in her delicate little hand. It made it seem as if it were a lot bigger than it was. "Are you sure it's important? It just looks like a kaleidoscope?" She put it up to her eye and squinted, twisting the coppery siding back and forth while it made clicking noises.

I snatched it away from her and heard voices as two of Hunter's men came around the corner—one of them Rosco. I dropped my purse at the sight of his cruel face. Caitlyn jumped forward to get it while I threw the cylinder behind my back, the whole time I inwardly cursed my stupidity in not waiting to do this at the cabin.

Rosco snickered at the sight of us. The other guy with him I knew worked for Hunter. They were muscular, tall men, prone to violence from what I'd seen, and they were looking restless. That spelled trouble. I was sure that Caitlyn and I looked suspicious. She clutched my purse, the one Rosco knew had my journal, and I had my hands behind my back.

The men exchanged glances then swaggered forward like cage boxers entering the ring. They blocked the way out. I could threaten to scream again. That had gotten me pretty far last time, but they hadn't done anything yet, and that would seem pretty ridiculous.

"Why are you hiding out here?" Rosco asked, mopping off his sweaty face.

"We're just figuring out our next song for karaoke," Caitlyn said.

I cringed at the lie, even as both men chuckled mockingly. "Why don't you songbirds sing something for us now?" the other guy asked.

"You're just going to have to wait," I said, "like everybody else."

"No special treatment?" Rosco sidled next to me, giving me a close up of his blond, scraggly chin hairs. Apparently, I was the one he chose while his friend wordlessly decided on Caitlyn. Did they always work this closely together? It wouldn't be too long until Rosco would see the cylinder. I stepped back and found myself pressed up against the kitchen door, trapped. "What do you have behind your back?" he asked.

"Girl stuff," I said. "If you don't mind—we've got to go." I tried to wriggle free, but I didn't have anywhere to go where he wouldn't see what was in my hand. "I need you to move."

By now he watched me suspiciously. "Not until you show me what you've got."

"Not cool."

I looked up to see who had spoken and saw it was Hunter. Heat warmed my cheeks. Normally I would've easily escaped a lout like Rosco before he even got close, but my hands were a little busy. I hoped Hunter wouldn't see with what.

"I can't leave you alone for a second," Hunter said. I wasn't sure if he was talking to me or to his men, but then he said, "Step away from the girls."

Rosco didn't like to be told what to do—I could see it in how his eyes narrowed at the order that he wasn't obeying. "She's hiding something." He made a move for me and wrenched back my arm, his rough fingers digging into my flesh. "You see?"

Looking up, I saw Hunter's eyes widen at the cylinder in my hand as Rosco tried to wrestle it from my grip, but I slipped sidewise, not really sure what I was going to do. I was so caught.

"I said step away." Hunter tugged Rosco back with a rough jerk. His man turned from me, growling, the glint of violence in his eyes showing that he did not appreciate being thwarted from harassing a Payne twin again. With a howl of anger he threw a punch at Hunter, who blocked Rosco's fist from his face.

Pushing up against the wall to get away from the fighting, I felt the door handle against my back. It was locked and I had nowhere to go. Rosco crashed hard into me, and Hunter's hands wrapped around his arm and threw him back from me so that the two had plenty of room to go at it.

Caitlyn screamed at each punch. Rosco was getting the worst of it, though he got in a few good blows himself. Hunter's lip and cheek were bloody. I only got a glimpse of it before Hunter knocked Rosco hard in the face then dragged him upright to shake him. "Get out of here. You're through."

Rosco snarled out in response but stumbled and fell to the

ground. The other man who'd been with him reluctantly stepped forward to get him out after Hunter gestured fiercely at him. Hunter supervised their departure with his eyes, then turned to me.

I straightened, knowing I was next. He held out his hand to me. He didn't have to say anything; I knew what he wanted. Feeling ashamed, I held it out to him.

He jerked it from my hands, and I saw that he was angry. "You're good," he said. "I never suspected it of you." I felt horrible—for a lot of reasons, but the main one was that I looked worse than he did. "And here I thought I played too rough with you last night." He pocketed the device. "I'll remember that in the future."

My mouth opened, but I had nothing to say for myself. He had rescued me—again—and I had stolen from him. A noise behind him made me glance over and catch sight of Bill. Frank was with him in his deputy uniform, and I remembered that he'd also be here in an official capacity. I'd gotten too used to his deputy uniform to recognize it anymore. Harlan stepped out from behind them, also shocked, but mostly amused... and very approving of Hunter. I should've known they'd take his side.

Hunter didn't try to turn me in. He walked away instead. "I can't process this right now. I'm sure we'll have it out later. We always do."

"Wait!" I grabbed his arm, and when he flinched, I stepped back, feeling like I was drowning in my guilt. I wanted to make up for this somehow. "Are you all right?" I asked. "There's blood." I touched my lip to show that his wasn't looking so good. "Let me help you!"

Fully aware of the old men's grins, I dashed to the napkins and came back with them. I held one up and Hunter nodded in permission so that I edged forward to dab at his bloody lip. I winced when I saw his bruising cheek and tried to get the scratches there too; a part of me annoyed that I liked the excuse to touch him, the rest of me not caring. After all, hadn't Brek told me to get closer to him? Hunter had already taken the device. It was very important to finding this treasure. I felt it—and I wished that was truly the reason I was so drawn to him.

153

I ran out of battle wounds to tend. Pulling back reluctantly, I met his eyes. They were trained on me. "I'm sorry that I took your tech," I told him. "I was angry after I almost lost the... journal. And I wasn't thinking. I'm sure it's pretty expensive." I wondered if apologies counted if some of it was a lie. I was sorry, but I knew exactly what I had taken. "If it's any consolation," I said, "I was trying to figure out how to return it." At least before I found out its significance... and maybe I still might have? Honestly, I had no idea what I would've done.

His gaze didn't waver through my stumbling speech, and I thought that he was too angry to respond until he said, "Let's talk about this over food." Now it was my turn to hesitate. It was what Brek wanted, but did I? I had a soft spot for this man. I noticed a dark smile dance over his expressive lips. "You owe me that, at least... unless you don't count this as a rescue either."

"Ah come now, Ivy," Bill called out. "Don't leave us hanging!" The other old men behind him shouted out their encouragement. "Thank Aiden for rescuing you!"

Frank nodded. "He saved me a spot of trouble. Glad you took care of things, Aiden."

Hunter accepted the compliments, his eyes on me. I tried to hide my smile and looked down before the amusement completely overtook me and I agreed to it. "Yeah, I owe you that, I guess." I chanced a peek up at Hunter under my lashes, and his gaze had softened on me. He put his hand behind my back to lead me out of the hallway before I noticed Caitlyn was recording the whole thing. "Caitlyn!" I cried. "What are you doing?"

"This is *really* hot," she said. At my stern look, she shrugged. "It's for the ratings!"

"Are you hungry too?" Hunter asked her.

She seemed torn and finally, with a laugh, explained herself. "I already ate, but I also want to get this on my phone... so sure."

Bill perked up with excitement. "You got that on film?"

154

"The whole fight!" Caitlyn said proudly.

"Put that on your YouTube!" Frank said.

I was sure that Hunter was sorry he'd asked Caitlyn to come after that, but he was duty bound now. The old men followed us out of the hallway like Hunter was the Pied Piper. We came to a table and Bill was the first to clap him on him on the back to congratulate him. "That's the kind of fighting for your lady I like to see!" I blushed, and Bill patted my shoulder as if sensing my discomfort, still pouring the flattery on Hunter. "You're all right, kid!"

Frank mumbled something about "Aiden" not being one of those snowflakes he was used to seeing nowadays. Harlan was translating for Pat who had toddled over to us with the help of his cane. "Now, let's give them some room," Bill said. "You deserve some good alone time with the girl."

That got a giggle out of me. *Tell that to Caitlyn and her camera.* She took the hint when Bill asked her for some help with the internet downstairs. Before leaving with her, he said, "I've been blessed with daughters, but if I had a son, I'd have him be like our Aiden."

That was coming on a little strong. "Oh, come on!" I met eyes with their new favorite, who was grinning broadly. "If it wasn't for Hunter, those guys wouldn't be here!"

Bill came to the defense of his hero. "He's got work to do in these mountains—those were good solid men. But he knows the number one rule: you don't hire anyone you can't lay out with a good, hard punch."

"Yep," Hunter agreed, though he didn't attempt to defend himself further. He didn't need to with these eager supporters on his side.

"So he punched someone," I said. "That doesn't make him a saint."

Guffawing, Hunter pulled out my chair at the table and Bill wisely didn't answer; instead he wished us a "Good evening!" and left with his posse of old men. I glanced over at Hunter and then at the proffered seat. Now that my pride was tweaked, I wondered if I was doing the right thing. This man was no different than the one who had set those

155

same guys after me to steal my journal.

Watching me under lowered lashes, he asked, "What do I have to do to prove that I'm the good guy?"

I took a steadying breath, trying not to blow this. It was like I couldn't decide whether this would work for or against me and so it made me indecisive. With no other options, I just sat.

Hunter took the seat next to me, leaning forward at the table. "I've got a new name for you."

Great! He was renaming me like he did the lakes. "Yeah, what's that?"

"Poison Ivy. What do you think? It's got a ring to it!"

That forced another laugh out of me—an uncomfortable one. He was still angry at me. "Absolutely not." I tried to think of a way to turn this back to my advantage. "I've got a name for you," I said. He looked intrigued, but warily so, as he should. "Fortune Hunter."

He turned silent and watched me like he wasn't sure what to do with me. The feeling was mutual. The attraction between us was unmistakable, but I was pretty sure we were a bad idea. I took a deep breath and thought of the dearest thing to my heart. "What do you think of karaoke?"

"Drunk people singing into a microphone? I don't think so."

"What!" I was indignant. "It's not like that at all!"

He was already shaking his head. "My life is complete the way it is."

"That's because you don't know what you're missing." I pushed my leg underneath me to sit up taller so I could meet his challenging gaze. "It doesn't matter if you can't sing. In fact, it's better if you can't. I mean, it's pretty awkward if you're actually any good..."

"That's why you won't catch me doing it."

"Oh really?" I was determined to figure him out. "Okay, out with it. What's something about you that's super geeky... even if you won't admit it to anyone?"

"I thought looking for treasure was enough."

"No!" I dismissed that with a wave of my hand. "Something that no one suspects about you! Out with it."

He pressed his chin into his hand with a sardonic lift of his brow. "I feel like you'd just use it against me."

"Maybe."

He pressed his lips together like he was weighing the essence of my soul then said, "Geocaching is interesting."

I didn't really know what that was and so I nodded slowly. "I'd google that," I said, "but I don't have a phone." He laughed and I waited for him to tell me. He didn't. "Well?" I asked.

"Nah, I'll let you discover it on your own."

"That is not cool! Tell me now."

"You're a curious thing, aren't you?" He leaned closer to me, touching my bracelet. My attention was caught by the feel of his fingers against my wrist. "Nope, not telling you," he said.

I hated not having a phone or I could search for it. "Okay, then maybe you might tell me what that thing was that I stole?"

"So you're admitting that you stole it?"

He was winning this battle. In fact, I wasn't able to get a straight answer from him, except for his dislike of karaoke. "Just tell me," I said.

Seemingly unaffected by the conversation, Hunter slid through the charms on my bracelet, only to stop on the camera. Studying it a moment, he dropped it and his gaze slid to mine. "What will you give me if I do?"

I could barely concentrate on what he was saying, but I desperately grasped onto the thread of the conversation. I had to get this information out of him. "If that cylinder is important then… maybe I might have something important too."

He looked smug. "That's what I like to hear."

I almost groaned. I wasn't sure what Brek was thinking putting me on this mission in the first place. He knew how awful I was at this stuff. Hunter would run circles around me if I wasn't careful. I slipped my hand from him to gain back my poise, fidgeting with the charms on my bracelet as I did so. Hunter's eyes drew to it before I broke the silence. "What's your game, Hunter? What do you want out of this?"

"Same thing you do."

"I don't believe you, not the way you talk."

He studied me then licked his lips before saying, "It's personal. There are some people I care about who are lost. This treasure swallowed them."

That was the last thing that I expected to hear. I knew exactly what he meant. I'd lost my own father to this treasure, and the rest of my family had been obsessed with it. I wondered who he had lost. "I'm so sorry," I said.

He shrugged, feigning a flippant air that I saw through. "It was a long time ago. I'm just trying to find answers, mostly for those who were close to them. I hardly knew them..." He ran his hand through his scraggly brown hair and abruptly dropped the subject.

I felt frustrated. I wished that he'd tell me more. "That's all you've got for me?"

"With that camera in my face? Yeah."

Raising my eyes, I spied Caitlyn behind us. She shrugged and put her phone down and took a chair on the other side of us. "How about off the record?" she asked.

Hunter had on his wry expression that he reserved especially for Caitlyn. "Sorry, that's all you're getting..." he caught me in his hazel-eyed gaze, "unless you agree to work with me?"

I hardly heard the offer as his story began to connect in my brain. "You're related to those brothers! Those ones Bill and Frank and Harlan were talking about. Back in the 90's... but no, it was '89." It had to be. When he looked startled, then guarded, I knew that I was right. "I lost family to this too." I realized what it meant. "Do you know anything about my dad?" His eyes widened. "I mean," I tried to explain myself, "I think those brothers worked with my dad. I'm not actually sure, but he was looking for the treasure about the same time. Bill said they were with this guy with dark hair."

"I'm sorry, I don't know," he said.

"It would be a really big coincidence," I said, starting to doubt myself, then bit my lip before saying, "This treasure is like a curse. Everyone who goes after it disappears."

Caitlyn's sucked in her breath. "Then why are we doing it?" she asked.

"Because we have to know," Hunter said, finally finding his tongue in all this; it had taken him a moment to gain his usual grasp of the situation, but as soon as he did, he used it to his advantage. "If our relatives worked together, there must've been a reason."

"I'm probably wrong about that," I amended. I shouldn't have said anything. "What would be the odds that they'd both be here at the same time?"

Hunter wasn't letting it slide. "The way I see it, we need each other. My family knows the meaning of those symbols. We have notes on that Spanish priest who hid up the treasure. My records are family heirlooms. My grandfather guarded them with everything he had. And... you have Eden's journal. She talked about her search for the treasure, didn't she?"

I tucked my hair behind my ear, trying to buy myself time to think. He was omitting that the device he had in his possession was integral to this mission, which meant that he still wasn't willing to put everything on the line. Still, I could see the advantage of working together. We truly had different pieces of the puzzle, but would he betray us?—take everything we had without being completely transparent himself? There was only one way to test him. "Spanish symbols?" I asked. "We might've found some today."

"Where?" he asked. I didn't answer, not sure how much I should spoon feed him, though it wouldn't be too hard to figure out, considering how far we'd be able to travel on foot in one day and return. "Was it out by Skunk Lake?" he asked.

I flushed at the reminder, but it was also enough to defeat my reservations against trying to trick him. Brek had stumbled on those trees with the false symbols on them. I had stuck his map into the pages of Eden's journal. I'd let Hunter believe it was the real thing. If anything, it would test how much he knew about those Spanish symbols. "I'll give you a clue if you give me a clue," I said. "Tell me what that device is? What's the writing on the sides?"

"Greek and Hebrew."

"What do they say?" I asked.

"You tell me what you found first."

He was making this really hard. "There are trees with Spanish symbols. We have a map. I have a copy of it... if..." I didn't have to finish my sentence.

"They're GPS coordinates," he answered almost immediately. He took out his device and I tried to pretend that I wasn't too interested in it, but it was near impossible. I studied the copper siding. When I had looked through the glass, there had been Roman numerals. "That's what's engraved on the sides," he said.

My heart fluttered with excitement, and I tried not to give away how important this was. GPS coordinates were better than anything we had. There was no way to get a picture of the writing without my phone. Caitlyn could... if I could give her the signal to do it. "Where do these coordinates lead?" I asked.

"It just takes us to another clue," Hunter said. "The Spanish Priest was a tricky guy. We haven't been able to decode it yet."

But if I could see the clue, Brek might figure it out. "What are the coordinates?"

"You'll give me a map of these trees?" he asked carefully. I nodded. Gladly. It was completely useless. "Fair enough," he said. "The map's on you?"

"Yes."

He took out a piece of paper and took his time writing down the coordinates. I searched through my purse, careful not to show that I had Eden's journal as I slipped Brek's map from its pages. As soon as

160

he was done writing, he set the paper face down on the table. "Okay," he said this with a half laugh, "You push the map to me, the same time I give you the coordinates."

"You're making this a little dramatic," I said.

"You've got to play right," he said and for a moment I thought he wasn't taking any of this seriously, but I didn't have anything to lose and so I played by his rules. Our fingers brushed as we swapped papers. He folded up my map without looking at it, and in my own show of trust, I deposited the coordinates into my purse sight unseen.

"That's it?" I asked.

"Unless you can think of anything else?"

Well, dinner, though now I felt guilty about it. Hunter ordered for us this time, refusing to let either Caitlyn or I get salads and loading us with lots of carbs. Caitlyn denounced all hiking in general, but Hunter wasn't taking any chances. He regaled us with stories of Jeep and ATV accidents.

"And you still refuse to wear a helmet?" I asked.

"I've got a hard skull."

"That's crazy," I said. "You won't get me on one of those."

He gave me a considering look. "And you give me a hard time for not trying new things."

"Fine. You karaoke, and I'll go on an ATV." It was a safe enough promise.

"With me?" he clarified.

I hesitated, not sure what I was getting into. "Yeah," I said, then tried to make sure he'd never take me up on it, "But you'd have to sing the most drippy, cheesiest song in existence to make it worth my while."

"That doesn't seem like a good tradeoff. One is fun; the other's not."

"I completely agree," I said.

Caitlyn almost choked on her noodles when she laughed. I'd almost forgotten that she was there besides the times when she turned on her phone to record without our knowledge, though I knew every time she did it. She wasn't that stealthy. Eventually dinner ended and still there was no sign of Brek. I started to get worried. "I think Angel kidnapped my brother," I said.

The mere mention of Brek was enough to drain Caitlyn's happy spirits. "Are you sure it wasn't the other way around?" she muttered.

Hunter swallowed the last bite of his hamburger, seeming to assess the situation when he looked over at my best friend. "Angel is…" he paused to think, "let's just say that there are girls who are real, and others who don't know how to be. You don't have to worry—she's got nothing on you."

Caitlyn beamed, and I was grateful Hunter was trying to make her feel better, but he should tell that to my brother—not that it would make a difference. Brek would be less likely to listen to him than to me, if that was possible.

Hunter took the check and paid it, waving away our offers of help. It didn't seem right; he'd rescued me tonight and had the bruises to prove it. If I'd felt guilty for the trick I had played on him before, now I writhed in it. He'd be furious after this—at least when I'd stolen from him, I'd been driven to it. This time, I was purposely being duplicitous. "Hunter…?" I began.

His forehead wrinkled when he looked up from the receipt. "This is number seven," he said.

"Excuse me?" I asked.

"Rescue number seven. That's how many times I've saved you."

I jolted upright in my seat. "No, it isn't!"

"Sure it is." He counted off on his hand while Caitlyn giggled the whole time, which only served to encourage him. "One, I pulled you out of the Jeep; two; I kept you from getting trampled in the cabin; three, I gave you my trucker's hat and saved you from getting burnt to a crisp. It looked quite cute on you by the way. You should wear it more often. Four, I paid for your dinner; five, I returned your journal; six, I took a couple of punches from Rosco because you stole my stuff;

and seven, you're getting another dinner out of the deal."

I was dumbfounded. "Dinners count as rescues?"

"Yeah," his eyes invited me to play, "and I'm just wondering when you're going to rescue me?"

"I can pay for dinner!" I argued, trying to figure out how to get the upper hand.

"No." He smirked and I tried to ignore how good it looked on him. "I like you owing me."

I fumed. "Next time I'm paying for dinner!" I said. I might have to use Brek's card, but Hunter didn't have to know that. My pride was on the line.

"Okay, when's our next date? Tomorrow?"

A date? "You know what? You can't use this against me," I said. "I will find a way to rescue you, Mr. Bighead Knight in Shining Armor, and I will get you back for this!" I felt the laughter bubbling up inside, and some of it escaped my lips. He totally deserved to get tricked. I could hardly wait to part ways so I could read those coordinates and find that clue. I'd get some respect when I figured out what it meant before he did. I stood abruptly, but before leaving, I decided to give him back some of his own medicine. "I cleaned up your blood—that was rescuing you! And I allowed you to sit with me while I ate—twice—a definite rescue. You would've had to eat with Angel. I wore your hat all the way back to camp so you wouldn't feel bad. I helped you see Rosco for what he really was! Oh, and one more thing." I leaned over him to whisper in his ear, "I'm going to find out the mystery behind those coordinates." I smiled slowly and pulled away.

His eyes were heavy lidded as he watched me. "You still owe me one more."

"Put it on my tab," I said sassily and walked away.

Caitlyn took this as the cue that we were leaving and trailed after me, but not before undermining me when she told him, "Yeah, she definitely likes you!"

My shoulders stiffened, but I kept walking, not wanting to

encourage either of them. Of course I liked that troublemaker. It didn't mean that I should do anything about it. Caitlyn and I headed for the staircase while she chuckled and wouldn't stop talking about Hunter. It was like she had forgotten that we were the ones who were supposed to charm him, not the other way around!

"So good news," Caitlyn said as soon as we reached the stairs. "People have enjoyed what we've uploaded online so far, especially this commentator called Hybernater!"

"So you mean we have one follower?" I asked.

She dissolved into giggles. "Five!"

"Are the other four Bill, Frank, Harlan, and Pat?" I asked.

She slid her hand over the railing, smiling serenely. "It's a good start, Ivy! He knows all kinds of things like he warns us not to get too obsessed and he talks about the curse. Oh yeah, and how you can only find the treasure at certain times of the year when it's not flooded."

"How do you know Hybernater isn't a she?"

She shrugged. "He's kind of a geek. I don't know! Anyway, we need to figure out a way to get more hits. Maybe a better name for the webisodes or something."

"I know what will do it," I said and pulled out the paper with the coordinates from my purse. "Let's find these tonight!"

She winced a little. "How? I could just punch it into my phone, but I don't have service."

But we happened to know a few adventurers that didn't rely on their phones. We went in search of the old men. They were so supportive of Hunter and whatever they thought he had going on with me that I was sure they'd do what they could. We found them at the table at the café downstairs. They had set up a card game and were teasing each other relentlessly. They glanced up at the two of us and stood like the fine gentlemen they were. It was a little embarrassing. "Sit, sit, at ease, soldiers," I joked.

Bill indicated the chairs next to them and Caitlyn took one, but I remained standing. "Do any of you have a way to find coordinates?"

"Why yes, yes." Bill shuffled from the table to go into his back room. He had ditched his shoes for his house slippers that he had worn a few nights before. It had seemed so long since then, like I'd known these old guys forever. Bill brought out a gadget that looked suspiciously like a phone. I thought it was at first until he turned it on and flipped on the screen. "You got the coordinates?" he asked.

"Yes!" I drew forward. "Can we borrow this?"

"Doesn't anyone buy anything around here?" Bill teased us. "Why do I even bother having a store!"

"Oh, sorry!"

"No, no, he's fine," Harlan cut in. "He just likes to complain. Just nod and give him sympathy. That's all he wants."

Bill argued that while I picked up the gadget and put in the coordinates. It pinned a spot onto a map. "Caitlyn," I said. "It's near here. Not too far actually, by the lake outside!" It made sense. Eden and her treasure hunting friends would've been staying near here when they first came to look for that gold. This clue could be from them.

"Doing a little geocaching, are you?" Frank asked.

That got my attention. Hunter had talked about geocaching as his geek hobby. "What's that?"

"Why, it's just finding treasures that people leave behind for others to pick up." Frank seemed to be warming up to his favorite topic. "It's about all an old man can do anymore."

"Yeah, yeah." It was a good enough explanation as anything. "We're going geocaching."

"Without your boyfriend?" Bill asked with keen eyes.

"Well, this is from him," Caitlyn said, enjoying the joke at my expense.

The old men became more interested, and I glared at her, but they were quicker to help us than before and provided all sorts of flashlights and shovels to make it easier. We set off for the lake amidst their cheery farewells and calls for luck. Twilight had taken hold of the horizon, and I tried to hurry so we could beat the darkness. I had no idea what was in store for us, but perhaps if it was anything like those symbols we'd found at Sinkhole Lake, I could take some pictures of it. The lights of the sunset bathed the lake and trees in a warm orange glow. A mist rose up from Grizzly Lake. If I'd had more time, I'd have spent the evening taking pictures of that instead.

Of course, Caitlyn decided to film the experience. "In case you didn't catch it," she told our Vlog audience, "and I suppose my recording was sketchy at dinner, but I can't be completely socially unacceptable—I mean Ivy and Hunter were really hitting it off!"

"We were not!" I pointed brutally at her. "Do not put that in there!"

She giggled and I knew she had no intention of listening to me. "This is the lowdown." She talked into the camera phone. "Ivy and Hunter have switched clues." She swung the beam of light from her flashlight to me. "Why did you do that? Brek is going to kill you!"

"I wouldn't give him a real clue," I said, mostly for her benefit. The unseen audience made me nervous; we could be talking to Angel for all I knew.

"You didn't!" She erupted in laughter. "Why?"

"I don't trust him. If his clue is any good then… maybe I'll give him something real. Who knows?" I felt kind of lowdown about it. Maybe Brekker would surrender and let us work with the other team if they proved indispensable. I couldn't stand the thought of spending any more time with Angel, even though Hunter was growing on me. I studied the glowing screen for the directions and announced with some trepidation, "The coordinates are leading us into the forest."

Caitlyn turned quiet. It was getting darker by the moment, and it didn't seem very smart to go in by ourselves. The memory of Rosco's leering face came to me, and for the first time, I wondered where he had gone after Hunter cast him out. If Hunter had to rescue me one more time… But worse, what if he didn't? I looked over at my best friend. "You want to get Bill to come with?"

"What's he going to do against the skunks?"

I giggled a little. If that was all Caitlyn was thinking about, I shouldn't worry her. I checked out the map again and saw that it wasn't too far in. "Let's just do this," I said. I'd beat myself up with regrets if I returned to the cabin without at least checking this out for myself.

"We're going in," Caitlyn told her cell phone. I imagined that her footage would be jerky and sickening. I hoped some people liked that.

We plunged into the pitch black of the forest and I cringed, too prideful to back out now, though I held tightly to my shovel. Caitlyn followed me, narrating my every move, and I had no doubt she'd post me running away like a scared little chicken if I called it quits. We pushed our way through, following the footpaths for the most part, but near the end it led us away from that too. The dot showed we were getting closer to the coordinates, though we were farther out than I had originally hoped. I was no longer worried about Rosco, but wild animals. What had I been thinking? But we'd gone too far in now. I heard a snapping twig and stopped in my tracks.

Caitlyn ran into my back. "What are you doing?"

"A twig."

"Oh no, a twig," she mocked, but I noticed that she didn't volunteer to go on ahead.

I listened for anything else, and when there was nothing, I gingerly took another step. A bush shook roughly in the darkness. "And now we've got a bush," I said.

Caitlyn wasn't making any jokes about bushes. Her hand went to my arm, and I knew she'd try to bolt. "Don't make any fast moves," I said. "We'll get lost." I tilted the screen and noticed that we could punch in the name of the Grizzly Bear House to get back, though the clue was only a few feet away. "It's here," I said. The bush had ceased its shaking. "There's nothing there."

"Or it's waiting for us to turn our backs on it."

"Then let's not turn our backs." I took a step forward, and another.

After the bushes and twigs remained silent, Caitlyn followed me too, her voice more subdued with her narration. "It just figures that we'd get this information in the dead of night instead of during a bright summer morning. Makes me wonder if Ivy is afraid that Hunter will figure out the clue before she does."

She was absolutely right. The GPS tracker showed that we were almost there... and the clue would be underneath that bush. The same one that had been shaking. "Put your light on the bush, Caitlyn. I'm not going in there if there's an animal."

Caitlyn did so, her hands shaking. I saw a green metal box hidden in the leaves, which seemed strange because if it had been so portable then Hunter and his men would've just stolen it away, but a few steps closer and I saw that it was cemented into the ground. I didn't know what this was. I searched for writing outside of it or symbols. Anything out of the ordinary. Circling it, I determined there were no wild animals before touching the lid. It was unlocked, and as I opened it, I knew that this couldn't possibly be from Eden's era. There was a note inside. I retrieved it and saw that it was the same map I had given Hunter at the pub. "That dork," I said. There was writing on the bottom and I read it.

"What?" Caitlyn asked. Rolling my eyes, I put it into her hands and she read it out loud. "Dear Poison Ivy, did you really think that you could fool me with an internet joke? I might be some stupid southerner, but we use Google from time to time too. Signed, Fortune Hunter." Caitlyn peered up at me from the letter. "So... he saw through you?"

Obviously. I was angry and intrigued all at once. Stupid Fortune Hunter! And Brek thought I could charm information out of this fool? "Let's just go," I said.

"This is definitely going on YouTube." Caitlyn was enjoying this at my expense.

"Don't even think about it."

Another twig snapped further into the woods and I froze. I had been so caught up with his trick that I had forgotten we were still in the middle of the forest with wild animals and possibly Rosco. Punching the name of our cabins into the GPS, I saw that there was a faster route through the forest, and I took Caitlyn's hand. "Let's get out of here."

She didn't fight it, but we didn't get far before there were loud footsteps behind us. "It's probably Hunter," I told Caitlyn. *Or deer. Or mountain lions. Or Rosco.* She nodded, too terrified to speak. "I don't want him to catch us out here and rub it in," I said as way of explanation, and we rushed over the pathway. Luckily the resort's forest was better cultivated than the ones in the mountains, but we still ran into our share of brush. The steady walking behind us switched into running. Caitlyn and I both picked up our speed in response. What if it wasn't Hunter? I didn't want to wait around to find out. I saw our cabins in the distance, and the familiar ATVs in front of Hunter's place, and with a sinking heart, I saw Hunter. He wasn't behind us.

Caitlyn saw him too. "Hunter!" she screamed. A part of me almost would rather die than call for his help, but I saw the wisdom in it when I turned to look at the shadow looming behind us. It had stopped next to a tree to peer at us. It was definitely a man with broad shoulders, and tall. Taller than me, anyway. "Rosco?" I asked.

The man's head tilted, in such a strange way that thoughts of Bill's Bone Man came to mind—the shadow of this man in front of us felt too narrow in my mind to be human, but then again I could just be freaking out. I prayed that whoever it was, they'd stay back. I tried to edge away, and it suddenly came bolting after us. I took Caitlyn's hand again, and the whole time she screamed for Hunter to come save us as we whipped around. We slammed into Hunter's hard chest the next moment and his arms went around us. Caitlyn grabbed him from one side and I did on the other. It was everything he wanted and didn't, since, technically, it was another rescue, but this was something real behind us. "Why did you have us go out there!" Caitlyn cried. "Someone's out there! Did you send someone to chase us?"

I had a feeling that he hadn't, especially when he looked up into the forest and the shadow fled at the sight of him. Listening to the steady pounding of his heart, I felt it quicken at the sight of it and he made to move after it, but Caitlyn held him back. "Do not leave us!" she cried.

He sighed and put his arms around our shoulders. "Why didn't you wait until morning to go out?"

Remembering his cruel trick, I threw the paper against his chest and pulled it back, replacing it with me. I buried my face against him. "Better yet, you could've *not* done it in the first place."

"And miss out on the opportunity to save you again?" His lip curled, but his heart wasn't in the joke, I could tell. Now I heard the faint sound of barking dogs in the distance, like that shadow had run through someone's campsite and startled them too. Hunter kept stealing glances in the darkness, and I did too. The fight had drained from me, and I fell silent. "C'mon," he said. "Let's get you back inside. Your brother got home about fifteen minutes ago and stopped short of accusing me of murder. I'm sure he'll be happy to see you're alive."

Chapter eleven

I woke up to my alarm again—four o'clock. It was still dark outside. Caitlyn groaned and turned over in her bed and I envied her for the millionth time in the last twenty-four hours. Last night I had forced myself to bed while she stayed up late and edited into the wee hours. She had taken to making documentaries like a duck to water. She'd always been into entertainment and social media, so going into film was a natural transition. At least she'd found her niche in life on this trip. I was still struggling.

Pushing my covers far from me so I wouldn't be tempted to pick them up again, I stumbled out of bed and headed for the bathroom. I passed a silent Brek in the living room. He sat on the couch chewing on an apple. My brother had refused all our prying about his night with Angel when we'd come in with Hunter after our adventure in the forest. Even after Hunter had left, he hadn't wanted to hear about how many times the guy had saved me or what happened with Rosco, and he'd scoffed at the shadow in the forest.

"Did the shadow come back to haunt you last night?" he asked from the couch.

I was annoyed. He had no sense of fear, but it made him stupid sometimes, especially where I was concerned. He might be big and strong, but I had limitations. "You know what your problem is?" I said. "You can't accept that I can get hurt."

He bit into his apple, and I felt his mounting irritation emanate from him. If it was possible, he was in a worse mood than he'd been in yesterday. Hunter had let him have it last night; he had said all sorts of things to Brek that hurt his chances of ever working with us. I was torn

171

between proving myself and really wishing that Brek would listen and not drag me into so much danger--and if he did then he should train me better. But to say so would make him question my dedication, and the more we searched for the treasure, the more I wanted to figure out the mystery behind it all.

I grabbed a toothbrush in the bathroom. "Tell me what happened with Angel?" I asked, poking my head into the hallway.

He swallowed the last bit of his apple and threw it one-handed in the trash bin. "She's the same as ever."

I wanted to scream. Why wouldn't he confide in me? "At least tell me if you got any information out of her."

He smiled secretly. "Not quite."

"So she got everything she wanted and you didn't?" I surmised.

"I wouldn't say that."

I glared at him. A few kisses from Angel and he was putty in her hands. He read my expression and scoffed. "Like you're any better. You were supposed to wrap Hunter around your finger, and now he wants me to wrap you in bubble wrap. That wasn't what I meant for you to do."

"So you want me to be more like Angel?" I asked.

"Never," he said with more conviction. So that's how it was? What was good for him wasn't good for me. "I can't believe you let him get the artifact back from you," he said. "Why were you carrying it around with you anyway?"

"Oh, did you want Angel to steal it from you instead?"

He put on that secret smile of his again and I rolled my eyes and slammed the door between us. If he thought he could justify spending time with her under the guise he was helping the cause, he was fooling himself. I didn't have the energy to lecture him about her. This morning we were going to our third lake, and I was worried. It was an overnighter, which meant hauling more in my pack, and, well... the obvious. I wasn't much of a hiker and I definitely was not a camper. To make it worse, our destination was Lake Adam. That was where Bill

172

had spied Bone Man, and though I didn't particularly believe in ghosts or anything like that, I'd seen something last night that made me more terrified about what was out there. I didn't want to walk in the forest when it was dark, let alone sleep in it. I threw my hair in a ponytail, applied sunscreen, and spied Hunter's green trucker hat on the counter. It would keep the sun out of my eyes. Not caring what Brek thought anymore, I put it on and looked in the mirror. It was pretty cute. Maybe I'd rescue Hunter by wearing it again. The thought made me dimple and inspired me to take a couple of selfies.

"Ivy?" Brek called impatiently. "You almost done?"

I swung the door open. "Rude!"

His eyes widened on my hat. "You're going to wear that?"

He didn't listen to me about Angel, then he had nothing to say about Hunter. "Yep!" I brushed past him and went to get my backpack in my room. I was prepared to find it in the dark, but Caitlyn switched on the lamp when I entered.

She stretched luxuriously in her bed. "Get me some good footage out there."

"I am!"

"And I'm not talking about narrating what you're doing… exciting stuff, like anytime anything goes wrong or if you interact with interesting people."

So roll the camera when Hunter came into the picture? That felt a little too personal. "Oh c'mon," I argued, "this isn't the Kardashians in the mountains!"

She rolled over to her side to look at me. "Why not? People like that kind of stuff."

"My life isn't that exciting anyway," I said into my backpack while I rummaged through it.

"That's what editing is for," she said.

I raised a brow at her. "Well, aren't you the natural."

"Yeah, and the stuff you brought me back yesterday was pretty boring."

I'd give her that. Swinging my backpack on, I grimaced at the weight of it. "Fine, I'll get you so much footage, you'll be sorry. Happy?"

"Yes."

I slid the camera strap over my head so that it was in easy reach and smiled sardonically at her. She waved me away and rolled over in her bed. She'd have a nice couple of days without us in her hair—not that she'd want to be away from Brekker, but he'd been horrible lately, so maybe she was through with him.

Walking back into the living room, I saw that Brek was already outside. The front door gaped wide open, leaving a chill in the air. I headed out. Hunter was talking to my brother. He stood on the ground outside the balcony in a white Henley shirt and faded jeans, his arms resting on the railing. It made me realize how muscular they were. His eyes rose to me, and I blushed. I hadn't realized I'd get caught wearing his hat so fast.

"Lake Adam?" he asked. Brekker was telling him where we were going now? He'd probably already spilled the beans to Angel, which would explain why he was so free with his information. "We've been all over that place," Hunter said. "We didn't find a thing."

Well, they weren't Brek, but I didn't voice that. Let them think there was nothing there. "Watch out for the ghosts," Hunter said with a smirk. He'd been there for Bill's wild tales.

"You afraid of Bone Man?" I asked, giving him a challenging look.

He shook his head. "That's where the ghost of Eden resides. I heard she doesn't like the Payne family."

Brek made a sound of disgust and retreated back inside. I couldn't believe he'd left me alone with him… but then again, maybe I could. Hunter's hazel eyes turned appreciative when they lingered on his hat that I wore. "You're feeling sorry for me again?"

"Yeah, I don't want you to feel bad that I never wear it. By the way, the rescue last night doesn't count since you sent us out there."

His expression turned serious and I was sorry that I'd brought it up. I knew he felt bad about that. He'd said it often enough on our way back to the cabin. "You got Bill's GPS tracker?" he asked. I nodded. He put his hand out. "Let me see it." I didn't know why I obeyed, but it was early and so I dropped my backpack and found it in the front pocket and handed it to him. He started punching in numbers.

"What are you doing?" I asked.

He handed it back. "Just in case you need rescuing."

Looking down on the screen, I saw that he had written down his coordinates. Was he serious? I cracked a smile. "I can't figure out if you think highly of yourself or just low of me."

"Being accident prone is no laughing matter," he said. Then why was he laughing? "We'll be at Reflection Lake—not too far away from Lake Adam; screaming distance, really."

"You're awful!" I said. "I can take care of myself." But I kept his coordinates anyway. I hoped he didn't notice, but I'd use them in a pinch. His men were outside his cabin, packing up their things for the morning. My attention veered to their ATVs. "Is Rosco still around?"

He shook his head. "He left last night... without his things, which was strange."

Great! My mind went back to that shadow demon from last night. That thing had either been Rosco after us or it had gotten him. "That's comforting," I said.

Hunter looked surprised, but before he could say something, Brek came back outside with one of those frame backpacks on. It was a lot bigger and a lot heavier than mine. "Are we done flirting out here?"

I stiffened and glowered at him, but he was still in a bad mood so he'd be saying more of that kind of thing for the rest of the morning if I fought back. I decided to make him sorry. "No, can you give us a few more minutes? I need to work my charm."

Hunter smiled slowly and Brek pushed past me on the stairs. "We don't have that long."

I stabbed a glare into his back then turned to Hunter. At least he looked amused. "Sorry," I mouthed to him and trailed after my brother, but not before Hunter buttered me up with a look that was as sweet as warm molasses. I wasn't sure what I should do about that. Probably nothing. He was like Brek—angry one minute, affectionate the next, on and off again. And they thought girls were hard to understand?

The trail to Lake Adam was difficult, and I didn't know how Brek was managing it carrying five times more than me and still forging ahead. I listened to the engines of the ATVs with jealousy as they grew louder on the trails alongside ours then faded away as they left us far behind. We trudged up the mountains without a break until the trail opened up into a meadow. Spring had touched the green grass with its beauty. Here and there tiny wildflowers popped through the skin of the mountain with their flashes of color. Brek left the main trail and cut through nature's garden. I followed closely, not sure how he knew the direction since there was no pathway that I could see. He had a natural sense for these things—one I didn't understand—and as we cleared one peak after another, we finally reached Lake Adam by mid-afternoon.

This place was eerier than the other lakes where we'd been. It was surrounded on both sides by tall granite mountains. One end was devoured by forest, the other desolate and flowing over with rock slides. Somewhere on the top of these rock canyons would be an old Spanish mine. Everybody knew it existed. It was caved in and covered in water, though we could travel farther into it this early in the season.

I was exhausted and set down my pack on a rock. Brek began the process of unbuckling himself from his backpack while I stretched out my shoulders. We had the place to ourselves. I couldn't hear any of Angel's men with their motorized vehicles, only the sound of birds in the trees and an occasional pika squeaking angrily at us from the rock slides. Their tiny furry bodies dove through the rocks for cover like we'd come to eat them for dinner. I wasn't hungry enough for that yet.

From the distance, I heard a loud cry, almost like the sound of a dying dog. I grabbed Brek's arm without realizing I did it. "What's that?" I searched the surrounding mountain of white granite, not seeing

176

where it came from until I spotted something furry and brown and gray with a long tail. It was on four legs and big. "There are cougars here!"

"No, no, that's a fox."

It bayed at us some more, making such an odd cry. It was terrifying. "So that's what the fox says!"

Brek's mouth split into a grin. The fox abruptly stopped its wailing when it locked eyes with us and then, as if it had proved its courage to us by its shouting, it turned with a whip of its tail and strutted away. Brek assured me all was well, but it made me worry about what else was out there. Nothing but caverns and mines. We approached the most famous of these caverns and saw that it was caved in, its secrets buried inside. "Has anyone tried to get in there?" I asked.

"Plenty of times." Brek looked cocky. "But they're not me."

They certainly weren't. I got out my food while Brek got out his climbing gear and explored the place until he found the abandoned mine. After that, he made me hold the line while he dove in the water and explored. I was bored out of my mind. I almost wished for a return of the fox, or Eden's ghost. I'd even take Bone Man. Remembering that I needed to be filming and almost positive that Caitlyn would lecture me for being so unexciting, I flipped the camera on record and made a running documentary of everything around me.

After I'd spent too long talking about the fox, Brek emerged from the water carrying his usual finds—beer bottles, a cell phone, but then something interesting... a man's wedding ring. Brek tried it on and his lip curled in disgust at how it looked on his finger and he tossed it to me. I put it on my thumb, and it still slipped around it was so big. Still, my foolish heart melted at it. This belonged to a man madly in love, I decided on the spot. And I unhooked my charm bracelet and added the ring to the other random charms on it.

Brek snorted out a laugh and pulled out from the water to lie on the sandy beach, staring up at the sky. "Did you hear anything about this place from Hunter?"

"Only that he said there was nothing here."

He turned quiet and I was sure he was thinking the same thing I was. That could mean there was something here that he didn't want us to find. "How about we set up camp," Brekker said, "and then I'll poke around. I have a feeling whatever is here will only show up at night."

That spooked me. "You mean Eden's ghost or Bone Man?"

"Well, you know what they say?" Brek turned on his stomach, looking up at me, the water from his hair dripping down his face. "Where there's smoke and mirrors, there's a fire." He'd mixed up the analogy, but I was sure that he'd done it on purpose, especially when he said, "As soon as I heard Bill tell his story, I knew we had to go. There's something out here."

"You took us here to find a ghost? I wished you'd warned me! What does Bone Man have to do with the treasure?"

"Maybe nothing. Maybe everything. I'm sure there's a scientific explanation. Maybe a natural phenomenon up here, which could be worse than any phantom." He raised a shoulder in a shrug. "A lot of people keep disappearing when they look for this treasure. You don't mess with nature. It can crush you."

So then what were we doing? I stared at the tall rocky peaks around us. It made this a solitary tomb with its walls jagged with boulders. Had Eden died here? If her ghost was rumored to haunt this lake, could that mean Lucius started that rumor? Or Adam? She was a tragic figure. She might've found what she was looking for, but in the end what she'd really wanted was love that she never got. Her last words to Lucius had been our curse, but they were wisely prophetic. Our hearts were never set on the things that would make us happy.

Brek peeled off his wet suit and grumbled something about an abandoned campsite that he'd found on a map on the internet. Sighing, I followed him into the forest to the east of us, and there we found a clearing that held rotting picnic tables overgrown with weeds. To the side was a locked outhouse with a big hole punched through the back of it. It looked like the set of a seventies slasher. That's where we set up our tents—mine was bright orange and Brek's was a neon green. There was a place for a campfire where we could cook whatever fish Brek caught for us, and we began setting up a perimeter against wildlife with strings and bells that would wake us up to danger. I had no idea what Brek had to use against wild animals, but I was sure that it was stronger than my bear spray. I set up my pack in my tent, spread out my sleeping bag, then tested it out on the hard forest floor with a wince. This would not be a good night's rest.

Brek took out his fishing poles and headed for the lake. "Watch out for Eden!" I called after him through the tent flap.

"If people see ghosts, it's in the forest when they get left behind," he said cheerily, and I growled out an insult that he didn't hear. Grunting in dissatisfaction, I rolled over on my sleeping bag and tugged my pack closer to pull out Eden's journal and flipped it past her fawning over a grumbling Lucius, past her bonding moments with Adam that she was too oblivious to appreciate, and to the time she finally looked outside of herself and started to see the world that she now lived in. It was very different than the filth of the city tangled up in the gold rush.

Eden's Journal: July 3rd, 1855 — Mountains of the Deseret

I never reckoned when I lit out of that city I'd see the like of its splendor again, but this territory is plenty pretty. I can't put the words to it proper, except the beauty of it tugs on my poor, undeserving soul. Life seems more livable in these parts—not crushing, not hopeless, not dark like it was in that bright city. My eyes warn't able to see the world around me before; I only slumbered like an old dog. But what was there anyway in that boom town that warn't clouded by dust and a steady flow of men in that hot and miserable saloon? I feel a change a coming. It feels like life has something for me now. If I only dare take it with both hands and not let go, I'll be the fine lady my mother always dreamed I'd be. If that is putting on airs, then who can blame me? Why can't a body dream... and love—even if he don't love me back. Lucius might see I'm worth something. This mountain is alive with

179

endless possibilities. And they're big, bigger than me.

But sometimes I git a sense there's another way to go; one that ain't as pretty. The forests breathe it out to me in them mournful cries that carry along the wind. They make a mighty sinister ruckus through the branches, mostly when I'm the only one around to hears it. And I hate when I git all alone like that—it's the worse feeling to endure. There's something out there, and when the trees shift above my head like they's all cramped up, they whisper my name and go on a stretch about what will come of me, like my end will be sorry and lonesome. And I don't want to be alone with it where it can swallow me. I want to live out my days.

Sometimes I think I git a peek at that bugaboo like it's standing in my own shadow, like it stayed on too long after I walk a piece from it. My blood gits hot and cold at once and I feel too weak to run—I told Lucius, but he shakes his head and calls me a ninny. But that shadow ain't a part of me. It ain't! It's too tall, too thin, and walks too unnatural. Maybe, I reckon, it is the soul of an old Spanish miner or one of them slaves long since dead. The Shoshones told me there was awful happenings back then, cruel, unnatural deaths of their people. I'm of a mind that it could be the land groaning out its complaint against so great a wrong. The ground's been traumatized by mighty wicked doings.

Lucius laid into me for fretting such nonsense. It ain't fitting, and if I can't quit it, then I'm to only bring my worrying to him so no one else thinks me leather headed. I obliged as best I could—there's nothing out there but Lucius, he says. And he don't believe in such things. Why do I fear being sorry and lonesome? I've got him here beside me. He yells at me a turn and strokes my hair and shushes me, and tells me there ain't nothing wrong.

But everything was wrong. I let out a breath that I hadn't known I was holding. I'd always thought Eden had let her imagination get the best of her. Perhaps in a way it had. These fears of dying alone and being alone were real, especially with a man like Lucius—how could she not sense it coming? It was the worst possible thing in her mind and it ended up being true. So tragic. On the other hand, she had taken a chance coming here. Eden had truly had two pathways. She'd pushed herself; she'd dared hope. She'd been a pioneer, leaving her old life behind and setting out for adventure—she'd lived life, not just posted about it! It could've ended a raging success, but it hadn't.

Yet who of us knew the end from the beginning?

Now, as I walked through these same mountains, her pathways became mine, and I could understand how she thought and why she'd made the changes she had. And what about me? I hadn't pushed myself enough before this; I didn't dare hope or make a change because I feared it might be worse. Eden's love might not have been requited, but she'd loved. I had only played with it, but on the whole kept my distance from it. Now I was experiencing life, and despite Caitlyn's insistence that I document this trip, I wasn't here for anyone else. These sights in front of me were for my eyes; these sounds were for my ears.

I felt grounded, for the first time in a long time, like I was really here and not floating in a virtual world somewhere. And yes, I could feel Eden's fears too. What if there was something to it? These shadows she talked about sounded like Bill's stories of Bone Man. He'd said it had run down these boulder slides like an unnatural demon. I shivered at the thought, sitting slowly up to stare through the flap of the tent at those same rock walls that surrounded us. Brek said that where there was smoke and mirrors, there was fire. These hauntings could just as easily be something someone had set up to scare people as it could be a natural occurrence in these mountains or it could be the unthinkable—something more sinister. Whatever it was, I didn't like it.

Stretching out my legs, I felt something ram hard up against my side and I screamed as I saw a tiny furry body scurry across me to get to my pack. A squirrel! Evil, Crazy Squirrel to be exact! I screamed again and it scrambled away like I was the biggest party pooper in the world. I held my heart, seeing Brek run back into the campsite with his fish. "What happened?"

I wasn't sure if I wanted to admit it, but he spied the chattering culprit for himself and got in a good laugh. "That's not funny!" I cried, although it kind of was. "Your animal perimeter didn't stop that little beast!"

"If that little guy is the worst of our problems, I'll count us lucky," he said. That ruined the mood. I didn't want to be reminded that I might have to fight for my life. Brek noticed my sour expression. "What? You've got your bear spray."

I pushed out of my tent, trying to force myself to be brave. It was crazy how much living off the land was a part of Brek's life and not mine. I inspected the fish that he had caught from Lake Adam. He had caught three big and juicy trout. I'd never cleaned a fish before—I'd refused to do it on our grandfather's misadventures—but I was sure Brek could do it in his sleep. For once, I was getting a glimpse into what he did and, in a way, I was impressed. This was what he lived for, and I was his city girl sister. How twins could be so different was beyond me. "Show me how to clean it," I said.

He looked astonished. "Really?"

I nodded. He went to work, cleaning out the guts on a rock, and I joined him on the other side, trying to do what he did. It was a messy process, and if I hadn't built up an appetite from the day, I probably wouldn't have been able to eat it. He showed me how to do the campfire next, and we spent a companionable evening frying up fish and devouring them. They were surprisingly good. In fact, I found myself in much better humor with my brother than earlier that day. We were no longer searching for a treasure that had ruined our family, but just bonding like siblings should. We laughed and told stories about Uncle Jack and our crazy grandpa and how they'd fight over where to store the dynamite from their mining adventures and how Uncle Jack accidentally blew up the shed with it.

It reminded me of my discussion yesterday about our dad. "Hunter's relatives were those two guys who disappeared out here back in the 90's," I told Brek. "What if our dad worked with them?"

Brek threw the remains of his fish into the fire. "Does it make a difference?"

"Maybe." I set my plate aside, resting my shoulders against a tree stump. "He wouldn't tell me much, but what if he knows something about what happened to him?"

We both turned silent as the sun settled lower in the sky until it finally disappeared behind the somber rock canyon that surrounded us. I retrieved my hat and gloves from my pack in my tent and joined Brek back by the fire, watching from a distance as the still water from Lake Adam turned black in the darkness then disappeared from sight altogether as night descended. For now the granite mountains blocked out the wind, so that it felt virtually silent at our campground.

Seeing my somber looks, Brek attempted to cheer me up by joking about the family curse and how none of us could quit while we were ahead. When that finally got a laugh out of me, he fed another log into the fire and warmed his hands over it with a sigh. "It's not all about the treasure for me, Ivy." His expression, for once, was open and vulnerable. "You remember that dog that got lost?"

I threw my mitten-clad hands under my armpits to warm them, thinking about that day. Lily, the little neighbor girl had come crying and pleading for help to find her dog. "You were only eight years old," I said, "but you took one look at that little girl's face and you wouldn't give up looking for it. You were always a softie."

He smiled so that the creases next to his eyes broke over his cheek. "I might have had a crush on her a little bit."

We shared a laugh. I poked a stick into the fire, enjoying how the flames licked against it, turning it black. "That's when I knew you were going to go into the family business," I said.

He seemed surprised at the revelation. "Then you knew before I did. Mom always made me promise not to do it."

"She knew you had to in the end. It's who you are, and you know what? You're good at it. I'm proud of you."

The light from the fire danced over his face, and his eyes glittered in the darkness when he turned to me. For once he looked truly pleased. "Sometimes I wonder what it would've been like... well, I wish you would've joined me before now."

I had never liked roughing it, but being out here felt different than before. "I'm not sure how cut out I am for this kind of thing, but..." I smiled at him, "I'm having a good time."

He made a pleased sound. "It feels right having you with me, Ivy, like a part of me was missing the whole time and now you're here."

I smiled. This was the first real conversation we'd had since before college that didn't involve crushes, just real feelings and vulnerability. He was certainly open enough to talk about Angel right now, but I decided I didn't want to ruin this moment. It wasn't too long before we stretched and called it quits. He killed the fire and stored our food in bear containers further away from camp. I got ready for bed, bringing a flashlight with me into my tent where it lit up the insides in a cozy orange glow.

"Ivy?" My brother's footsteps approached from outside.

I poked my head out and looked up into the beam of his flashlight. "Yeah?"

"Don't worry about lions or tigers or bears, all right? I've got it."

I broke into a smile and covered my eyes from the bright light. "You'd better be right."

He made some wry comment about me being high maintenance and retreated to his tent, his flashlight making the nylon material turn into a green ball of light.

I retreated back inside, pulled off my hiking boots, and inspected my sleeping bag for bugs before getting into it fully clothed. I pulled the warm material up to my neck and reached for my water, drinking it and making a face when I realized that it tasted like campfire. I turned off my flashlight. A light tapping on the nylon above my head made me realize it was raining outside, and as it poured harder, I prayed it wouldn't get inside. They must have made tents more rain resistant since my childhood days, because I stayed dry. Adjusting my position about a dozen times, I finally dozed off.

Chapter twelve

I woke to bells crashing on our makeshift perimeter outside. The rope sounded like it ripped from the tree, the bells clattering to a stop on the ground. Whatever had come through was big! It was still dark outside. Taking deep breaths, I grappled for my flashlight and pushed outside the same time Brek was pulling on his shoes outside his tent. I didn't bother with my hiking boots, but scrambled to stand on the muddy forest floor. Rain poured over me. "Wait, wait," Brek put his hand out to me. "I've got it!"

Well, I wasn't about to chase after it, I only wanted to see what it was, but when I saw he had every intention of going after whatever had come crashing through our camp, I panicked. "No!" I tried to grab at Brek's arm. "No, please! Just stay here."

"It's okay." He showed me his bear spray and then, when I freaked out, he tried to reassure me. "It's not a bear. Look at those prints. Those are human."

They didn't look quite right in the mud. It wasn't a bare foot, but those didn't look like shoes either. "I don't know…"

"Just get back in your tent and wait for me. It's fine. You're getting all wet."

"Yeah, so are you…" I let him lead me back into the warmth of my tent, and then he took off. The moment he did, I was sorry that I'd let him go. Five minutes passed, then ten—that turned into an hour. I zipped up my tent, imagining the worst. What human would go through our campsite like that? Hunter might be into cruel jokes, but he didn't like scaring me. Angel might send one of her thugs, but she was trying to woo us onto her side right now. My mind went to Rosco and my stomach clenched. Hunter had never found him. What if he'd come back here for some kind of revenge?

No, he wouldn't go to all that effort. It couldn't be him, but the more I tried not to think about it, the more I wondered about that shadow that had followed Caitlyn and me into the forest near the Grizzly. If that had been Rosco, then he was out for revenge. What if crashing through the camp was meant to lead Brek away and then, when he was sure my brother was far enough away, he'd come back for me? Ridiculous. No, no, I couldn't think that way. It was stupid.

I took a deep breath and waited longer, playing with the charms on my bracelet as I listened for his return. A noise sounded outside the tent. The bells that had tipped from the line to the ground rolled. "Brek? Is that you?"

When he didn't answer, I pushed my head into my knees. My whole body had tensed until it ached with exhaustion. Huddling inside a tent wouldn't keep me safe from anything. With my hands shaking, I went through my pack and found the GPS tracker. It still had Hunter's coordinates to Reflection Lake. I turned it on just to see how far away he was, and I let out a breath of relief. He was less than a mile and a half from here. That wasn't far at all. I walked three times that distance at the shopping mall downtown. I could be gone and back within the hour. But did I dare? What if I ran into trouble? Did I have a choice? Brekker could be hurt. Hunter could help us. That decided me.

I unzipped my tent and peered out. "Brekker!" I called. Fear made my voice hoarse. "Brekker? Answer me!"

There was only darkness outside, and it hit me like a powerful force. Anything could be hiding out in the shadows. The threat felt almost palpable.

Clasping onto the laces of my boots, I began the laborious process of getting them on, hoping that by the time I did Brekker would be back and teasing me for my worry. I loaded my backpack next, making sure I took my bear spray and flashlight. My whole body shook. I took my camera too, because I didn't want anyone stealing that while I was away. I had my priorities. Still, there was no Brekker.

My rain poncho went on next and I cautiously pulled out of my tent. "Brekker?" With my newfound suspicions, I said his name quieter this time. He couldn't have gone far. Still, he had to know that I'd be a nervous wreck. Why would he be out there for so long if he wasn't hurt? I listened to the sounds of the night and, besides the rain, it felt unnaturally quiet. I worried that if I left to find Hunter that Brek might come back and find me missing then go looking for me again. I ducked into his tent and found the pad of paper that he used to record his finds out here.

Brek—I left to get Hunter. I have his coordinates. Don't be mad—you took too long to come back and I'm worried! Hunter will know what to do.

I left the note on his pillow next to the tent flap so he'd be sure to see it. And then I ducked back out of his tent, zipping it up. I hesitated outside, staring into the dark night, not sure if this was the best move. The rain dripped down the sides of my poncho while I tried to decide. Brek might need me. I couldn't chicken out now.

I did my best to stay on the path while still following the coordinates, but nothing followed a straight line here. I knew there'd be water, forests, cliffs, and boulders standing between Hunter and me. The ground was muddy, and I kept slipping so that I had to force myself to slow down and pick my way through it all. I was cold and miserable, even with my stocking cap and gloves. I hoped that meant that all the nocturnal creatures had checked in for the night too, but I heard every sound they made and more. The night did strange things to my mind. My fear was driving me batty. Every shadow, every sound was magnified in my mind. Wandering the forests outside the Grizzly was nothing to this; this was terrifying, and I didn't have Caitlyn to keep me company. Feeling the camera under my poncho, I tried for the next best thing to a friend. I pulled it out and started to film, using my flashlight to show the way.

"Okay, Caitlyn," I whispered hoarsely. "This is for you." My voice trembled and I tried to steady it. I had my vanity, after all. "I am wandering in the middle of the woods looking for Hunter because Brek disappeared. He went running after something that went crashing into our campsite in the middle of the night... and now it's two in the morning and he still hasn't come back. I'm going to find Hunter to get some help. Where's my pride?" I asked. "Good question. I don't have any—you know that. Besides, this isn't for me."

A sound in the darkness ahead made me stumble to a stop, and I listened closely. I heard a howl in the distance followed by barks. Hunter's camp didn't have dogs that I knew of. Coyotes? I didn't know if I should call for Brek or not. I could alert whatever was out there to my presence, and if it was something wild, it didn't seem like a good idea.

I strained to hear anything else and trained my flashlight ahead. The beam of light only went so far. I wanted to cry in frustration and terror. I couldn't stop thinking of Bone Man and the shadow in the forest that had chased me. It always seemed to rile the dogs. Was that what had caused the barking? Then there was Rosco and ghosts. All my fears crowded my mind so that I could barely think straight. Glancing at the GPS tracker, I saw I was more than halfway to where Hunter camped, and I took a steadying breath. I could do this! Stepping forward, I fell in a hole and screamed with all the horror that had built into me while my feet landed firmly against the ground, not too many inches down. My shins knocked painfully against a rock.

And that was one powerful scream. I groaned, pretty sure that I had alerted the whole mountain to my presence. Hopefully I'd terrified all the wild animals off, and not alerted them to a meal on legs nearby. I tried to gather my thoughts and remembered my camera was still on and attempted a joke for my YouTube audience, "So now you've heard my horror movie scream. I'm still alive... in case you're wondering. It's just a little nerve-wracking wandering the forest in the dark. I don't recommend it to anyone."

Even the deer were terrifying. A doe and her fawn came careening down the pathway, and I scrambled back from them, letting my camera swing at my neck while I grappled for my bear spray, which I should have had ready the entire time. I only knew that they weren't mountain lions because I blinded them with my flashlight and they sprang away. Still, they were intimidating with their powerful movements. They splashed through the mud, more agile than I was.

Mud caked my boots and I slid after them along the trail. I didn't bother with the camera now, but I left it on and occasionally narrated my adventures into it. It was pretty stupid, but at this point I figured that someone could play it back like a pilot's black box to figure out what happened to me. The closer I came to Hunter's camp, the more worried I became that he wouldn't be there. Also, how would I find him? There would be multiple tents and I didn't want to run into any of his men... or Angel for that matter.

Another crack of moving leaves and breaking twigs sounded in the forest. It could be anything. By now I was used to the fear that filled me at the potential predator, and I stilled and searched through the darkness to find what was out there. A beam of a flashlight blinded me, and I held up my hand with the bear spray to shield my eyes. I didn't know if I had run into trouble or not, but I would know as soon as I heard the voice of the person in front of me. "Who is that?" I asked.

"Ivy? Is that you?"

With relief, I lowered the bear spray. Hunter had found me—he was made for his name. "Hunter!" I stumbled over to him while he came to meet me. The first thing I wanted to do was hug him for comfort, but I was wet and covered in mud—besides that, I turned shy at the rush of affection that filled me at the sight of the man. He reached for me instead, his hands sliding down my arms as he took me in. "Ivy? What happened?" The first thing I noticed was his gun. I tried to remind myself that it could potentially keep us safe. He hadn't tried to kill me before, so I figured I could trust him... actually, I had no choice but to trust him.

"My brother's gone!" At his startled exclamation, I hastened to assure him that I didn't mean he was dead, and explained what had happened and why I had come, my flashlight moving with my hands.

His face grew grimmer while I talked. "Okay, let's take you back to your camp and wait for your brother there. If he comes back while you're gone, he'll think the worst."

I didn't appreciate his lecturing tone. "Yeah, I know the feeling."

He grumbled out a laugh. "Well, I didn't say he doesn't deserve it." He put his gun in a holster at his side and covered that with his coat before picking up a walkie talkie to get a hold of Angel. "It was Ivy," he confirmed to her. Angel was awake too? I had *really* woken up the whole mountain with my scream. "Yeah. I'm going to take her back to her camp and wait with her until her brother shows." At Angel's tense questions, he informed her that Brekker was missing. She actually sounded worried, which surprised me, though I supposed they had a strange sort of love going on that I knew nothing about. After Hunter ended his conversation with Angel, I promised myself that Brekker and I would get walkie talkies after this was all over. It could've saved me a lot of trouble.

I noticed Hunter studying me. "You ready to go back," he asked, "or do you want to get warmed up first?"

"Let's go back."

He was right. Even with my note, Brek would freak out once he found me gone, and I felt a ton better with Hunter at my side. My head barely reached his shoulder. The fact that he dwarfed me was no small thing since I was a tall girl. He was bigger than anything in this mountain. At least it felt that way. His strong arms brushed against mine, and I remembered those were the same arms that had taken out Rosco. *Easily.* No, I'd be fine. I couldn't get back fast enough with him by my side, which was difficult with all this mud. We slid all over the place, the both of us taking turns slipping in the mud until finally Hunter grabbed my hand and wouldn't let go.

"Believe me, I need the help as much as you do," he said.

I eagerly took the excuse to hold onto him in this cold, black night, while he kept me from rushing to get back, which was probably better since it kept me from hurting myself. We reached our campground. Brek wasn't back. It was still dark, and there was no sign of Brekker returning. I got seriously worried. "It's okay," Hunter reassured me. "He knows what he's doing. Even if he's hurt, he can take care of himself."

But what if he was knocked out cold somewhere or had fallen off a cliff? I didn't want to say any of these things aloud for fear of making them true. "Something big ran through our camp," I said, showing Hunter the ripped perimeter and pointing out the marks in the mud— the rain had washed most of it away. "Look at those footprints."

"Not big enough for Big Foot." He cracked a smile, looking up at me. "I get it—we all want to believe."

I grunted out a noncommittal answer. "It's all part of the Payne family curse."

"Yeah, Angel told me all about that," he said. "Don't take it personally; my family didn't hold up so well when looking for Eden's treasure either."

I shivered. "As if sleeping outside wasn't scary enough, we have to deal with a ghost?"

"Bone Man or Eden?" he asked. I shrugged and he muttered, "Maybe they're the same." I didn't like this line of conversation when it was so dark and Brek was missing. Hunter must've sensed it, because he attempted to lighten things up, "Well, if you can take on Evil, Crazy Squirrel, you can handle anything."

That got a reluctant laugh out of me, and I told him about the squirrel that had attacked my leg that day. "Oh?" he said. "You made a friend." The rain was getting heavier, and I knew that we couldn't stand outside much longer, though he politely said nothing.

"Okay," I said. "Let's get rid of our boots and wait for Brek inside my tent."

Hunter gave me a wry grin. "He'll love that."

"He has nothing to worry about."

"Are you sure?" Hunter always had to turn flirtatious, and I didn't want to admit it, but I loved it.

"Positive!"

He chuckled, taking off his muddy boots. I unzipped my tent, threw my backpack and flashlight inside, and sat on the edge of it, working mine off my feet. The bottom half of my legs were spattered in mud but there was nothing I could do to get warmer. At least not until Hunter sat next to me and took care of that, too. He was like one of those human heaters, and I relaxed against him, unabashedly stealing his heat while trying not to be too obvious about it.

He pointed at my camera. "Are you going to hold your camera all night?"

I made a sound of surprise. "Oh wow! It's still on!" The red light was still going steady. I pulled off the strap from around my neck and checked the battery. It had a good one. It was only half drained. I didn't stop it from recording. This was probably the best lighting of the whole night. I looked up to meet Hunter's questioning look. "Well, you know, Caitlyn and I are trying to make a documentary. She wanted me to get her some good footage. She said it was too boring last time."

"So you got her some screaming in the darkness?"

"Yeah," I admitted.

He reached for the camera, and turned it to show his face so he could cross his eyes at it. "Hi Caitlyn," he said with a smirk. He turned to me. "Can I see what you have in it so far?"

Well, besides some useless night footage of me freaking out in the wilderness, I'd taken a lot of photographs of the scenery while Brek had been at the lake. I didn't see why not. I turned off the recording and handed it over and was immediately sorry when he found my selfies with me wearing his trucker hat that morning. I flushed. "No, not that!"

He held me back one-handed. "No, I want to see." He studied the picture with a widening grin. "My hat looks good on you."

I decided to tease him back. "Yes, it does! Are you jealous? Do you want it back?"

"Never... unless it smells like you."

I knocked my knee against his in my attempt to make him behave, but he only took it as permission to move closer. I didn't pull back. I liked him being so near—stealing his warmth was only half of it.

That didn't stop me from trying to get the camera back from him, but I discovered I couldn't do that without putting my hands all over him, and so I let him have it, squinting in embarrassment at my close-eyed pictures. He enjoyed every one of them. As soon as he was done with the selfie portion, he found my pictures with Caitlyn on our first day on the trail. We looked miserable, but we had tried to amuse ourselves with taking pictures up our noses.

"Okay, okay, that is enough!" I said. Laughing, he gave it back, and I decided to get him back by pressing record. "Now that Hunter has found every embarrassing picture of me and knows every secret moment of my life," I said, "it's time to find out what makes him tick. What inspires your excellent taste in hats, Hunter?"

"Are you kidding? This is going into your documentary?"

"Caitlyn loves this stuff, don't you, Caitlyn?" I turned the camera back to me.

When I tried to turn it back on him, he put his hand over mine to pull us both into the frame. It was a good compromise. "What do we do now?" he asked, "take pictures up our noses?"

"Let's refrain," I said. "Why do you always have to catch me doing something embarrassing?"

I was having a hard time not picking up his southern accent, and he noticed with a snort. "You from the South now?"

I nudged him with my arm. "That's not fair," I drawled. "It's addicting." Seeing he wore a red stocking cap touting some expensive brand, I decided to play with that to distract him from stealing his accent. "You see," I pointed, "more sophisticated headwear." With great daring, I leaned across him and peeled it from his hair. His hair was messy beneath, the good kind. "Now we know why he wears so many hats," I narrated. "He doesn't want to do his hair." To

193

demonstrate my point, I ran my hand through his thick hair; I'd wanted an excuse to do that since the moment I'd seen it.

He directed a wry look at the camera. "It was because I was rescuing her again," he explained, "and she woke me up in the dead of night with her screaming. It was harrowing. This is the eighth or ninth time I had to run in to save her."

I gasped. "Not that many!" I argued.

"Honestly, it's really hard to keep count."

"Most of the time he's causing the trouble!" I said. "I blame him entirely for having to rescue me."

That was when he stole my hat. My blonde hair went every which way, and I swatted playfully at him, but there was no way I was getting it back from him. I stuffed his hat over my head instead. It swallowed my ears. He tried to put my hat on, but it didn't have the same effect because it was much too small and it kept popping off. I burst into laughter. He joined in, but finally turned to me, his eyes probing mine. "You're going to run out of batteries."

"I have more battery packs in my tent."

"Of course you do."

I took that as my cue to turn the camera off. That would be a good enough peek at our adventures for Caitlyn. Now that I had gotten my boots off, my toes were cold. My socks were all wet and I struggled to get them off. "Remember how you said you liked how I smelled?" I reminded him. He groaned when I got them off, and then he gingerly touched my toes. "They're ice! We're going to have to amputate them. Let me find my knife."

I shrieked, but instead he blew onto his hands and reached out to warm my feet, his big hands wrapping around them. It felt so good. "Please don't ever stop doing that," I said.

"Number ten," he said, looking up at me under his thick dark lashes.

I groaned, though I didn't really care that the tally was going up. At least not tonight. I just liked having him here with me until Brek was back. I didn't want to be alone in the middle of the wilderness. Hunter was a comforting presence; also an exciting one. I couldn't quite figure him out yet. He switched from protecting me to teasing me like we'd known each other forever, and it almost seemed like we had. *Almost.*

Still, he didn't try to make a move on me, which was probably best since I kept my eye on the world outside to see if my brother had returned yet. Every time I heard a noise, I'd peer outside and get depressed when it wasn't Brek until Hunter obligingly lifted my spirits again with another joke. We talked until the night sky began to fill with light and I felt my eyes droop. I must've dozed against his shoulder until I felt him straighten and I opened my eyes to see Brek coming through the trees. He was hobbling, and Angel was with him, supporting him as he walked towards camp. I gasped and stood, my head running against the top of the tent. "Brek?"

My brother's eyes widened when he saw who was with me, but he had nothing to say with Angel's arms looped around him. I'd think it was too coincidental, except I had been the one to find Hunter and alert them to Brek being missing. That meant Angel had gone in search of him as soon as Hunter reported him gone… and she'd found him. I was actually impressed.

Hunter followed me out of the tent, holding me back from my brother until I'd put on my boots. Brek watched the cute interplay between us with wary eyes, but he was too hurt to do much about it. He sat at the creaking picnic table, putting most of his weight on it. Brek's hand went to his ankle as he tested it with his fingers and winced.

"What happened?" I asked.

"Just a sprain, I hope. It was a bad night!"

"I told you not to go running after whatever came through here!"

"Now's not the time for 'I told you so,' Ivy. Give it a rest."

Well, yeah, but… "How did you sprain it?"

"I got chased up a tree by a moose." Brek chuckled a little under his breath, and Angel watched him with adoring eyes, which I hated.

They seemed as thick as thieves right now. "I was stuck up there all night until Angel came by and figured out a way to scare it away."

It was hard to imagine Brek getting chased up a tree by any wild animal. "But, but... I thought you had some bear spray."

He rolled his eyes. "I dropped it."

"Not to say, 'I told you so,'" Hunter said, "but why did you leave your sister?"

Brek glowered at him. "I wasn't going far, but someone was calling my name when I got into the forest. Who knows my name out here?"

Chills spread over my arms when I remembered Bill's story about Bone Man, and then a more likely suspicion came to me. Hunter had heard that story too. He turned to Angel. "Did you hear anything out there?"

She shook her head. *Like she'd admit it.*

Looking over at me, she asked gruffly where the first aid kit was. I pointed to Brek's tent, and she left to get it like she had the run of the place. She came back with it clutched between her slender fingers, and she took out the bandage wrap with the ease of a professional. I fought the urge to wrestle it from her. Brek already looked resentful. A sprained ankle—heaven forbid, a broken one—would put him out of commission for maybe a week. "Don't put pressure on this," she said. "You won't be able to walk on it for a few days." Let alone hike.

"We'll see," he grumbled.

She turned to lecture him like she actually cared. "Brek, you're not superman! So you're going to lose a few days—it's not the end of the world. You'll be back on your feet stronger than ever." Then she put her hand on his knee, and I was immediately suspicious this was an act. "Let's help you off this mountain."

"No! We've got it," Brek said.

"What are you going to do—limp all the way home?" Hunter asked. "Think about your sister."

That was the wrong thing to say. Brek lashed out at him. "I can

196

take care of Ivy, okay?" He was furious. A night of being stuck in a tree with this injury would do that to him.

Hunter pressed his lips together and went to get his things, leaving Brek to Angel and me. I tried to reason with my brother. I wanted out of here. "Let's just take them up on it."

His eyes glittered stubbornly and I knew that look. "We can stay up here until it gets better."

That shocked me. No way did I want to be up here another night left to our own devices, especially when he was hurt. Angel soothed him with her gentle touch, and for once I hoped her seductions would work on him. "You need to get that ankle checked at least," she said. "You don't want it to heal wrong. It could affect you for years if you don't do something about it."

Hunter came back with his things from my tent—just his flashlight, the walkie talkie, and his coat. The gun was hidden out of sight. "C'mon man," he said. "Let's just work together on this. We can find the treasure faster if we join sides."

Brek pinned him with a glare. "What are you still doing here?"

Hunter's mouth clenched shut and the muscle on his jaw worked overtime in his effort to keep his cool before he answered, "Sure. I didn't want to babysit you anyway." He left us, marching down the hill for the forest beyond, his shoulders that had rested against mine earlier looking broad and strong in the daylight. Angel pursed her lips, raising a defined brow at Brek. She gave a regretful shrug and heaved on her backpack before quickly joining Hunter.

They were really going to leave. I turned to my brother in a fury borne of desperation. "Brek! I am not staying on this mountain another night! They offered to help us down. Let's just take it!" At his stubborn look, I had to put my foot down. "If you don't do this, I'm out!"

"Who was calling my name last night?" he rasped in a tense undertone. "They lured me out there."

His words filled me with fear. "Are you sure it was them? It could've been anyone."

"Who, Ivy? Huh?"

I looked over at Hunter as he disappeared into the distance. "Even if it was them, you're hurt. Do you really want me to be out here another night if this is happening?"

Brek leaned his head back and groaned, then he shouted over the distance. "Hunter!" To his credit, Hunter stopped to listen. "We'll take your help off the mountain," Brek said. "Just stop looking at my sister." Hunter grinned and looked over at me. "Like that," Brek muttered angrily.

Hunter gestured over to their campsite. "Stop crying! We'll come back with the ATVs and get you sorry losers home."

Brek hunkered over the table, glaring down at the splintered wood. I was sure that if it hadn't been for me, he'd have gone through with his threat of living out his days on the mountaintop until he healed. I felt slightly bad that I was dragging him down. His eyes traveled to the stocking cap I wore, and I realized it was Hunter's. I hurriedly took it off and rushed to my tent before he could say anything, my boots slapping through the mud as I took it down. I tackled Brek's tent next, though he made for a poor supervisor. Nothing was good enough for that perfectionist. It was why he always did his own thing.

I snapped insults back at him while still managing to gather all our things together. The picnic table made a perfect place to set our supplies. The morning was already turning warm, though there were puddles of mud everywhere.

I popped the green trucker hat on my head, and Brek took exception to that. "Ivy! I take it back. You should leave Hunter alone." In light of his suspicions, he could be right, but after last night, Hunter didn't seem the type to do something so lowdown like luring Brek away from me to get us hurt. Of course, there was nothing like seeing Angel with Brek to throw doubts on everything I had with Hunter. Angel used what she had to get what she wanted out of my brother. Hunter could be just as tricky, but with a ton more charm.

The sound of ATVs got louder in the distance like a swarm of angry bees, and for the first time I realized the extent of what helping us out entailed. Hunter's stories of all his accidents filled my head as I watched him and his team ride up from the back way where the motorized vehicles were allowed. I watched them close in on us, Hunter at the front of them like the Alpha in a pack of dogs.

"If we find out they did this to you," I said. "I'll drop him on his head." I turned to Brek. "Happy?"

"Not yet."

They came for us, and together we wordlessly packed our things on the back of their four-wheelers. I avoided Hunter's eyes, though he pinned me with a questioning glance that I avoided until I remembered his stocking cap and retrieved it to slide back onto his head. "I almost forgot to give this back."

He caught my hands in his, which finally forced me to look at him. "Thank you, Ma'am," he said in that irresistible drawl of his. I bit my lip, not knowing what to think as he let my hands slip from his. Circling to Brek, I saw he hadn't noticed. At least that. Hunter caught me checking for my brother's approval, and his expression turned amused. That annoyed me as I moved away to pack up the rest of our campsite.

We finally got everything tied onto the back of the four-wheelers, and Angel drove alongside Brek with a flirtatious toss of her black hair. "Get on, hot stuff." His suspicions didn't stop the hypocrite from climbing onto the back of her four-wheeler. So weak!

Hunter collected me next, and it was my turn to face my rival, except I was filled with trepidation. I hadn't been kidding when I'd said these made me nervous. I noticed Hunter had dumped his jacket in the back and wore only his white t-shirt and jeans. He must be freezing, but the only sign that he was even moderately cold was the hair standing up on his muscular forearms.

"Where's my helmet?" I asked.

He studied me and tugged playfully at my shirt. "I didn't know you were coming back with me or I would've brought it. Just hold tight."

If that was some sort of come-on, I wasn't falling for it. I got behind Hunter, using the minimal amount of pressure to hold onto his back. Too late, I saw his lip curl up as he leaned forward and pressed the gas. We lurched forward, and one of my arms wrapped around his waist, the other his neck as I clasped my hands together with him in between. The charms on my bracelet crashed together. He smirked in response. The faster he went, the tighter I held to him. He was doing this on purpose. We left his men, and then Angel and Brek, far behind. Of course Angel didn't try to catch up. She was in no hurry to play chaperone, not when she had Brek in her clutches.

I felt the wind catch at my hair. "I'm going to lose my hat," I shouted.

"What?"

Leaning against his back with my lips against his ear, I tried again, "My hat!"

"*My* hat!" he corrected. And he didn't care. My hand clutched at his stomach. I let go of his neck to grab the hat one-handed and tore it from my head to keep it from blowing away. I grabbed onto Hunter again, this time with both arms around his waist, my hair flying around us in what was turning into a horrible tangled mess. He hit a bump, and I screamed and hid my face in his back.

"Don't stop looking. You're missing it," he said.

"Go slower!" I shouted. "You dork! I told you I don't like these things."

"That's because you've never gone with me." But he slowed down anyway. My heart started to calm down, though I didn't dare loosen my hold on him. He laughed, and I could feel the vibrations of it under my hands. "Easy on the loving," he said. "You're squeezing me to death."

I swatted his arm with his own hat, and found myself laughing. He had done this to himself. I rested the side of my head against his back, watching the countryside blur past me. It was a faster way to travel, and the countryside was beautiful on the trails meant for the ATVs. The trees to the side of us were caught up in the mist of the morning next to each lake we passed in the distance, and I couldn't help but think how Brek and I were making this hard on ourselves. What took us a full day to hike, we traversed in less than an hour in a vehicle. If I'd had a helmet, I'd have felt much better about it. We reached the forested trail from the clearing, and Hunter plunged through it and down the mountainside until we reached the Grizzly Resort on the other side.

Our cabins were a welcome sight ahead of us, though we passed the café first where Bill was on the porch with his fellow hecklers. Of course they'd have to witness this—all their hard-earned time at playing matchmaking was paying off, and they waved as we passed. Hunter waved energetically in return, knowing full well what he was doing, while I forced a smile. I'd never hear the end of it.

Hunter parked us in front of the cabin and turned off the engine. The sound of it still echoed in my ears as I raised my head from his back. "You can let go of me now," he said.

I did, but my arms were still shaking as I pushed off the seat and almost lost my footing in the mud. He grabbed me to steady me, looking concerned. "Are you okay?"

"I'm fine!" But my voice sounded testy even to me. I guessed I was mad, but really more disoriented than anything. The alarm spreading across his expression cleared the moment he checked out my face, and he broke into a laugh. "You might want to clean up."

I pushed away from him, feeling unsteady on my feet. Caitlyn came rushing out of our cute little cabin like a gnome in a clean summer dress. She had made the place her home. Little potted plants from the Grizzly decorated the railing outside. I recognized her fine hand in everything. She stopped short when she saw me. "Oh, you might want to do something…" she pointed to her eyes. "You've got mascara running down your face." At my sour expression, she again hastened to defend herself. "Friends tell!"

I brushed under my eye with the back of my hand, pouting a little, then tipped back on my heels to check out Hunter's back and saw it was all over the back of his white shirt. He really deserved it. "I'm not the only one who has to clean up," I said.

He arched his back, trying to catch sight of it. "You mascara-ed me?"

Caitlyn helped me get my stuff from the back of his four-wheeler. I couldn't even hear anyone else in the distance, we'd gone so fast. "Now you have to sing a really cheesy, drippy karaoke song," I told him.

He broke into a grin. "Why?"

"That was the deal, except you got it backwards."

"Wait, let me get this right," he said. "I save you and now I have to humiliate myself?"

I nodded. "Yes." And then I went inside with my stuff and slammed the door behind me. Caitlyn knocked and I let her inside before heading wordlessly for the shower.

Chapter thirteen

*A*fter scrubbing my cheeks free of my running mascara, I came out of the shower and wrapped the big, white terrycloth towel around me. The warmth of the shower and the feel of the soft towel on my skin was my first real comfort in the last twenty-four hours. My whole body ached from wandering the forest and slipping in the mud and not sleeping all night. I wanted to crawl into bed and not emerge until the next day. I threw on a baggy t-shirt and gray joggers and trudged out into our bright orange living room.

Brekker was already set up on the couch. Caitlyn bustled around him, trying to make him more comfortable, putting up his foot and talking about getting a doctor. For a moment, I wondered if she had been absolutely right when she'd decided to pull out of the hiking. I'd thought Brek would be put off, but now he had something nice waiting for him at home. She was still full of energy, and she looked fresh and beautiful in her summer dress. Her sweet concern would win any man's heart. But Brekker's? I wasn't sure. It was a tug of war between the sinister seductress and the sweet girl next door.

My brother held a glass of ice water next to his aching head and let her play nurse. If I didn't know better, I'd have said he actually liked it, though Angel was still not distant enough a memory. Brekker looked over at me, wincing at the effort. He had it worse than I did. "Your boy drives fast."

"Yeah." I didn't want to be reminded. "He couldn't wait to get rid of me."

"That wasn't how I saw it," he said. I rolled my eyes and left for my room. Brek's voice stopped me. "We're going to have to work with them."

After Brek's suspicions? I threw my hands on my hips. "But... what if they were the ones who did this to you?" Caitlyn looked confused, and we quickly explained to her what had happened the night before. Predictably, she didn't like the idea of us working with Angel. And if Brek was right and they had lured us away, then I didn't want to do it either.

"I don't know what else to do, Ivy." Brek glared at his ankle. The frustration leaking into his expression gave me pause. "Did you ever wonder why I dragged the two of you into this when I needed a real team?"

Insulting, but accurate. I sat on the edge of the hard tweed couch. "What's going on, Brek?"

He downed the rest of his water bottle and set it down on the side table. "Six months ago, we were looking for a lost artifact—a famous one. If we had found it, we would've gone down in the history books. None of us would have ever had to worry about money again. It was the Crown Jewels of Ireland, stolen in 1907."

"I... have no idea what those are," I said.

"Yeah, well, they're really famous among intellectual circles." I let the insult slide and waited for him to tell me the rest. "We got a tip that maybe it went down in the Carruthers, a ship lost in the White Hurricane of 1913."

"I don't know what that is."

"It doesn't matter." He looked grumpy about it. "Most of those ships ended up in shipwreck alley in Northern Lake Huron, so that's where we went. I took out a big loan to do it. We found a backer who was super emotionally invested in it and we took with us a whole slew of diving crews and historians... and Ivy, we found it."

But he wasn't any richer, and so I got nervous. "What happened to it?"

"Angel." Brek slunk down into the couch. "I think she sold it to the highest bidder."

"How do you know she did?"

"She said she lost it. I mean, how stupid does she think I am? Angel thought she could weave some story that I'd believe because I loved her." *Love?* It was quite the revelation, and used in past tense. I noticed Caitlyn straightened at that. "She betrayed me," he said. "I'm ruined. The team blamed me, the creditors are after me. I lost everything, my house, my deals, my reputation. The only reason I still have my Jeep is because I haven't stayed still long enough for the bank to take it."

The both of us had been backed into the corner—that's what had brought us here. This didn't mean fame or endless riches to us. Sure, I had my credit card debt, getting mom a better place for a few years, maybe showing an old boyfriend or two that I was worth something, but Brek had so much more at stake than I did. He might be in the hole for millions. He stared despondently at his hands. "The backer I had worked with before this? Rooney? He thinks I'm the one who cheated him. He's powerful in the business. He'll make sure I don't work after this."

This was horrible in so many ways. Seeking the lost treasures of this world was the one thing Brek loved, and it was now denied him. "Why did our new backer not stay away?" I asked.

"I don't know. I think Walker knew our father, honestly because no one else would go up against Rooney. Walker's people approached me out of nowhere. I was desperate. I'd always wanted to know what happened to dad, but after losing those jewels, I thought I'd never find a backer for it. If I didn't agree to do it now, everything he worked for would be lost. We'd never know what happened; but now?" He stared at his ankle despairingly. "I don't see any other way out of this."

Caitlyn hurried to reassure us that things weren't as bad as we thought. "We are getting more hits on YouTube. This thing could go viral and then you won't have to worry about money." She pulled up pictures from her phone. "Look at these numbers." Glancing over her shoulder, I saw she had taken pictures of the screen from the computer in the resort lobby. "It just kind of blew up." There were at least 10,000 hits. I scanned the comments in her pics. Hybernater was getting all sorts of replies. He was the star of the internet.

"Wait." I noticed what she had called the series. "Poison Ivy and Fortune Hunter?"

"Isn't it great?"

Brek snorted, but he was stuck where he was so he couldn't walk out like he was used to doing. "There's no reason to be desperate," Caitlyn said, "—just get me lots of footage. If you don't find the treasure, we have this."

Brek's mouth firmed before he attempted a civil answer. "That doesn't exactly solve anything."

"Where's your footage from yesterday?" Caitlyn asked, snapping her fingers at me.

Reluctantly, I retrieved the camera and she turned it on, watching through the footage. It wasn't exactly groundbreaking. Brek set his head on the arm of the couch, looking up at the ceiling with crossed arms like he was the most put-upon man in existence. When the segment came up with Hunter and me in the tent, he turned angrily away.

"This is so good!" Caitlyn said. "He saved you and now you're hitting it off!"

"How cute," Brek said sarcastically. "The only problem is that he was behind everything. You want to know what we're really facing here? The funder behind my last expedition thinks I cheated him, and he's powerful. I wouldn't be surprised if Rooney sends his thugs after me. And Angel knows exactly what she did. Hunter does too."

I remembered that Hunter had hinted Brek had a secret when Hunter asked us why he had recruited us and not his usual team. No, Brek was right. Hunter knew. I had to quit lying to myself just because I didn't want it to be true. And if he was capable of working with Angel after she'd stolen those jewels, then he'd be low enough to be behind the Bone Man scare. It changed everything. "Then we don't have a choice," I said. "We have to do what it takes to get that treasure."

Caitlyn tried to object again. "But join them? Angel will steal your find again!"

"She won't… not if we steal it first!" The words left my mouth before I could think about the implications, but if she was crooked then so was Hunter. And if we fought back dirty then they deserved it. I tried to forget how Hunter had found me in the darkness last night and had comforted me until my brother had returned. If my twin's life was in danger, nothing else mattered. "Let's just work with them," I said. "We pretend that they've got us, that we fell for their little Bone Man trick in the wilderness, lull them into security, and when the time comes, we take what belongs to us!"

Brek's backer wanted the whole find—70/30 wasn't good enough for us, though I'd pretend to ask for 50/50 to look legit. After a moment, Brekker nodded. "We have to do it."

Caitlyn looked panicked at the thought. "You're horrible at lying, Ivy. He'll see right through you! Both of your faces are open books. Angel will see through you too, Brek!"

The unspoken fear was that she didn't want my brother spending any more time with Angel than he already did—Angel was tricky in more ways than one. Even after she'd cheated him of his last find, ruining his lifelong dreams of being a famous treasure hunter, he still had a soft spot for her. It would be difficult for me too. I wanted nothing more than to sleep off my rough night and maybe think a little harder about what I wanted to do; but I had a lot of work ahead of me. I threw on my coat, and Caitlyn watched me with worry, Brek with confusion.

"Where are you going?" he asked.

"I'm going to make Hunter think he convinced us to work with him."

"I'm filming!" Caitlyn chirped. I squeezed my eyes shut in frustration. That would make it even harder. "I'm not giving up on my idea," she said. "If none of your stupid tricks work, you'll thank me!"

Sure, I preferred making money on a documentary more than stealing it, more than treasure hunting, but now I had every reason to work with Hunter. Not only that, but he had that artifact, and we wouldn't find anything without him. I was ready to play hardball.

"Wait, wait, wait." Now that Brek had gotten his way, he still wasn't happy. "I'm still laid up. You think you're just going to do this on your own?"

"How else is this going to happen?" I asked. "We're at our lowest point—they won't believe that you gave in otherwise. You'll have to make Angel believe that you don't suspect her of taking that find anymore. Let her take care of you while you heal or something. I've got Hunter."

His eyes clouded with concern. "I'm not leaving you alone with him."

"What other choice do we have?" I pushed out the door, and the door swung a couple of times before Caitlyn was following me.

"I told him that I'd watch your back," she said breathlessly. She fiddled with her cellphone before asking me the plan. First things first, we had to get some coordinates. She was patient while I set up what I was going to do. She even forgot herself enough to act like I was just a regular girl with a regular interest in a guy. After getting everything that I needed at the Grizzly, we headed to Hunter's cabin. If he was anything like me, he'd be asleep by now—which I partly hoped for—but when I saw the blur of activity on his front lawn, I set my teeth, knowing that I couldn't put this off.

I sighted his broad shoulders as he leaned over his four-wheeler to unpack. He had showered and his hair was wet; he'd changed from his white shirt into his black one. Appropriate since he was now the villain in my mind. He caught sight of me, and when I didn't immediately run away, he looked confused then intrigued as I walked his way. "You cleaned up the…" he indicated a finger under his eyes, and I scowled, not wanting to be put at a disadvantage. I crossed my arms. "Fifty-fifty," I said.

He gawked. "What?"

"We work with you if we split the find fifty-fifty."

Immediately he took a relaxed position, and I knew he did it to put the fire out of me. "So you're the emissary now, are you?"

"My brother can't seem to find his feet." I tried to ignore the fact that it was probably Hunter's fault. "But yes, if you must know—this is his decision. We kind of don't have a choice."

"Sixty-forty," he said.

I knew he'd try something like that, and I had to make this seem real, so I put up a fight. "You can't do this without us. We've got Eden's journal."

"I've got the 'device' you stole from me, and you know it has significance. I saw that look on your face when you lost it." My stomach clenched at his words. I hoped he couldn't read me as well as he professed. "We also have the manpower," he said. "Sixty-forty is generous."

"We don't want the others to work with us—just you and me." I stood a better chance against him if I wasn't surrounded. "Until my brother is back on his feet, everyone else stays back. I'll show you what we've found so far, then you show me what you've got."

He looked intrigued. "And you'll let me read Eden's journal?"

I gulped. "If you let me use that device," I returned.

"Fifty-five, forty-five split," he said. "That's my final offer."

"I'll only agree to that on one condition," I said and held my hand out. "Where's your GPS?"

"Why?"

"Just get it."

He went through his bags to dig it out. Before he could ask "why" again, I took either side of it, my hands over his as I punched in coordinates. His attention seemed to be more on me, but then he studied the numbers and smiled. "You're sending me geocaching? Is this to get me back?"

"Partly." I stepped back, sliding my hands from his.

He caught sight of Caitlyn filming behind me and broke into another laugh. "Am I going to survive this?"

"Considering that we need your help, I'm going to bank on a yes," I said.

He leaned back on his heels, resting his hands on the four-wheeler behind him as he studied my face. Lifting my chin, I tried to prove that I was serious. This was the moment where I could make or break this. Angel came out of the cabin and stumbled to a stop. No doubt, she hadn't expected to see us out so soon. Hunter's eyes narrowed on me and then he turned to his men as they went about their way, some of them shooting us curious glances. "These girls are stealing me for a bit," he called over his shoulder. "I'll be back in..." he turned questioning eyes on me.

"An hour."

"An hour," he repeated.

Angel stepped up against the railing, and I tried to ignore her. She knew I couldn't stand her, but I couldn't have her guess what we were up to. Hunter either. I tried to pretend that he wasn't the main suspect behind Brek's injury, and it wasn't hard when I got lost in his easy charm. "Let's do this, then," he said and picked up the GPS tracker to follow the coordinates. We trailed beside him as it took us away from the cabin and towards the Grizzly. The bells at the entrance rang merrily as the coordinates led us inside.

We passed Bill and his compadres on the ground floor. They perked up in excitement. Frank was polishing his badge and looked over it. "What is this?" he asked.

Hunter shifted his attention from the tracker and gave them a sheepish shrug. "Ivy put me on a treasure hunt."

"Oh? She did, did she?" Bill was beside himself with excitement. No doubt he thought that Hunter and I were hitting it off, but if he knew the real story, he'd be as shocked as I was.

I couldn't let my anger show on my face, so I forced a smile. "He's proving how trustworthy he is."

Hunter looked up from the tracker. "Is that what this is?"

"Oh, yes!" I nodded. Caitlyn dimpled and agreed, her red curls bobbing up and down.

Suddenly Hunter wasn't so in charge of the situation as he began to suspect foul play. His mouth tightened as we went up the three flights of stairs with the old men following us the whole way. As soon as we got to the Bear Den, Hunter spied the karaoke stage and groaned. "No, no, I don't do that."

"I don't go on ATV's either," I said. "But if you want me to get on another one tomorrow then you'd better do this." The old men started to catcall, and Hunter leaned his head back in an embarrassed laugh.

"You have to prove that you're one of us!" Caitlyn called behind her camera. "How else can she trust you?"

"If I have to be vulnerable then so do you," I said, picking up the mic. "Backstreet Boys or we go back to fifty-fifty."

"And you're going to film it?" Hunter's voice choked on another bark of laughter. "What is wrong with you?"

I flipped on the player and the familiar nineties music filled the empty loft. There were people downstairs that would hear it, and the open balcony door would carry it a little farther than that—maybe to the cabins. I held out the mic and he didn't take it. I shrugged and stepped onto the stage, speaking into it, "Then it's fifty-fifty, folks."

Hunter jumped on the stage after me and took the mic. "Every—bodeeey!" he sang. "Rock your bodeeey."

I was shocked as he talked/sang the oldie-but-goodie. Then he went into the chorus, which wasn't so bad, though a little off. My arms dropped to my sides as he completely blew me away. He was super cute. Though completely out of tune, he made up for it in energy, and I was really attracted to him right then. He threw his hands up in the air to go with the lyrics of the song, and I realized the guy had some rhythm. He took one of my dangling hands and serenaded me with the last warbling lines of the song. Then as it ended, he held up the mic and

211

STEPHANIE FOWERS

pumped it in the air before stuffing it back in its holder with a war cry. I didn't want to like him, but I did.

He came back for me and almost bumped foreheads with me to whisper, "You didn't think I could do it, did you?"

Hunter pulled away as the old men clapped and hollered and shouted for "Aiden" to do an encore. I watched him, stunned. I couldn't answer. I just wanted to wrap my arms around this cute man and kiss him for being so adorable. And I was mad that I felt that way. Why did I have to find the perfect man when he was so wrong?

"Duet! Duet!" Bill shouted to us. "Do a duet!"

Attempting to gain back my poise, I picked up the mic and smiled at him. "How about it, Hunter? You want to sing some *Hamilton*?"

"No! You've tortured me enough!"

Caitlyn skipped over to us. "That was so hot! I am not going to lie."

Everything was so hot with her! I felt tense and prickly as I tried to fight my softening heart. At the same time I listened to the clatter of hiking boots behind us, and circled to see Angel enter the Bear Den with one of Hunter's minions. She attempted a giggle when she saw us at the stage, but I could tell she was really bothered. "What are you doing up there?"

Hunter slipped my mic from my fingers to seize it in his hands again. He put it to his lips and said, "Just a little hazing before we welcome Ivy and her brother onto the team."

Angel looked shocked, her eyes going to me. I tried to conceal my dislike, but I didn't do it very well. I supposed it was fine since I'd made it clear that we were basically doing this against our will. "Rent her a four-wheeler from the Grizzly," Hunter said. "We are working together now."

Heaven help us, we were... but would he really make me drive one of those things? Things were going from bad to worse. Hunter had survived me, now would I survive him?

212

The morning came faster than I wanted. After sleeping all day and arguing with Brek all night, I found myself throwing the last of my things in my pack. By now I had layering down to a science—I wore sweats over my shorts and a windbreaker over two shirts with varied sleeve lengths. I wore a beanie hat, but I had packed Hunter's trucker cap for when it got hotter. Hunter and I were only going to Sinkhole Lake today—it was where Brek and I had found the Spanish symbols—and so we wouldn't have to camp overnight, but I wasn't taking any chances of not running into water, mud, or skunks, so I packed an extra pair of socks and sweats.

Brek didn't think that I had to show Hunter what we had really found, but I wanted to make sure that we made this look good. Besides, if we wanted a chance to *steal* the treasure, that meant we really needed to *find* the treasure. We'd actually have to try.

When Brek heard that it would only be Hunter and me, I wasn't sure if he was more relieved or more worried. On one hand, I wouldn't be outnumbered; on the other hand, it gave Hunter more of a chance to work his magic on me. "What happened to me working my charm on him?" I asked in a fit of pique.

"The problem is that it keeps working both ways." Brek rearranged the rice bag on his ankle. He had stripped down to basketball shorts, a workout shirt, and had tied a bandanna over his hair in a skull cap. He had made for an ornery patient, and I didn't envy Caitlyn. He was a permanent fixture on the couch, and she fetched him ice to take down the swelling.

The doctor from town had made a house call at Bill's insistence and determined that it really was a sprain, but the ligament had likely been partially torn, which meant that Brekker could be off his feet for at least three weeks. I was sure that my brother would be in full commission sooner, but even a week was a long time for me to be spending with Hunter alone.

"I've got it covered," I said. "Just watch out for Angel."

"After what she did, you think I'd mess with her again?" he asked.

"Yeah, I do actually. I've seen you two together."

I knew Caitlyn agreed, but she didn't want to be a nag like I was. She had tied her red hair into a sloppy bun and dressed down today in a long-sleeved button-down thermal shirt and black stretch pants. Collapsing on the other side of Brekker on the couch, she sighed. "Don't forget to get me the footage, Ivy. The last stuff was gold!"

That possibly made Brek more upset with her than with me. He popped two Tic Tacs, looking restless. Yeah, he'd be off of that couch much sooner than the doctor prescribed. "I got us some walkie talkies," he said.

"You did?" They'd make things way more convenient. The Grizzly had everything.

He dug them out of his bag near his sprained ankle. "You take one and I'll take the other. It has a fifty-mile radius. Then you can let me know you're alive. Don't look at me like that."

"Brek! I'm going to be fine!" Before we could get into it, someone knocked on the flimsy cabin door, and I stood, expecting Hunter. Instead, we got Angel. Caitlyn straightened on the couch, and I wondered if I'd witness a catfight.

Angel was looking at me, her arms crossed. "You want Hunter to yourself, do you?"

What did she want me to say? I didn't like her or any of her men? "Look, it's easier to just do this one-on-one until Brek gets off his feet."

Her beautiful dark eyes narrowed. I should've known she would be just as restless as Brek. Those two were made for action. She sauntered into the room. "That's fine. I'll just make sure your brother heals sooner rather than later."

Uh-oh. Brek predictably glowered up at her, but his body language told me that he was desperate for the distraction. Caitlyn and I exchanged glances. I wasn't sure which of us hated Angel more. Brek downed more Tic Tacs. "In case you haven't noticed, Angel, I've got someone here who's capable of taking care of me."

I felt limp with relief. Was he finally blowing her off? Angel looked insulted. "I don't know why you don't believe me! You can't possibly think that I'm still to blame for... for..." She looked over at us like we were an inconvenient crowd. "We need to talk."

"We've done enough of that," Brekker stated.

"Is that why *she* won't work with me?"

"Ivy trusts Hunter, not you," Brek said. "How's that for honesty?"

Well, it was only a half-lie, since I didn't trust Hunter either, but still brutal in its near-honesty. And Brek actually pulled it off. Angel sucked in her breath and stormed out. After a few moments of staring at the door—perhaps a bit reluctantly—Brek turned to me. "And that's how it's done, Ivy."

I'd remember that. I put my pack on over the bulk of my windbreaker. "She'll be back," I warned.

Caitlyn looked stunned, like she could scarcely believe that Brek had finally shown Angel her place. She waved weakly at me as I peeled open the warped door. "Ivy!" Brek called. I looked over and he attempted a weak smile. "Thanks for doing this."

I nodded as he nervously finished off the Tic Tacs. He was going to have a hard time sitting still. My best friend would have her hands full, which she might be looking forward to—we hadn't had any time for heart-to-hearts lately, so I didn't actually know.

Walking out onto the cold balcony, I saw Hunter on the front lawn. He hadn't bothered with his coat this morning. He wore a dark khaki button-up shirt layered over his usual tee shirt and more of those faded jeans that looked great on him. He was still packing up the four-wheelers. There was a new one parked there, and I cringed. He had gone through on his threat to rent the extra one from Bill. "Where's my helmet?" I called out to him.

He turned and smiled at me. "It's on the seat." He'd thought of everything. I approached it suspiciously, having never run one of these things before. It was surprising, since Brek had been born to ride. "Bill said the gas gauge is off," Hunter flicked the glass on the display board, "but he filled it up before I took it."

A creak on the balcony alerted me to my brother's presence. He had hobbled out the door despite Caitlyn's protests. "Hunter!" he said, holding out some walkie talkies. "Take one of these so I can keep tabs on my sister."

I groaned inwardly and met Hunter's incredulous eyes. "He's a little protective," I said.

He broke into a grin. "Can you blame him?"

Well, yeah, kinda. I wished I'd taken the walkie talkie myself to avoid this humiliation. Hunter dashed up to the balcony, and the two exchanged some tense words before he bounded back down, returning to my side. My brother disappeared back inside his cabin. "What did he say?" I asked.

"That's just between us *girls*."

My eyes narrowed at him—his jokes weren't going to get him off that easy, but past experience told me that I'd get nothing from prying. I threw my hands up in the air and went to the ATV. "Okay, I have no idea how to drive this thing," I said.

"It works a little differently than a car. You turn it on and control the speed through the handlebars."

I tied my pack to the back of the four-wheeler, using the netting like Hunter had done with his things; then, putting on my helmet, I straddled the seat, staring at all the buttons and gauges. "How do you turn it on?"

He snickered a little and came over to my side where he leaned over me to pull a cord like it was a lawn mower. The engine was just as loud when he got it started. "This is an old-school one," he shouted over the noise. "Now, you disengage the parking brake," he reached his arm around me, which was a little unnecessary, but he was taking advantage of every opportunity to touch me. I was bothered that I

216

didn't mind. He flipped a switch back by the handlebars. "Then you put it in drive. "You can go forward by twisting the right hand grip."

Without hesitation, I tested it out and flew forward. It was poorly thought-out, because I wasn't sure where the brakes were. There was nothing by my feet. "The brake," he shouted. "The brake!"

Too late, I saw Brek's Jeep in front of me and I swerved, barely missing it and going down the ravine to the side. I was too busy trying to guide the ATV around the trees to figure out where the brake was, and with relief, I stayed alive as I flew through the trees and onto the Grizzly parking lot. There were a lot of cars there for a Tuesday morning, and I tried to figure out the parking brake. At least I knew not to twist the handle, so that the ATV got slower and slower. A loud engine behind me showed me that Hunter had somehow caught up to me, and he pointed at the handlebars. "The handle! The handle, push it down!"

Glancing down, I saw what looked like an extra layer of handlebars, and I took a chance and pulled it. The ATV lurched to a stop, and I ran into the dashboard. "Ouch!" I rubbed my arms.

Hunter was immediately at my side. "Are you okay?"

I was alive. Did that count? Bill came sleepily out of his café to watch the commotion. He was in his cowboy hat, though he still wore his night slippers. We had turned into a sideshow. "You ever ride one of these things before?" Bill asked me.

It was a little obvious that I was a newbie. I grimaced. "I'm kind of new."

"Those are some bad trails up there." He looked over at Hunter. "Aiden, you sure about this?"

"Yeah, yeah." Though Hunter didn't look so sure anymore.

"Be sure to pack tents if anything happens," Bill said.

What would happen? Hunter gave him a distracted look. "I've packed some extra gear for that. We'll be fine."

Bill was shaking his head. "These vehicles are touchy. This one's not the best."

"You gave me the touchy one?" I accused Hunter.

"No, no, look, just follow me and you'll be fine." He gave me a quick tutorial again, looking a little harried. By now we had gained a following. His men, bereft of anything to do this morning, gathered to watch. I tried to ignore that, but it was hard since they had resorted to hooting and hollering every time I attempted a practice run. I got slower and slower each time since I was losing my confidence. Angel took the opportunity to cast me superior looks. After following too far behind Hunter one last time, he hopped off his four-wheeler and untied his stuff from the back. "Angel," he said. "Take mine back."

For a second, I thought he had given up on me. "What are you doing?"

He threw his gear on the back of my ATV and hopped behind me to share my seat. "Okay, drive. You're going to get this."

My ears burned. This was so embarrassing. Bill waved us happily on, and with my pride on the line, I tried again, but my heart was racing and I crawled along at a snail's pace. Hunter reached around me and took over the throttle to make us go faster. We raced up the trail we had gone down the morning before, and soon Hunter backed off and let me take over, his arms intermittently going from the guardrail at the back to around my waist to guide me. I was sure this was what my brother had been worried about, but the ride wasn't so long, considering, and we reached Sinkhole Lake in no time at all, from the back side where the cliffs weren't so steep. Hunter hooked his chin over my shoulder and indicated the brake to the side of me. "You remember where that is?"

How could I forget? I eased us to a stop and breathed a sigh of relief. Hunter pushed me forward so he could get out and stretch. I took my time climbing out, feeling super jittery. "Hey?" he said with a reassuring look. "You did it."

"Yeah." And I felt like I was burning up. Either it was because I'd been so close to that human heater that Hunter turned out to be or the cooler part of the morning was over. No matter the reason, I couldn't

218

get out of my sweats and windbreaker fast enough, and I got rid of my next layer after that, too, so I was in my hiking shorts and a cool floral top. I still fanned myself.

Looking over, I saw that Hunter watched me with an amused look. "Should we let your brother know that you're alive?"

"Am I?" I asked.

"Hmm." He stepped closer to me to check my pulse at my neck. "Yeah, you're still breathing. Really fast, actually."

And his nearness made my breath hitch. He knew what he was doing. Laughing at his little joke, Hunter picked up the walkie talkie and contacted Brek. "We've reached the lake, and you're in luck. Your sister hasn't fallen madly in love with me yet."

I swatted him in the arm. "Don't tell him that."

"Oh, you mean you are in love with me?" he asked.

"It's not happening, Hunter," Brek came through, his voice surprisingly clear on the other side. "Let me talk to Ivy."

I gave Hunter a severe look before taking the walkie talkie from him. "Don't even put that in Brek's head," I said. "He'd kill you." I pressed down the button and turned from him. "Brek! We're here. What do you want me to show him first?"

"The symbols on the other side of the lake. See if he knows what they mean. I've only worked out a few of them, but together they might mean something else."

"Got it." I put the walkie talkie in the mesh pocket of my backpack where I'd have easy access, and I slanted a wry look Hunter's direction. "And you thought they were all a hoax here."

He didn't look convinced, like he thought I'd play the same trick on him as before. He hauled his pack onto his shoulder. It was full of all his instruments and cameras. "Lead the way."

The ATV trail had taken us a back way, but I did my best to lead him through the same side paths Brek and I had traveled before, through the forest fringing the side of the lake, hoping that it would be as easy to find the spot where I'd found the symbols last time. I was desperate to get this over with. They had been on a flat rock near the cliff's side between the two lakes near that glacial red limestone wall. As we traveled to it, I noticed that the ground was still muddy from the rain. I slowed, remembering how much I had slipped before, and how much Hunter had caught me. I'd been so grateful—before I'd known he had been behind it all. Inspecting each lookout where I might have taken a picture, I jerked back when Hunter started to crowd me. "You didn't get the coordinates?" he asked.

"I'm sure that Brek did, but we're almost there."

We wandered aimlessly for about twenty minutes before Hunter stole the walkie talkie from the mesh pocket in my backpack. He pressed down the button. "Brek, where are the coordinates to these symbols?"

There was a hesitation before Brek told him, a little defiantly. Hunter set his tracker and we found it within minutes. I'd miscalculated the distance, but as soon as we walked into the area, I knew it. The glacial boulder that held back Sinkhole Lake was so tall it cut off all wind and sound. It reminded me a bit of a slot canyon—at least on one side, with tall pines blocking us the other direction. It was a wonder I'd found the flat rock in the first place. He knelt next to it and inspected the X etched into it, then the holes on either side of it, along with the triangle pointing to the lake. "How did you find these in the first place?" he asked.

"I kind of stumbled across it. I was taking pictures. I probably should take out my camera now." I put down my pack and slipped it out. His eyes found mine. "Must you?"

Oh, a little camera shy? I'd do it even more now. I was desperate to get him back for everything. "We got to make the big bucks somehow," I said.

"You don't think you'll find the treasure?"

I shrugged. "Even so, we get a flat rate and the funder of the expedition gets the whole find."

"Forty-five percent," Hunter reminded me.

"Right," I said, feeling myself flush. "But that's better than our backer getting nothing, so…"

"Who do you work for?" he asked suddenly.

"He goes by Walker."

Hunter looked up sharply, but before I could ask why, he turned back to the rock. "I'm not familiar with this sign." I was disappointed. "The cross, I know," he said. "It's a symbol of the church; but what are these two circles on either side?"

I turned on the camera to catch this moment. "We don't know what that is, but it's on the coin Eden had." I reached for her journal one-handed, then stopped out of habit. We had agreed on sharing everything, and so, after locking eyes with Hunter, I pushed through my initial unwillingness and pulled it out and showed him the coin Eden had illustrated in it. He picked up the journal and studied it.

"And there's more," I said, pushing between him and the journal to find the entry Eden had written about this place. "The Spanish symbols show the way to the treasure. It is a way to return the land to what it once was."

"Return the land to what it once was," he repeated as if it were a clue.

I got excited, wondering if he really could help us. "She also talks about a shiny stick."

He read through her entry. "A shinny stick?"

"No, that artifact you have—I'm sure of it. She says it's a tool to find the treasure, like a compass."

His face flushed with interest, and I knew that I'd found something important. Digging the artifact from his pack, he stared at it. "Before my uncle disappeared, he was the leading expert on the Spanish Priest who hid this treasure. The priest's name was Gabriel de Padilla, and he sailed to America in the 1500's with his monks and the Spanish Conquistadors. They were searching for souls and gold."

"Wait?" I held up a finger. "Your uncle… was he one of the lost brothers you're related to?" It was a closer relative than I'd thought. I wondered about the identity of the other brother. Had we both lost a father to this? It seemed too crazy a coincidence.

Thrown off track, Hunter digested the question fully before he nodded. "This uncle knew everything there was to know about this Spanish priest. Rumor was that the conquistadors got this far north, and that's where legend of this gold came from. The priest taught the good word of God while the conquistadors imprisoned his converts and forced them to work in the mines. When Gabriel de Padilla found out, he was furious. He repented of coming to this land, and he hid up the Spanish Treasure so that the one to find it would be a better man than he was. The Conquistadors discovered his deceit and tried to torture the secret out of him, but his death brought it to the grave."

He handed me the device. "Whatever this is—it's religious. That writing on the side is written in Greek and Hebrew, the language of the New and Old Testaments. See this first phrase on the side?" He pointed to θησαυρός του βουνού. "It says 'Treasure of the Mountain.' And this," he ran his finger over the האלוהים אוצר, "reads, 'Treasure of God.' Gabriel de Padilla wanted a religious man to find this treasure."

"Oh!" I held the device up to my eye again and looked through it to see the Roman numerals placed haphazardly over the screen. Hunter's story seemed like a romanticized version of this priest. "Are you sure he didn't want the treasure for himself? He just got killed before he could get to it?"

"You should read some of these translations of his writings. He feared for his soul. He sought a chosen vessel—a man of intelligence, a man of bravery, a man of sacrifice, a man who did not set his heart on riches. Only he would be the one worthy to find this treasure and use it for the interests of the church—as he said, a man of God. This whole treasure hunt is to test his worthiness. It's all in my uncle's notes."

I didn't know what that all meant, but it felt like we were close to figuring this out—even if we were definitely not chosen vessels.

"We just need to figure out how this artifact works." Hunter took it back again. "I think my uncle might've figured it out, but he died

222

before he could tell anyone."

Or he wasn't found worthy and he failed the priest's test. I didn't say that aloud. There were times I feared finding this treasure more than failing. My father had died looking for it too; so had Eden. She probably wouldn't have gotten close to finding it if it hadn't been for that trapper she'd befriended. "Adam figured it out, too," I said without thinking. At his curious look, I explained, "It's all in Eden's Journal. Unfortunately, she didn't say how Mr. Black did it, only that he took the shiny stick and made it happen. You can read it."

Hunter pulled it over to him and read through the whole entry, then he turned the page and read the next and the next, then glanced up, his eyes going to my camera. "You're still filming?" he asked. "Turn that off—you don't want to blast all this to the world."

He was right. This would be stuff that would end up in the documentary *after* we found what we were looking for. Still, in lieu of arguing about my intentions, I turned the camera to the view instead, then turned it off to make myself comfortable on the rocks, staring off into the horizon in the distance with its rolling clouds tinged with blue. It reflected perfectly off Moonlight Lake below, along with the fringe of trees, making an upside-down world in the water. On the other side of us, Sinkhole Lake was held back from us in a natural dam made of rocks and boulders. And then I found myself watching Hunter, his brow furrowed, his hazel eyes focused on the words in Eden's journal, the sensitivity of his strong hands as he turned the pages. I wondered if this was how Eden had felt with Lucius. She'd been drawn to his dark looks with his French Canadian origins, but he'd been so completely wrong for her.

Hunter glanced up from the journal and met my eyes with an expression that put me to mind of a wild man. "Ivy, there should be more symbols here."

"More? Why do you say that?"

"Adam discovered seven." He handed me the journal and pointed to the entry:

Eden's Journal: July 6th, 1855 – Mountains of the Deseret

Mr. Black's uncommon smart—but for a man who reads the Bible so much, he sure knows more than is decent about that shiny stick. I don't like it none, especially after feeling the wickedness of certain places up hereabouts. Lucius told me to listen to no one but his self, but sometimes Mr. Black can be real entertaining. He says there is a pattern in the Bible, even the numbers mean things, like one is the alpha and that there's the firstborn; two is the pairing of man and woman with Adam and Eve in the Garden—Oh! How I wish Lucius would listen to that one! Three is the godhead; and seven is completeness and perfection—because that's how long it took God to piece together the world. He said that the Spanish Priest talks in numbers and codes, like his voice talks at us from the dust, and that the symbols is also complete and perfect. Such talk is wicked, but Lucius told me not to bother Mr. Black none. He's gonna find us that treasure, and then what should Mr. Black do? He found all of them symbols one after another and now he just gits to figure out what they means.

"Why seven?" I asked.

"Seven means completeness and perfection, and Adam said that's what the symbols are, so I'm going by Mr. Black. And if we found one, then the others should be nearby."

It was a stretch, but what did we have to lose? Brek and I had already searched the area, but when we hadn't found anything last time, we had assumed that the symbol was a standalone. There had been so many rocks caused from centuries of rockslides that finding anything else seemed futile, but spurred on by Hunter's confidence, I explored the area around us for more. He was already shaking his head at me. "No, we have to search above us. Mr. Black never would've found it on the ground 350 years after the priest hid it up."

"Maybe he convinced his Shoshone friends to start digging," I said.

"Look at the date between the time he found the shiny stick and the day he found the symbols," Hunter said. "Three days isn't long enough to unearth this mountain. No, it's above us, uncovered."

I stood up on my tiptoes and stared up at the glacial boulders holding in the lake like a natural dam. The rock was smooth and polished. Lacking anything better to do, I filmed the side of it while Hunter pulled out his gear. If the symbols were indeed on the side of this mountain, they would be almost impossible to find. The bottom half was covered in moss and shrubbery, and the top half looked eroded from years of wind and other weather-related problems.

Hunter took out two black pieces of plastic equipment from his bag. One looked like a fancy flashlight, and the other was a remote of sorts. He handed me the flashlight-looking one, and I realized it was an external flash unit for cameras.

"What is that camera, a Canon?" he asked.

"Yes."

"Do you mind?" He reached for my camera, and, confused, I handed it to him. He took it with the ease of a professional and slid the piece of equipment onto it before adjusting the settings. "We've been doing off-flash photography on these rocks to try to uncover engravings. It's what people do to uncover writing on tombstones—this is just on a bigger scale. The etchings used to be easy to read, but they aren't anymore. If you can stand near the rock wall and just hold out the flash box, I'll take care of the rest."

I was dumbfounded. "Have you found any more of these symbols around here?"

"Not at all," he said. "We haven't gotten any leads like these." He stood at an angle and started popping off pictures. "Hold the light a little closer to the wall there." I did. "Good, now just bring it down the wall. I felt like I was with Brek; the role of assistant came easily to me. Each time Hunter finished a shot, he'd look at the picture and shake his head, until he stopped with a grin. "Ivy, we found one."

I almost dropped the flash box in my eagerness to get to him.

Looking over his shoulder, I saw what time had eroded over the years. It was a petroglyph. Of what? I wasn't sure. He stared at it. It looked like horns over a circle stacked on top of a cross. "It's Wednesday," he said. "This symbol represents Mercury."

"So we have the days of the week?" I asked. "I thought that the priest would only deal with religious symbols?"

"The Romans invented these symbols for the days of the week— but Christians adopted them. This is where the Roman Catholic Church came from. Emperor Constantine established the Roman calendar that we use today."

"So then there should be seven symbols here that represent each day of the week," I said.

"Yes." He found the spot where the picture had been taken. The actual petroglyph was faded and stood out like pocked marks against the rock—nothing like what the flash photography had brought out. It was truly a modern-day miracle of technology. Hunter wrote Wednesday over it with chalk so we'd know where it was.

I went back to my position, and we took more off-flash photography until Hunter shouted out that we'd found two more. This time, he came to me to mark the spots off as Tuesday and Monday. They were more or less in the correct order, though not spaced evenly or on the same plane, which was odd.

We worked on this all afternoon until we finally found Sunday, which had been the most difficult one of all—I was sure it was no accident. It was a circle with a dot in the middle that represented the sun. Hunter marked off the last one and let out a heavy breath. By now we were giddy at the find. Brek would be mad with jealousy. This was the kind of thing that he lived for. Hunter had more than earned his name. He retreated to his pack and took out a map and began making all sorts of annotations and notes, still wearing my camera around his neck.

I picked up the walkie talkie near his bag to report to my brother. "Brek, we found the symbols!"

He answered back almost immediately. "The old ones?"

"New ones! Seven of them. Hunter figured out that there would be seven from Eden's journal."

"He did, did he?" I couldn't decide if he was happy or not, but I knew this would be bittersweet for him. He finally got back to me, "Well done. Are you headed back soon?"

I glanced over at Hunter and he shook his head. He lowered his notes to his side to gather the walkie talkie from me. "Your sister and I still need to celebrate," he said. "I just haven't found a secluded romantic getaway yet."

I stole the walkie talkie back. "I thought you had something serious to say!" I lectured. Pushing down the button, I tried to reassure my brother. "Don't listen to him—he's just really giddy."

"I don't blame him." Brekker sounded resigned, and I felt terrible that we'd discovered it without him. "So, what's your plan?" he asked.

Hunter held his hand out for the walkie talkie again, and I shook my head. "Just tell me!" I said.

"My uncle's notes mention a geyser—we've been looking for it; even if it is dried out, it's a landmark. And it's probably somewhere around here. I've got a few ideas. We'll take the ATV."

The geyser. Brekker and I had long since given up on that. I held the walkie talkie to my lips. "We're going to look for the geyser, Brek."

My brother's answer was almost immediate. "Don't get sprayed by another skunk."

I grimaced. "I think Hunter will do everything to avoid that—he has to ride back with me."

Brekker didn't like to be reminded of me riding with Hunter and so didn't remark on it. "Let me know when you're headed back," he said.

Hunter slid the walkie talkie from my grip, his hand brushing over my charm bracelet, making the little miniatures clash together. "I will let you know her every move," he assured my brother.

Giving him a warning look, I stood up and gathered my pack. He was making things worse, and he knew it. I couldn't figure out his game. Seeing my camera still hung around his neck, I reached for it, and his eyebrows lifted like he'd complain. "I'll give you copies of these pics," I promised and lifted it carefully away from him. His eyes were steady on mine as I rested my arm against his and flipped through the pictures. That's when I noticed that everything before that was gone— all his talk of the Spanish Priest, and whatever I had said about Eden. "Hey!" I complained. I was seriously ticked. "Where's all the footage I took this morning?"

"Oh, is that gone?" he asked too innocently.

I was immediately suspicious and pulled from him. "You erased it!"

"C'mon," he said and shrugged, "you can't release this stuff. So far Caitlyn took out anything relevant, but you never know..."

Of course we wouldn't put in anything that would ruin our chances at getting this treasure first, but how did he know what was in the webisodes? "Wait, have you watched the show?"

"Well, yeah... just to see if you found anything." And we hadn't. "So far, it's a big fluff piece. Nothing we could go on. It's why we had to actually join sides in the first place. But, I have to say, the two of us make really cute frenemies on the show."

I flushed. What was Caitlyn actually putting in the webisodes? I could guess. And it would only get worse with the tent episode from yesterday. "You can never borrow my camera again."

"Don't be mad."

"You could've asked," I said. "We're not stupid."

"I told you to get it out of my face."

So now we were back to that again. I flipped on the camera; I had to make up for lost time. "Hunter is apologizing for deleting all my footage from this morning. Right, Hunter?" He looked stubborn and he picked up the walkie talkie. "What are you doing?" I asked in some panic.

"Hey Brekker, Ivy's taking useless footage and wasting valuable time. Just thought you wanted the latest update."

I rushed to get the walkie talkie from him and slipped on the mud and squealed as I fought to stay upright. Hunter lurched forward to steady me. As soon as I got my footing, I knocked him away. Hunter got right back on the walkie talkie. "Oh, Ivy slipped in the mud. Should I do mouth to mouth?"

That forced a laugh out of me. "Give me that." I tried to twist the walkie talkie from his grip, but he refused to give it back.

"Now Ivy is abusing me," Hunter dutifully reported. "I think Ivy wants to give you a message, but I won't give her the walkie talkie."

"Ivy," Brekker said through the speaker—I could almost hear him rolling his eyes, "don't encourage him. Back off."

"Me!" I shouted. "It's not me. It's all him!" I wasn't sure if he got that message or not.

It wasn't too long before Caitlyn took over the receiver. "Tell Hunter he can't escape my camera. I got some good footage of him this morning chasing after you on his ATV. You looked terrified, Hunter. Were you afraid Ivy was going to run away from you?"

Hunter stilled, and I realized that this was the way to get him. "Anyway," she said, "you'll have to sneak back tonight to get rid of me. I'll be hiding in the trees with my camera. I'm your worst nightmare."

I stepped back with a satisfied look and crossed my arms at his disgruntled expression.

"Don't get into too much trouble, you crazy kids." She giggled. "Brek can't get to you right now. He's too proud to speak, I think. We're just going to relax inside our cabin where there isn't a bunch of bugs and dirt and stuff." She signed off, leaving us to ourselves.

Rolling my eyes, I went back to my camera and realized that I had left it on, which was probably fitting for the way our documentary was going.

"All right," he said suddenly. "I'm sorry for deleting your footage without asking."

That was unexpected. I lifted the camera and trained it on him.

"See, that wasn't so bad."

"Now can I see your camera?" He held his hand out.

I quickly turned it off and put it away. "Not a chance." Swinging on my backpack, I headed back for our ATV and kept my distance from Hunter. He was incorrigible; I was mad and pleased and mad and pleased with him all the time. It was a recipe for disaster. But we made the perfect team—I wouldn't be surprised if we not only found the Spanish symbols, but the geyser too—all in one day of being together.

Chapter fourteen

*W*ordlessly, I packed my things back onto the ATV, knowing we'd have to get close again to drive to wherever Hunter wanted to search for that geyser. Cringing that he had watched Caitlyn's webisode, I wondered if he was annoyed with our little romance in it or had just used it to his advantage.

"You driving?" he asked me.

That was a "no." I climbed onto the back and gestured for him to do the honors, since being in charge of our lives gave me the heebie-jeebies. I strapped on my helmet while he took the driver's seat, and I wrapped my arms around his midsection. The muscles tightened on his stomach when he leaned over to pull the lawnmower string, making the engine roar to life. My grip tightened convulsively over him, and I saw his amusement play on his cheek when he recognized my fear. At least I was comforted by the fact that he knew what he was doing, and I rested my forehead between his shoulder blades as he expertly guided us up the summit above Sinkhole Lake.

The trails twisted into a blur of switchbacks until it opened into a clearing and we were able to break free onto a trail that looped over a meadow where there were no scary cliffs on either side. It was still not the tallest part of the mountain, but we were high enough. The green grass swung from side to side in a soft breeze as we headed for the saddle in the distance.

As we neared the lookout, Hunter slowed and turned off the engine. I lifted my head to see the valley below us was blanketed in pines. I wasn't sure if Hunter had taken us up here to get a bird's eye view before we really dug in to find this geyser, but it was gorgeous.

The rocky land made a terrace from one lake to the next. Sinkhole Lake was a perfect oval, while below that, Moonlight Lake was an uneven crescent dripping with tributaries and lagoons. From this distance, the cliffs between them looked like a stairway where one could step from one to the other. It was like a painting. I dug out my camera.

"Wait," he said. "Take a moment and enjoy it through your own eyes."

I laughed. He had the soul of an artist, and for once I decided to listen and put my camera away. Neither of us spoke as we stared over the summit. I let the view below consume my thoughts, though it left one thing untouched: my thoughts of this man in front of me. He was still a mystery. One minute open and trustworthy, the next closed off and irritating. My arms itched to go back around him, to feel the warmth of him next to me, but since we were no longer in motion, I was out of excuses; except one. I hooked my hand over his arm to use him as my leverage to get off the four-wheeler. Immediately, he guided me with his hands on my waist, and he set me easily on the ground. My skin tingled at his touch, and I stepped back to get control over my emotions, noticing that his hands only left me when I moved away.

"Are we searching for the geyser here?" I asked. *Or was this his secluded romantic getaway?* He took out his map from his back pocket and unfolded it from the tiny square he had made of it. "Well, we've combed through a lot of this area. The trees are thicker together down there near Skunk Lake."

"Say what?" I turned so quickly that my hair swung with me.

"Skunk Lake," he repeated nonchalantly, studying the map.

"You wrote that down on your map?" It was one thing teasing me about renaming Moonlight Lake after that unfortunate incident, but making it permanent? Looking over his shoulder, I saw that he had scratched out the real name and that Skunk Lake was printed neatly under it. I crowded next to him to see his map. There was Angel's Fall, and Evil Crazy Squirrel Lake, and Broken Cellphone Trail. "You've renamed everything on your map?" I asked incredulously. I gasped when I saw he'd written Mascara Ivy for Lake Adam. "You brat!"

"But here on Romantic Getaway Saddle, there's also a group of trees we haven't explored yet."

I met his eyes and cracked a smile. I'd make him pay for that one. "We'd better get on it. My brother needs to hear every move you make."

He gave a self-conscious laugh and pulled off his ATV to get his pack, but not before unbuttoning his khaki top and stripping down to his chocolate brown tee shirt. He leaned over to rummage through his gear, giving me a view of his broad shoulders. We were getting back to the excavation business, and I felt a twinge of regret. Retrieving my pack, I followed him into the stretch of wilderness to the side of us. It was a cheery afternoon; the light was bright between thin trees, and the way was easy to navigate.

"In my uncle's notes," Hunter said, "he found a cool-water geyser out here in the thickets of trees on the same mountain where he found the Spanish Symbols. When the geyser was active, it fed from the lake above it in the spring. Lake Adam is just over that summit up there," he pointed. "So if we don't find anything in this wilderness, we'll go to Moonlight Lake next."

Besides facing off with a skunk, my instincts had served me well. "Why is the geyser important?" I asked.

He stuffed his map into his back pocket. "I don't know. These notes were before my uncle disappeared. He didn't even leave coordinates. Most of what he knew disappeared with him."

We were both looking for answers. It occurred to me that maybe when he found them, I'd get mine too. Brek and I could finally figure out what had happened to our father.

We spent the better part of the afternoon combing through the forest in a much more organized way than Caitlyn and I had at Moonlight Lake. Hunter marked off the land that we'd covered. We stopped to eat around three and then went back to work. It was easier with Hunter. In some ways, he was more patient than Brek, who depended on his skill and gut instinct alone.

The light slipping through the trees turned pink, which meant that we hadn't had as much luck at finding the geyser as we'd had with the symbols. I was a little disappointed, since the taste of success was addicting, but we always had tomorrow and the next few days to do this.

Twilight settled over us as we made one last sweep through the forest on our way back. I had begun to think that we were the only ones out here, so I was startled when we stumbled onto someone's campsite. I stopped short when I saw the blackened campfire. To the side there was a stack of logs built into a teepee and a dirty sleeping bag. "Oh, someone's here."

Hunter stared around us. "This campsite has to be a few months old, at least."

That was creepy. Pots, plates and cutlery had been set on rocks that were made into makeshift tables. There was even a hammock. Hunter picked up a metal dog bowl and emptied it of rainwater. There was a jacket to the side covered in a thick layer of dust, like someone had shuffled it off with every intention of coming back and hadn't. Hunter wandered over to the black nylon hammock and shook it free of dust. It was a nice one. This would've been a pretty place to camp. There was a nice view of the valley below. Looking over at him, I wondered what he was thinking. "People get lost up here a lot." It was probably the wrong thing for me to say—it didn't bring up the best of memories.

"They do," he said slowly.

I bit my lip, thinking about how many lives this place had taken, including my father's, and I sighed. "I never met my dad, so it wasn't so bad. My mom was pregnant with Brekker and me..." my voice drifted off. It was actually pretty bad, and I hadn't meant to share that.

No words passed from his lips. He squeezed my arm instead. The comfort he offered was sincere, and strangely, I was touched. I gave him a weak smile in return. We were quite the pair. He dug into his pocket to take out his map, and I felt like we stood on holy ground at this forgotten campsite. The horizon settled into hues of pink and orange with darkening clouds snaking through the misty air. Hunter recorded the coordinates, and we made our way back to the ATV.

I tucked my pack onto the rack while he pulled at the starter cord. It took me a bit to realize that it wasn't turning on. "What's the matter with it?" I asked. He made some inarticulate grunt and went at it again. "Wait?" I asked. "It's not out of gas, is it?"

"No, Bill said he filled it."

The first thing that ran through my mind was that the matchmaking Bill was at it again. Hunter snapped off the seat and some panels while I pulled our supplies from the back. He went into the engine, and I realized it was something more complicated. It was getting darker and colder around us, and I dug out my flashlight so Hunter could see better. He checked the battery and plugged and unplugged a few cords and wedges that looked like Legos, checked the oil until he spanned the whole radius of the ATV and groaned when he got to the fuel tank and opened it. "Um, yeah, gas. We're out."

"But... but..."

"Bill," he said his name like a curse word.

"Maybe the fuel connection leaked."

"It's possible." He didn't sound convinced. Hunter found the walkie talkie and, staring down at the four-wheeler, grimaced before making the call. "Brekker, you there? We ran into a problem."

There was no answer. Brek hadn't turned off the walkie talkie after our little squabble, had he? Hunter tried a few more times and then switched it to another channel to get to his team. "Angel? You've got your ears on?"

Nope, she did not. Maybe she had wormed her way in with Brek? I got nervous. He'd be furious when I didn't get home at the appointed time. And it wasn't like we could leave a message either. My stomach sank. Hunter's hazel eyes were steady on me as he listened for an answer and got none. He lowered the walkie talkie. "Um, so it looks like we're staying out here tonight."

That startled me. "What?"

"It's fine. We can take the abandoned campsite. It might be warmer over there."

I didn't like the thought of spending the night out in some haunted campsite—not after what had happened last time. "Or we could hike back," I suggested.

He gave me a look like I was crazy. "Is it me?" he asked. "You still have your bear spray, don't you? If I get out of hand, feel free to use it on me." When I broke into a smile, he gave me a devilish look. "And I have my pepper spray in case you get out of hand."

I broke into a laugh. Still, the decision seemed a little premature. "We can't get a hold of anybody?"

"It'll be dark soon. We were pushing it already, but I get it. I get it. I know you hate the idea of sleeping out here after last time."

I couldn't defend myself. I was terrified. Plus, I was already exhausted from no sleep the night before last. "I have a tent you can use," he said. "I can take the hammock. I even brought a sleeping bag."

"Two?" I asked.

He shook his head. "But I'll give it to you." He didn't offer to take the old one we'd found on the ground. It was probably filled with all sorts of horrid things.

I couldn't stand the thought of him being outside without a sleeping bag. "I can use my coat," I said.

"Not a chance," he said. "I packed my coat. I'll use that."

Now we were going to be arguing about who lived or died from exposure. "You take the sleeping bag," I said, "and I'll take your coat in the tent." It seemed reasonable.

He pressed my hand with his before he started to gather our things. "We'll figure it out."

I helped haul his gear. He'd brought a whole lot more than I did, almost like he'd been prepared for the worst. I should've been too, but I was new at this. I slid the walkie talkie into the mesh pocket of my backpack and waited for Brek to call in a panic as I followed Hunter back into the woods where we had first found the abandoned campsite. My worst fear was that it was actually infested with one-eyed aliens who looked mysteriously like tall, thin shadows and knew our names. I knew I was being dramatic, but until I found out for sure that Hunter and Angel had been behind our scare the night before last, I wouldn't sleep well. And if it *was* Hunter, how could I trust him?

But we were stuck together. With the help of his GPS tracker, we found the campsite easily. The view that I'd found so beautiful before was now cold and mysterious as the stars began to pop up on the horizon, brighter and more glorious than they'd been even at the cabins. Hunter placed a flashlight on one of the rocks near the blackened fire pit and left to look for kindling. I put on my warmer layers and found a few twigs here and there but didn't wander too far. Hunter came back with a load of branches and began breaking them in half to put in the pit. Before long, he had a raging fire. Finding his coat, he put it on and zipped it up then helped me set up the tent next. It felt so odd that we were doing this.

"Do you think we're too far for the walkie talkies to work?" I asked.

"He said they had a fifty mile radius."

A part of me hoped that it was Brek's fault that he hadn't gotten back to me, that he was out eating somewhere and had forgotten to check up on me, except I couldn't imagine him leaving the cabin in his condition. Hunter threw his sleeping bag inside his tent.

"Hunter! You can't! You'll freeze."

He chucked me under the chin. "This coat has protected me in zero-degree temperatures, and it's hardly that cold right now. I run hot. I'll be fine."

I felt horrible and vowed to be as helpful as I could. He went to the hammock next, and I helped swat it free of all dirt and dust. Brushing out a few pinecones, I gave him a weak smile that I was sure he hardly saw through the darkness. "I'm sure it will be really comfortable."

"Yeah? Let's check it out." His accent seemed especially thick as he settled gingerly into it. The bungee cords to the side strained, but it held, so I figured the hammock couldn't have been abandoned too long in this weather. "It's great," he said and shifted to sit sideways so that his legs touched the ground like he was on a suspended couch. "It's okay, Ivy, it's not the end of the world that we're stuck here together." He patted the spot next to him where I could sit too. "Relax. The view is gorgeous."

I knew it was, but I hesitated, not sure if this was the best idea. Besides the worry that the weathered bungee cord wouldn't hold, I knew that I liked Hunter too much to resist his charm when I was near him. He seemed to read my mind. "If I wanted to make a move on you, I would've by now," he said.

"Who said I didn't want you to make a move on me?" I asked impishly and immediately regretted it. "No wait, I take that back! I take that back!" I hid my laugh with a hand. "This night is already going to be uncomfortable enough without me making awkward jokes. I'm sorry!"

"You're right." He held his hand out to me. "Here, help me out." This I could do, but the moment I put my hand into his, he wrapped his fingers around mine and slowly pulled me in to sit by him. The temptation was too much, and I let him tug me into the hammock, where I slid into his arms. It happened so quickly that I hardly knew what to think.

"Hunter!" I turned a teasing smile on him, and my nose almost ran into his so that I had to move over, giving him a face full of my hair instead. He pretended to choke on it, and I shifted around until I got more comfortable. The hammock felt like a bench swing and was surprisingly comfortable, especially after hiking all day. I tried not to think about what would happen if it snapped open beneath us, and I anchored my feet on the ground next to his to guard against falling. His arm was behind my neck, and, feeling the hammock sway but not give,

I relaxed against him. He was warm, like he always was. Yeah—maybe he would be all right without the sleeping bag. I snuggled closer to him to try to steal his heat while I could.

The fire crackled to the side, and the view of glittering stars on the horizon made this really nice. I'd never been out in the woods alone with a man before—well, two days ago didn't count since I'd been scared out of my mind. If I hadn't been so worried about Brekker or that Hunter had been behind Brek's sprained ankle, I'd be having the time of my life right now.

"Hunter," I said. I had to know the truth. "Who called Brek into the woods?"

He stilled with surprise at my chosen topic, and he rested his chin against the top of my head as if giving himself time to think of an answer. How hard could it be? I started to doubt that he'd have a good explanation for me. "Just tell me it wasn't you," I said.

"What?" He pulled away. "You think that was me?"

"Tell me it wasn't and I'll believe you."

"It wasn't."

"Then who?"

The line between his brows furrowed. "It could've been anything; maybe even you—you called him, didn't you?"

I gave him a disbelieving look. That seemed a stretch. "He knows my voice."

His eyes probed mine, and he rubbed my arms. "The night can mess with your mind."

It really could, especially right now. I wanted to believe him. He'd said he was here on a personal mission, just like me. He was trying to find the truth behind the disappearance of his family members—maybe even a father. Maybe the only thing wrong with him was that he hung out with the wrong crowd. I found myself wanting to know everything about him. "You said your grandfather raised you? Did your father leave on that expedition with your uncle?"

His lips tightened. "I think my dad was trying to prove himself to

239

my grandfather. Gordon—that's my grandfather's name—he funded their expedition. He's one of those scary elitists who collects useless artifacts. He lived through his boys' successes. Gordon... he always goes on about my Uncle Charlie; he was the smart one in the family—a linguist, archaeologist, geologist. I don't think my grandfather cared too much for my dad, you know? I think that's how my father got pushed into it. He didn't have the smarts, but he was the fearless one. In the end, he got blamed for everything."

The story of the missing brothers was more tragic than I'd thought—a son trying to measure up to the expectations of a disapproving father and dying in the attempt? "Oh Hunter, how did you deal with it?" I asked.

"I was just a kid—only two when it all went down—but when my mother left me with my grandf... with Gordon, he tried to raise me to be everything my dad wasn't. He'd lost his favorite son, so I think he was trying to make me into *him*."

I imagined Hunter as a small boy, haunted by memories and never able to move past his grandfather's loss. Hunter was a man now, but I could see the child he'd been from the pain on his face as he tried to tell his story as indifferently as he could. "It wasn't so bad," he said, and I felt his shoulder lift behind me. "I learned multiple languages and studied lost civilizations. Gordon took me on expeditions as a kid— treasure hunting was in the blood and I took to it—but I was always too much like my dad for Gordon's comfort—no matter how much he tried to get it out of me. He'd go on about how worthless my dad was for not being smart enough to save Charlie, and what a coward. I guess I always believed him... that my dad was somehow at fault and that I was just like him, but... well, I found out a few things that told me differently. Anyway, you don't want to hear how messed up my family life is."

"I don't exactly have the perfect family either," I said, wincing. No way would I bring up what mine had done. "Do you still keep in contact with your grandfather?"

"From time to time." His answer seemed guarded, and I became suspicious that Gordon was funding his expedition here. Had he put his grandson in charge of finishing the job that his sons couldn't do? It might explain Angel and all this riffraff with him. If Hunter was raised to do this very thing, it might also explain why he was willing to do anything to get this treasure, even trick us. "Ivy?" he seemed to sense my unease and turned to me. "I'm trying to vindicate my dad. Gordon blamed him for what went down, and I want to know what happened here—I wouldn't—I wouldn't hurt you or your brother."

Staring into his eyes and watching how the firelight played with its hazel depths, I sensed the sincerity of his words. We were tied together in so many ways—with our loss, our shared experiences, our family histories. It was as if our meeting was meant to be. The guilt ate at me that my whole reason for working with him had been a farce. He'd just had a few bad hands dealt him in his life—that was all. I wanted to believe it as much as I wanted him to be the man who had rescued me from the Jeep on that first day we had met.

He reached out and pushed my hair from my eyes, maybe to see me better, maybe to lean over and kiss me. I wasn't sure how much of that he'd planned when he'd brought me to sit with him, but I felt his mouth up against mine, his lips as soft as I'd imagined they would be, his cheeks as rough. I smiled against his kiss and pulled back to look at him, the sparkle of his eyes running heat through my veins. "Wait," I said. "You said you weren't going to make a move on me."

"I changed my mind," he drawled in that thick accent. He kissed me again and I melted. I'd changed my mind too. The hammock swayed beneath us as he caught me between his strong arms and pulled me closer. I ran my hands through his thick hair, loving the feel of it. This didn't feel like a mistake. This was so different from anything that I had felt with the guys I had dated before. I didn't have to work overtime to get his attention; he was drawn to me like I was to him, and we fit. But what if I was getting caught up with another player and tomorrow he no longer wanted me? I opened my eyes to take a longer look at him—as much as I could in the firelight. He stilled, like he was caught up in my beauty. No one had ever looked at me like that before, and my heart went wild for it. I reached for him again, and he obligingly caught me to him. That's when the walkie talkie went off somewhere next to me.

"Ivy? Ivy? Do you hear me?"

Oh! It was my brother! I disentangled myself from Hunter's arms to find the receiver somewhere near my coat pocket. Hunter tried to take it from me, and- I pushed him back with my elbow, knowing he'd try something mischievous. "Brekker!" I said into it. "I am so sorry! I tried to get a hold of you earlier."

"Where are you? Why aren't you home yet?"

Hunter played with my hair, and it was hard to concentrate. "The ATV ran out of gas," I said, trying to sound natural. "I guess Bill forgot to fill it."

"I don't believe that for a second—if you're smart, you wouldn't either. You're staying up there in the woods with *him*?"

"It's okay. We found an abandoned campsite so it's more comfortable. I'm taking a tent. Hunter has a hammock. I have a sleeping bag. I'll be warm."

"That isn't what I'm worried about."

Hunter slipped the walkie talkie from my hand before I realized what was up. "Brek," he said into it, "your sister is fine. I'll bring her back to you in one piece."

"You haven't kissed her, have you?"

I made a sound of protest, and Hunter smirked a little before he pressed down the receiver. "I might've, but not much."

He wasn't supposed to admit that. I tried to wrestle the walkie talkie from him, but it went the way it normally went when I tried that, and I only got more wrapped up in his arms. It must've been too much for Brek because Caitlyn took over again. "I hope you got some good footage for me, Ivy."

I giggled nervously, and Hunter obligingly held down the receiver for me. "Actually, it's been pretty bad," I said, "but I've been thinking that we should change the theme of this documentary anyway. We could make this more of an intellectual piece."

"No," Hunter whispered into my ear. "Those aren't any fun."

"I heard that," Caitlyn sang, "and I completely agree. I'm holding you both to that."

"See what you did?" I said to him. He might not care tonight, but he would tomorrow—he was the one who wanted the camera out of his face. "You might change your mind when you see my footage tomorrow," I told Caitlyn.

"Ivy!" Brek had gotten the walkie talkie back from her. "Don't be stupid, okay? Go to bed."

Great pep talk. Hunter dropped the walkie talkie on the hammock behind me and pulled me in for another long kiss, the whiskers on his cheek rubbing against mine to remind me of what a man he was, until I pulled away with a shy smile. "I'd better do what my brother said."

He studied my face and took my wrist and helped me find my feet, pushing himself out of the hammock with me too. He was really walking me to my tent, just like the Knight Gallant he had been from the beginning; he even unzipped it for me and made sure I had my flashlight and my bag. "Take all the food out of it," he said. "You don't want the bears after you—I don't like the competition."

Man, he was cheesy and cute. I was loving it. "No worries," I said. "I've got nothing."

His hand trailed to mine and he traced his finger over my wrist. "Do you need anything? Water? Chargers? More light?" Now he was just stalling.

"No, just this." And I stood on my tiptoes and kissed him demurely on the cheek. He grinned and caught me by the waist to give me a slightly more thorough kiss before letting me go. I backed toward my tent and ducked into it to get inside, and he zipped it up behind me. My heart was on fire, and I lay on the sleeping bag, my thoughts a giddy mess. I had kissed him! Well, he had kissed me. I replayed everything in my mind and tried to find something off, but I couldn't, and my mouth split into a wide smile. Brek was wrong about him. He was being honest with me—I knew who to blame for all the trouble, and it was Angel. I closed my eyes and I saw Hunter. I opened them and I saw Hunter—his teasing looks, his forehead creased in concentration, the way his eyes sparkled when he looked at me. My cheeks burned where he'd rubbed his bristly cheek. I'd have to get him to shave. Giggling, I was too wired to sleep, and so I did the next best thing and pulled out Eden's journal and turned it to my favorite part.

Eden's Journal: July 8th, 1855 – Mountains of the Deseret

By and by, Mr. Black asked if he could see my journaling, and I showed him a page, to which he said it was a fine bit of writing and how he wished he'd had his books from home to pile on me because he knowed I'd enjoy them as much as he does—books like Moby Dick and Pride and Prejudice. He told me the tales in them when we set around the fire at night. Poor Lucius don't believe a word of it, and stalked around all stiff and grumbling, like we had insulted his honor when we told him they was only make believe stories.

Mr. Black told me I should call him Adam, and so I've begun to do so though I reckon it hurts Lucius' feelings some, but I can't help it none. The more I talk with Adam, the more my eyes open to the beauty in these parts. For a man who deals a lot with that shiny stick, he talks plenty of God and all his creations on this mountain. He tells me to appreciate every color, every sound, every experience, the rain on my face and the sun, and the trees whispering in the wind (though I can do without all that whispering!).

Adam don't make me feel lonesome when I'm with him. Even when he ain't around, I reckon he's made it a habit with me to git me more comfortable in my own skin. I walk through these mountains and feel God with me, and everything feels so fateful, like my ancestors are with me, and the generations of children to come after me walk along with me too. What a blessing this world is—that we can feel sorrow and joy and love, even if it

244

ain't returned.

And I gots a secret boiling up inside me that I can't tell a soul—especially Lucius—because the more I'm out in this wild, the treasure don't seem all that fantastic a find no more. It pales to all this around me. I've been blinded by the flash of gold. What was it inside me that made me hanker for it? And after I git some of that gold, what then? It won't fill that gaping hole in my heart. Why'd I deceive myself with this rot? I wanted the world; I yearned to be something to them nameless, faceless people out there—they don't care what I do. They can't have a part of my life. They can't have me. Not no more—not for a flake of it for an evening, not bags of it for my soul. It's only those who count I reckon I'll hold close. Part of me fears that this beautiful town outside these mountains and these friendly folks might change if we find this gold, like maybe it'll turn into that dirty mining city we runned off from. I don't want to bring nothing about that boom town here with me. This gits me to thinking that maybe gold ain't gonna buy me freedom, that maybe I'm free already.

The more I listen to Adam, the more I believe such miracles. I knowed it's maybe wrong, but Adam's got a way of looking at me that makes me feel like I'm something, and I've never been something before to anyone that counts. It's not how Lucius looks at me all—rough and angry and hungry—but more of a soft gentle way, like Adam wants to hold me in his arms and protect me from everything bad. It's like he don't see me grimed in dirt and filthy, but like I'm something better. Such a look from a man like that is worth more than a hundred futures with a man who's lesser. And I want to hold that with me and keep it with me forever.

I weres thinking these thoughts when I went trekking through the wilderness with Adam and we stumbled over that spot where the water bubbled up from the ground. I couldn't fathom how it would return to what it once was, though Adam talked of strange places where the land was awash in heat and steam and covered in geysers where water shot up to the sky in great fountains. Some—like the Steamboat, he said—were so big that they drained the lake near it. He judged them geysers fed from the water in the ground, and he said I should take a look at it myself. I told him I'd rather stay here with him, and he looked at me tender and asked me what I meant. I felt shy and would've talked more, but a skunk come up real sudden like and scared us good so that we cleared out, laughing and shouting back to the others. He took my hand and said it was the softest he ever did hold. I didn't mind the feel of his neither—though in no way was his soft. But then we seen Lucius and we both pulled back. Lucius looked at us darkly and we explained we runned on account of a skunk. None of us liked them varmints, least of all Lucius. They hanged out by the swamps and made things real nasty. Lucius staid mighty huffy and wouldn't talk none on the way back.

I stopped there and reread that last paragraph. The geyser *was* near a swampy area full of skunks? I remembered splashing through that meadow before I'd gotten sprayed. The geyser was at Moonlight Lake! It had to be. I was sure I could find that spot again. I briefly thought of running to tell Hunter about my hunch, but it could wait until morning, and I turned off my light and nestled deeper in the sleeping bag, determined to get more sleep.

That night, my thoughts didn't revolve around hunting treasure, they lingered on Hunter and his kisses—how he'd given me the tent and the sleeping bag, walked me to the tent and taken care of me. He was definitely not a Lucius; he was an Adam. Reflecting back on my usual taste in men, it disturbed me how many guys had been like Lucius. But Hunter was different. The secret was in how he looked at me—like he would protect me, he appreciated me, and he couldn't wait to hear what would come from my mouth next; not like I was a nuisance at all. Eden should've stuck with Adam.

Chapter fifteen

I woke up to the smell of a campfire and peeled my face from the sleeping bag. The air was still crisp, and I put on my coat before going outside. The morning light was blue and hazy against the trees, but that could just be the fire. Hunter leaned over the pit. Being truly hot blooded, he had discarded his coat, having procured a long-sleeved, red flannel shirt and a clean pair of jeans. He had found some packs of oatmeal in his bag and was in the process of boiling them up. As soon as I emerged from my tent, he smiled, his eyes crinkling up at the sides. "Hello beautiful!"

I blushed and his smile got wider. Immediately my hand went to my hair, since he had that look he got when there was mascara running down my face. "What's going on with my hair?" I asked.

"It's huge. I love it." He pulled up from the campfire and tentatively reached for it and ran his fingers through it, patting it down and then rubbing the mascara off my face while he was at it. That got rid of my fear that he would lose interest in me the next day. Soon I was laughing and swatting him away, but he caught my wrist and pulled me in, kissing me on the cheek. "We're still doing that, right?" He murmured the question against my ear.

I hid my face in his chest with an embarrassed chuckle. "You're gonna let me brush my teeth first?"

"Well, I wasn't going to say anything." He went to his bag and threw me a sample tube of toothpaste. This guy had everything—he made me look like a minimalist.

I dipped my finger in it and scrubbed away, laughing when he tried to get me to talk through it, but finally I couldn't keep quiet any longer. "I've been reading Eden's journal and I've got an idea." That got his attention. I explained about the skunks and the references to swamps and standing water, and how I'd splashed through some down at Moonlight Lake. "Do you think the geyser could be where I got sprayed by that skunk?" I asked.

"We could try," he said and handed me his bottled water. I assumed he was offering to let me rinse out my mouth with it and I squirted the water against my tongue and swished it around. As soon as I spit out the rest of the toothpaste, I wiped my lips and went back to my theory. "I mean, how crazy would it be if it was down there all along. That skunk was guarding it…"

He didn't let me finish and pulled me in for another kiss. The tips of his fingers explored the skin at the back of my neck, though the feel of his arms around me felt familiar now, like we fit together like two pieces in a puzzle. He ended the kiss with a whisper against my mouth. "That was minty fresh." He pulled back to peer into my eyes. "I'm sorry, but since the moment I woke up, I could only think about kissing you," he admitted before releasing me, but not without laying claim to my hand first. "What were you saying?"

I couldn't remember. He led me over to the fire pit, where we sat down and he handed me the oatmeal in a tin cup. I smiled at it—this was adorable. "No spoons. Sorry," he said.

Dipping my finger in that too, I tried it. "This is excellent," I said. "It almost tastes like real oatmeal."

"Is that so?" he asked with a teasing lilt to his voice.

I nodded and proceeded to devour it while he left to pack everything up, and I almost felt sorry to go. Despite my suspicions that it was a haunted campsite, my experience here had been nothing like the scare I'd had with Brek.

"I'll call Angel to bring the team to pick up the ATV," he said. At the mention of Angel, I froze as real life intruded into my thoughts. This wasn't his way to introduce the rest of his rough team back into our lives, was it? Kissing me didn't mean he could go back on our deal. Seeming to sense my unease, he glanced over at me. "Until then, let's hike down to Moonlight Lake."

He had been listening to that, at least. I weaved my unruly hair into a fishtail braid while he got a hold of Angel and explained the situation. She had been a whole lot easier to get ahold of this morning. I wondered what had happened while we were gone. Getting rid of my layers so I was back in shorts and a white t-shirt, I found my socks in my pack and put them on. They were incredibly long, making me feel like a girl scout. Meanwhile, Hunter took every opportunity to touch me whenever I passed him to pack things up. It became a game so that I returned it with gusto until we were finally laughing and knocking each other on the elbow and messing up each other's hair.

Finally, Hunter put away the walkie talkie and we stared at the hammock that was left behind. "I think it belongs here," I said in a hyper-solemn voice.

"Indeed," he said. "It will serve as a resting spot for all couples." He was calling us a couple already. That was so different than any guy I had dated. I looked over at him and saw him squinting with laughter. "That is okay, right? I can call us a couple?"

"Oh boy," I moaned. "My brother is not going to be happy."

"I could care less," he said flippantly. "I'm happy about it, are you?"

"Yes," I admitted.

He began to stack his bags over his shoulder. I helped him, swinging a few over my arms so that we were both loaded down. We headed through the woods and came to the meadow where the ATV was parked and began to tie it all down, excluding the supplies we'd take with us to Moonlight Lake. Hunter gave the four-wheeler another once-over. He checked out the fuel line and touched it cautiously. "There's a rip," he said. "We can't blame Bill entirely. We might even thank him."

"We didn't need him to get us together," I said, chuckling at the idea. "We were almost there."

He gave me an incredulous look. "Really?"

"Well, I was." I adjusted my pack on my back.

"You little minx," he said.

I was too giddy to care what he said and let the teasing roll off my back. Soon enough, Hunter went back to his walkie talkie and gave Angel the coordinates to the ATV. "Bring a new fuel line with that gas," he said. "Mel can fix it. Bring him too, and a third person to drive it down to us at Skunk Lake." That earned a glare from me, and he pressed on while biting down a snicker. "We're checking out a lead."

Angel handled the orders with clipped professionalism, and I wondered about her relationship with Hunter. It was much different than the one she'd had with Brek when I had known her. She had been gooey and impossible to deal with back then. Without realizing it, I made a face at the memory. He put away the walkie talkie with a laugh. "Don't worry. I'm not asking Angel to join the party."

"You better not." I turned away with a little more sass than I'd intended, and he gamely caught up to me with a smart-aleck remark about wanting to see that catfight.

We made our way down the trail we had come up, and it was a lot longer than I had bargained for. Maybe it would've been faster to wait for Angel, but I wanted some time alone with Hunter; plus, it felt good to stretch out my legs after sleeping on the hard ground last night. We spent the trip trying to figure out how Hunter's artifact had anything to do with the Spanish symbols on the walls that held up Sinkhole Lake.

"Where did you find that, anyway?" I asked.

"My mother had it for a long time. She got it from my Uncle Charlie. I'd had no idea. I hadn't seen her for years." He turned serious at the turn of the conversation, and instead of hiding his pain with a mocking remark like I'd noticed he did, he revealed everything. "She had this whole other family—just kind of started over like my dad and I were just an unfortunate smudge on her life. At least that's what it felt like. I'm not going to lie; it hurt a lot."

"I'm so sorry."

I touched his arm, and he turned quickly away like he couldn't handle the sympathy. "Um... anyhow, I stopped some people from stealing it from her." He was censoring his story, which made me uneasy. "That's when she told me a few things about my dad. I didn't believe her at first, but then... I found it was true. My grandfather has been lying to me my whole life."

"You stopped people from taking it? Who? How did you know they were after it?"

"I overheard someone talking about it and figured it out before it was too late."

His ambiguity revealed everything I needed to know. "Your grandfather?" I asked.

"On the phone at the dinner table, actually." He shrugged. "Gordon has always been suspicious my mother was up to something, kept tabs on her—not that he'd ever have let me know if he'd found anything good. Like I said, Gordon's *real* family-oriented."

"What did your mother tell you?" I felt like I was prying, but it seemed important for me to know. This whole business with his grandfather felt shady.

"She didn't leave me because she wanted to... she left me because my grandfather blackmailed her. I know, it's a weird story. Things like that don't happen to real people. He hated her for what happened to his sons. At least that's what I thought."

That's what he thought? I didn't have time to ask what he meant, because right then Angel and her team of mechanics came speeding up the way. Hunter and I pulled over to the side and waited for them to meet us. The others passed us, but Angel stopped. Her suspicious eyes went from Hunter to me, and I stood up straighter, trying to seem in no way romantically involved with her boss. Knowing her, she'd try to use it against me. "How was your night?" she asked.

"Cold," Hunter said with a smile.

My eyes slid to him. "You said you weren't! I told you to take the sleeping bag."

"Oh no," Angel interjected. "He'd never take a bag from a lady—

he's got southern manners. Next time, you'll have to share."

That stunned me to silence, until I gathered my wits and tried for a casual tone. "Ha—how many next times do you think there will be?"

"It depends how many times you plan on playing damsel in distress?" she returned.

I stiffened.

"She's a lady," Hunter interrupted as if that ended the argument, "and I was happy to oblige."

Angel's lip protruded at my southern gentleman. "Yes, so I see. That's just perfect." She turned on the motor of her ATV with an expert flick of her wrists and rushed past us after the others to the broken ATV.

I wasn't sure how to broach the subject as I watched her turn into a speck in the distance, "If you wouldn't tell her that we, uh..."

"Kissed?" His lips curved up.

"Yeah, I'd be much *obliged*."

"I think she's already figured it out. Anyhow, we have nothing to hide." I supposed not, but Angel was an angel of vengeance, and I feared what she'd do with any information on me. We headed back on the trail, passing Sinkhole Lake on our way to Moonlight Lake. "What do you call Sinkhole Lake?" I asked with sudden interest.

"Hmm." Hunter pretended to consult his map. "That's what I like to call Where I Almost Kissed Ivy the First Time Lake."

"No!"

He shrugged. "You're the one who said we didn't need Bill's help."

A giggle bubbled from my throat. "I mean... when?"

"Right before I got in trouble for deleting your footage, so that wasn't going to work."

"You're right," I said. "You're still in trouble for that." We passed the time teasing each other as we made our way down the rock slide between the two lakes. Hunter lent his hand to me multiple times to help me down the boulders. Mostly I didn't need it, but I accepted all that southern gentility anyway. When we reached Moonlight Lake, I found the thicket of woods where I had run out with Caitlyn at my heels. Staring into the wilderness, I set my shoulders. "So, I think it goes without saying to watch out for skunks."

He pretended to steady himself for the great task ahead, and I bit my lip, hoping he'd get sprayed by a skunk for that. "Let's do this," he said, and we plunged into the forested area. Despite the jokes, I noticed how seriously Hunter took my input. Brek wouldn't have even checked it out, but if this actually worked, Hunter's patience would benefit us all. I tried to backtrack as much as I could, first finding the cairns of rocks I'd used as my trail of breadcrumbs, but eventually those ran out and everything looked like that meadow where Caitlyn and I had splashed into the water. Hunter entertained himself by pointing out all the different vegetation and how we could survive if we got stranded here indefinitely. I assured him that I'd pick him to be on my team if we were stuck in an apocalypse. Soon, Hunter took to picking up rocks and throwing them. I didn't figure out why until one of them made a splash.

I gasped and grabbed his hand. "You're brilliant!" Stepping gingerly to the spot, we inspected the area. Sure enough, we'd found the marshes. The heavy reeds had hidden them from us. Hunter got to work, taking out his gear. One of his supplies was a telescoping pole that he slid out to make full size. It had a white cup on one end, and he started out by taking samples of the water. He stopped when he noticed the orange-ish sedimentation on the bottom of the cup. The machete came out next, and I felt like we were on a safari as he hacked away at the reeds and revealed a still pool beneath. The rocks under and around it had an orange tint. "Travertine deposits," he said. Next he tasted the water. "And that's the CO_2 in it," he said. "It's like the carbonation in soda. Taste it." I passed on that. He hardly noticed, he was so preoccupied. "Have you heard of the serpent sightings at Moonlight Lake?" he asked.

I nodded. Bill had talked about it.

"That could be bursts of CO_2. Judging by this spot, the ground underneath has a substantial reserve of it." He took his machete and hacked away at the reeds until I noticed the water bubbling at our feet. I shrieked and jumped out of it onto dry ground. Hunter didn't move, just watched it fizz around his ankles. "Ivy," he whispered. "You did it. You found us the geyser."

I could scarcely believe it, but it was wimpy and barely did anything. Just like Eden had described it. After a few minutes, it stopped bubbling and went back to nothing again. "Are you sure?"

He laughed under his breath. "Oh, it's active... but there could be a blockage under there stopping the CO_2 from fully erupting or it just has no underground water to feed it."

I pointed the direction of Moonlight Lake. "There's a whole lake over there. Why doesn't it feed off that water?"

"Well, these tunnels go down hundreds of feet—they might not connect, or if they do, it's at a weird angle... it's complicated." He was already pulling out his notepads and making notes. He checked his watch. "What time did it go off?"

"Um... about 2 minutes ago?"

He immediately went to work measuring its eruption pattern. We spent most of the afternoon doing that. I sat down on the bank, watching him. It was another find that Brek would've killed for, and I toyed with how I'd break it to him before I found the walkie talkie and called him. "Brekker, you won't believe it."

"You're getting married."

"Close. We found the geyser."

He got silent on the other end before saying, "You sure?"

"Positive. It was where I got sprayed by a skunk. Crazy, huh?"

"Well... that's great. That means that the caves have to be at Moonlight Lake," he said. Hunter looked up from his measurements to listen.

"Yeah, but you went diving there," I said. "You didn't find anything."

254

"I'll do it again." He sounded excited. This was his specialty. Also Angel's, but I wouldn't bring that up. "It has to be there," he said. "Eden wrote that it was."

Yeah, but they'd known the geyser was there long before Adam had figured out how to open up the way to the treasure by using the symbols and the shiny stick. He had returned the land to what it once was, whatever that meant. It was all still a riddle.

"Who would've thought?" Brek said.

Hunter sat on the bank next to me. "Skunk Lake holds the treasure," he muttered with a smile. I nudged him with my shoulder.

"I'll start diving," Angel announced over the same channel. I stiffened. She wasn't with Brek—we had just seen her—but of course she had just switched over to the same channel we were on. Brekker went ominously silent on the other end.

Hunter held his hand out for the walkie talkie, and I relinquished it. "That would be perfect," he told her. "Look for false bottoms, not just on the sides, but in the middle of the lake."

"I'll get my diving gear as soon as I bring you the ATV," she said. "By the way, your fuel line was cut. Just thought you should know." She sounded smug when she ended the call.

"Cut?" That was Brekker this time. He was not happy.

It took a moment for Hunter to answer. "I'll look into it. Over." He turned off the walkie talkie and glanced over at me. "You think Bill would go as far as to cut the fuel lines?"

I shook my head. "No way." He might be a matchmaker, but he wasn't crazy. I immediately suspected the most devious person I knew. She'd enjoy reporting it like it was everybody else's fault, too. She was the classic gaslighter. "Angel, I bet."

"What?" He seemed genuinely surprised. "Why do you think she'd do that? What's your deal with her anyhow?"

If he didn't know by now, then he should. She was taking everything from us, even the thrill of the hunt. The way she had cut into Brek's excitement broke my heart. Watching Hunter closely, I

255

decided to test what he knew about Angel. "She stole a find from Brek."

His forehead wrinkled. "That's a serious accusation. Even if it were true… why would he trust her enough to work with her again?"

"That's why I said I'd only work with you. Brek might think you're shady, but… there were these Crown Jewels of Ireland—they were stolen in 1907. He found them, and she sold them, so…."

"I know about those," he said softly. So he did? I tried not to let my disappointment show. He looked thoughtful, tried to speak, shook his head, then finally said what was on his mind. "You don't just let something like that go—it's priceless. Are you sure he's not here to get the crown jewels back from Angel?"

"Wait? You think that he's here for some other reason besides what we're doing now? How long have you thought this?"

"Now. Just now. I didn't know Angel took those jewels until you said something."

"You didn't?" *We had suspected he had.* Hunter shook his head and I believed him, but now I scrambled to make him believe me. "Well, Brek isn't here to steal those back. Going after Eden's treasure is in our blood."

"Then why hasn't he done it before now? Interesting timing, when the artifact shows up."

"Oh no," I held a finger up, "Brek did *not* know anything about that." The accusation gave me pause. Had Hunter been suspicious about that? I tried to reassure him. "My brother told me to throw it in the lake when he first saw that I had it. He had no idea what we had."

"What about the person who hired him? Walker? Who's he?"

I was starting to get uncomfortable, like I shouldn't have brought any of this up. Brek had told me not to trust Hunter, and here I was blabbing out all of our suspicions to him. Now I had to clean up my mess. "He says he's a family friend—Brek's trying to pay back creditors."

He let out a sound of disbelief. "You don't pay back creditors for the Jewels of Ireland."

No matter how much I tried to stop it, I let that sink in. Was Brek's backer these thugs he'd been talking about, and this was all a trick to get to Angel? But no, Brekker had been enraged to find Angel here, so he wasn't here for her. That didn't mean that his mysterious backer didn't know. They could be keeping tabs on us now. "What do you think is going on?" I asked.

"Does it matter?" He sighed and stared at his hands. "If she stole them… we can't trust her again."

"She stole it!" He had better believe me!

"Yeah, maybe." At my angry look, he took my arm. "Okay, she did. Let's just keep to the original plan, just you and me working together… unless you try to double-cross me, too?"

I stilled. It was a nasty accusation, but true before I'd known he wasn't working with Angel. "Brekker thinks he's going to make everything right by finding this treasure," I said. "When he saw Angel here, he thought she was betraying him all over again." At his doubtful look, I explained. "He's my twin. He can't hide anything from me. He believes Angel is out to cheat him, and she probably is, but we thought we could outsmart her." I put my hands up in defense since it was basically admitting that I had been planning on doing the same thing to him. "All I'm trying to do is help my brother—but I don't know how to do that anymore."

His eyes were steady on mine. "Easy. We expose Angel and make her tell us where she sold the jewels—that'll free you from your backer's thumb, since that puts the blame on *her*. Then we can still split our find forty-five, fifty-five, like before."

Now that I wasn't planning on stealing the find from Hunter anymore, I realized that I hadn't negotiated well enough. We were bringing a lot to the table, and Brek might need everything he could to buy those priceless jewels back. I stood and straightened my shoulders. "Fifty-fifty—even split."

He looked surprised, and then his lips twisted in amusement. "I sang for you. Are you going back on our agreement?"

"No, but…"

Before I could state my case, he interrupted me. "On one condition." I tensed. I had forced him to sing, and I couldn't imagine what he'd come up with to get me back for that. He gestured me closer and took hold of my shirt. "Kiss me."

I laughed, but uneasily. He wasn't taking this seriously, and I wondered what he was playing at. "Just like that and we're fifty-fifty?"

"Just like that, yes."

I felt a slow smile spread across my face, and I reached down, my fingers curling through his hair as he sat on the banks before me. "I only kiss someone if I want to."

"Okay." He wrapped his arms around my waist, bringing me even closer. "Then kiss me like you know you want to kiss me and then I'll make it fifty-fifty because we're both decent like that."

I liked that deal much better. I relaxed in his embrace. "And you're wearing a helmet when you're on a four-wheeler."

He jerked in surprise because I had no negotiation power right now, but then, to my astonishment, he agreed. "Deal… as long as we don't tell your brother about this."

"But—but, why?"

He stood up. "Do you want to expose Angel or not? Brek's too close to her. He's been nothing but obvious about what he wants."

"Yeah." I knew my voice lacked conviction, but I was halfway there. I saw the wisdom in what he was saying.

"Promise me," he said. "If you really want to help your brother, you'll do it."

My forehead wrinkled and I nodded. "Okay, yes, you're right."

Trailing his fingers through my hair, he looked deeply into my eyes before we sealed our deal with a kiss. The loud engines from the ATVs sounded on the trail next to Moonlight Lake. A part of me wondered if I was making the right decision. It all rested on trusting Hunter completely, and no one else.

It was late afternoon when we got back to the resort. Brek and Caitlyn had left a message to meet them at the Grizzly café where Bill was feeding them a special dinner before the Raspberry Festival tonight. I'd completely forgotten about that. Brek had complained a little bit about it over the walkie talkies. He was mystified to be invited and didn't want to be bothered, but Caitlyn was all gratitude and graciousness. I wondered if Bill was back to his matchmaking ways, but with my brother this time. I hoped so.

Hunter dropped me off at the cabin first, where I was able to clean up before he came back to take me to the Grizzly. Since the cold was beginning to take over the air again, I came out in a paisley sweater over my red midi dress and knitted stockings that went over my knees. I couldn't get warm. Hunter looked great in a black button-up and his signature worn jeans. When I got onto the back of his four-wheeler, I inhaled that woody floral scent of him, and I might've rested my head against the broadness of his back just to breathe him in.

We came to the Grizzly, and Hunter swiveled sideways to help me down like we were going to the prom. I loved his southern manners. As I stepped to the ground, Caitlyn came out from behind a wooden post on the balcony, holding her camera to her eyes and grinning. "I told you that I'd get you!"

Hunter and I exchanged glances, but before we could say anything, she retreated back inside to get her own man. I'd known that facing Brekker was going to be difficult, but my best friend was not helping things. Hunter licked his lips as he regarded me. "Hey, it's going to be fine. He'll be mad at you at first and then he'll get over it."

Brekker wasn't the kind to get over anything; plus, I had one job, to betray Hunter and I'd failed that, but I smiled weakly and nodded. We came into the main room, and I saw Bill had indeed arranged a little dinner in the café. It was adorable, like a Thanksgiving setup. They had pushed the tables together. The other old men had joined him, with Brekker placed next to Caitlyn. Brekker kept rubbing his forehead. To his credit, he was attempting to act pleasant, but I knew the stress of being out of commission with a sprained ankle, Eden's treasure being found without him, and Angel's interference would hardly put him in a romantic mood.

"Aiden! Ivy!" Bill brightened when he saw us enter the room, and he stood and beckoned us over. "You were gone longer than you said."

"Yeah, the fuel line..." Hunter began, but Bill didn't look interested, just made everyone scoot over so we could sit down. I found myself across from Brekker, who was pinning me with an accusing look.

Caitlyn was trying to get him distracted by anything else. "Bill was telling us about the festival tonight at Dry Gulch—Raspberry days! There will be a dance and live country bands."

Brek looked anything but interested. All he wanted was to talk about what had happened today—I could see it in his eyes.

Hunter's hand went to my lower back to lend his support. It was the wrong move. Brek stiffened. Since no one had replied to Caitlyn, Hunter politely attempted it. "Raspberry Days sounds fun." He turned to me with a warm expression. "Will you save a dance for me?"

He danced, too? I couldn't imagine anything more romantic, but I tried to contain my excitement for Brek's benefit. "I've never done country dancing—you're going to have to teach me some moves."

"Hasn't he already?" Brek murmured into his food.

Bill laughed. Frank and Harlan followed suit. Caitlyn cleared her throat. "Hey! I put together your footage from your night in the woods. It's got a lot of views. There's this commentator, Hybernater—I think I told you about him? He has a lot to say. I think you should read his comments for clues."

Bill seemed interested, or he finally understood that we should change the subject. "Hybernater? What is that, some old bear?"

Caitlyn laughed heartily at the dad joke, which meant she was desperate. "Take a look." She traveled over to the computer desk behind the counter and started to pull up the video.

"Oh!" Bill stood, throwing his napkin down. "Sign me out first."

"You're using YouTube?" Caitlyn asked. "I'm so proud of you!" She looked up at his notifications and saw he was signed in to a bunch of cat videos. No wonder Bill wanted her to sign out of his account. His Dogo Argentino would get jealous... if Skip stirred. He lay motionless on his doggy pillow. Caitlyn tactfully signed out Bill and got into our account. "Look, 5 million views already. We're so going to go viral!"

"What?" I shot up in my seat. "What did you put on there?"

Even Hunter looked nervous. "You're taking out the important stuff, right?"

"Oh, you mean don't give away clues and stuff? Yeah, Brek told us that already."

"Then what's in there?" my voice broke.

"Just sleazy reality TV stuff," Caitlyn said. I tried to remember everything we'd gotten in there—Hunter's fight with Rosco, the scary geocaching episode, me getting stuck in the woods, and Hunter saving me. I hid my face in my hands. Caitlyn snickered. "What? It's making us a lot of money." She pulled up her dashboard to check our stats. "At least $6,000 so far."

Not quite enough to pay for Brek's debts, but it could mine. On the whole, not bad, especially if the treasure hunt ended up being a bust. I was mad and pleased and mad all at once. Hunter snorted. "I'd pay you that amount for you *not* to do that."

"It's only going to compound on the views," Caitlyn said. "We could get hundreds of thousands of dollars. You can't afford us."

Angel strutted into the room, her black hair still wet, slinging her weighted scuba jacket over her shoulder—looking all sexy and capable. It was completely unnecessary, and I knew she was rubbing the fact that she was diving in Brek's face. She peered at the screen. "What's this?"

"The kids got some virals," Bill said as if that explained it.

"We've gone viral," Caitlyn said with a reddened face.

Angel scoffed when she saw the hits. "That's hardly viral."

Caitlyn's fingers curled into fists at the keyboard. "This is just the beginning." Glancing up at me, she said, "but I really need more footage."

My mouth opened and closed like a fish. All I had was me forcing Hunter to apologize for deleting my footage. I wordlessly handed her my camera. Hunter watched the exchange with some misgiving.

"Next episode should be titled Hunter cuts the fuel line to get some alone time with Ivy," Brekker said acidly.

Hunter's attention trained on him. "Is that what you thought happened?" he asked. His eyes veered to Bill, who suddenly concentrated on his food.

"I'm not stupid," Brekker said. "I told you not to mess with my sister."

"Brek," I held out my hand. This was getting ridiculous. "I can take care of myself."

"With your bear spray?" Brek asked with a roll of his eyes.

"She only used that the first few times I kissed her."

Brek pushed away from the table, but he couldn't get far with his ankle, and he grimaced and fell back into his seat. I stood, shaking Hunter's hand away from my back, feeling horrible. "Brekker, are you all right? Let me help you."

"No, I don't want your help. Go enjoy your Raspberry Days."

"Brekker!" Angel dropped her scuba equipment and rushed to his side. "I'll take you back to your cabin."

He refused to dignify that with a response—which at least meant he was angrier with her than with me. Squinting against the pain, Brek looked over to his most sympathetic ear. "Uh, Caitlyn, can you give me a hand?"

It took her a bit to gather her wits. Casting an apologetic look at me, she nodded. "Of course." She pushed my camera back into my hands.

Brek got up slower this time, grimacing. He spared a contrite look at Bill. "I'm sorry. The dinner was fantastic. I just need to get... out of here."

I was still standing as he left. Angel's lip pushed out in a pout, and she turned on her heel and went the other direction. Frank nudged Bill in the side. "That girl's trouble."

"Someone's keeping up on their episodes of *Poison Ivy and Fortune Hunter*," Hunter muttered.

I collapsed back into my chair, staring at my untouched food. What was I doing? I had wanted to patch things up with Brek, and that just kind of exploded. I was doing everything wrong. I stuffed my camera into my purse, barely seeing it. "Hey?" Hunter asked. "You want to get out of here?"

"Yes, yes," Bill supported that idea. The other men agreed, almost desperate to repair things. "Why don't you two go out? There's a country band playing right now by the lake. Go teach the girl how to dance, Aiden."

Hunter watched me while I played with my napkin. It didn't feel right. He pressed his lips together and scooted closer to me. "You want me to apologize to your brother?"

I snorted. "That would only make it worse. He needs some time."

"We can give him that," he said.

"Yes, yes," the old timers fell all over themselves in agreement. "Just give him some space. Let Caitlyn have him for the evening, and you go out and let him cool down."

Their words caught my attention. This was possibly more for Caitlyn's benefit than for ours. Were they rooting for Caitlyn to score some points with my brother? I draped the strap of my purse over my shoulder. Hunter still waited for my answer, and I slapped my hand into his, letting him out of his misery. "Let's do it."

Our sweet matchmakers erupted into cheers and herded us out the door, pointing out the festivities by the lake. Now that we were outside, it was hard to miss. The sound of dancing, loud laughter, and music drifted to us over a soft breeze. The stars were out, though they were not nearly as bright as they had been on the mountains. Had it been a whole day since I had first kissed Hunter? I allowed him to take me to the party near the lake, consumed by memories of sharing the hammock and being held by him. Everything was happening so fast, but looking over at him, I didn't want anything else except to be with him now. My hand tightened on his. He seemed to understand, his hold strengthening on me too.

"I guess we need Bill more than we think," Hunter said in an undertone.

I wasn't sure if I was meant to hear that, but I glanced up at him with a miserable cry. "That didn't go well at all."

"I'll make it up to you," he said. "Next time I see your brother, I'll let him yell at me until he gets it all out and then we'll go hunting together. We'll be as thick as thieves at the end of this."

I smiled. They did things differently in the south. The band was playing a slow country song I didn't know. The singer had a deep, gritty voice that reminded me of Hunter's, though it sounded like velvet to my ears. Hunter guided me closer to the dancing, and he swung me around so that I laughed in response. He held me close, looking into my eyes as we swayed to the music. "Not bad," he said. "You've got this already."

"I doubt it, but I appreciate you saying so anyway." I rested my head on his shoulder, watching the light from the torches on the dance floor spread over the lake. I was falling in love with this place like Eden had. She was right, the treasure was within, not without. I only hoped that my fate was different than hers. Feeling the steady beat of Hunter's heart under my ear, I already felt like I had chosen the right man. "Hey!" I said, pulling back. I found my camera in my purse and snapped a shot of us. He laughed and stole it, slipping it back where it belonged, then kissed my upper lip before saying, "Let's have a moment that only belongs to us."

I laughed up at him. "What?" I teased. "How am I supposed to make everyone jealous of me back home?"

His smile turned grim and he swung me around again. "Who are you trying to make jealous?"

"Oh, maybe an old boyfriend who never treated me right."

He pulled me closer. "You're still not over him?" He whispered the question. The breath of it tickled my ear and made me smile. "You can't care what he thinks of you post-breakup," he said. "Your life is yours now."

Even though I'd been half joking, his words struck a chord in me. He was right—I'd never felt freer. Not having my phone, along with my social media sites, up here in the mountains was the best thing that had ever happened to me. I only needed to get rid of those webisodes, and I'd be left to myself to run wild through these mountains where no one controlled me. My thoughts flew back to Eden, and I felt like I was missing something. It had to do with Adam, and again I wondered what had happened to him after she'd disappeared. My heart broke at the thought.

The music slowed to a stop, and Hunter taught me a few fancy moves where I got wrapped up in his arms. He laughingly gave up and crossed his arms over me and kissed my ear before spinning me out. I was having the time of my life, my skirt swinging around me. My socks over the knee were having less luck, and they kept sliding down my leg so that I had to stop and pull them up. He tried to help me, and I swatted him playfully away and caught his pinky in the process—having nothing better to do with his hand, I set his arm over my shoulder and led him to the side of the dance floor like I was a cavewoman taking my man to task.

He followed willingly. We found some chairs and sat down, talking about everything but looking for treasure. I laughed about my last job, and he told me a story from when he was little and first discovered he wasn't a cat. My cheeks hurt from smiling, until I heard a growl in the darkness. It sounded like a dog. Circling, I caught a movement in the bushes to the side of us. The slender shadow of a tall man blended against the black lake. I gasped and my hand went to Hunter's arm. He turned so quickly that I could barely get out my words. "Do you see...?"

Hunter took after the man like a shot, and I stood. "Hunter! Don't!" My pulse raced as I saw him chase the shadow into the night. I ran after him, slower, stumbling through the tall grass and rocks.

"Ivy!" Hunter glanced briefly back at me to shout over his shoulder, "Don't go after us!"

He disappeared into the woods, and I stopped, not knowing what to do. The dogs barked again, though closer than they had before. My heart raced with fear. I stepped back, but that felt wrong. I stepped forward, not knowing what I was walking into. "Hunter?" I called tentatively.

A hand landed on my arm and I screamed. "Ivy! Sheesh!" I recognized Caitlyn's voice. "It's me!"

"Caitlyn," I took a hold of her hands. "Hunter just ran after that shadow that followed us the other night."

"Rosco?" she asked. That made me nervous. Maybe. Hunter had beaten him once, but what if he had friends lying in wait for him or a gun?

Searching for any kind of help, I spotted Bill standing by the refreshment table; he had his Dogo Argentino. "Bill!" I called. "Can we borrow Skip?"

He came over, too slowly, while we explained the situation. His expression changed into something fierce, and he told us to stay there while he tottered after the action in the forest. Of course, we didn't listen, and we flanked his sides as he fumbled with his flashlight and showed it through the darkness. "Aiden?" he called.

Caitlyn and I followed that in a chorus of "Hunters," summoning him with our voices. Suddenly, he tumbled out of the darkness, his frustrated expression illuminated by Bill's spotlight. Hunter leaned forward, his hands on his knees while he took deep breaths.

266

Bill approached him. "What were you chasing after, boy?"

Hunter didn't seem like he wanted to say, but finally muttered, "Some guy in the forest. He keeps bothering Ivy."

"Who is it?"

"I don't know. We only see his... shadow."

"Oh!" Bill grew solemn. "You're talking about Bone Man. You brought him back here from Lake Adam, did you?"

Now I understood the reason Hunter was reluctant to say. He met my eyes, but neither of us contradicted his superstitions. Bill seemed oblivious to our discomfiture. His keen eyes rested on Caitlyn next. "I thought you were cooling that stormy boy's temper with your sweet words?"

Now it was her turn to be embarrassed. "No, um, I'm supposed to bring you back, Ivy, so Brek can tell you sorry."

"Oh." That was unexpected. I had imagined their evening going a different way. "I thought you guys would have a nice night off."

"Yeah, right!" her flashlight moved angrily with her expressive hands, "When all he can talk about is how much he despises Angel and goes on and on about her every move. I wouldn't be surprised if he calls her in a fit of passion and she's back there when we return."

"Is that what happened last night?" Hunter asked quietly. Was that right? My blood boiled. What a hypocrite my brother was!

Caitlyn reddened under Bill's flashlight and shook her head, and that cooled my temper somewhat. "We were having a really good time. That's probably why we didn't hear you had troubles, Ivy; sorry."

Suddenly everything made sense. "How good of a time?" I asked with a growing smile.

Her eyes got big and she tilted her head at the mixed company, and I understood the code. Brek had kissed her! "Does it matter though?" she asked. "Angel came around asking for you and Hunter and pretending like she was so worried and made him feel all guilty."

Bill's romantic heart couldn't take it. "I don't understand why he'd go for some wildcat when he's got a girl like you around. I'll tell you what, I've got something that will turn things around for you." Bill insisted we go back with him to the Grizzly, even though we desperately tried to get out of it. I claimed a headache, and Hunter took it so seriously that I had to admit that it wasn't as bad as all that, so we gave into Bill's entreaties with a shrug. We left the light of the dance party and traveled across the pathway to the Grizzly, the country music fading into the background of revelers. I felt a pang of regret to be leaving so early, but I wouldn't have felt easy out there anyway, with that shadow watching us.

I found Hunter's hand in the dark and squeezed it. "Don't go chasing that shadow anymore."

"Were you worried?" I heard the amusement in his voice.

I jogged his hand to show him I was serious. "Yes! It could be Rosco!"

He hugged me close, which felt good, but it wasn't the reaction that I wanted to my warnings. "His stuff was gone when I got back to the cabin," he said. "I think Rosco's gone for good."

A chill ran through me. That meant he'd been here while we were gone, and doing what? I clutched tighter to Hunter while we followed Bill into the warmth of the Grizzly. The store was deserted inside. Bill hadn't put away his dinner yet. He wove around it, scraping past his computer to poke around the DVDs on the shelf behind the counter. "You want to know the way to a man's heart?" Bill asked.

Caitlyn threw her hands deep into her coat pockets, not knowing how to answer.

"What's he got?" Hunter muttered. "A love potion?"

I wouldn't be surprised.

Bill finally found the video cassette tape he was looking for, pulling it out from the shelf with a grunt. He waved *The Man from Snowy River* at Caitlyn. "The man doesn't know what love is. Show him this and he won't look at another woman but you."

She sighed. "Honestly, Bill, I'll be happy when he's back on his feet and out of my hair."

That sounded like Brek. I was sorry that he had blown it with Caitlyn, though. He didn't know what he was losing.

Bill wasn't giving up on them; he wouldn't take no for an answer, so Caitlyn snatched the movie up to keep him happy.

My eyes drifted to the plaque above Bill's video shelf. It displayed the first coin spent on his business, except the more I stared at it, the more I realized that it wasn't a regular coin. My heart raced. It seemed too good to be true. It matched the illustration of Pratt's coin in Eden's journal. "Bill!" I interrupted his ramblings on love. "What's that coin?"

Hunter slid the *Die Hard* video back onto the shelf. I never could hide the urgency in my voice, but he was reading me pretty well lately. He straightened to see it for himself.

"Oh, that?" Bill settled onto his couch behind the counter. The Dogo Argentino buried his nose under Bill's knees, and he rubbed his pet's head absently. "That belonged to my ancestor, Adam Black."

Even Caitlyn knew what that meant. She drew to attention.

"He was a trapper," Bill told us like we didn't already know. "Quite the adventurer, he was. He made all sorts of trades with the Shoshone Indians."

He had one of those coins, too? Or had Eden given it to him before they had parted ways? She had never mentioned that in her journal. "Did he ever talk about looking for that treasure in the mountains?"

Bill took on a sly look. "Is this for the YouTube? Where's your camera? I'm not doing an interview without a camera." He winked at Caitlyn.

Hunter's arm ran into mine in his haste to help me get out my camera. For once he had no compulsions against it. We struggled with it until I had it trained on Bill. He puffed himself up at the importance of making an appearance on our documentary again, and he straightened his plaid shirt, muttering something about changing into something more suitable. Before he could, I said, "Tell me everything you know about Adam Black."

"That's a broad question," he lectured. "You gotta simplify it a little."

"Right—tell me how he's related to you."

"He's my great, great, great grandfather. He settled Dry Gulch—that's where his business took off. He lived comfortably for the times, not too extravagantly, but never in want. He set up a cabin not far from here. He's buried out there, you know. I've heard tale that he was in love with Eden, that drowned girl."

I should've just let him ramble on—we were getting way more out of it than by asking questions—but when he stumbled to a polite stop, I asked, "Did she give him that coin?"

"Nah, that? No. His wife was from Europe somewhere. What was her name? Eva? That was a family joke," he chuckled, "—that they were the first people living here in these mountains. Adam and Eva?" He chuckled. "But that's one of those foreign coins. I'm guessing Spanish. He always said not to put your heart on the treasures; said he'd choose his wife over that coin anytime, and he did, which is why he ended up with it. It was the key to the greatest treasure. But he loved that little girl he married after all that hoopla. She's buried near that family cabin too, side by side—quite the love story that turned out to be. He said she was the love of his life."

That didn't sound right—he had loved Eden, hadn't he? How sad would that be if even Adam hadn't considered Eden one of his great loves? It was heartbreaking, and hurt me more than I'd thought it would. I fought the idea. He'd loved Eden—he had!

Bill was still talking, and0 so I turned my attention to him. "Probably why I'm such a romantic," he said. "It's in the blood. You should take your camera to that graveyard. You'll find all sorts of history out there. Eden's grave's out there too."

"Wait, wait... he found her body?" I asked.

"He must'a," Bill said. "You'd think his wife would have something to say about her being in the family plot. Yup, gotta love history. It's one big, fat, juicy book of gossip."

Hunter had been stunned to silence up to this point. "Where's this cabin?"

"Why... lessee... a little past Lake Adam. I haven't been there in ages... ever since Bone Man."

How had we missed the biggest clue yet? Obviously the lake was named after Adam. It made sense that his cabin would be near there, and Adam was the key to all of this. He was the one who had figured out how to uncover the treasure, not Eden, not Lucius. They had been along for the ride. Had he left it all behind after losing Eden to it? Even so, if there were remnants of clues leftover from what he'd done, we'd have this treasure within the week.

"Thank you, Bill," I said.

"Did it make the cut?" he asked eagerly.

Caitlyn hurriedly assured him that it had while I stuffed my camera back into my purse. Hunter leaned over to me. "Don't you dare put that out there."

"Never," I whispered. It was much too important of a clue to share with the world. He'd only make the director's cut. I hoped Bill would forgive me.

Chapter sixteen

*B*rek grumbled something from the couch when I left in the morning, but he was exhausted from watching the *Man from Snowy River* the night before, plus the sequel and the knock-offs, and so he just waved me out the door, his hair standing on end.

He had been apologetic when I had come in after our discovery at Bill's, but judging by his grumbled comments about the broken fuel connector, he still hadn't gotten over his suspicions. Still, we were used to hating each other's significant others, and he had been interested in hearing about Bill's coin. "He's related to Adam Black?" he asked. "Figures."

I told him about our plan to go to Adam's grave the next day, and he had gotten quiet, a longing look in his eye that made me feel bad that he was missing out on so much. He asked me if Angel would be diving, and I admitted that she would. "Keep an eye on her," he said.

"Isn't that what you're doing?" I asked pointedly.

He'd ignored that. We had settled into an uneasy truce by the end of the movie that night, though I'd put my foot down after he'd called for the sequel. I'd noticed that he sat a little closer to Caitlyn by the time I turned in. Maybe Bill was onto something. The *Man from Snowy River* truly was magical.

Hunter waited for me on another ATV that morning, wearing his black puffer jacket and the helmet he'd promised he'd wear. He gave me a wink as I came closer, and I laughed. The engine grumbled low in the background. He had my helmet ready for me, and he handed it over. It was no longer a question that we would share the vehicle. I had let go of all pretenses of wanting to learn how to drive one. This ATV was a newer model, however not his usual, and I guessed he wasn't taking any chances this time. I looked over at the supplies he'd packed and laughed, seeing that he had brought a lot more after our last adventure. "Aren't we going overboard?" I asked.

He shook his head. "Well, maybe if you stop cutting the fuel line."

I squeezed his arm when I got in behind him. "Sorry, you're going to have to blame someone who knows a little more about engines than I do."

He turned serious, but before I could ask him what was up, he lowered his head and put on the gas to take us out of the resort, slowly as we passed the cabins then picking up speed on the trail. I was glad that he was taking it easy now that he wasn't trying to terrify me into his arms. At least that's what I'd hoped he'd been doing. I still held tightly to him, watching the scenery fly past us as we headed up the mountain and followed the coordinates Bill had given us last night.

It wasn't too far from Lake Adam. The trailhead was tucked behind the granite mountainside a little further east. Seeing there weren't any trails for motorized vehicles leading from there to Adam's cabin, we had to hike the rest of the way. It was a beautiful morning, but the trail was overgrown, steep, and difficult so that Hunter had to take out his machete to clear it. The sun grew hotter, and we peeled off our clothes until we were both in short-sleeved shirts and shorts; then, with our packs already open, we stopped to eat lunch before pushing on. It was late afternoon when we reached the cabin, sweaty and covered in dirt.

The scene before us took my breath away. Adam's cabin was a charming setup in the middle of a meadow with a stream rushing past it. The peaks in the distance were frosted with snow. The vegetation was sparser out here, which meant that we were high up, though to the side there was a patch of forest made up of aspens and pines. We walked into that idyllic setting under a cloudless sky—besides a few jet streams to remind me that we were in the present, though for a moment, it felt like we were back in time and living off this glorious land.

Hunter turned silent as we headed for the cabin. My heart rushed with excitement. It hadn't really sunk in that we were going to Adam's cabin until I'd seen it. This was where Eden had stayed all those months. She had listened to and told stories over the campfire. It would've been crowded with her and Lucius and Adam.

It was one of those one-room cabins where it was hard to believe anyone could live so cramped up in there. The roof was caved in, though Adam had added a few frills here and there with a big stone chimney and a covered patio, and even windows with dilapidated leather flaps. How had this looked back in the day with his Spanish wife sweeping it clean and putting her own feminine touch to it?

Peering through the missing door, I saw the cabin was partially furnished with an old bed that took up half the room and a fireplace that doubled as an oven made of crumbling stones to the side. I ventured inside, my hand brushing over the bed, though I was careful for bugs and spiders—my greatest fear when it came to these old places. There was no mattress, only a frame. Hunter picked up some discarded plates from a warped plastic foldout table. Those looked newer. Still, that wouldn't be too surprising. A place like this would attract anyone who needed a stop to rest.

We didn't say much—I felt too worn with sentiment. Hunter must've sensed it. He let me take the lead as I wandered through the cabin. We stepped outside, where I spied what was left of the stable. This was where Eden had met Adam. She'd thought he'd been a lawman and held him up with her shotgun. I smiled. Like the memories, only remnants of the stable remained. A weathered corner stood alone, buried deep into the earth. I didn't explore too much. With the day waning, we decided to find the graveyard first.

Brek hadn't bothered us too much with calls yet, but I knew that if we took too long, he'd harp on us about getting back. If he did, I'd ask after Angel; not that his stupidity justified me. We were quite the pair, except I believed and trusted Hunter... or I wouldn't have taken him here. This place was too special to me.

We searched the surrounding countryside for the gravesite, wading through tall grass. It shouldn't be too far. If Adam had buried Eden first, then he'd want to keep her close to him. I didn't explain my reasons to Hunter because it didn't make sense, but I tried to find the prettiest place, where he could sit for hours by her grave, immersed in his mournful thoughts.

Hunter was the one to find the graveyard, and he called me over into a pretty grove of trees. Once inside, I found it breathtaking in its solemnity. The stones were old, some of the writing blurred out from time—though I supposed Hunter could bring them out with his off-flash photography. The people, however, could not be brought back, their bones mostly wasted away—the last vestige of their lives slipping from mortality.

The brush crunched under my feet. The graveyard was overtaken with weeds and moss and ivy. Aspens had grown between the headstones. There were more graves than I'd thought there would be. At least twenty, and they held the family name of Black, and then some Strongs and Lahns. This held Bill's ancestry, right here. What would it be to have your family line laid out for you and in such close proximity? It was the luxury of living in small, obscure towns such as Dry Gulch. How sad that Bill had stopped coming here after Bone Man; but the hike was a strenuous one, and he was getting on in age. Perhaps it hadn't been too much of a sacrifice.

My eyes had drawn to a gravestone at the center of it all, and stepping through the dead grass, I found Adam Black's name on it. It was taller than the others, with weeping angels on either side of him. His wife must have loved him dearly to put up such a memorial. Her grave was next to his—the two had been buried side by side.

Hunter pulled next to me, his mouth tight, his strong jaw thickening as he bent to stare down at the two graves. He seemed especially dark in this grove, his features shadowed by his facial hair, his concerned brows bringing out the soft expression in his tender eyes until they widened. "Whoa!" He pointed out the dates on the graves. "Eva was a much younger woman."

Startled, I studied the dates. She'd been born in 1855. Adam had been born in 1829. He'd been a full twenty-six years older than her. "She was born the same year Eden died," I said. That meant that he'd been alone for years until he'd found his Spanish beauty—at least until she was eighteen. "He was about forty-four when he married her," I said.

He grimaced. "If he waited that long." He studied the dates. "He died in 1899 at the age of seventy. She died a year later in 1900. She was forty-five. He was practically twice her age."

"Maybe she really loved him?" I said, desperate to make this story happy. "Look what his stone says—'my life.' If he died before her, she put that there..."

"And he wrote that on Eden's grave over there." He indicated the spot where he'd come from. I froze. That was odd. Why would Eva repeat the words her husband had put on his first love's gravestone? It made me want to cry. Had he never gotten over Eden? Had Eva suspected it from the beginning?

"You still think Adam and Eva had a love match?" Hunter challenged.

I read the wording on Adam's headstone and looked at the chiseled angels on the sides of it. She'd put her heart into this memorial. "Yes." It couldn't be any other way. If he'd lost Eden in such a horrible way, I desperately wanted him to have been happy with this Spanish Senorita. "It was a different time," I said. "And she was foreign."

"First of all, the only reason Bill thought she was Spanish was because of Pratt's coin," he said. "Secondly," he reached out and ran his hand down the back of my hair, no longer looking at the stones. "You're a romantic," he decided.

"Well..." I couldn't explain my connection to these people—I'd grown up on stories of Eden and Adam and stupid Lucius. I couldn't bear thinking of Adam dying of a broken heart. Groaning at the tragedy of it all, I stole a hug from Hunter, and he rubbed my back, looking a little puzzled. "Her death must've broken him," I said into his shoulder. "How could he have gone after the treasure after that?"

He peered over my head at the gravestone. "Did he give up? He had the coin."

Too many secrets had been buried with Adam. "Her headstone is back there?" I asked.

He nodded. Sliding his fingers through mine, he brought me to it. I felt like I needed the emotional support, and I was right. This one made me swallow at the sadness of it. She had died on July 16th, 1855—the last date in her journal. Had Adam found her body, or was this just a memorial to her? Her headstone was a simpler design than the one Adam's wife had made for him. I stared at the inscription on it, "My Life." A heavy chain was wrapped around the tombstone, which added to the eeriness, but the stone was made by a man with little means. It wasn't from someone who had just hit the jackpot.

Hunter let me go to pull out the artifact from his pack. At my questioning look, he raised a shoulder. "You never know. Maybe he left a clue on how to use this thing." He held it up to his eye and peered through it at the graveyard. When that didn't yield results, he tucked it in his pocket. "Maybe we should dig the bodies up?" That horrified me, and he bit down a smile. "What?" he asked. "Does that take the romance out of it?"

Yes! Trust Hunter to do that, but somehow it also made me feel better. I wandered through the graveyard, taking footage of all the gravestones. I was making a collection of clues that we could put into the documentary after we found Eden's treasure… or called it quits. Apparently people enjoyed the drama between Hunter and me more. The interest in us would die down when we became a boring, happy couple. I smiled at him over my camera. That would be fantastic—in a lot of ways.

He found some gravestones that were tipped over and began to right them. "I'm going to get these ready to do some off-flash photos. Maybe we can find some clues. You in?"

"You're not touching my camera after last time," I said. "Use your own."

"What happened to sharing?" He didn't hide his amusement well. "Selfish! And after I gave you my sleeping bag?"

"I paid for that in full!" I said, laughing. "Brek won't let me forget it!"

His hand brushed my charm bracelet. "What is this anyway?"

"It's something my brother gave me. He finds a trinket from every place he's been to remind me of him—this is a pot of gold he got in Ireland, an Eiffel Tower, a wooden shoe, a double-decker bus. A camera. And…" my hand rested on the gold wedding band. "This is just some ring he found at the bottom of Lake Adam."

"Are you going to fill your bracelet with any of your own adventures?" he asked.

"Like what?"

"Maybe a mini ATV, or a skunk, or a canister of bear spray?"

I shrieked out a denial, and after giving me a hard time, he busied himself with his work, the tendons standing out on his strong arms as he righted the heavy stones. I took footage of it, enjoying more than just his companionship.

My thoughts invariably shifted to Adam—a lone man in the wilderness. How long had he been out here alone after Eden's death? It was only him and her grave here until he'd met his wife… maybe even ordered for her in one of those mail-order bride gigs. If his wife had been born around the same time Eden died, he'd been alone for a long time. There had to be some evidence of it. "I'm going to see if Adam left anything at the cabin," I said. "Love letters? Journals. I don't know."

"We should ask Bill if he has any of those too," he said over his shoulder. He heaved another heavy stone up.

That was a great idea. I left, the tall grass tickling past my legs.

278

Aware of my duty to Caitlyn, I narrated my travels back to the cabin and tried to recreate the moment when I had first come upon the place. "Eden was crazy to turn down Adam's proposal, even if it was just to get a chance to live with him here. It's charming—hidden away from everything—pretty much deserted."

I strode through the door like I owned the place, and stumbled to a stop when I saw a scraggly old man devouring a bowl of chili. His back was turned to me. He wore a long jacket that reached the ground. It was the same one that had rested on the ground near the hammock at the abandoned campsite.

"I'm so sorry," I said, feeling like I was intruding for a moment.

He didn't turn, but he stood, and he was tall—really tall—but thin, so maybe he couldn't overpower me if it came down to it. I wasn't sure where that thought came from, but I stepped back slowly and quietly while trying to keep my cool. He was probably just a hiker, but when he didn't take notice of me, I got nervous, especially when I backed into a wall. He turned at the sound of that, and the second he met my eyes, he silently ran at me.

That was wrong. The silence especially. If there was anything I was good at, it was a good scream, and it came from my very essence. Brek always called it my triple-vocal-chord scream. It was enough to scare the old man, too. He stopped suddenly, looking so terrified that I flushed with guilt. "Eden," he asked with some confusion.

"No!" I held my hands out. "I'm Ivy."

"What did you do!? What did you do to Harry?"

"No, I'm Ivy," I repeated helplessly, not sure who Harry was. The splintered wall of logs was hard against my back, and I wasn't sure how to escape without pushing the man back, and I didn't want to touch him and set him off again.

"You got your revenge on all of us, didn't you?" he raved. "I see you! I see you walking through the mountains! I see you in the trees! I see you dancing!" His hands landed on the cutlery next to the bowl he'd dropped. He let it all slide noisily to the floor until he clutched at a

STEPHANIE FOWERS

knife. My blood froze. It was a sharp fillet knife with a long, wicked blade used for skinning animals. I didn't want to put him into a frenzy with another scream. The man was off his rocker. "You won't take me," he said, softer this time. "You won't take me!" His fingers shook, and he touched my face with the hand that wasn't clutching at the blade. Was this really happening? I felt paralyzed, and I closed my eyes as if that would make it all go away. He now had a hold of my hair. "You're real," he said.

"Yes!" My eyes opened, a sudden hope taking hold of me at his words. Maybe he just didn't like ghosts. "I'm just hiking here."

"No, no, no, you're looking for Eden. You're looking for her. She'll hurt you, too." He looked wildly from side to side like he'd see her ghost, and then his hands went around my wrists and he dragged me to him. "I see you! I see you walking through the mountains! I see you in the trees! I see you dancing!" he repeated it verbatim like a broken record. There was something loose in his head.

A panicked sound gurgled from my throat, as I was very wary of the knife in his hands, but I tried to stop myself from screaming as I lowered myself to the ground so it was harder for him to get me, but he was strong and his bony fingers tore into my wrists. "Stop it!" I cried.

"You can't go after Eden!" he said. Before I knew it, he'd hauled me to my feet and shoved his shoulder into my stomach, propelling me off the floor like he fully planned on carrying me away. Where did he get this strength? He was so thin.

I felt like I was in shock. I fought through it. "Hunter!" I screamed. "Hunter!"

He dropped me flat on the floor at that and my eyes went to his feet. They were wrapped in rags. He knelt next to me, looking confused. I felt like a bug he was inspecting. Breathing heavily, he ran his hands down my face. "Don't trust anyone!" he said.

"Whoa!" Hunter rushed through the door. His eyes went to the knife in the old man's hand and then to me. I was covering my head. "Ivy!" he said.

280

The old man looked up. "Ivy, Ivy, Ivy!" he repeated. Now he knew my name! And he wouldn't stop saying it. "Ivy! I see you!"

Hunter held his hand out to the man. "Don't hurt her. Let her go. Just… stop." He slowly maneuvered himself between us.

"Hunter!" I whimpered. "He's got a knife."

The old man's eyes drew to Hunter and his eyes narrowed in befuddlement. "Harry?" he called out to Hunter, whose head tilted at the name, his arm still out, the muscles on his bicep pulsating reflexively. "He's going to hurt Ivy," the old man said.

"Who is?" Hunter asked.

Then the man caught sight of the artifact in Hunter's pocket and he pointed at it. "The man kills! The man kills who took that stick! He wants me dead. He will kill you again. He doesn't know you lived!"

"Okay," Hunter said, keeping his voice controlled. "Who wants to kill me?" That wasn't what I'd expected to come out of Hunter's mouth. I forced myself to watch the exchange between them. Hunter didn't seem as surprised to see this guy as he should. "Tell me what happened," Hunter said. When the man didn't answer, Hunter's eyes filled with emotion. "Who are you?"

The man's hand tightened on the knife, and moaning in a pathetic, feral way, he stabbed it into the plastic table to the side of us and knocked Hunter back with his shoulder on his way out the door. Hunter fell into the wall then used it to propel himself forward to go after him, but Hunter stopped at the frame of the door when his gaze drifted to me.

I gasped for air, still sprawled to the floor. It was weird, but I couldn't move. Now that the threat was gone, my eyesight was going weird. And I heard dogs barking and growling—I put my hands to my ears. Hunter landed on his knees beside me and pulled me to him. "Are you okay?"

I nodded. It was all I could do for now and I let him gather me to him. I hid my face into his strong shoulder. "Let's get out of here."

"Tell me what happened?" he asked.

"I walked in here and he attacked me. I didn't do anything. He thought I was Eden and he thought I did something to Harry." My forehead wrinkled. "He thinks you're Harry. Who is Harry? And he knows my name now. Bone Man! Bone... Bone Man!" Nothing I was saying was coming out right.

"Did he say anything else?"

What did it matter? He was a crazy old man who'd been wandering these mountains for decades if he'd been the one tormenting Bill. And Hunter only cared about what he said? It only made me suspicious that Hunter knew more than he was letting on. "He told me not to trust anyone. That was it."

Hunter cursed under his breath and helped me to my feet. He found my camera somewhere on the ground and pushed it into my hands. I saw it was still on and almost rolled my eyes. More footage for Caitlyn. Not wanting to think about it, I turned it off and leaned heavily on him while he half-carried me outside. The both of us couldn't get out of there fast enough.

Searching wildly for anything threatening coming at us in the distance, I saw that the man had disappeared into the fields of tall grass. He could be anywhere. And there was still that sound of dogs barking. It grew fainter. "He was trying to keep me safe from Eden," I remembered. "I don't think he was going to stab me... when he thought I wasn't Eden. He did try to take me though."

He made a sound of dismay. "He's out of his mind. We need to tell someone about him."

"He's Bone Man." I said it clearer this time. At his look, I tried to explain myself so I could make sense—but my mind was going crazy from the danger like it was firing all sorts of neurons through me. "He's wearing that coat that was crumpled on the ground at the old campsite. He's tall and thin and... I think he's been following us."

Hunter looked worried. "He picks up names pretty fast. Calls them."

"Wow," I said. "And here I thought it was Rosco this whole

time."

"You did?" his voice cracked.

"I thought Bone Man was all sorts of people. I'm just glad it wasn't *you*."

Normally, he'd let me have it for that with a mocking comment, but his expression stayed grim as he hurried us back down the trail. There was no way I was staying out here tonight. I was gradually getting the strength back into my limbs after that little encounter, and my adrenaline was rushing through me as we ran headlong down the mountain. The ATV at the end of the trail was a welcome sight, and Hunter made a big deal over me as he packed me in, making sure I was comfortable. The last straw was when he found my helmet and stuffed it over my head.

"Hey!" I said, tugging it off, and felt my pony tail tip over to the side.

He looked confused. "You don't want it on?"

"Come here." I tugged at the collar of his shirt and pulled him onto the seat with me. "What was that?" I asked. "Is that eleven or twelve?" He still didn't know what I was saying and watched me like I had lost it. I had, but that was beside the point. "That's your eleventh or twelfth rescue," I said. "I mean, I can't keep track anymore, and I've never thanked you properly!"

I knelt up on the seat and put my arms around his neck and went in for the kiss. My forehead ran into the bill of his hat. We both laughed, and I turned the hat around his head and tried again. He eagerly returned my kiss, his mouth on mine. He held me close, and it felt comforting after my scare earlier.

The loud sound of a helicopter shook the air as it flew over us, the reverberation of it shaking into my bones as it disappeared over the tall granite mountains past Lake Adam. I pulled back. "Brekker!" We both said it at once.

Had he assumed the worst and called a helicopter on us? "Where's the walkie talkie?" I went searching for it. It was in my pack. So he could've gotten to us if he was worried. I pressed the button. "Brek?" I asked. "You there? We're alive! What's your problem?"

"Ivy," he said after a moment. "I think you'd better get here." I tried to get more information from him, but as usual he preferred the more dramatic way of relaying news. "I'll explain when you get here."

"Brek!" When he didn't answer, I picked up the fallen helmet and stuffed it back over my hair.

Hunter looked disappointed. His hand went to my back, and he rubbed it in his comforting way before getting back on the ATV. I climbed on after him and we rushed home, the sound of helicopters following us the whole way.

"It's not my fault exactly!" Caitlyn held her hands up defensively.

Hunter and I peered out the window of the cabin at the crowds of hikers who'd shown up at Dry Gulch. There was a downside to fame. The town was swarming with people interested in finding the treasure, some a little scary. I imagined this would've been like the gold rush in the old west.

"It's just that things went pretty crazy," she said. "The views for our webisode doubled overnight, and now it's quadrupled, and then boom. We have more than 100 million views!"

My hair felt like it was standing up on end. I didn't want to go viral—I had just unplugged. I wanted a normal life now. "How?" I asked. "What did you put in there?"

"They loved Hunter apologizing for deleting your footage, I think." She grimaced. "So I blame him for being so cute... I don't think they care about the treasure hunting stuff exactly, but the fact that this is going on and it's live is driving them crazy!"

Hunter looked stressed out. He pushed his hair from his face, for once ticked off at Caitlyn. "How can we look for the treasure with all these people?"

Caitlyn knew she was in trouble and so she tried to flatter him. "Most of them can't keep up with you anyway."

Brekker snorted; he was watching the show we'd turned into from the couch, not softening towards Hunter at all. In fact, the angrier Hunter got, the more he enjoyed it.

Casting him a distracted look, Hunter shook his head. "I saw some pretty sophisticated units out there. I don't think they're all here for the romance between Ivy and me."

He wouldn't even look at me now, and I didn't know how to make this right.

"Most of them are... the reporter I talked to from..." Caitlyn was beginning to realize that she'd messed up big time, and she stumbled to a stop until she caught sight of my camera and snatched it from me. "What do you have today?"

I protested weakly, feeling overwhelmed. "But..."

"What? You're giving her more?" Hunter cried. "We have a problem here. Stop feeding the vultures! We've got to figure out a way to get rid of them." Hunter refused to listen to any more explanations or apologies from Caitlyn and moved for the door.

I hoped he'd listen to mine. "Hunter, I'm sorry."

His eyes were hard on me, and I was momentarily stunned. "You don't know what you've done." He pushed out the door to the loud cries of spectators—quite a few beautiful girls at that. I had a little bit of an idea of what I'd done. My stomach hurt with it. The door slammed behind him.

"Good," Brekker announced loudly. "I didn't think he'd ever leave." He readjusted his leg on the couch and picked up the stick he'd designated as his poking stick and dragged a pizza box closer to himself to dig out a big slice of pizza. He made short work of it, swallowing half the slice in one bite. He was going all the way with this couch potato thing—the evidence in the stacks of pizza boxes, empty ice cream cartons, and VHS covers from the Grizzly. "Ivy, I'm sorry, but I've got some bad news for you."

He didn't seem that sorry to me. I sat on the edge of the couch, inching from the crumbs. "What?"

"Yeah, we've got to figure out how to get rid of these people, but… at least one good thing came out of this." He pushed his phone at me where he'd put a picture he'd taken of Bill's computer. "The spotlight has a way of bringing the truth to light. Some followers dug up some old newspaper headlines from a few months ago. They make your boyfriend look pretty bad, I'd say."

I read the wording on the fuzzy image. *Aiden Hunter, 32, arrested on suspicion of breaking and entering. Possible burglary and arson charges pending. Motive unclear.*

Caitlyn bit her lip. "He got caught for breaking into a warehouse and setting it on fire. Nobody knows why he did it, but the charges were dropped mysteriously. A lot of commentators online think it's because his grandfather is Gordon Hunter. He's an oil tycoon—he runs the offshore oil industry off the coast of South Carolina. He's pretty unethical from what I hear. Some say he put Hunter up to it. Brekker's been doing a lot of research on Gordon the past few days. He's kind of a slime."

I glared at my twin. He had nothing better to do than turn all Sherlock Holmes while we were gone? He had graduated from finding things in the ground to finding things online. Hunter might be working for his grandfather, but he was still after the truth like we were.

"That's not all," Brek said, looking very satisfied with himself. "Look at Hybernater's first comment." Ah yes, the famous online commentator. "Caitlyn showed this to me yesterday." Brek pushed another fuzzy picture from his phone at me, and I read it with some misgiving:

I know that treasure well. There is a copper cylinder that has been passed down through the generations of my family that was rumored to have some connection to Eden's treasure. One day, I lent it to a young man who vowed to return it to me, along with the treasure. I never saw him again. It left a bitter taste in my mouth, but

I find myself commenting here out of sympathy for the young lady.

"Hybernater might be anonymous, but I trust him more than some guy accused of setting a warehouse on fire," Brek said.

Hunter had told me that he had stopped some men from stealing it from his mother. "Wait," I said. "You think that Hunter stole it from Hibernator?"

"He has it now, doesn't he?"

"Hunter's face is all over the webisodes," I said. "You'd think Hybernater would know if he loaned it to him or not."

"So? Hunter's got a lot of riffraff working for him. Rosco isn't gone yet, either."

I let out a startled breath and Caitlyn nodded. "We saw him with Angel."

"Looks like he pretended to get rid of him," Brek said.

"I don't buy it!" I said, shaking my head. "No, no, it's all Angel— she didn't answer the walkie talkie that night we got stuck up there. Maybe she's working with Rosco or something."

"She didn't answer?" Brek scowled. "They're playing you for a sucker."

"You didn't either!" I accused.

Brekker and Caitlyn exchanged guilty glances, and I almost called them on it before my twin scooted closer to me. "Look, I know I haven't been the best brother to you the past few days, but Hunter is not who he says he is. He's involved in something shady. I'm thinking he's just as bad as Angel. Maybe worse."

"Oh, that's convenient for you!" I snatched up my camera and retreated to my room before he could rub it in more. Sitting on my bed, I pulled my blanket around my shoulders and tried to decide what to do. Hunter was involved in something he shouldn't be. Was it because of the artifact? Someone had been after his mother before he'd stepped in. Soon after that, he broke into that warehouse? Who was he going up against?

I didn't have enough information. I'd have to ask Hunter, which wasn't possible when he was so angry, and then with all those YouTube fans in the way? Not to mention the people on his team would hate me now. As I sat there, I remembered how that hermit had talked to Hunter like he knew who he was. And it was all in my camera. Picking it up, I played it back.

Brek came hobbling into my room in a panic the first time he heard me scream on it. "Are you okay?"

"Oh, sorry," I said.

"What is that?" He sat on my bed, looking more contrite than he had when he'd been gleefully relaying all Hunter's indiscretions. Caitlyn and he must've talked after I'd left.

"You know Bone Man?" I asked. "I think we met him today." I showed him the video, and his mouth fell open when the hermit came running at me and I dropped the camera. It was actually pretty good footage because it fell at just the right angle. I mean, it was from below, and so it wasn't exactly flattering, but it caught everything. Caitlyn crept into the room next and she was gasping with horror when the hermit picked up the knife and tried to grab me. When she watched Hunter run into the cabin to save me, she turned unresponsive, her eyes following everything.

Brek watched closely, digesting everything that was said. "Who's Harry?" he asked.

"I don't know."

Brek's hand went to mine and he took it. "Why didn't you tell me this happened today?"

"I was going to." The hermit was off his rocker, but he knew that someone had been killed. "I think he was trying to warn me. Also, the name Hunter meant something to him."

"Yeah, that's weird." Brek rewound it to the part where I shouted for Hunter and the man dropped me to the floor of the cabin. I rubbed my hip in response. It still throbbed.

"The whole thing's weird. Play it to the end," Caitlyn complained.

"I think he was the one who called you in the forest," I told my brother. "Once he heard my name he kept repeating it."

Without being crumpled up on the floor in a defensive position, I could see the hermit point out the artifact in Hunter's pocket. Someone had been killed for it, and now whoever had done it was after Hunter. "Are you getting this?" I asked. "I think we're dealing with some bad people."

"It could mean anything," Brek said, but he wasn't as sure of himself as before.

"You trust Hybernater now?" I asked.

"Not really," he said. Brek played it over again then met my eyes. Caitlyn took the camera after he was through with it, nervously playing it back, perhaps for lack of something better to do. This had become bigger than us. Hunter was mixed up in something.

"Who's funding our expedition, Brek?" I asked. "Are they dangerous?"

"No! It's Walker, like I said. A family friend."

"Do you even know who that is?"

"No," he admitted. *Typical Brek.* There was more to this than people who wanted their royal Irish jewels back—the hermit made that clear. The artifact was proof that people were willing to kill for Eden's treasure. I had no idea what was going on, but Hunter did! I was sure of it. I had to get out there to talk to him. But how would I find him in this crowd of people? And when I did, could I get him alone? He might not tell me the truth, but I had to try.

Chapter seventeen

I pushed my way through the Grizzly on my way to the Bear Den upstairs. Hunter wasn't at his cabin so this would be the next most likely place to find him. I'd entered a media circus. It was the Thursday before the Fourth of July weekend, making it the worst time to go viral. There were so many people at the resort that it reminded me of a concert, and I was one of the main attractions. It would be dangerous to get discovered. I'd borrowed Caitlyn's coat and one of Brekker's beanie hats. I even tucked my hair up into it. It was a hideous look, but I reminded myself that that wasn't the point.

Brek had no idea I'd slipped away or he'd be worried out of his mind. I'd left him dozing on the couch in front of episodes of *Murder She Wrote* on the old tube TV. If he woke up, he'd just have to learn what it felt like to watch everything from the sidelines.

Poor Bill looked harried behind the counter of the café. I'd hoped that he'd enjoy the extra business, but it was clearly too much and he wasn't prepared. His friends had secured their table nearby and watched the whole proceedings with interest. The cane shook in Pat's hand.

Bill rang up yet another sandwich, and I kept my head down, intending to apologize to him later. The only bright spot of the night was that he had plenty of listening ears for his stories, and he was in the midst of regaling the tale of Bone Man to the interested crowd. Behind him, the computer lay dormant—the one place to get the internet. Considering that these people were here because of what they'd seen on it, I found it ironic. My only hope was that they couldn't stand being unplugged for long and would go home.

Working my way up the stairs, I searched through the crowd to find Hunter. This whole thing was impossible! Of course he wasn't in his usual spot. Angel and her cohorts had been replaced at the pool table with a group of young adults, though a few of Hunter's men were on full display and having the time of their lives with their faux celebrity status. The karaoke machine was in constant use. I was pleased about that, at least. The bar was full with hands beckoning for service.

I felt a touch on my back and turned. Hunter had found me. He didn't look the worse for wear, at least, and he hadn't bothered with a disguise like I had. His eyes swept over me and he snorted. "You trying to hide from what you did?"

I guessed that meant he was still mad at me. I sighed. "We need to talk."

"How?" he gestured to the crowds. "You comfortable with complete strangers having a piece of our lives?" He shook his head in frustration and looked at me with his piercing eyes, almost pleading, "Don't you want to have something that only belongs to you?"

Now he was starting to sound like Eden's journal, but he'd read it, hadn't he? My hand went to his arm. "They'll leave soon," I said. "These people are dependent on their internet."

"The media brought their own cell phone towers here," he said. "You didn't see? They have access to us all the time now."

We were attracting an audience, and I heard our names whispered through the crowd. Caitlyn had done it. By just spotlighting us in frozen moments of time, we'd become celebrities, and to know Hunter was to fall in love with him. I wouldn't be the only one. He drew me aside. "How can you live with so many eyes on you?"

"Are you saying you care what other people think?"

"No, not at all. They don't own me. And I don't care what they think of you either. It's part of growing up—being secure in yourself. But don't you want to say stupid things and be wrong every once in a while without the whole world thumbing it down or commenting on it?

Some things were meant to be private, like now."

Somehow he had turned this all on me. He was calling me a child for oversharing, and he was dead right. "I agree," I said. "I messed up." But he also had his problems. Hunter wanted everything shrouded in darkness because he had secrets to hide. "I just... need to ask you something," I said.

"Oh? What do you want from me now?"

"We've got to find a place to talk."

He gave me a disbelieving look, and it was almost as if I could hear his thoughts—*now I wanted privacy?* After a resigned sigh, he took my hand and pulled me closer to whisper in my ear, "There's no place to go."

He was forcing me to say this here? And so I tried to be as private about it as I could and I leaned over him, my cheek brushing against his, "It's just I've been looking at that footage and you haven't told me everything."

"Yeah, why would I?" he asked louder this time, "—with everybody listening to everything I say?"

"The camera wasn't on the whole time," I said, still trying to keep my voice down. "And you know something about the guy we're working for!"

"He's a bad man." He wasn't bothering to keep quiet anymore. "I told you that already."

"You know him personally," I said, "and he's after you."

The crowd was getting thicker around us, and glancing up, I saw the cellphones trained on us. This whole moment was getting recorded. Hunter couldn't take it anymore. "I can't do this here!" He pulled from me and the whole crowd groaned in disappointment.

"Hunter!" Some girls tried to get his attention and he brushed past them. They turned to me, pouting. "You don't deserve him—do you do everything your brother says? Show some independence."

I didn't appreciate the unsolicited advice. Another girl grabbed my arm and almost pulled off my charm bracelet with her roughness. I clasped it protectively against my stomach. "Is your brother single or he still not over Angel?" she asked.

My mouth moved, but no words came out, as the full extent of what I had done came over me. More hands landed on me, and I was slowly getting mauled by adoring and not-so-adoring fans. It felt like I was up against the hermit again, but way outnumbered.

"Ivy!" I got shoved from behind. These hands were stronger and male—possibly boyfriends who'd been dragged here by romantic girls. "Ivy!" My hat was torn from my head, and it ripped out a few strands of my hair with it. The rest of my hair went flying over my face. "You going to scream?" No, not boyfriends, troublemakers.

"Get away from me!" Trying to escape them, I circled and saw the real danger as the crowd shifted—Rosco was lying in wait inside of it; his watery eyes were on me and I saw something in his hand. A knife. A hand jerked me back and I looked into the face of one of my hecklers. He was an overly tall, hard-faced teenager. Snickering, he took me by both arms. "Don't scream!"

Hunter was on him in a second, and shoved him back before dragging me away. There were a few "aww's" in the crush of people, but it became indistinct from the jeers. I was very aware of Rosco ramming his way through the crowd like a bulldozer as the phones caught Hunter's latest rescue of me.

"I guess it's not the best idea to split up right now," Hunter said into my hair. Before I could tell him about Rosco, Hunter's hand went to my elbow, and he fought us through to the back where one of the workers let us through to hide in the kitchen. We locked the door.

I leaned against Hunter. "Rosco's out there! He had a knife."

Hunter's expression tightened, but then he checked his phone—it wasn't quite the reaction I'd expected. He wrote something back, and put it away. "I haven't been telling you everything," he said, "because I don't know everything. I only have suspicions." His phone went off and he picked it up to read his text through, frowned, then punched back another reply.

"Who is that?"

"Your brother—he wants to know if you're alive."

This was what happened when I broke my phone—no one could get to me, except by cheating. "You told him I was fine, right?" I asked. He smirked. "Hunter!" I said in a lecture. He wasn't taking anything seriously.

"Yeah, yeah—I let him know that we're trapped in the kitchen, fighting for our lives behind a barricade. Your mom called him and told him what had happened to us out in the bar, so... I guess that went viral too."

"My mom?" How was that possible? "We've got to get rid of these people!"

He licked his lips. "Ivy... what if they could help us find this thing? The more eyes we have on this, the better chance we have of solving this." That was different than what he'd said before, but I was eager to make this right so I was all ears. "Once they help us get this treasure, we'll have our privacy," he said. "I'm ready to tell you everything now. I have a lead that I haven't told you about. I couldn't trust you before. I'm sorry about that."

This sounded so weird—it wasn't his words that were wrong exactly, but his whole manner had changed and he seemed fake, or maybe it was because he was giving me all the information that I wanted without a fight. I got uneasy. "This whole thing between us has been a lie," he said. "I mean, not what's between me and you. That's real. At least it was to me." His hands went to my hair and I felt numb as he stroked it back with his thumb. "But I'm supposed to distract you while my team finds the real treasure. They've been diving in Creek Valley this whole week. And, Ivy, they've found it. Everything fits together like a puzzle."

"But what about all the things that we've found...?"

"We planted it. All of it." I didn't believe him and I scowled at him. He acted like I wasn't and smiled the smile of a mad man. "So, tonight, let's get out of here. We'll take you and Caitlyn and your brother and we'll go to Creek Valley and finish this thing."

"Brekker would never…" I began.

"He knows everything. See." Hunter showed me the texts between the two of them, and I read through it all:

BREKKER: *You're streaming on Facebook Live. Someone is hiding behind the fridge and filming you. Give them a false lead and get this crowd out of here.*

Hunter was good. He was too good. I gulped. The nerves that had built inside me from his fake revelations now prickled through me at the thought of going through with this act. It all rested on my shoulders now. "I'm really mad at you," I said—and realized that wasn't a lie.

"I guess we both have a reason to be mad. Hey, look at me," he said softly and his fingers gently touched my face as he studied me. "But we can forgive each other. Right?"

Did he mean that? I didn't know what was real and what wasn't, but I knew I wasn't kissing for the camera. "I'm going to need a little time."

He nodded. "Me too." And he kissed me gently on the lips before pulling back. "Was that enough time?"

Well, yeah, but… jerk! I couldn't help it; I smiled, and he acted like he was going in for another kiss when his head jerked up like he'd become aware of the intruder. "Hey!" He roared and ran at someone hiding behind the fridge. A grown man peeled from his vantage point, which was confusing since I'd expected a kid. He skidded out the door, shouting out his rights. I guessed he wanted the next viral video. Well, he'd gotten it.

"C'mon, let's go," Hunter said under his breath. Taking possession of my hand, he tugged me to the door. "We don't know how many rats are hiding here." He was back to his brusque ways, and I was filled with even more confusion. I didn't know what to believe anymore.

"Rosco," I whispered in warning.

He nodded grimly, but stayed silent. After a moment of searching the premises for Rosco, we escaped back into the hallway, where he stole my coat and put his stocking hat and coat on me instead. We dumped poor Caitlyn's coat near the trashcans. "Put your hair back up. I almost didn't recognize you last time."

I tucked it into his hat before we rushed down the crowded stairs, having no other way to retreat. Hunter had me walk ten steps ahead since people were looking for a couple, but it was close enough for him to keep an eye on me. Already I heard people talking about Creek Valley around me. I really hoped this worked, for all our sakes.

We got outside and felt our way through the shadowy back side of the Grizzly. When I knew we were alone, I caught Hunter's arm. "You're good," I accused.

"Now you know what I feel like," he said under his breath.

"No! Everything I said to you was..." Looking around and still not sure if we were alone, I whispered into his ear, "real!"

His cheek lifted in a grin. "Good," he said.

Good? That didn't answer anything. We rushed through the shadows of the trees to get back to our cabins. Hunter's was closest, and so we headed for his first. I prayed we wouldn't find Rosco there. Hunter's men were basking under all that attention at the Bear Den, and for the first time that night, I spared a thought for Angel, wondering if she'd be back at the cabin. If she was working with Rosco, that could be dangerous.

As we neared, a man walked from the shadows and we slowed. This had better not be someone with a camera... or worse. "Aiden?" the man asked. I saw the red ember of a cigarette shining through the darkness.

Hunter straightened. "Father?"

But he was supposed to be dead? The shadows concealed the older man, but I could see he was tall and had broad shoulders like Hunter. My head whipped over to Hunter to see if he was as surprised as I was to see his father living and breathing, but he had turned stiff and defensive, not at all overcome with joy. I'd gotten that one wrong—I'd thought that the Hunter brothers had both disappeared looking for the treasure.

"I told you not to come up here," his father said. He had that thick South Carolinian accent that Hunter had, though his was huskier from years of smoking.

"I heard a few things from my mother that made me change my mind," Hunter said. His voice had lost all its passion, though I knew that meant he was hiding it. "Why did you believe grandfather over her? You knew her better than anyone. She never looked at another man until you divorced her for it, but I think you knew that."

"I'm not so sure about that." His father took another shaky puff of his cigarette. "She got pretty close to Charlie, as I recall, before the end—he'd given her that artifact for safekeeping, I'd heard."

"You didn't try to get her back." Hunter sounded disgusted. "You never cared about her side of the story."

"She was better off without me, to be honest."

The resignation in his father's voice seemed to tick Hunter off. "Was I better off? Is that why you left me? Or did Gordon threaten you too?" The cigarette stilled in the air as Hunter's father stared over at him in astonishment. "Yeah, I know what he did," Hunter said. "What does Gordon know? What is he holding over all your heads?"

"She doesn't need to hear this." Hunter's father tried to wave me away so he could get his son alone. "Let's go inside."

Hesitating, Hunter's hand went over my arm then loosened. I knew he was divided because he didn't feel he could leave me out here alone, and I wasn't about to volunteer to be in the dark—in more ways than one. "Whatever you're going to say," Hunter said, "do it."

His father dropped his cigarette onto the ground and rubbed it out with his foot then headed for Hunter's cabin without another word. His boots crunched into the gravel. Wordlessly, we followed him. So far, I was getting that Hunter's home life was messed up. Did this have something to do with what he wasn't telling me?

We moved into the cabin, and at the flick of a light switch, I saw that his father looked like an older version of Hunter, though the years had been very, very bad. He didn't look comfortable with his age like Bill, but it had ravaged through his face all the same. His cheeks and nose were ruddy with broken veins caused by years of heavy drinking; his skin was otherwise pale and soft like a man who had given up on the sun long ago.

The cabin was deserted of inhabitants. Hunter left us to make sure that was truly the case, and I found myself alone with Mr. Hunter. I knew too much about him to be at ease. Before, he had been a ghost story, the tragic figure who never measured up to his father's exacting standards. He'd been the brave, dashing brother who had died mysteriously young—a retro image of Hunter from the late 80's, in my mind. Except instead, he'd survived, and the years of abuse from his father had dragged on long after that. The guilt of his brother's death had settled into him like a disease that showed in the resigned bend of his shoulders.

Hunter returned from the back and asked his father to sit, but the older man shook his head, looking uncomfortable with such hospitality. Not appearing to know the niceties of small talk, he got straight to the point, "This is what killed Charlie. I never wanted you out here."

"Why?" Hunter returned the candor. "What are you afraid I'll find?"

His father's brows drew in, the pain shining in eyes that were paler than Hunter's. "I see you've been living too long with that old oil tycoon."

Hunter scoffed at the insinuation. "I don't listen to Gordon."

"Then why are you here? He's funding this, isn't he?"

"Does it matter? I'm here for the truth—whether you like it or not." Hunter hesitated before asking, "Did you leave your brother behind to die?"

I was shocked at the accusation, but I didn't know enough to intervene. This man could be the one the hermit had warned us against. His father, on the other hand, only seemed annoyed by this talk. "Is that what you think?"

"I think there's someone out there who knows what happened," Hunter said, "and if you don't tell me, I'll find it for myself."

"No!" His father's hand shook, and he straightened in a pitiful attempt to overpower his son's show of spirit, but his shadowed face only revealed a man in hiding. The years had broken him. "Leave this alone."

"I met an old hermit out there in those mountains," Hunter said. "He asked about Harry—he knows your name." That was one mystery solved. His father's name was Harry. Hunter didn't act like this was an important revelation. He pressed for more. "I think he saw everything that happened out there to you and Uncle Charlie!"

"I told you everything."

"That's a lie. Gordon has something he can use against you—that's why he can move you around like his puppet—all of us like puppets! Something bad happened that night."

"Yes, it did!" The veins running through his father's cheeks and nose reddened, and he roared out, "My brother died!"

"Did you kill him?"

I drew in my breath, my gaze running to his father. Such an accusation could break a man, and if it were true? He could be the one behind all our misfortunes. If that hadn't stopped us, would he try something more drastic? Against his own son? But Hunter's father didn't look like a killer, and I watched him wince. "You don't know me at all."

"You never gave me a chance." Hunter's eyes watered with pain, and I felt helpless against it, not knowing what to do.

His father dug around his jacket for more cigarettes, lost without them. "Everyone keeps talking about how Charlie was so perfect! Charlie's gonna put us on the map. Charlie's got it all figured out! He was my younger brother. I knew what he was! Looks like I was the only one—if you even knew the half of it." His head and hand shook with emotion. "I wasted my time coming here."

Hunter looked stricken, and he tried to touch his father, who flinched from him. "Dad."

"No." He moved away. "You're more Gordon's than mine—he's got all the money, all the power."

"You think I care about that?" Hunter shouted.

His father retreated to the door to escape, his arms swinging with abandon, too full of emotion to see clearly as he missed the handle far too many times for me to think he was okay. He rammed his shoulder against the frame on his way out. Hunter watched Harry go, his mouth trembling with emotion.

I hopped from the barstool. "Hunter!"

He put his hand up to ward me off as he wiped at his eyes. "That's a big reason why I didn't want that camera in my face." He was angry. I understood completely now. His upper lip was red from forcing back his grief, and I wanted to hug him, but I knew he wouldn't let me. He was beside himself with wretchedness and rage. Making a strangled sound, he picked up his coat and handed it to me. "Let's get you to your brother."

How could I leave him like this? "Please, let me help you!" I said.

Shaking his head, he headed for the door, blindly, just like his father had. He'd always rescued me, comforted me, shared what he had, and he wouldn't let me help him in return? He'd been taken from his parents and brought to live with some sadist of a man when he was two, and he was still under his grandfather's thumb. Who'd ever watched out for Hunter? Even if he worked for Gordon, he had told me the truth from the beginning. Hunter wasn't doing this for the treasure. Something horrible had happened—to Charlie, to my dad, maybe even to his own. If anyone wanted to stop him from finding out what had happened, they'd have to stop me too.

"Let's find that hermit again and figure out why he knows so much," I said.

"No, I'm not taking you back there."

"If you don't, then I'll do it on my own," I said.

It was the wrong thing to say, and he blew out in frustration. The last thing he needed was more stress, but I wanted to break through that to reach him. "I thought we were in this together," I said. "How else can we know what happened to your uncle and father? My dad disappeared too." He stilled in thought. I was making him work through this logically, and I pressed my advantage. "Let's just go."

"Absolutely not." But he no longer looked so wracked with frustration, and I worried that I'd gone too far. Maybe he might leave without me. He dropped me off at my cabin. I wanted to refuse to go, but he wouldn't be reasoned with. And I didn't want to make things worse for him either, so I let him walk me to the door.

When the door opened, Brek looked up from his couch. "It's about time!"

Hunter nodded once and left. I was afraid I'd put something in his head that I shouldn't have.

I woke up to gravel hitting my window in the wee hours of the morning. Caitlyn jumped up with a tired chirp of fear, and I hurried to push the curtains to the side. Hunter stood out there in the darkness. I'd have recognized his silhouette anywhere.

Working the window open, a cold gust of air met me as I leaned on the sill. "Hunter?"

He shushed me and held up his glowing phone in the darkness.

"Oh!" Caitlyn said as her phone beeped with our newfound phone service. She held it out to me. "I guess he doesn't want to wake up your many admirers." The partiers had been obnoxiously loud throughout the night, but they had begun to fade as the night wore on. Cabins were scarce, camping wasn't as fun as they'd originally thought, and rumor was that we were taking off for Creek Valley in the morning. They'd begun to drop off, but the lawn still looked like the setting for Woodstock. "He's giving you coordinates," Caitlyn said.

We were going to find this hermit. I got dressed, finding the last of my clean sweats to pull over my shorts. I barely had time to pull my hair back when Caitlyn stopped me from going out the door through the living room. "Brek's out there!"

"The window," we both said. She had meant it when she'd said she wasn't trying to impress my brother anymore. I felt like a runaway, but Brek might rouse the neighbors with his complaints.

She giggled and slid her phone to me. "Don't break it."

"You don't need it?"

She shrugged. "I got so used to not having service that I'm fine. Just don't lose it; you know, for when I come back to my senses."

"Thanks." I threw my leg over the window, balancing my backpack over my shoulder and trying to judge the distance from it to the ground when two hands clasped around my legs. I let out a surprised grunt before Hunter shushed me. Finding his shoulders in the darkness, I held on while he transferred my legs to the ground. Now Brek could add kidnapping to his list of complaints. We traveled around the makeshift campgrounds, past the Grizzly, and finally reached the thicket of trees near the trail opening. There, he'd stashed his ATV, complete with helmets.

I took mine, feeling amused. "I thought you'd go without me."

"I couldn't," he said, getting into his seat. "Who'd watch out for you while I'm gone?" Good point, though it was lowering. He helped me into the seat behind him. "And just maybe," he said, "I want you with me." That was more flattering, and a smile touched my lips.

As soon as the engine was on, we took off at full speed to avoid anyone tailing us. The Creek Valley cover story would explain our disappearance, but if we got caught it would all be over. It felt like we were sneaking away from the kids after picking up the sitter. Brek's headlights guided us through the trail. We passed Moonlight Lake and Sinkhole Lake in the dark, and we were moving up the mountain to Lake Adam when the light from the morning sun descended over us. It made the whole forest light up like it was caught up in a fire. It was breathtaking, and we traveled straight for it, going east where we passed the granite mountains to reach the trailhead to where we'd found Adam's cabin before. I got out of the four-wheeler in the meadow, stretching.

Hunter watched me like he wanted to say something, and finally he did. "I'm sorry you had to see me and my father go at it last night."

"That was my fault for not leaving," I said. "Though to be honest, I thought he was dead."

He looked baffled. "Oh? Because of Bill's story. Not many people know what happened. My grandfather sent search and rescue teams for months and they found nothing. Then a year later, my dad returned home out of nowhere, a broken man. He couldn't talk about what had happened. Everything about that night and that expedition was lost. My grandfather was enraged."

"Do you really think your dad killed Charlie?"

"I have no idea. From what I've heard, they were inseparable. My dad was the adventurous, athletic one. Charlie was the intellectual. They weren't rivals; but why can't my dad talk about what happened? How is my grandfather getting my parents to do what he wants? Maybe something did happen between my mom and Uncle Charlie; but to give me up?" He kneaded his forehead. "I think there was foul play. I think it had something to do with this." He pulled out the artifact, tossing it in his hands.

"Someone else is angry about that," I said. "Hybernater." At his confused look, I explained, "Our most devoted online commentator... well, you know, before it went viral. He said some guy took it from him to go after Eden's treasure and never returned it."

"When?" he asked. I admitted ignorance, and he dug more. "Can you write private messages to commenters? We need more info on that."

That made me think Hunter hadn't taken it. I had one other question. "Brek showed me something that he found online about you. You set a warehouse on fire?" It sounded ridiculous saying it aloud.

He blew out and it ended a laugh. "My past isn't exactly stellar."

"That was a few months ago. It wasn't that long ago."

"Well, sometimes it pays to have connections or I'd still be in jail for that."

He wasn't going to tell me, was he? My mind filled with suspicions—he could've been after the men who had gone after his mother as much as he could've been playing errand boy for his grandfather. But the answer-questions session was over. I threw the backpack on my shoulders and he pulled away just as quickly from the ATV. He'd blown the moment by not explaining, but he didn't try to make it right.

We headed back up the same path Hunter had cleared yesterday, and it was much faster traveling to Adam's cabin this time. As we entered the meadow, I felt that same sense of awe from yesterday. The refuge made its own little world surrounded by a wall of mountains, and I imagined Adam coming home from his fur trading, retreating from the cold snow to a warm fire in the hearth. It would be a cozy place to live when he wasn't haunted by memories.

Hunter had gone silent, and I guessed why. "If you find out your father did something bad," I asked, "what are you going to do?"

"I don't know." He directed a mocking smile at himself. "Gordon will probably just use it to blackmail me too."

"Would you ever turn your father in? End the blackmail?"

He shook his head, looking ashamed. "No," he whispered. "Never."

So this was just a quest for answers. Nothing else. We approached the abandoned cabin where we had last seen the hermit. A soft growl next to the porch made me fall back into Hunter when I noticed a pack of dogs waiting for us there.

"Whoa," Hunter stepped in front of me and held his hand out between me and the angry pack. These were the dogs I kept hearing when I caught sight of Bone Man. One of them gave a low growl as it came crawling forward, sniffing and rooting with its ears pulled back until the old man came storming from the cabin in a rage and set them off again.

The curious dog leaped back in a little dance, yapping and growling. "Call them off!" Hunter shouted. "We came to talk to you."

The hermit didn't seem like he'd have the sense to do that, but to my surprise he circled to the dogs and shooed them away with a hiss between his lips. He watched us with that same unblinking intensity from yesterday.

"Do you live here?" Hunter asked.

The man nodded once and slowly. Under the light of the sun, I studied him. His ragged hair and beard was spackled with white and gray. He was shockingly thin, and his clothes hung in tatters around him, including the long black coat that fluttered like a cloak. I could see how he could be Bone Man, and depending on how long he'd been here, that gray hair would've been black when Bill had seen him. He'd look like a shadow at night as well as in the day.

Hunter seemed at a loss, but taking a deep breath, he asked, "Is your name Charlie?" My eyes shifted to Hunter in shock. I hadn't suspected that at all. Were these two truly uncle and nephew? I studied one then the other and saw no similarities except for the strong jaw and heavy brows.

"I drowned," the hermit said. "I came out the other side. She saved me."

"Who did?" I asked.

"Eden." Not only was he back to ghosts, but his vague words weren't exactly telling us who he was either.

"What happened to... Harry?" Hunter seemed more hesitant now. The answers about his father might be hard to hear.

"Eden swallowed him up," the hermit answered matter-of-factly. "She thought he was Lucius, but he would never leave Charlie to die. He never would. Charlie! Charlie! Charlie!" He started to moan out the name.

Hunter let out a breath. "But you survived?"

The hermit abruptly stopped his cry and gave him an impatient glare. "I melted through the rock." He looked up at the sky, staring up at the fluffy white clouds in the sky and pointed to them. "I came out the top!"

Hunter pulled out the artifact from his pocket and showed it to the man again. Like last time, the hermit was mesmerized by it. He reached out hesitantly, his hands shaking like I had seen Harry's do last night on the door handle. "It opened up the earth," he said.

"How?" Hunter's voice turned hard.

"It is..." the hermit's forehead creased in concentration, "it is...Tehillim, Corinthios, Bamidbar. Seven, seven, seven."

Meeting eyes with me, Hunter scooted closer to the old man. "What does that mean?"

"Mean... mean..." The hermit closed his eyes now. "Nathan. He wrote it 1448, Stephanus, he wrote it 1551. Chapters, verses numbered. Hebrew, Greek, Hebrew. Open!"

"What? What?" I asked. Clearly, this man had once been a great thinker—information poured out of him like a sieve. What had happened to him? The numbers and figures were inside his mind, but all other rational thought was gone.

"Gabriel de Padilla lived in the 1550's," the old man said. "Stephanus was his friend. He knew the translations. Tehillim, Corinthios, Bamidbar. Seven, seven, seven."

"He's talking about the bible," Hunter said with some excitement. "Nathan and Stephanus were translators of the Bible. They were the first ones to number the chapters and verses."

"Why is that important?"

"I... don't know."

The man snatched the artifact and twisted it to the side like we always knew we could do, but then he tugged it up so that the copper slid over itself and we saw new writing inscribed beneath it. I still couldn't read it, but Hunter gaped and was quick to retrieve it again, turning it over to stare at it. "This is written in Hebrew and Greek. He's naming off books in the Bible! The Old Testament was in Hebrew and the earliest version of the New Testament was Greek."

The hidden engravings on the artifact were scriptures? "Can you translate what they say?"

He nodded. "Being raised by a complete psychopath has its advantages. Gordon trained me to be both of his sons—the intellectual and the daring one. He'll be sorry." Hunter went back to questioning the hermit. "What is seven?" he asked, but the man wasn't attending.

"We found seven symbols," I said. "Maybe the scripture verses have clues about what to do with them."

The hermit snatched the cylinder from Hunter and put it to his eye. "Seven, seven, seven."

I put my hand out to him, and he set it into my hand. "That is not yours," he lectured me.

"I know," I said, trying to pacify him. Looking through the artifact, I saw the seven Roman numerals on the screen ahead of me and gasped in sudden understanding. "These are the seven numbers... in the same pattern we found on the rock wall. This is a map, Hunter!" I rose to my knees in my excitement. I couldn't believe it.

"And we found them ourselves by taking off-flash photography," Hunter said with a disbelieving laugh. "Do we not need the cylinder then?"

"No," I said. "There's more to it—or we'd have the treasure already."

"Pushhhh," the hermit told me.

"Push?" I pushed on the lens on the cylinder, but nothing happened.

"We need to look up these Bible verses," Hunter said. "Then we'll know. Got a Bible handy?"

I didn't, but there might be one in the cabin. If not, the closer we got to the satellites in town, the more chance we had of picking up the internet to look them up, and I had Caitlyn's phone. It was a good one.

"No, it's not yours!" the hermit was getting angry now, and he pointed at the artifact in a state of agitation. I knew better than to push him. Remembering that he had the strength to drag me off, I lowered the cylinder and almost handed it to him.

Hunter stopped me, though he still tried to humor him. "Is this yours?"

"Not your stick." The hermit seemed quite sullen. "It is David's. David. David Payne."

A shock ran through me at the sound of the name. "That's my father! Hunter!" My hand landed over his forearm. "My father is David Payne! Did he work with you?" I asked the man.

The hermit showed no surprise—in his world everyone would be related—but Hunter seemed stunned. We'd already suspected my father had been on the expedition, but he was lost in thought before he inched closer to the hermit. "Are you David?"

My breath caught in my throat, until the old man shook his head.

Disappointment filled me, but it would've been too incredible. "My dad died in an explosion," I said. "I guess it couldn't be."

"No," the hermit said. "No. He did not." *Yes, he did!* I knew better than to argue with a crazy man, however. "He has a stick," he said. "He knows how to melt into rock."

An explosion then. I was furious with this man, even if he was crazy. Bringing up my father was a sore spot, and to say he melted into a rock was heartless; yet he thought the artifact belonged to *David?* Then my father had been the one to borrow this from Hybernater. This had happened years ago. My father had never returned it because he had died.

A line creased between Hunter's brows as a look of grimness took over his face. Everything came together for me too. All my suspicions were confirmed. My family history was entwined with Hunter's, and the closer he got to this, the more we uncovered from that night where we had both lost so much. Hunter's family had inherited the artifact after my father's death, and they had never returned it to the rightful owner. Perhaps they never knew who that was.

The hermit pointed to the artifact again and said in a voice of such sternness that I was taken aback. "Do not use that. That is Pandora's Box. You cannot close it again. I got stuck. Harry got swallowed."

It was enough to give me pause. We'd walk straight into the thing that had killed them—my father, Hunter's uncle, and whatever had changed Harry forever. Turning to Hunter, I was about to point this out when he leaned forward and tried one more time. "Are you Charlie?"

The old man's whole body shook with rage. "Charlie is bad, bad, bad. He died with us and he'll never, never go away." Then he let out a loud, mournful cry and punched Hunter in the face. Hunter fell back at the impact and then, when the hermit wrestled with him for the artifact, he hurriedly jerked away from him.

I shot to my feet. "No!" I shrieked. The old man didn't listen. "Stop!" I pulled out my bear spray, but Hunter shouted me back and put out an elbow to knock the hermit back, but I knew from experience that he was strong, like a wild animal. The dogs began to bark in the distance, coming for us.

"Hey! Call back your dogs," I cried to the hermit, hoping that would bring him to his senses like last time. His gaze lifted to me and his hand stopped scraping for the cylinder. "Your dad is David?"

"Yes, yes!"

His eyes went back to my wrist. "You're wearing a bracelet. Ring!" He grappled for it. "Give me that!"

Dodging back, I spoke softly, "Yes, it's a wedding ring." It was the one Brek had found in the lake—it had meant so much to someone at some point that it felt like it belonged with the rest of the charms on my bracelet.

"She was pregnant," he said.

I didn't know what to say to that, but since he was being so grabby, maybe I could satisfy him with the ring instead. "Okay, do you want to see the ring?"

I unclasped the bracelet and dropped the ring in the old man's waiting palm, despite Hunter's warnings, and he was right, because the old man caught a hold of my arm, too, and didn't let go. "You're a girl."

"Yes, I have a brother too. I'm a twin." I didn't know why I said that, except to warn him back.

"Twins, twins, twins," he said.

I panicked. "Okay, let me go. My brother is just over there and he's real big."

His eyes widened and he dropped my arm, and I scrambled backwards, running into Hunter, who righted me. "Don't melt into the rock," the old man warned me before he put on the ring. It fit perfectly. Seeing the dogs were almost on us, I retreated with Hunter to a safer distance. "What do we do with him?" I asked.

The hermit wandered over to his dogs, as calm as if we had only stopped by for tea. "He's survived out here for years if he really came up here in '89," Hunter said, catching his breath and touching his reddening cheek. "I have no idea who he is. A lot of people were lost in that. We'll send someone for him."

There was nothing for it. We left the man for his dogs and retreated down the trail and headed for the ATV. "My father *was* on that same expedition your family was on," I said.

He nodded wordlessly, seeming a little preoccupied, his expression darkening like he blamed himself for that too. He seemed to take a lot on himself. "He chose to do it," I said. "He knew it was dangerous and he went for it. The same thing for your dad and uncle. It didn't end well for them, but… who knew the worst would happen?"

"Yeah." He cleared his throat. "If we're doing this, then we need to be smarter. If anything, *anything* looks shady, then you need to back off."

"You too," I said quickly, not liking the turn of this conversation.

He was silent a moment, seemingly deep in thought. "Melt into rocks?" he asked. "What does that mean?"

I rolled my eyes at the offensive description. "He's talking about an explosion."

"That old guy said *he* melted into a rock, too. I didn't see any burn marks on him."

"He also said he was dead," I pointed out, "and that he got stuck and he came out the other side. I hope we don't find out what that means."

"We won't," he said with a stubborn look, but the further we left Adam's cabin behind, the more distant and agitated Hunter became, and more preoccupied. There was something about that conversation that bothered him and he wasn't telling me, no matter how I tried to get it out of him.

"We'll just take this one step at a time," I said. "If we get over our heads, we bring in the big guns."

I wasn't sure who the big guns were, but it wasn't me. He nodded distractedly. We reached the ATV, and he took us to Sinkhole Lake from there. It was mid-afternoon by that time, and we reached the rock wall where we'd found the Spanish symbols. Hunter's chalk marks with the days of the week were still written into the rocks. Before tackling it again, we sat down to eat, and I called Caitlyn—well, Brek, since I had her phone. I could've used the walkie talkie, but there was no telling who was listening in. Plus, it was a great way to test if the satellites were still working. Brek answered on the first ring. "Why didn't you tell me you were going this morning?" he asked.

"We didn't plan it. We talked to that old man in the mountains again."

"You did what?"

"Relax! He only punched Hunter this time."

Hunter glanced up with a smirk at my choice of wording. His cheek was bruising, and I knew it probably still throbbed. "He confirmed everything!" I told Brek. "Dad worked with Hunter's dad and uncle. He knew all their names and everything."

"He's pretty good at copying names," Brek said sullenly.

"He knew about the artifact. It belonged to dad, and he told us how to use it… sorta. I mean, he's not all there, but the shiny stick is supposed to help us figure out what those Spanish symbols on the rock wall mean! We're going to try it out." He turned silent and I tried to fill it in with my talking. "We thought he might be Dad for a minute. The guy said dad didn't die in an explosion, he melted into the rock—which is the same thing, in my opinion."

Brek cut me off. "If this goes south, I want you to stop."

"We know that," I assured him. "We would never put our lives in danger." He made a grunt like he didn't agree, and to get him off my back, I asked for Caitlyn. "Let me speak to her."

Caitlyn got on the phone, bright and chipper. It was like night and day to talking to my brother. "Guess what?" she asked. "All the YouTubers are packing up and going. They're about to take their satellite dishes and cell phone towers down though, so that's kinda bad." She giggled. "We're trying to keep up the appearance of moving out to Creek Valley, so Brek and I have been pretending to pack up all day. Brek's forcing himself to walk around the cabin now."

I got worried for his ankle. "But it's too early!"

"That's what I said; he won't listen to me. I think he's hit his crazy point. He's been hobbling all over the place and avoiding admiring fans… although I think he kind of likes the attention."

Brek barked out a denial, which meant that Caitlyn hadn't bothered to wait until he was out of the room to talk about him. There was a flirtatious lilt to her voice, which meant we were due for another heart-to-heart about her feelings for Brek. "Also," she continued. "Angel isn't anywhere. I haven't seen her for two days."

Hunter looked up. With all the excitement, I had completely forgotten about her.

"And," Caitlyn added, "I know you hate this online stuff, but we heard from Hybernater again. I think he's from Dry Gulch. He noticed that Bill's coin is missing after all these people came into town—he thinks someone stole it. He says it's a key to the treasure!"

What? "But we didn't put up that footage that talked about the coin!" Things were getting worse. I glanced over at Hunter. "Someone stole Bill's..."

"Got it," Hunter interrupted me, looking somber. "Your phone is pretty loud."

I went back to Caitlyn. "But how would the coin have anything to do with that? What did Hybernater say exactly?"

"You'll have to look at what he said. You've got internet on my phone, don't you? You'd better hurry; the towers won't be up for long. On the bright side, I think your plan really worked, you guys. I was starting to miss my quiet little resort town."

Caitlyn hung up, and I looked over at Hunter. He was gone. "Hunter?" He tapped me on the shoulder on the other side of me, and I jumped then laughed, taking a hold of his hand and liking the touch of his muscular arms as they folded over me in response. "Hybernater left another message on our videos," I said.

Hunter smiled at me like that was the last thing on his mind before kissing me with all the passion I'd ever felt in him. He was excited for this find—it was that same giddy elation that got a hold of Brek. I knew it well, except there was more behind this, too; a resignation to the inevitable, a desperation, and I remembered what this find would mean to him. It was that for me, too. We'd know what had happened to our fathers. Hunter pulled back, studying my face. "That's for luck," he said as way of explanation.

"We're really going to do this?" I asked.

"Let's use this internet while we can."

He was right. Armed with the internet, the artifact, and Eden's journal, we'd figure this out. I spared a passing thought for Brek, who'd be horribly jealous of our success. I tried to remind myself that this was for his good. We had to buy those jewels back.

Hunter stood and scanned the perimeter of the rock wall. "We need to get into this priest's head. He sacrificed his life for this. We've got to think his thoughts, feel what he feels. That's the only way we'll be able to get through his series of tests."

These tests made me nervous—if we failed them, I hoped the consequences wouldn't be as terrible as *Indiana Jones* made them out to be. "What test is this one?" I asked.

He picked up the artifact and studied the inscriptions on the side. "He wants a scholar—not just any scholar, but a brother of the cloth. Only monks and priests read the bible at that time, and none of them but his contemporaries divided the Bible into chapters and verses—which was unheard of back then; it would be quite the code. He'd have had no idea that it would be adopted throughout the world."

"So these are only scripture references?" I asked.

"This first one is in Hebrew." He pointed to the writing: תהילים. "This means Tehillim, which is in the K'tuvim. Um, so that's Psalms in the Old Testament," he translated for himself. Grumbling out a laugh, he said, "Not having a childhood has its tradeoffs. This!" He tapped the symbol, סב, "—means sixty-two, and this," his finger ran to the ז symbol, "is verse seven."

Pulling the scripture up on my phone, I read it through. "My salvation and my honor rest on God, my strong rock; my refuge is in God."

"No, wait," he said. "We need to look at Nathan's original translation—he's the Jewish Rabbi—there might be subtle clues we're missing."

With some difficulty, I did the search on Caitlyn's phone, aware that we could lose connection any moment. I found it. "This translation says, 'Only He is my Rock and my salvation; my stronghold, I shall not falter.' Yeah!" I had both translations open. "It seems like that works closer to verse six in the English version."

"So, the verse divisions aren't completely on par with ours today," Hunter said. "Good to know, but I have an idea of what the priest is trying to tell us. We need to find a rock."

"The flat rock in the ground with the X on it," I said—the one with the mysterious circles on either side of it. Searching behind us, I found it easily, near the bushes. "X marks the spot."

"On line of treasure—that's what that means," Hunter said, studying the flat rock. "The scripture uses 'not falter.' That means don't move." He straightened. "That's it! We stand on it."

"Both of us?" I asked.

He gave a laugh. "One of us."

Not wanting to melt into any rocks, I stepped gingerly onto it and was gratified when it didn't move or explode. I put more and more of my weight onto it until it supported me completely. Nothing too crazy was happening, and I looked up at an amused Hunter. "Now what?" I asked.

He refrained from teasing me, only turned back to the artifact again. His dark looks from earlier had brightened at the challenge. I'd always admired his passion, and now I felt it energizing me too. I hadn't realized how much I'd lost mine until Hunter had brought it out in me.

I watched him study the next bit of writing. "This is Greek." Looking up at me, he cracked a smile. "Never my favorite subject, but Κορινθίους is Corinthios. One ad, um," he must've realized he was talking gibberish. "First Corinthians," he translated aloud. "Their numerals are simple because they're Roman, so it's First Corinthians chapter twelve, verse twelve. You got that?"

"Yes." We made a good team. I googled it, feeling like I had a New Age translating device. "For now we see through a glass, darkly;" I read, "but then face to face: now I know in part; but then shall I know even as also I am known." Looking up at Hunter, I felt like I was getting the hang of this. "So, that's simple," I said. "We look through the glass of the artifact."

"While standing on the rock and not 'faltering'," he said. He gave me the cylinder, and I lifted it to my eyes. The roman numerals on the glass didn't fit where we had marked them off on the wall. "It isn't matching up," I said. Hunter took it from me and peered through it. "Are we standing on the right rock?" I asked.

"Kneel," he said suddenly. "You do not stand in holy places, you kneel. It's best if you do it—they were shorter back then, so you'd have the same body type."

With some excitement, I took the artifact and knelt. Sure enough, the numerals matched perfectly with our finds, a roman numeral overlaid over each one like an X. It was a map. Yet, we had circumvented this part with our modern technology. It gave me hope that we could avoid the traps that everyone else had run into.

Hunter tested the lens out for himself, ducking his head to make the map match the symbols through the device. When he pulled back, he seemed confused. "The roman numerals don't match up with the days of the week. The first numeral should be Sunday... or Monday, depending on the calendar; but it's on Wednesday. You see that?"

I got nervous. Were we missing something? "That's okay," he said in a sudden hurry. "That might be part of the puzzle. Let's just do this last scripture before we lose the internet." Pressing his finger onto the last bit of writing, בְּמִדְבַּר, he whispered, "Bamidbar, that's in the Pentateuch... the Torah, so Numbers, and for chapter we have," he ran his finger across the symbols כ and א. "Chapter twenty and verse eleven."

I put the scripture, Numbers 20:11, into the search engine and read, "And Moses lifted up his hand, and with his rod he smote the rock twice: and the water came out abundantly, and the congregation drank, and their beasts also." Circling to him, I asked, "We smite the rock?"

"Yes." He stared at the wall. "We strike the symbols... somehow."

"And water comes out?" I asked doubtfully. That sounded dangerous. "Is this where the coin comes in?" I got excited at the idea. It was the key, wasn't it? "The artifact shows us the way and the coin opens it somehow? It makes sense, right? The symbol on the coin is on this rock I'm standing on." And then I remembered what Caitlyn had told me, "Let's look at Hybernater's comment!"

I opened up YouTube and got an error message on the phone.

Losing internet had been bound to happen, but it was disappointing. "Uh-oh," I said. "The reporters took their satellites with them!" Sitting down on the rock, I tried to think.

"How about Eden's journal?" Hunter asked. "Does she say anything about it?"

I crawled over to my backpack and shuffled through it until I found the journal. Opening it up to the illustration of Pratt's coin, I studied it but found nothing. Then I flipped it over to the journal entry where Adam had figured out how to use the shiny stick.

Eden's Journal: July 11th, 1855 — Mountains of the Deseret

Adam come to me real excited like, and he said, "Eden, my girl, I've a surprise for you!" And he brought me over to them symbols we found and started talking all sorts of gibberish about how they was in a certain order but they warn't. And that we should listen to the shiny stick on this one. "It's all about the order," said he. "That's the way to git at that treasure. We'll return the land to what it once was!" I reckon he got wore out yammering on about it because he ran to git Lucius next, but there was no sign of him neither. So he shinned down the hill to the Shoshone Indians, and they looked on it with powerful suspicion, but what should you know? Adam got it done with their help. They found the way to the treasure!

"She's not really great at explaining anything," I said, which was probably why we hadn't figured this out yet.

At Hunter's beckoning fingers, I gave the journal to him and he read it through himself. "In a certain order," he mused. "Yes! That's it—that's what the roman numerals stand for—we strike them in a certain order."

"Even if we figure out what 'striking' is, then what?" I asked. "The land turns to what it once was? That seems a little risky." Maybe this was the part where we'd melt into the rock. My knees went weak at the thought, and for once I considered bringing in Hunter's team for this.

Hunter shrugged. "Adam didn't die, Eden did... after they got it open. This part should be fine."

He was right. Stretching to my feet, I brushed the pine needles and dirt off my bare legs and took back the artifact before getting on my knees again. Looking through it, I was able to point out the symbol that was marked with the first Roman numeral. "Strike that one first."

"This one?" His hand brushed the wrong one.

"No, that one, to the right, Wednesday! Yes! That one!" Heaving against the stone, Hunter pushed it and it fell inward. We listened to the low growling of chains push into place. The ground shook beneath my feet. I almost dropped the artifact. "What's happening?"

Looking mystified, Hunter threw his hands in the air. "I have no idea."

"Roman numeral two?" I asked. "Do we really want to do it?"

"Yes."

Having no idea if we were doing this right, I guided him to the next, where he pushed it in again. It made the same grinding sound. "We're not breaking anything, are we?" I shouted.

"I hope not." He laughed a little to himself, and I couldn't help it, I was so terrified I joined in. If we messed this up, Brek would literally kill us—this was his baby, and he had told me to be careful, but we kept going, like it was a puzzle where we couldn't stop until we put the last piece in.

Eventually, I heard the roaring sound of streaming water behind me. I climbed over the dirt to look over the embankment to stare at the cliff below. Water pushed out from around the boulders below us in a massive waterfall.

"We're opening culverts," Hunter said. "The whole side of this mountain is a manmade dam."

I stared at it in horror. "Is that going to cause an avalanche or mudslide or something?"

"No, look, it's running through those tunnels and disappearing into a sinkhole. I mean, the water is literally disappearing."

"Is this showing the way?" I asked.

"To what?"

Then it hit me. "Maybe, maybe... this is 'returning the land to what it once was.' All the water melting from the snowcaps would be caught in Sinkhole Lake because of this dam, which would make this lake bigger than it ever was hundreds of years ago. If we're draining it to what it was during the time of Gabriel de Padilla then... it would uncover the caves that hide the treasure." So it wouldn't be in Moonlight Lake like we'd all thought?

"Let's finish this," Hunter said. We pushed each stone in, which started another succession of flowing water. We experimented to see if the order mattered, and found that it was impossible to push one stone in before the proper one before it. It was magnificently engineered. As soon as we got the last one shoved in, the first one closed; the next one followed ten minutes later, like clockwork, and I imagined the rest would follow suit over the next few hours.

We didn't waste any more time. We ran up to the surface of Sinkhole Lake and watched the lowered levels, but there were no caves to speak of. The exposed surfaces bubbled with mud.

"Where's the treasure?" I asked.

"Maybe in another hour or so?" Hunter retrieved his walkie talkie and tried to get a hold of his team to call them over. "Perry? Thomas?" When no one picked up, his expression went tight with suspicion. I noticed he didn't call for Angel.

There was nothing to do but wait as we watched the banks slip further down, uncovering more mud. The pondweed drooped like a nasty green comb over. We sat for a full two hours, throwing rocks and watching the murky lake dwindle to less impressive heights. As the water lapped up against the parts that lay bare, there was nothing there—no opening, no hidden caves, only mud and weeds. Finally, I stood up in frustration and waded into the lake, feeling the slick grass slide under my bare feet.

Hunter scrambled to his feet. "What are you doing?"

"I'm just going to see if I can see anything through all this mud." Maybe standing on the lake floor would give me a better view of what we were dealing with—I might be able to get past all that debris on the banks. Hunter sighed and began taking his shoes off too. As I waded further into the lake, I managed to get past all that nasty pondweed while still keeping to the shallow sections. I promised myself that I would stop if the water reached my waist, though it was getting harder to move. The mud stuck to my feet like heavy glue. It was time to go back. I turned, but as I headed towards the bank, I felt myself sink deeper. I strained to free myself and managed to lift one foot up as the other got stuck. My heart raced. Being an avid documentary watcher, I knew that if this was a type of quicksand, struggling would make it worse.

"Hunter," I said carefully. "I think I might be in a sinkhole." He cursed under his breath and tried to go after me. "No!" I called. "You'll get stuck too."

"Don't move."

"I'm not." And I felt like I was going to cry, because even though I wasn't moving, the mud was sucking me in, and the further I got lodged into it, the worse chance I'd have of getting out. The hermit's words came back to me, and I realized with horror that he could've meant this when he'd said that Eden had swallowed up Harry… but Harry hadn't died.

Hunter traveled around the bank to get as close to me as he could. He tore off layers of his clothing, jacket, hoodie, until he was only in his jeans. His shirt was the last to go, and he tied it to the rest of his clothing like a rope. I didn't think that would hold me. He knotted the end of it and threw it at me so that it landed against my shoulder. "Put that around you," he said, "around your waist."

I did, trying not to freak out. He jerked hard on the end of it, and it tipped me forward. The clothes slid out of their knots and I groaned. He jumped into the water with a splash. "Hunter, no!"

But he was swimming through the deeper waters—not where I

had come—so he wasn't touching the ground, which helped him get to me; but then he planted his legs on either side of me and tugged, ripping us both out of the mud. It worked since he was so much stronger. He growled at me to lift my legs above the mud and swim, and I did. With his arm across my back, he led me through the deepest part of the lake where we didn't have to touch ground.

I'd never been a strong swimmer, but this time the adrenaline coursed through my body and I clawed my way to the bank, feeling the mud at my legs the closer we got to shore. I grabbed at the weeds on the sides. Hunter took one of my legs and pushed me out and dragged himself out at the same time. We breathed heavily on the blanket of weeds, on our stomachs side by side. One of my legs still dangled in the water. I didn't have the strength to pull it back in, but it was too much for Hunter, and he shoved me all the way out of the water as if it might snatch me back in.

My horrified gaze went back to the lake. "What was that? That's not normal! Is that why they call this Sinkhole Lake? Brek said there might be a cavern under all this—plugged up with all that mud."

"What?" Hunter's breathing came out ragged. "You mean he thinks that there's some secret passage in all that sludge that leads to the treasure? A tunnel or something?"

A horrific thought came to me—Harry had been swallowed by it. The hermit talked about coming out the other side—the other side of what? To be sucked into one of those things and not know if you'd make it anywhere else, until you did? No wonder it had turned him mad. "You don't think that all of those people tried to go after the treasure by going through some kind of sinkhole?"

"I don't want to find out." Hunter wiped the grime from his face with the back of his hand. "Is it really worth it? That old man said he got stuck in it. All those people drowning and getting swallowed up and melted into rocks? Do you really want that for us?" His rush of words was interrupted by a fit of coughing, and he cleared his throat and stared at me, his hand going to my cheek to rub off the mud there. "Or we could really live? When I saw you go down, I didn't care about that treasure, Ivy. I didn't care about the gold or even about what happened all those years ago. I don't want to lose you too!" He kissed me on my cheek, my nose, my mouth, and pulled back. "I've made too many mistakes in this—too many—but losing you would be the worst one. Let's call in this hermit to search and rescue, and then we'll live out our lives together. We can have a future."

His muddy hand went to mine, and I stared at it. Like Brek, he had lived his life to the fullest, and just being with him made me more adventurous than I had ever been, so it was funny to think that I was the thing that made him want to settle down, to want to live a normal life.

"But what about Brek?" I asked. We had to get this treasure for him. "He's in trouble."

"Don't worry about that." He sat up with a grunt, pushing his wet hair from his face. "I'm the reason why Angel made a run for it. She and Rosco were the ones behind cutting the fuel line. I thought Bill had loaned us a defect so he could play matchmaker, but when I tried to take out my ATV the next day, it was dead. The fuel line on it was also cut. It wasn't Bill. And you know why she didn't pick up the walkie talkie that night? She was too far away from us to get reception. She'd left the resort to meet up with someone out of town."

"Rosco?"

"Among others," he said, his voice low. These were the people Hunter had been going up against—I knew it. "I took care of it," he said. "I told the rightful owners about where their missing jewels ended up. That's all Rooney needed to know. People only steal from Rooney if they don't think they'll get caught. Believe me, she'll cough up the jewels in no time."

So if Rooney was our backer, that meant that we'd be square. Hunter, Brekker, and I really didn't have to go after this treasure. Whoever Angel and Rosco worked for would be too busy running from Rooney to go after us anymore. The secret of Eden's treasure would die out once the descendants of Lucius put their hearts on something else, and my heart was here with Hunter.

"Okay," I said, laughing out in relief. "Let's live." I wrapped my arms around him and kissed my rescuer.

Chapter eighteen

*W*e came into the Grizzly late that evening, spattered in dry mud from Sinkhole Lake. Bill almost dropped the cup he was cleaning behind the café counter. "I thought you was off to Creek Valley?"

The other old men watched us like we had returned from the dead.

"No, sorry for all the commotion." Hunter leaned on the counter. "We were just trying to kick out the unwelcome guests in this town."

Bill nodded, setting down the cup. "That's good, because the treasure is not there; it's here."

Both of us turned silent. We knew that, which made the decision to not go after it all the harder.

"How about we celebrate?" Bill asked, perhaps sensing our subdued mood. "I've made a Crème Brulee. You can tell us all about your adventures." Despite losing out on the treasure, we had a lot to celebrate—Brek's freedom from his creditors, my relationship with Hunter, and pretty much being alive.

"That sounds perfect," Hunter said. "Let me go back and get on some clean clothes, and I'll take you up on that."

Bill turned to me, and I also accepted the invitation, though I also needed to check up on Brek first. Bill informed me that he had been up and walking already. "He's a strong one, that brother of yours—determined to get back on his feet."

"Well, that's Brek for you," I said. "He gets claustrophobic inside. He's not housebroken yet." Chuckling, I retreated to my cabin after paying Bill for a bottle of orange juice. Hunter and I parted at the middle of the lane where it forked between our two cabins. When I had first discovered that he was going to be our neighbor, I never would've imagined this scenario, as he folded me in his arms and brushed my lips with a kiss before leaving me to dress for dinner.

Opening the door to the cabin, I saw Caitlyn was gone from the back room and that the couch was empty of Brek. He moved around upstairs and I shouted up to him. Brek carefully made his way downstairs, leaning heavily on the railing. I expected him to be happy to see me, but he grabbed me in a hug, completely surprising me, his looks desperate. "What happened?" he asked.

That's when I remembered that I was still covered in mud. We had returned the land to what it once was. And it was a messy thing. Had he sensed that he had almost lost me? I licked my lips, trying to find a way to break my decision to him. "You know how you said to back off if things got too dangerous? We backed off."

He guided me into the living room to hear the story, steadfastly avoiding the ugly orange couch. I explained everything, from opening the culverts to the lowered lake and its muddy bottom that was like a sinkhole and where it had almost dragged me under.

"I'm glad you're okay," he said, touching my cheek. He steadied himself and I cringed at his next words. "I've got to finish this. You know that, right? I can't drop my deal with our backer." He might be blaming 'Walker' for needing to go in, but I detected that eager glint in his eye. This was more dangerous than anything he'd ever done. I had to make him see that.

"You don't need to go in," I said. "Hunter knows Angel took the jewels and he proved it to Rooney—he's our backer—and that's all he wanted. He'll let us go."

Brek looked confused. "Rooney is *not* my benefactor."

"How do you know? You told me he only goes by the last name 'Walker.'"

"Because I know Rooney. Wait." He peered at me like I was crazy. "You lowered the lake and you left it like that with no plan on finishing what you started? You realize we have to strike now while it's still exposed?"

I tried to defend myself. "It's not going anywhere. How is it going to fill back up again? Not until the next snow melts in the spring."

"A sinkhole?" He was still trying to take it in. "Was I right then? Does it lead to caverns or tunnels or something? Is the water going to drain from that whole lake?" he asked, almost to himself. "That would make it easier to get into it." He headed for the stairs to get to his supplies. "We've got to get to it before someone else does."

No, it was too creepy. I tried to stop him. "Brek, please don't try to do it. That hermit we found today said that he got stuck down there. Charlie died and that guy was talking about how he got sucked out to the other side. It sounded horrible."

"Like there is a subsystem in that sinkhole—maybe a whole underworld." He looked excited. I should've seen this coming. "Did you record what he said?"

"No, I kind of learned my lesson from before."

He was frowning. "From who? Hunter? That's what I needed to tell you. You might need to sit down for this." He shoved his phone in my face and I stared at the screenshot. He had taken a fuzzy picture of Hybernater's latest comment. "Read this."

I wasn't in the mood for more accusations, but I needed to know what I was up against and so I read through it:

Anyone hear about Adam Black who first settled Dry Gulch? I heard tale he had a coin that he called the key to the greatest treasure. Of course, after all this media hoopla that's come into town, I didn't see it on the Grizzly wall like it's been. Seems like someone's stolen it. It got me to thinking that maybe someone's figured out something that we hadn't—like maybe we should've taken Adam Black's words more literal. Is the coin an actual key? We'll never know because some fool of a thief don't got the smarts to figure it out. I'm done with this. This whole business rots the soul.

"Hunter brought his bad habits here," Brek said. "Don't you get it? He stole Bill's coin. The cops have been poking around here. They're asking for him."

Were they at his cabin then? I stood up quickly, peering through the windows and noticing the collection of vehicles parked around Hunter's place. "Why didn't you tell me?" I ran out the door, leaving the door swinging on its hinges as I headed for Unit #3, quickly outpacing Brekker in my haste to help in any way I could. Hunter would never steal from Bill.

Brekker called after me, angrily trying to keep up. "Ivy! Don't go over there! He's guilty." Brekker was wrong! Hunter had given up on the treasure to keep me safe, hadn't he? Or had he not needed my help anymore and would go after it when I was out of the way? No, those were my doubts talking. I rushed up the stairs to Hunter's cabin and walked into chaos.

The place had been torn apart. Hunter stood in the middle of it in his muddy tee shirt and jeans, glowering at the group assembled inside. Angel was back, along with Rosco and a few other burly men that I didn't recognize. My heart quickened. There were two uniformed officers there too, which was possibly the only reason that things were still civil. When Hunter saw me, his whole manner changed to concern and he tried to get to me.

An illustrious, elderly man blocked him from going anywhere. He was too well dressed to be an inspector from Dry Gulch. He looked to be mid-seventies, had a high, freckled forehead with a sparse head of white hair, and wore a tailored suit made for a man half his age. His collar was free of a tie and unbuttoned. But it was his eyes that caught my attention. They were hazel like Hunter's, but menacing. His brows rose at me like he knew who I was.

Brekker came through the door behind me and stopped short. "Walker?" he asked.

The sophisticated man coughed into a hand covered in rings, and he glared until he found his voice. "You working against me with my grandson?" *So, not Walker. This was Gordon.* Did that mean that he was

327

our backer? I froze as the truth hit me. Hunter didn't work for him—we did. And Angel and Rosco were also under him. Had Hunter known? For sure, Brek hadn't. He looked as confused as I felt.

Gordon stepped toward us, putting most of his weight on one leg as he did so. Hunter's grandfather easily took the role of patriarch of his family, though the years had been kinder to him than to his son. "How long has this been going on?" he spat out at Brek.

My twin still looked bewildered, but he'd always been fast on his feet. "Hunter had information that we needed to find the treasure," he said. It didn't make us look good, and I listened to Brek repeat my words. "Fifty-fifty is better than nothing."

Gordon snorted. "Fifty-fifty?" His tone made it clear he had no intention of honoring the deal.

My gaze veered to Hunter, and his jaw tightened, though a thread of uncertainty broke through his defiance. I tried to put together how much he'd lied, but I still couldn't figure out what was going on.

"Aiden tells me that you've given up on finding my treasure," Gordon said, a thick crease hardening between his brows. "You better believe he was getting ready to sneak back and get it."

"I wouldn't do that to you." Hunter's words were only directed at me.

"You wouldn't?" Gordon's voice turned rough. "Then why did you take that coin from the Grizzly? Angel told me what you did." He swiveled from his grandson and went for me. "Did Aiden give it to you, little girl? I want the coin and I want that artifact too."

I stood my ground, but a part of me wanted to run at the rage permeating through his wrinkled face, like he could turn me upside down and frisk me and no one would question him. I glanced over at the officers, but they didn't interfere.

Brek was quick to get between me and his backer. "She has nothing to do with this."

Gordon snorted. "What about you? You thought you could stop me with Rooney? I made Rooney!"

"That wasn't Brek," Hunter said behind him. "I contacted Rooney. I thought he might want to know who stole his find."

Turning with the viciousness of a wounded coyote, Gordon backhanded his grandson hard, rings and all. It was done with the ease of a hardened abuser and scraped up Hunter's face. Hunter took it with a grimace like he was used to it. "Such a stupid move, Aiden. Have you learned nothing? No one gets out of working with me—not even you."

Angel stood stiffly behind him, and I wondered if that was true for her too. Had she been corralled into this or was she just greedy?

"Yeah?" Hunter's mouth bled, but he stubbornly refused to wipe at it. "Did Rooney take it lying down?" His lip curled. "I don't think so. You're on the run." His hazel eyes narrowed at his grandfather. "I have to say, it feels real good to get out from under your thumb."

I thought he'd get hit again, but Gordon's eerie silence felt scarier before he broke out into a goofy grin that didn't fit the vicious tremble in his jaw. "Oh? So that's how you want to play it? I thought you were better than your old man—but you're just as stupid. Do you prefer jail? Is that it?"

Hunter's eyes veered to the two officers. He didn't look impressed. "Are those even real?"

"You bet they are. Should they read the charges out loud? Let everyone know what you did? Better yet, let's talk about your father."

Hunter's lips tightened as if forcing himself to stay quiet.

"You want to know about that night, boy?" Gordon taunted. "I'll tell you about it... every sordid detail, every little thing your daddy did. Oh wait, you don't want to hear it anymore?" His spiteful gaze slid over me and Brek, like the move was meant to toy sadistically with his grandson. Whatever Gordon knew, whatever he'd used to keep Hunter's mother away from him, played at the tip of his tongue. "Aiden always thought he knew better than me—you were just a kid when it happened," he shouted over his shoulder to Hunter. "What did you know? But you've guessed it now, haven't you? I see it in your eyes— you haven't started your usual whining with me—'Leave my dad alone,'

" he mocked. "Yeah, Harry got Charlie killed. He was behind a few other deaths, too, some of them not so innocent." Gordon's bulbous eyes found mine and they were full of broken veins and malice. "You know where Hunter's dad got that artifact?"

He'd gotten it from our dad, but what had that to do with anything? Brek was silent beside me, which meant he was listening intently.

"Aiden knows, don't you?" Gordon asked. "You know and you didn't tell your little girlfriend? She is your little girlfriend, aren't you darling? Is that how he got you to work with him? I've seen the videos. He was using you…"

"Don't listen to him," Hunter said.

"Stop pretending to be a boy scout—I've put you on missions that would make hardened criminals blush."

Hunter tried to deny using me like that and then, meeting my eyes, lowered his and said, "I thought you knew about Gordon at first, but I figured it out real quick. You were in the dark."

"And you thought why not use this little girl to help yourself out, get a little sugar on the side?" Gordon spit out the disgusting insinuations through cracked lips. Rosco grumbled out a laugh to the side, leering. Gordon snorted at his grandson. "You were never going to help her get the treasure when you wanted it for yourself. I get it, Aiden—you're afraid if she knew the truth that she wouldn't work with you… that she'd hate you? That's real sweet. *You like her…* in a way."

I didn't know what secret his grandfather was getting at, but I wouldn't let him use it against us. Lifting my chin, I prepared to hear the worst. Gordon stopped, inches from me, his breath rancid. Appropriate, since everything from his lips was rotten. Studying my face, he straightened and smirked. "Tell me where you stashed the things you stole, Aiden, and I'll leave it there." He paused a mere second, not giving his grandson time to decide, before the cruelty of his nature took over and he blurted out, "His dad killed yours to get that artifact."

A gasp tore from my throat. Hunter closed his eyes, his teeth clenching against the words.

"What?" Gordon let out an easy laugh. "You didn't want me to tell her like that? I'm only being honest—it must be so refreshing for her."

"Your son killed our father?" Brek's hand clamped over my arm. *"Some friend of the family.* And you hired us knowing what he did?" It was obvious Gordon only wanted us because we had Eden's journal. Angel leaned provocatively against the table, watching us with interest. Rosco grinned like a mad man. They were the scavengers who'd sweep in after we joined our clues with Hunter's.

Brek eased me back towards the door with him. "We're out," he said.

"You shut up," Gordon told Brek like he was an annoying fly, "you never knew your father anyway." To my alarm, his men moved to cover the door. "But, I'll make it up to you. I'll take you kids in like you're my own—your mom's had a hard time of it. I've watched her over the years. Taking on two brats like you hasn't been easy on her. How'd you like me to take care of her too?"

This man was insane. Brek had gone stiff. "What do you want?"

"Here's the thing—I have those Irish jewels. I bought them fair and square from Angel here, but I'm a good guy. I'll give them back to you, Brek—give you anything you want, even take care of your mom for you—if you and your sister work with me."

Hunter cut in. "You don't need them. I have the artifact. I'll give it to you if you give me the job. I'll throw in the coin for good measure."

I searched his face and he kept it free of emotion. Was it true? He had the coin? If he did, had he really planned on double-crossing me this whole time? The part of me that wanted to believe that Hunter was looking out for me wondered if he interfered to keep us safe, but I wasn't sure.

Brek snorted at him, already hating him for everything before this. "No one needs the artifact anymore. You and my sister already opened the culverts and drained the lake."

Angel made a happy sound. "Is that true? Now you and your sister can go in."

Brek shook his head. "No, she's not that good. I'm not taking her."

Gordon grimly saw the sense in that. "Angel will go." He shot a glance at his grandson. "You happy now? Little Ivy will be safe. See, I'm on your side."

In her excitement, Angel also tried to patch things up. "Brek! I told you I'd make it up to you." She inched toward him as if approaching a wild animal. "He stole from his grandfather. He took the artifact... you couldn't get in without it. This was your life's work."

Brekker ignored that, and I knew exactly what he was thinking. My brother wanted to go into these caves in a bad way, but the other part of him was well aware of who we were dealing with and what would happen to us once he worked with them... or didn't. We were stuck.

Hunter studied Brek like he wasn't sure how to take this new development. "Don't trust Gordon," he said. "He's using you like he uses everyone."

The man in question snickered. "It's called a business arrangement," his southern accent turned twangy when it dripped with sarcasm. "That's what people do when they don't lie and steal and set my warehouse on fire. Aiden, over here," Gordon explained to the room as if he were merely discussing politics, "stole his uncle's maps and clues from my warehouse." His brow rose in realization. "Is that how you knew about those Irish jewels?"

Hunter refused to answer that.

"You're lucky I didn't press charges."

"You didn't want to get caught," Hunter said.

Gordon sighed mournfully. "What must you think of me? Now, give me the coin. You won't be joining us for this find, I'm afraid." Hunter looked up quickly, and then his eyes ran to me in worry, like I might still be going in. "You would only get in the way," I heard his grandfather say. "I've talked to your father. He's in town. He can take you home and we can forget this happened."

Hunter stood his ground. "No."

A knock sounded on the door and Gordon stalked to the windows, peering out the blinds. A group of officers, including the sheriff of Dry Gulch, stood outside, illuminated by the light from the patio. Frank was with them, dressed in his deputy garb. Now these cops were real—though this was probably their first gig in years, and suddenly I felt nervous for them. Gordon nodded to Rosco to open the door, and he swung it open, squinting down at the unimpressive group of townsmen.

Bill stood to the side of them, looking stern in his cowboy hat. "I heard what happened," he said softly. His eyes found Hunter through the crowd gathered in the cabin and he took a deep breath. "Was that you, Aiden? You took my coin?"

For the first time that night, Hunter reddened with shame. "I didn't want you to get involved in this."

Bill looked disappointed, his eyes pinning him with the severity of a father. "Let me see it."

Hunter ran his tongue over his lips and, making a sudden decision, shook his head. "I can't."

"What's that mean?" Gordon demanded of his grandson. "You don't really have it?"

Hunter's voice turned harder. "It means, you're not getting it."

Gordon made a noise of protest, but there was nothing he could do surrounded by the police officers from Dry Gulch. None of these men were in his pocket.

The sheriff turned to Bill with a sober look. "You're pressing charges then?"

"Yeah, yeah, I guess I am." The men pulled out a warrant for Hunter's arrest.

Hunter backed up quickly, his eyes going to me like he was afraid to leave me alone with this group. Brekker had gone into this fully aware of the dangers, but I had no say in what happened.

"It's best you come without a fight," Frank said, his usual humor gone from his voice.

"Aiden!" Gordon called over with a threatening growl to his voice. "A night in jail will do you good. I might pay you a visit if you change your mind about helping us out here."

Hunter turned quickly away and moved past me on his way to the door. Bending over me, he whispered for my ears alone, "Come with me."

Bill's attention was on us and he cleared his throat. "You involved in this, Ivy? Should we take you in too?"

His words shocked me. How could Bill think that I'd do something like that? But meeting his sober gaze, I wondered if I should do what Hunter said. Maybe I should pretend I was an accessory to get away from here? Hunter begged me with his eyes to do it, but seeing my brother with this hardened lot, I knew I couldn't leave him—he'd become one of them without me. "No," I said. "I don't know anything about it."

"We could take her in for questioning?" Frank asked hopefully.

Now I felt they were ganging up on me. Gordon lifted a hand that shook with age, used to being obeyed in everything. "Unless you've got a warrant for her arrest, you're wasting your time here."

The officers looked disappointed. Frank took Hunter's arm, leading him out. I felt like I was losing my only allies, but most especially I felt a pang at losing the man I'd come to trust and respect. I was caught between wanting to cry and staying strong for Brek. Even with my twin by my side, I was scared. Was this how Eden had felt when Lucius had left her to die? Or did it feel even worse for her when Adam had walked away?

I'd have to step up. Hunter couldn't rescue me now. For some reason he'd blocked us from taking the coin. And if that was the key? Then maybe we couldn't go in anyway? The thought gave me hope, though I couldn't see how the coin worked. Eden hadn't mentioned it at all... and she had died. Could that be why? My nerves bunched up at the thought as the night turned into a blur around me.

Gordon and his men packed up for Sinkhole Lake. They pored over the maps and notes that Hunter had stolen from the warehouse, asking me all sorts of questions. It felt weird that this rough group would be finishing what Hunter and I had started. Our hunt had turned into a labor of love; theirs was cold and calculated. I kept an eye on Rosco, wondering if Gordon might try to send him after Hunter in jail to get that coin. I was sick with worry.

Brek was going over the maps when I approached him. "This isn't a good idea," I said under my breath. The mud at Sinkhole Lake had been sticky and heavy—maybe if they waited a few days for it to dry.

"I don't have a choice," Brekker said. "I need to get those jewels back."

From the man who had stolen them? Looking over at Gordon, I saw that he supervised the proceedings as part jailor and part benefactor. He walked crookedly over to Angel to whisper low, his back bent by age, his body twisted from the inside out. I wasn't sure why he'd told us about our father. Would Gordon really let Brek go after this? If this night didn't kill my brother, then being prisoner to the whims of a man like Gordon would. There was something else driving Brek tonight, and it had to do with the thrill of the find. It made me wonder how many men like this my brother had worked for over the years? He didn't seem a stranger to this kind of activity, and this time it might come back to bite him.

Something felt wrong, and I skimmed through Eden's journal to figure out what it was—knowing that they would take the journal from me soon. Angel kept casting it hungry looks, and I would be absolutely heartbroken to relinquish it to her. I reached the last entry, and instead of skimming it, I took my time. The cautionary tale seemed to fit with my life now. This was what came of trusting a bad boy.

Eden's Journal: July 16th, 1855 – Mountains of the Deseret

Lucius catched Adam kissing me and now I feel like a kid with a hand stuck between the cookie jar and the sugar bowl. Lucius got real red in the face and said he was getting around to making an honorable woman out of me, which meant we was practically married and I was going against God messing with another man. "You're plenty lucky, Eden," says he, "that I'm willing to take you in after what I'd seen of you in San Francisco—you who'd go with any man who'd asked it of you—I'm the kind of man to overlook what you are, but an upright fella like Adam would never if he'd seen what I'd seen. Even if he was fool enough, the honest town roundabouts would shun him for it."

I knowed Lucius was right, and I felt sour all over like old milk. Adam were a good sort of man and I was nothing to him. Lucius and I were more fitting. Sides all that, I was used to Lucius' ornery ways—being with him was like washing dishes in the river and cleaning the muck off boots. He could make me happy if he loved me, and wouldn't you know it? He told me he did. It warn't as if I didn't yearn for his love, but I didn't rightly believe him like I believe Adam.

It warn't long after that when Adam found the way to get to that treasure. We saw the water splashing out so much from the hole it fountained up to the skies, and soon we was able to see the rocky bottoms to where that treasure was hid. Lucius came strutting over, and he told me in his rough way to move. Adam took offense and said as how he didn't like how Lucius treated me, and when Lucius said he'd do what he'd like by me, Adam fought him. They punched and bled all over the rocks like a bunch of rabid varmints going at it, and me a hollering for them to stop.

Adam got Lucius a good one under the chin so that Lucius fell. Then Adam took my hand, his eyes ablazing, and he tells me how I gots to be the one who chooses between them. And I didn't know what I was fixin to do. I knowed I wanted to be with Adam—a full on man with strong shoulders and sober looks, and maybe I loved him, but that didn't make it right. I was poison to a good man's soul and I shouldn't do no such thing.

I told Adam I could never be the woman he wanted me to be, especially after my mom up and died and left me to the saloon to raise me up proper, except I warn't. I made him cry, but it was best he cry now than all the days of his life crying over a woman like me. He told me he'd never push me away if I came back, but I knowed I was no kind of woman for him. And so he left and didn't go after that treasure, leaving Lucius and me to the whole of it. We had to hurry into those caves or it would all be over. My heart feels so low. I keep telling myself that it ain't so bad I got Lucius. He said he loved me no matter what I was, but still there is a pang in my heart for what might have been.

And that was the end of Eden's journal. Soon afterwards, Eden entered the caves with Lucius and the rest of their history got lost in Payne family legend. The caves filled with water from the lake, and, fearing for his life, Lucius left Eden behind in the caves. Though she pled for his help, she drowned there, alone. He was the worst kind of man alive, but in my heart, I knew that Hunter would never have done such a thing to me.

I reread the part about the water that splashed out. It sounded almost exactly like the culverts Hunter and I had uncovered, besides the description of the fountain. And there was no mention of mud, just a rocky bottom. "Brek," I said. "Read this."

He sat down beside me on that ragged couch and read through the part that I had pointed out. "What about it?"

"It's not the same as Sinkhole Lake. Where's the mention of the mud? I was stuck there, Brek. I couldn't move. This says a rocky floor. There's nothing here about the lake lying shallow for days to dry before they went in."

"The geography has changed?" he guessed.

"No! When we let the water out of the culverts, it shot out the side, but it didn't fountain up to the sky. Brek, I think she's talking about the geyser, but how can that be?"

"Ah, don't you look so cute together. The twins." Rosco sneered at us and snatched at the book. I held it closer to my stomach and

337

glared.

Brek put a protective arm over me. I didn't want to think what would happen to me if any harm came to him. "Why don't you go and do something useful?" Brek asked, "Like pick on small woodland creatures."

That seemed his style. Rosco acted like he might retaliate, but then he turned with a vicious snarl. We watched him strut away, though he cast looks at me every so often. I wasn't sure what he was planning, but it wasn't good. "I know you don't listen to me very often," I whispered to Brek. "You're usually the one that goes by your gut instinct, but my gut's telling me something and I need you to hear me out. Hunter said that the geyser at Moonlight Lake had to have a water source, but there was no groundwater. That's why it was practically dead, because it couldn't pull from the lake either. Maybe it was attached to it like a straw at an angle, but the thing is… we just fed it."

Brek's arm tightened over me before he reached down to look at the journal again.

Everything that I had heard from Hunter came back to me in a rush. "After that, the CO2 would pressurize under it all," I said. "That'll make the geyser explode! It could lower the water surface there—at Moonlight Lake! Maybe that's what we're looking for. It makes more sense with what Eden's saying!"

Brek rushed after his maps to study the lakes that seemed to make a stepladder from one to the next "It could start a chain reaction that was so strong that it would suck the water out of the lake in its explosion," he said. "Yes! Like drinking through a straw. I think you're right on this one, Ivy. This was always about draining Moonlight Lake—not Sinkhole." Looking up from the map and where he'd stuck a pin on the geyser, he turned to me. "You've put it all into motion. This geyser is going to go off soon… if it hasn't already."

It made sense. Will Pratt, that mean old prospector who'd lost his coin to Eden, had said that the treasure could only be accessed once, and in the spring. Was that because once the geyser was fed from the culverts, then it would lose its access to more water after it blew? Eden had said that they had to go in right away or they'd run out of time. Sinkhole Lake would stay low for the rest of the summer, but once Moonlight Lake was drained, it would fill back up from the geyser's flow-off.

The thought of Brekker meeting his muddy death at Sinkhole Lake terrified me, but a nice rocky bottom on Moonlight Lake with a possible trapdoor felt more doable. For the first time that night, I breathed easier. My brother might live through this.

Chapter nineteen

*I*t was midnight when I left Hunter's cabin—my mind darted from my brother's plight to his. As far as jails went, I was sure the one in Dry Gulch was tame, but I feared that Gordon would try to get the coin from Hunter in any way possible. I didn't trust Rosco, and I didn't think Frank could fight him off. At the same time, that coin could potentially save my brother's life. I wasn't sure how, but Hunter might know. He might know a lot of things, and if what we had was real, then he might confide in me. That was assuming a lot. He came from a line of pyschos, and more than anything, I was afraid he was one of them.

The lights in our cabin were on, and I prayed that meant that Caitlyn was there. I really needed my best friend right now. I took the stairs, and my foot squeaked on the first step. Caitlyn came careening around the door at the sound. "Hybernater's been at it again!"

I didn't want to hear it, but if our favorite online commentator had something to do with keeping Brek safe, I *had* to be all ears. Caitlyn took hold of my hand and dragged me out the door with her into the night. She was taking us to the Grizzly. "When the police came around asking for Hunter, I ran and got Bill," she said. "My brother's a cop and, no, those guys were not legit. Bill got Frank, and they came to take Hunter away to rescue him from those fakes. Bill and Frank didn't know you'd be stuck in there too or they would've trumped up some charges against you and Brek, just to get you out of there!"

"Wait?" I couldn't keep up. "So they didn't take Hunter to the jail then?"

"Oh, they did," she said, halting outside the Grizzly. "He's got some outstanding warrants and so they've got to be above-board and all that."

A loud roar of engines sounded across the lot as Gordon's group of men passed us, their lights shining eerily into the darkness. Gordon trailed them in an oversized-mud-wheels Jeep, his dashboard light revealing his arrogance as he waved a hand full of rings at me, like he hadn't just informed me that his son had murdered my father. I didn't see Rosco with them at all. Angel and Brek were the last riders on the trail. My brother didn't see me as he passed, even though Caitlyn called out for him. Angel saw us, and she spared us a slow smile when she passed under the streetlight before disappearing up the trail after the other gold diggers.

Caitlyn gave a little growl in anger. "Angel! I should've known she'd cause more trouble. I thought, 'Oh, she disappeared, we're through with her!' Then when she came back with Rosco and that old guy, I about died. I don't know if I can take Brek's stupidity anymore."

"He thinks he's smarter and stronger than anything he's up against," I said. "He knows that these people are crooked, but he thinks he's going to come out of it without a scratch."

"Well, Hybernater thinks there's a trap inside the cave," Caitlyn said. "That's why I'm freaking out, but Brek won't answer my texts and won't take it seriously at all!"

She wrenched open the door and our eyes shot to Bill at the computer. His cowboy hat was a little askew. "Bill?" Caitlyn asked. I was surprised to find him here instead of near the action at the jail, but Caitlin wasn't at all. "I told Ivy what's happening!" she said. "And now I'm showing her what Hybernater wrote!" She hurried to the computer, and Bill pushed out of his chair, his knees creaking as he gave her his seat—they were getting quite adept at the computer switch. "See?" She pulled up the comment under the video. "Read this!"

Bill and I met eyes, and I tried to convey my apology. "I am so sorry about that coin."

He waved that away and shuffled into the back room. "You have worse problems."

"You do! You do!" Harlan said. He sat next to Pat at their usual place at the table, not looking tired at all. They were a nocturnal bunch. Pat's shoulders hunched over his cane, which was also usual. However, Frank was missing, which meant he was guarding someone at the jail. Caitlyn was tugging on my arm as soon as she pulled up the site, and I leaned over her shoulder to read:

Surprise! The Hybernater is back again! This whole treasure hunting business won't leave my mind. People who go looking for that treasure don't come back from it. I think this has something to do with the fact that this treasure was hidden by the Spaniards—they were known for their devices of torture, especially during the Spanish inquisitions, which was at this same time. I ran across an article on "el Draque"—the pirate who constructed a crude structure based on the barbaric practices of his Spanish slaves to entice those searching for his treasures by putting that treasure in actual touching distance. It was the bait, so to speak, so that any poor seafarer would reach inside a hole to get to it and set off a mechanism that would lock the hand inside like a monkey trap. It was called the Spanish Lover's Trap because another mate could put their hand into the hole on the other side and free the first victim at the expense of his or her life. And on and on, the two would take turns freeing the other until the trap clenched down and chose its victim. In el Draque's cave, the tide would eventually come and drown whoever was left. The symbol of this trap is a cross with two holes on either side of it—this is found on the back of Bill Pratt's coin—I no longer believe that the coin is the key to getting the treasure, but escaping it.

"There's not more?" I shouted. "What does Hybernater mean it's the way to escape? Write him back! Write him back! I want details!" But how soon would he get back to us?

Hunter had said that the Spanish priest had set up a series of tests to measure the mettle of a man and whether he was worthy of the treasure. Was this another test? What were we supposed to prove here? It seemed to me that the person who sacrificed for the other in this

Lover's Trap would end up dead! Like Eden!

Hunter had stolen the coin. That meant he'd kept this back from me too. Now it was my turn to pull at Caitlyn's shoulders as she finished off her message to Hybernater. If I wanted Brek to leave that cave alive, I'd have to figure out how that coin worked.

"Um…" Caitlyn leaned back with a surprised look. "We're not signed in as ourselves… we're signed in as Hybernater."

Bill heard that as he walked in and lurched to a stop, caught. His friends at the table jeered at the fine joke. His face reddened.

"You're Hybernater?" I asked.

"Well," he blustered, "who did you think it was? Some fourteen-year-old punk?"

"Not exactly," Caitlyn muttered.

"Then… then…" my words crashed over each other, "you were the one who gave that artifact to my dad. David Payne? Was that really him? Was he the one?"

"Yes." Bill leaned next to his Dogo Argentino, rubbing his ears. "The whole sad affair left a sour taste in my mouth, but when you kids came into town, I couldn't help but take on your cause. I guess I have a soft spot for you."

Caitlyn stood up from the computer, sighing. "I should've known that was you."

We didn't have time for a *Scooby-Doo* moment. I grasped onto Bill's hands like my lifeline. "What do you mean that the coin is the way to escape, not the way to get in?"

"I don't know, dear, it's just that no one gets out of this alive as far as I can see. It's a hunch."

If that coin had ended up in Adam's hands, that meant that Eden had given it to him before she'd gone into those caves. She hadn't stood a chance. "I'm sorry to take another thing from you, but we need that coin!" I said. And there was only one way to do that. "Where's this jail?"

He hesitated. "Now I don't know if that's the best course of action."

Harlan broke his silence at the table, gathering his coat and hat. "Of course it is. Don't you want to witness the big declaration of love, the apology, and the make up?" Pat backed him up with a smile and a nod.

I drew myself up. "That is not what this is about!"

Bill grinned broadly now. "No, no, of course not."

"This is serious!" I said, but they barely heeded me.

He turned to his compatriots at the table. "Who's ready to break Aiden out of the jail?"

"That seems a little dramatic," Harlan muttered. "We could just drop the charges."

"That ruins the fun a bit." Bill seemed downcast.

"Anyway, I don't like it," Harlan said. "This is all too dangerous for you, Ivy."

"I know you probably don't like Brek, but…"

They interrupted with shouts of denial. "We like Brek!"

"Yes, yes," Pat said.

That was surprising; he'd been so surly here. "Well, I'm trying to save his life." And then when I looked down at the charm bracelet on my wrist, I choked on my words and broke down crying. I was a little stressed out.

The old men made soothing noises and hugged me. "Let's see what we can do." Bill picked up Skip's leash like we were simply leaving to walk the dog, and he led us outside in a parade of stressed girls and old men… and then across the street to a cluster of small buildings, one of them a post office, which we entered.

"This is the jail?" I asked.

"Not bad, eh?" Harlan asked, stepping onto the wooden floorboard. It creaked like it was a million years old.

"Do you ever use it?" Caitlyn asked.

"Sure… if the occasion calls for it." We turned the corner and found Frank sitting at a little wooden table. I looked around for

344

Hunter, not finding him. I felt like I was in the Mayberry jail with Barney Fife.

"Where is he?" Bill asked Frank.

The man rubbed at his whiskers and sighed a heavy sigh of importance. He finally had a prisoner. "You're not getting him out," Frank warned. "This is over my head."

The other old men stiffened in excitement, like that meant a jailbreak was in order. I ignored that. "Can I at least talk to him?"

"Well, no one said anything against that," Frank said. "I s'poze so." Signaling for us to follow, he went down a long hallway and opened a heavy seventies-styled metal door. Hunter stretched out on a bench behind the bars, his arms crossed as he stared up at the ceiling.

"Hunter?"

As soon as he saw me, he scrambled to his feet. "Frank won't listen to me." He pushed against his cell, looking desperate. "I'm trying to tell him those guys are dangerous, and he keeps saying to save it for the judge." His hands found mine through the bars. "I am so sorry, Ivy."

"For which part?" I steeled myself for the truth. "Were we? Were we real?"

"What?" his voice broke on his emotion. "Yes, we're real! I'm just sorry about who I am. That my father did that..." he couldn't bring himself to say it, "to yours. It's unforgivable."

I put my hand up to touch his face through the bars. "You didn't do it. We're not meant to pay for the sins of our fathers."

"Oh, but we do," he said with some bitterness. "We do. My mother didn't know what she had done leaving me with Gordon. He likes to collect things—that includes people. He's warped. He'll do anything to manipulate us. He used me to find him priceless artifacts in these dangerous excavations—it's what he did to his sons. He made them what they are. My mom probably thought she was saving my dad from jail. He's so broken, Ivy. I'd thought the secret I'd find was maybe an affair between her and Charlie—she'd been on the expedition with them—but never this. I didn't know what he'd done. I didn't, not until today! When that hermit attacked you and said that a man had been killed for that artifact, I didn't put it together until this afternoon when he said that it belonged to your father. That's when I knew the secret my father had been hiding all these years. It was why my grandfather could blackmail everyone—of course he could! It was indefensible. I didn't know how to tell you after that."

"It wasn't your fault!" I held onto his fingers and wanted to kiss it all better, but nothing would make any of this better. "You can't blame yourself."

His fingers slid from mine and he looked down. "Don't forgive me. I used you. When I heard your last name was Payne, I knew Gordon had hired you. You had no idea who you worked for—I saw that—but I wasn't so sure about Brek... once I found out that Angel was manipulating him with those jewels, I thought I'd get rid of that threat and you'd be free."

"We're even," I admitted. "I stole your artifact once—I mean, I didn't know it was the artifact until later, but... and well, I was planning on double-crossing you too."

Caitlyn nodded to confirm it.

He looked surprised, and then amusement spread across his face. "You were?"

"Yeah... and that just kinda went away." I frowned. "Were you going to go for the treasure without me?"

"I don't know. That lake doesn't look like it's going anywhere."

"What about the coin?" Bill asked from behind me.

Hunter looked sheepish again. "It's somewhere safe—as soon as I get out of here, I'll get it."

"Just tell us where it is," I said.

"It's too dangerous. I'm not letting you do this alone. I knew Angel would try to take it when she left with Rosco—I had no idea why, just that my uncle wrote about it being a key. To be absolutely clear, I didn't know Angel was against me at first. I only saw the jewels

346

when I broke into the warehouse."

"That's what the warrant is about," Frank said.

Hunter looked confused. "Gordon dropped the charges."

"Looks like the city wants to look into it—probably to investigate Gordon, most likely."

"Why'd you set it on fire?" Bill was genuinely curious.

"Have you met Gordon?" Seeing he wouldn't be getting out soon, Hunter paced his cell. "He sent thugs after my mother when he found out she'd had the artifact all these years. Charlie gave it to her before he died. Just imagine how surprised her new family was to see me tearing through their house to go after those cutthroats. Here she was with this normal life with this normal family." He ran his hands down his face to stare bleakly at the wall. "We're from two different worlds. After I got rid of those guys, I asked her if this was the family she'd left me for, and that's when it all came out. She wouldn't tell me why Gordon was blackmailing her, but she said that he'd never liked her. He made her believe it was her fault for what my father became after that accident— he's real good at that. She thought I'd be happier without her. It's the other way around now. Gordon's made me into someone she can't stand. She pushed the artifact into my hands and told me to go. The first place I went was that warehouse."

"What's in there?" Frank asked. I wasn't sure if he was genuinely trying to do his job or just interested, but even Caitlyn drew forward to hear.

"It's where he kept all his most priceless possessions, everything he valued over us, and I took what was left of my uncle's notes—notes my grandfather assured me he'd destroyed because they caused him so much pain—and I set the whole thing on fire. Everything that I'd found and stolen for him over the years went up in flames." Hunter snorted in disgust. "Not that it mattered—he saved most of it."

"That's good enough!" Bill called. "Get Aiden out of there."

Frank fumbled for his keys. "I'm good with that." Caitlyn was overjoyed and clapped her hands. Hunter watched dumbfounded as

Frank threw the key into the hole to get that squeaky lock open.

"What are you waiting for?" Bill asked. "Kiss the girl!"

"No need to make it about that." My words were interrupted when Hunter caught me in his arms and kissed me, his eyes on mine, though I couldn't help but think it was also for the benefit of our little audience. The old men were giddy with excitement.

I stepped back, blushing. "All right." I ducked my head a little then gained my composure. "Where's that coin?"

"Has Gordon left yet?" Hunter asked.

"Yes, is it in your cabin?"

"No, I just need to get my stuff. I put it in your camera bag. I knew you were a little gun shy with that after going viral."

I gasped. "What? My bag is in my room."

"That's what I needed to hear." I heard Rosco's voice then felt him at my back when he grabbed my arm. He pushed a gun into my side. "We'll just be getting that camera bag and we'll get out of your hair."

Immediately I slid to the floor, like I'd done when facing the hermit, I was so scared. The gun discharged in Rosco's hand, the sound of it blasting out my ears as Hunter rammed into him. I covered my head and scrambled to the side, desperate to see if anyone was hurt. There was only twisting legs and shoving arms. Somewhere I heard Caitlyn scream. So far, no blood. Harlan had my shoulder and pulled me back, and I saw Hunter and Rosco going at it.

The gun skidded across the wooden floor, and Bill had it in an instant. Frank lifted his gun too, and they shouted for Hunter and Rosco to get down.

Hunter leveled one last punch into Rosco's face, and the man's head bounced against the floor while Hunter found my side. The old men herded Rosco into the jail, all of them shouting at once. Surprisingly, Pat was the loudest of them all, though he stood further from the action. "Who sent you, you rascal!"

Rosco groaned out, but I doubted he'd confess anything more

until he'd been subjected to a night of the old men's pestering questions. "You'll bring that coin to them!" he growled. His watery blue eyes pinned me with a glare. "Or you let your brother die."

Bill shut the cell door behind him and turned to Hunter. "Get that coin to Brek."

We were already on it. Hunter helped me to my feet while Frank and Pat guarded their new prisoner. Bill and Harlan led us to the ATVs, talking the whole time. I was shaking, but the fight had already gotten my adrenaline going so that I felt like I could run up that mountain to get to my brother. I explained about the geyser, and Bill swatted his hat against his leg, impressed.

The revelation made Hunter stare. "I knew we were missing something." He climbed onto the first ATV and I pushed in front of him. The urgency of reaching my brother overrode my fear of driving one of these things. "What are you doing?" Hunter asked.

"I'm saving my brother."

Before he could protest, Caitlyn took the next ATV. "I'm fine!" She preemptively cut off all arguments. "I go four-wheeling at my grandparent's farm every summer. I would've gone before, but I'm like these old romantics—I'm into matchmaking." She pressed down the gas and had me convinced in an instant when she expertly sped past us to retrieve my camera.

"I think that means she's going," Hunter said and turned to Bill and Harlan. "Get us some reinforcements. SWAT if you can. Not Dry Gulch. I don't want anyone killed."

Bill straightened defensively with an argument on his lips, but Harlan promised to do it as I put on the gas and drove away.

The moon was full tonight—so bright that we hardly needed the headlights of our ATV's—everything about this felt serendipitous. We weren't too far behind Brek. I just hoped we could figure out how to use the coin when the time came to it.

Chapter twenty

*I*t was after three in the morning when we got to Moonlight Lake. A thunderous noise rumbled through the ground as we approached on our ATVs—an appropriate explosion for the Fourth of July, though this was far more powerful than fireworks. The geyser had erupted. As we passed a clearing, I saw the mushroom cloud spiraling over the jagged cut of trees lining the horizon. The geyser was of epic proportions—shooting up into the sky in a powerful cascade of water, bigger than anything I'd seen, and I'd been to Yellowstone. It made a thick fog that moved in on the full moon.

Caitlyn held up her phone to record it. She shouted something back at us, but I couldn't make it out. We skimmed past the banks of Moonlight Lake, not necessarily following the motorized vehicle rules in our haste. The air sprayed us with its mist until we were sopping wet. Mud sprayed out from our wheels. I clutched tighter to my camera bag where I kept the coin safely next to me.

It took us a half hour to navigate closer to the banks of Moonlight Lake. And when I saw it, I caught my breath. It had lost its glitter under the night sky with its drained depths—now it looked like a gaping black hole. The geyser had drained it in the sections closest to the banks, leaving deep pockets of water elsewhere—dark blue cenotes that would never empty. No matter; there was no hiding the secret of these missing caverns below. Once Hunter and I had opened the culverts on the side of the mountain, anyone traveling this way would have seen it.

The bright lights Gordon's men had set up at the banks on the east side led us to them. Moonlight Lake was massive, with more than its share of sweeping lagoons, so finding the actual opening to the cave that hid the treasure would still be a challenge, but so far their beams of light were concentrated on one area. It meant they had found something.

We were past caring about alerting Gordon's men to our presence. It wasn't about who got the treasure anymore. I had to keep Brek safe. Eventually, the brush got too thick for our ATVs and we had to dump them next to a snarl of trees and run through the forest, taking out our flashlights, our words getting lost in the loud roar of the geyser behind us. It was taking too long, and I breathed hard at the scramble, feeling the branches and bushes rip into my skin as we tore past. I tucked the camera bag under my arm. Caitlyn was lagging behind, but she had her flashlight, and so I pressed on, hoping to catch my brother in time.

Eventually, the forest opened onto the illuminated banks. The spotlights brightened the east side like the powerful rays of the sun, highlighting every detail of the pale gray rock below so that I saw the moss and reeds in full display like a garden laid bare. The bottom of the lake was open to the outside world. It was a cavern of beauty, though its glistening surface seemed frozen without the buoyancy of the water lifting the seagrasses like it would the hair of a mermaid—now lying flat like a bad hair day.

Loud blasting waterfalls flooded over the sides of the bank as every drop the geyser had stolen from the lakes came pouring back in from the swamped lakeshore. It filled the lower sections first, but the water level on higher ground wouldn't stay shallow forever, even with the geyser still exploding out the contents of the lake. If Brek was already in the caves below, he could get caught inside like Eden and drown. Lucius might've left her, but I'd never let that happen to my brother.

I rushed forward. "Easy," Hunter shouted over the sounds of water around us. He took hold of my hand and pointed ahead at Gordon's men, and for the first time, I noticed their guns. We'd have to enter carefully, but we didn't have time.

Caitlyn caught up to us, and I figured out what had taken her so long as she narrated the events of the night into her phone. "We're sorry for throwing you all off the trail of the hunt," she told her future YouTube audience, "but it was necessary. This is serious stuff here." She turned the lens of her phone onto the activity below as we stood like shadows watching Gordon's men lugging cables and machinery.

That's when I caught sight of the opening below. The door was a huge slab of rock, which was possibly why Brek hadn't been able to find it with his previous diving; but free of water, the Spanish markings were clearly written over it. It would've been virtually impossible to open with the weight of the lake on top of it. Gordon's men had propped the door open with a thick stone wedge.

My eyes scanned the area for Brek, and when I didn't see him, I searched for Angel next and found her missing too. My stomach dropped with the horror of it all. They were inside already. It would be simple getting down there, but not getting out. There would only be a pocket of time that they could retrieve the treasure from the cave before it was all flooded again.

We snuck through the foliage to peer closer to the rising water. Gordon pulled out a cigarette, like his son had done when confronting Hunter. His fingers shook while he watched the hole below him—not necessarily from nerves. There was an impatient tilt to the unfeeling mogul's thick chin. The man next to him carried a walkie talkie, and I heard Brek's voice in it. The reception wasn't very good inside there, and he kept cutting out, but I got the gist of it. "We've cut through the twilight zone. There's not much to it. No roots to be seen," he reported. "The stalactites and stalagmites are especially thick at the entrance, where we've found a crude network of stairs cut through the stone. The air is heavy with CO_2. We're using our respirators as a precaution."

Brek said nothing for a few minutes, then reported, "We're traveling west, which is taking us to the center of Moonlight Lake, according to our maps, at a 22% grade. It's steep. It just keeps going down. There's a cenote to the side. It's a deep pool here." There was a long pause while he narrated Angel's dive in there.

Hunter's eyes narrowed at his grandfather, like he was trying to decide how to confront him. If we came forward with the coin, what would Gordon do? Another hulking man stood on the other side of him, acting like his bodyguard.

After a few minutes, Brek reported finding nothing unusual in the pool before moving on. "We've made our way through one of the branches. The tunnel forks and we're taking it to the right. It's opened up into a colossal cave chamber—at least fifty feet tall. There's water streaming down the walls; not sure of its source."

Everything Brek said sounded very clinical, until his words quickened in his excitement. "We've found another set of stairs. It's on the south side of the chamber, and it opens into an alcove. There are some strange symbols written on it..."

I pushed out of my hiding spot to stop the impending catastrophe. "Tell him not to touch that!" Too late, I noticed his men train their guns at me. I held up my hands.

"Whoa!" Hunter pulled forward, his hands raised too. "You need to listen to her. Tell him not to touch that."

"Please!" I begged Gordon. "Tell him now! He'll die!"

Gordon shook his head at me, and I made a pitiful yelp and tried to run for the walkie talkie to get it from the man standing next to him. Hunter's arms went around me, stopping me. "Hunter!" I shouted. "What are you doing?"

"I'm saving your life." He stared down the men with their guns, mainly Gordon, who looked narrowly at me. Caitlyn gave a cry as one of Gordon's men discovered her hiding, and pushed her forward to join us. Strangely, no one stopped her from recording—like they had no idea what a cellphone could do.

"My arm's stuck," Brek sounded through the walkie talkie in a panic. "It's like a metal handcuff. It's clamped over my wrist. It won't come off. Angel, hold that light still! There are symbols on this. Uh, there's a way out... Angel, come here. I think there's a way..." His voice cut out.

I let out a scream. "He's going to die! He's going to die! Just like Eden! Just like your son! Let me go, Hunter!"

He did, but reluctantly, and I paced the rocky bottom, not sure what to do with myself anymore, while Gordon tried to get a hold of Brekker again with no results. I threw my arms around my waist feeling cold and hot all at once. The strap of the camera bag where Hunter had hid that coin weighed heavily on my shoulder. "We need to go down there," I said. "The water's going to fill up in that cave. We don't have long."

Everyone ignored me like I wasn't even speaking, until Gordon looked up at his grandson and ordered him to keep me quiet. Hunter glowered over at him, though his hand did find my arm. "Ivy," he whispered. "You won't like what he'll do to you."

I stilled and met his wary eyes. What kind of things had Hunter seen his grandfather do?

"We've got professionals in there," Gordon snarled at me, but I knew I'd gotten to him, the way that his voice trembled and his eyes darted back and forth. The reminder of Charlie was too much—this was the same thing that had happened to his boy and he was reliving it in present time. "Let them take care of it!" he shouted. I knew his weakness now, but I didn't know how to use it to my advantage.

Angel wouldn't be able to get Brek out. She was like Lucius—no way would she sacrifice herself for my brother. She'd have to love him for that. The lake was filling up, and we could only watch in horror as the water surged closer and swept up against the bank walls in waves, swirling around us. We were standing on higher ground, but it would get us soon. Caitlyn watched the hole propped up by that wedge with stricken eyes. Being lower to the ground level, water streamed down the mouth of the hole, circling it like a drain before going in.

"Let me go down there," Hunter said.

Gordon snorted without looking at him. "No." He looked over at the hulking man with the gun and gestured at him and then the man holding the walkie talkie. "Go down there."

My eyes shot to them, and I got ready to give them the coin, but they held back until a scream came from the mouth of the cave. It was Angel. The two men ran forward as two hands appeared from the surging water and wrapped around their arms. They plucked Angel from the hole like a rabbit from a magician's hat. She was dripping wet. She'd lost her respirator mask somewhere back in the cave, and she collapsed to the ground, coughing hard and spluttering.

"Angel!" I shouted. "Where's my brother?"

She ignored me, her eyes on Gordon. "Keep your treasure!" she screamed. "Keep the jewels. I don't care anymore!" One thought raced through my mind—Angel had failed the lover's test.

No one was going to help Brek but me. Letting out a cry, I ran for the cave opening. Hunter was after me too—I wasn't sure if it was to drag me back or to join me. Gordon shouted at him. "No, no! Not *you!*" There was some rustling as he shouted at his man at the mouth of the cave. "Stop him! Stop him! I'm not losing another boy to this treasure!" And just like magic the pathway to the mouth of the cave cleared as the men went after Hunter. They tackled him behind me, and another one joined them to make sure Gordon's order was filled. Hunter didn't stand a chance. I kept going; the coin was in my camera bag, and I had to get it to my brother. I couldn't live with myself if I just let him drown.

"Ivy!" Hunter called for me to stop, but I landed like a cannonball into the pool of water. It froze up my limbs as it washed over me. I forced myself not to gasp out underwater. The churning water caught me up and sucked me through the hole to the other side of the cave where I met air. I landed hard against the stone stairs, sliding down a few steps as the icy water trickled past my skinned hands. A trail of flameless flares threaded through the length of the cave, ensconced into the wall through the means of Brek's fastener gun. It cast a glow over the limestone splashed in shades of orange, ivory, browns, and greens.

Stumbling to my feet, I felt like I was in a science fiction movie as

I entered the cave through the jaws of a great monster. Spiked stalactites hung from the ceiling. Sharp stalagmites jutted out from the floor like knives, and here and there were a few columns where the two met. I waded through them in chilly water that whirled around my calves, remembering how Brek had described this place only half an hour ago. He hadn't said anything about walking through water. It rushed down a steep incline. There should be a pool to the side, and following the flares, sure enough, I found it—its crystal blue depths swirling as the water sliding down the walls poured into it, forming an eddy. I splashed quickly past it, slipping down the rest of the incline before I reached the bottom and landed in a deeper pool of water. It was to my knees down here.

I hurried, my heart going through my chest as I wondered if I would make it in time to save Brek. If not, we'd go out of this world like we'd come in—together. I pushed my way through the tunnel next, feeling claustrophobic as it closed in on me. Layers of white calcite caked over the walls like the rough outside of a shell, some of it so thick that I had to squeeze myself through it. The flares were ahead. They would lead me to my brother. I just had to get to him.

Stumbling through the last of the calcite, I fell into what felt like nothingness. The water was high here. I sucked in my breath as its frigid temperatures lapped against my waist. The only light came from an alcove above, and it streamed down another set of stairs carved into the rock. Half swimming, half dragging myself through the freezing water, I cried out to him. "Brek! Brek! Are you here?"

I cleared the alcove and he knelt there on his knees like a sacrifice to the gods, his arm stuck in a hole in the wall. He groaned when he saw me, pulling the respirator from his mouth. "Ivy, get out of here!"

"No!" I didn't have time to argue. I stared at the carvings on the wall. It was full of Spanish symbols. A great stone cross was carved into the wall with two holes on either side—exactly what was on the coin and the flat rock. Brek's arm was in one of them, and the other was still free, waiting. But I had a better way. "I know how to get you out." I pulled the coin out of my bag.

He stared at it, not impressed. "How?"

"I was hoping you would know!"

He leaned his head back in frustration. "Please, Ivy, just get out of here while you can." He dug into his supply bag by his knees and handed me an oxygen bottle. "Please, for me! I don't want us both to die."

If this coin was the thing to release him, then it had to be a key of sorts. With my heart in my throat, I turned to the wall and saw Spanish symbols that I couldn't read and then at the corner of that, I spied the round indentation at the level of my chest. Perfect to fit a coin! This had to be it! And I stuffed it in where it seemed to fit perfectly. Still it didn't free my brother. "Tug at your hand, Brek!" I said. "That should've done it."

He jerked ineffectually at it, shaking his head. His eyes watered now, and he didn't bother to wipe away his tears. "Just listen to me, for once, Ivy. If you live, it will be like I did—you're a part of me. Please go! I love you."

"I love *you*." And I stuck my arm in the hole on the other side of him. The mechanism pushed against my arm as it clamped down on me in a vise before releasing my brother, who fell back with a grunt, rubbing at his arm. He looked panicked when his eyes ran to me. "What have you done?"

"I had to, Brek! Love over treasure, and I chose you."

"No," he said. "No." He went to stuff his own hand into the hole. I shouted out at him, "No, don't! Stop!"

"You're crazy if you think I'm leaving here without you!" my brother said. "I'm not!"

"Find a way to make that coin get me out then!" I cried. "It's supposed to work! If we keep switching places in the Lover's Trap, it will just choose who dies in the end."

Brekker listened to me—which was a miracle, because he never did. He landed against the wall, both hands moving the coin around to

STEPHANIE FOWERS

find some way of making it act like a key. By now water was pouring down the walls in a waterfall. My eyes had adjusted to the darkness, and by the light of Brek's flares I saw that we were in a cavern with walls going up about five stories above us. The tunnel where we had come in was almost sealed off from us, and we'd be stuck in this tomb.

And I couldn't help it; seeing that made me scream—that demonic, out-of-body scream that Brekker always complained about; but he wasn't now. His jaw clenched against it and he worked harder on the coin. No one would hear it, but my whimpers came from me all the same, out of pure fear.

"Ivy!"

I gasped and turned when I recognized that voice from the darkness. It echoed over the water. "Hunter?" I whispered, then called out, "Hunter!"

I listened to the splashes as he came for me, and it filled me with relief. Would he save me? I didn't know, but he was here, and I wouldn't feel as scared with his arms around me. Did I want him to die with me? No! I groaned, knowing I'd never be able to convince him otherwise.

The walkie talkie next to us shrieked to life. "Is Hunter down there? Is my boy down there?" It was Gordon. So now he cared? He sounded so desperate.

Hunter reached the stairs, pulling himself onto them, his jeans sloshing as he ran to get to me. The walkie talkie crackled as Gordon shouted after his grandson. "Turn around! The wedge won't hold that slab open for long!"

Hunter picked up the walkie talkie. "Keep it open!" he said then threw the receiver into the greedy waters below us before turning to me. "We don't have long. We can swim through the tunnel, but if that rock slab at the opening of the cave doesn't hold, we'll be stuck down here."

"The coin isn't working," I said, resting my aching arm against my head. "We don't all have to die. Hunter, take my brother and get out of here."

Both he and Brek made sounds of disgust. I guessed that meant a 'no.' "What kind of man do you think I am?" Hunter asked.

Was that a rhetorical question? He was a man who would protect me or die trying. I knew that now. He was no Lucius. Laying a comforting arm against my back, his gaze ran over the Spanish symbols engraved into the wall, and I wondered if he could read them. "Love over treasure," he read, and then, before I could warn him against it, he stuck his hand into the other hole. I'd known he'd figure it out soon, and it released me, making me fall back. Brek caught me. "Now, take her," Hunter said. "Do it!"

My brother hesitated. I knew he wanted to and that he'd never liked Hunter, but suddenly Hunter was sacrificing his life for me, and it didn't seem right. But I knew Brekker would do it if it meant saving me, and so I threw my hand into the other side of the trap to stop him from carrying me away. That freed Hunter, and he made a growl of frustration before throwing his arm back again and releasing me. "Brekker, you know what to do."

I fell back and scrambled away from my brother's arms and threw my hand back in, my charm bracelet clashing like eerie fairy music in the glowing light.

"Stop it!" Hunter shouted.

"You're wasting time!" I said. My breath was coming out short, and I felt dizzy in here. "We're going to keep going back and forth, and I'll keep doing it!" I warned. "Brekker, figure out how to get that coin to work!"

Brekker knew how stubborn I was. I kept my face turned firmly from the rising water below us, my cheek pressed against the cold stone on the wall. Brek cried out in frustration then turned to the wall. "It's not a key," he said. Hunter looked up quickly at that. Brek twisted the coin to the side to complete the engraving. "It's part of the symbol. It's instructions." Then translating it, he shouted, "Push! It says, Push! Quit pulling away, start pushing. Both of you push your hands into the trap."

I gasped out and shoved my hand into the hole as far as I could, feeling my fingers tap against a board at the end. There was a slit in it. "Nothing's happening!"

"Wait! Wait!" Brek scraped the coin from the indentation in the wall. "It doesn't belong there anymore—it *is* a key."

"Make up your mind!" Hunter shouted, his cheek smashed up against the wall.

"You sacrifice the treasure to save another. Who can pull their hand out?" We both drew back and my hand was loose enough to pull free. Brek handed me the coin.

"Are you sure about this?" Hunter asked.

Taking a deep breath, I stuck my hand back in, my whole body shaking as the mechanism clamped down over my hand again as I stretched my fingers up against the back wall and felt the tips of them brush up against the slit. I pushed the coin into it, listening to it slide down the side.

Please, let this work!

The mechanism clicked once and the clamp loosened from my hand the same time that the stone wall snapped open like a door on a safe, making us both fall back. We were both free! Hunter crawled over to me and took me in his arms as a black container pushed out of the wall. It scraped over the raised floor and pushed into us.

"It's a boat," Brekker said. In the middle of it was an iron box, as if the priest had planned for us to float the heavy thing out through the tunnels. It was everything too late—we'd never fit it through where we'd come. The tunnel was flooded and there was no sign of it. We were going to drown.

The water lapped against the walls, licking over the stairs to greet us. Now that the water had reached a certain point, the cave filled up faster, like some monstrous hand had pulled the plug on the drain and we stood helplessly beneath it. The flood surged over the stairs and into the alcove where we were.

Hunter reached down and steadied the boat as it bobbed in the

360

water. "Get in. Get in!"

And then what? We'd rise to the top of the cave and get smashed up against it and then die? We had to try to survive, but each stolen moment would lead us to the next and so, feeling Hunter's hand at my arm, I jumped into the boat. Brek snapped a flare to light our way and he dropped inside the boat next to me. Hunter pushed us out into the water before jumping in himself. The movement sent us rocking, and his arms wound tightly around me.

The current took us to the far end of the cavern. Our little vessel knocked against the rock walls as we rose to the top until there was nowhere to go. The heavy rock ceiling pressed against our boat and we dropped flatly to the hull. The wooden sides crunched. Water spilled inside and I felt it soak into my hair. I let out a groan and squeezed closer to Hunter, my cheek running into his hair, while I found Brek's hand. I would go with the two men I loved.

The boat let out a dying groan, and just as it looked as if there was nowhere else to go, the water beneath us gave one last shove—and the rock ceiling above us shifted in response. It pushed us through a concealed trap. That was all it could be, because one minute we were getting crushed, and the next, we were shooting over the water like we had melted through rock. And air—good, clean air—slapped against our faces as our small craft scraped and rammed over rocks. The savagery of the crashes punctured the sides of the boat in dizzying violence until we settled over a smooth patch of water on the surface of Moonlight Lake. We held onto each other, the sides of the boat... and the treasure.

None of it seemed real.

A pink sky spread over us in the dewy haze of morning. After the blackness of the cave, I'd never thought I'd see such a thing again, and I stared at it in shock. We were alive. Water had spilled over the canoe, and I was lying in a pool as we slowly lost speed. We floated slower and slower until we were drifting aimlessly over the top of the lake.

"Ivy! There they are!" That was Caitlyn. I lifted my head, seeing her on the banks high above us. The green pines spread out into a backdrop behind her. "Hunter! Brek!" her voice broke with her happiness, and she was crying out, "You're alive!" Brek pulled up from the bottom of the boat, and I did likewise, staring around in a daze. Caitlyn recorded our homecoming with her phone, not able to keep still at the excitement of finding us alive.

"Don't do anything stupid," Hunter warned us. "We're still not out of this."

I wasn't sure how much more I could take from this day, but I knew he was right. It wasn't too long after we were spotted on the lagoon for Gordon's men to make their way through the crags to pull us in. I leaned against Hunter while he watched them with an unblinking glare. One of the burly men had a bruising eye. I wondered if Hunter had given him that to get to me.

Gordon waded into the water, his breathing hard, his gait irregular as his thick hands wrapped around the end of the rope to join his men in pulling us over the sandy beach. He reached out and patted his grandson on the cheek. "I knew you would find me this treasure, my beautiful boy!"

Then he ignored that *beautiful boy* as his attention swerved to the treasure. There was nothing we could do as he ordered his men to haul it all in. They had the guns. We kept our hands up where they could see them. Their brawny forms bent to pick up the treasure and between them they brought it to the rocky shore. The water from the canoe dripped from it. Brek let out a breath as he watched it go. Hunter didn't look surprised. His eyes met mine in silent apology.

"Get that open!" Gordon rubbed his hands together. "It's been closed for far too long."

His man shot open the lock, then he lifted the lid. It groaned out its protest, and their hands piled into it at once to get at the treasure. It was sacrilege—these were not the ones meant to find it. Gabriel de Padilla's sacrifice had been for nothing.

Gordon shouted them back and lumbered through them to get to it first. Reaching down with his whole body cracking, he sifted his fingers through the find and brought out a handful of beads, rocks, and shells. He tossed those aside, his forehead creasing as he reached inside again and pulled out a leather-bound book. I straightened when I saw it. It looked exactly like Eden's journal.

The old man wasn't pleased with it. He flipped through the pages. "What's this?" I kept my silence, hoping that he'd toss it aside as he'd done the trinkets. The veins stood out in his neck, and spying Hunter, his tone turned dangerous. "You knew this was all there was!" Gordon chucked the journal at him. Hunter caught it one-handed.

"Where's the rest of it?" Gordon shouted. He raged at his grandson until I got nervous about what he might do. "Is this your way of getting back at me?" Gordon turned the box over and shook it for any hidden surprises. There was nothing else. "Do you know how much this cost me? The enemies I've made?"

That was on him, but for once, Brek and I followed Hunter's lead and didn't fight back.

I became aware of the low rumble of a helicopter flying in the distance. Lifting his head to squint up at the sky, Gordon cursed low under his breath. Caitlyn silently recorded that, further convincing me that this grandpa wasn't too technologically advanced. I didn't feel too bad about it since he still hadn't let us off the boat.

My attention went back to the book in Hunter's hand. He held it by his lap and I worked it from his grip. Peering down at me, Hunter lifted his fingers to release it so that I could covertly turn over the first page while using the wooden sides of the boat as my shield. It was a journal entry, and I recognized the writing. Eden had gotten to the treasure before we had. But how? She had died.

Gordon turned his wrath on Brek. "Don't expect me to pay you for this!"

As usual, Brekker was left high and dry. "What about those jewels you owe me?" he asked.

"I'll make you earn them."

My stomach felt like a boiling pit of nerves. Brekker could never work for Gordon again. This crook cared nothing for my brother's life. "What about Rooney?" Hunter called after him mockingly. "He's still after you."

The red veins in Gordon's face went purple. "Don't talk about him!" he screamed. I was inclined to agree—Gordon was unhinged, and there was no telling what he'd do.

The helicopter landed in the meadow to the side of us, the blades slowing their rhythmic spin. Gordon straightened and slid his hands down the length of his coat, his whole manner changing to that of a brisk businessman, with one difference—he gestured for his men to follow him with their guns as they approached the aircraft. "Rooney?" Gordon called.

That explained his altered attitude. For all his tough talk, I should've suspected he really feared Rooney. As soon as the man emerged from the helicopter, Gordon dropped his act of respect. It was only Hunter's father. Harry threw his cigarette onto the muddy ground. Brek and I couldn't look away from him. This was the man who had killed our father. In theory, he could've been taller than Gordon, except for his bent shoulders. The years of abuse showed in the droop of his mouth and his inability to meet his father's eyes. He scooted past Gordon, calling out for Hunter. When he caught sight of his son, he cried out. "Hunter! Don't go in!"

But his son had already faced the danger, and unlike his father, he'd come out virtually unscathed. "It's too late," Hunter said, his shoulders stiff as he faced him. "We lived."

"How?"

We weren't quite sure. Hunter pulled from the boat and gave me his hand. I followed him out, dripping with the cold water from the bottom of the hull. Caitlyn let loose a cry and went for Brek, still clutching onto her phone as she clung to him in a big hug and refused to let go. Judging by the slow smile crossing his face, he liked it.

"I'm sorry I wasn't there for you." Harry watched his son

364

pleadingly. "Tell me what happened?"

Hunter pointed to the empty treasure chest. "That's not all," he said. "I know what you did."

His father looked down, his insecurities flooding his pasty complexion. "I'm sorry I couldn't be as strong as you." My heart felt like stone when I studied him. He wasn't much of a man now, and if I hadn't known what he'd done, I'd feel sorry for him.

Now that Gordon had determined the helicopter would serve as an escape vehicle over impending doom, he called impatiently to his progeny. "We're leaving in thirty. Let's pack this up!"

Hunter refused with a shake of his head. "I'm not going anywhere with you."

"Bring him!" Gordon shouted over to his biggest man, then to Hunter, he scowled. "You don't want anything to happen to your friends, do you?" He stalked over to us as best he could, his left leg dragging behind him as he lowered his voice. "I'm sure our secret is safe with you." His veined eyes found me. "You won't say anything, will you sweetheart? Say your farewells, Hunter, and if you're good, I'll bring you visitors."

My mouth dropped. Did he actually think he could get away with taking his own grandson hostage? Harry shouted out in anger the moment Gordon's men stepped closer to his son. "No! This ends now! Step back!"

Gordon laughed and circled from Hunter to his father. "Where was that backbone thirty years ago? I know things about you that would make Aiden's toes curl. He'd never look at you again. You want us to start talking about that?"

"I don't care!" Harry cried. "I was a coward! I let my brother die. But I won't be a coward again—not anymore! You'll stay away from us!"

"You think you have a choice?" Gordon laughed again and walked away, but not before motioning to his men, who took threatening steps towards the rest of us.

"Harry! Harry!!" The chanting came from the woods behind us. I knew that disembodied voice. Brek did too, and his lips tightened when he searched the trees for it. A shadow stood at the edge of the forest, and it seemed the moment my eyes latched onto it that it lurched forward into the light to show us the thin form of the hermit. He stared at us, his arms hanging limply at his sides.

Harry's legs buckled as he fell against his son. "Charlie?" he asked.

Hunter steadied him, his head lifting up to watch the strange approaching figure. "No," Hunter said. "That man said Charlie was dead."

Gordon swiveled on his heel as the crazed man stumbled out of the woods. "Not Charlie," the hermit screeched. "Bad! Charlie has been bad. And now David is dead." He found me in the group and came at me before I could react. "You opened it again!" he accused. Flecks of saliva caught on his long beard. His eyes darted in rage. "The forest is alive again! Boom, boom went the air, and you!" His finger shook when he pointed at me. "The lake swallowed you." He growled and grabbed for me.

Hunter shouted out, but Brek was closer and jumped in front of me. "Don't touch my sister."

The hermit's face cleared. "This is your twin?"

I nodded, and the knowledge was enough to make the man cower from Brek in terror. I remembered that I had used Brek to threaten him. "Yes, he's big. Very big," the hermit whispered. Brek wasn't that big, but I'd take the illusion because nothing else had seemed to make this guy back off. I noticed he still wore the ring that came from my charm bracelet.

"Charlie?" Gordon's voice broke on his son's name. "That *is* Charlie!"

"No!" The hermit took exception to that and he raged until Gordon stepped closer, then the man ducked from Gordon to cover his face. "He kills. I died."

Gordon's face twisted with an undecipherable emotion, his eyes watering. "What happened to you?" He tried to take another step closer, and the man hissed him back, refusing to let him touch him. "What happened?" Gordon helplessly repeated himself.

"Charlie has been bad!" the man shouted. "I died... and David died. His ghost cries out."

His words were enough to forestall Gordon, and he asked quietly, "Is this why you didn't come home?"

"Bad, bad." Charlie said, his fingers shaking at his father, for this was definitely Charlie, though he didn't seem to know it.

Gordon shushed him, his voice soothing as he attempted to embrace his son again. This time Charlie scrambled away so that his father stepped back and held his hands up to stop him from running back into the woods. The old man's eyes shifted to his men with their guns, but what could they do to keep his son in place? Shoot him?

Behind them in the woods, a low growl came from Charlie's dogs. They pressed forward on trembling legs as if sensing their master was up against something they didn't like. Gordon's eyes shifted to them and the men started to shoot at them. The dogs yelped, escaping back into the shelter of the trees.

Charlie let out a shriek and glared at his father. "You! You shot him! I went in there." He stopped pacing to point his shaky finger at the lake.

Hunter's whole body was rigid as he watched his uncle then turned to his father. "He told us something... when we found him in the woods—a man was killed for that artifact. You killed David Payne, didn't you, Father?"

Harry watched his brother, aghast. "No," it came out a horrified breath. "No."

Caitlyn's phone camera was back up again as Charlie cried out in a loud voice, "I went in that water and got stuck there!" He loudly sniffed and ran a hand under his nose. "Harry ran away. Harry said he'd bring help, but he never came back!"

"I tried!" Tears escaped from Harry's eyes. His shoulders stooped lower, the horror of what had happened to his brother too much of a burden to carry. "I couldn't get the help I needed and before I could come back for you, the stone slammed shut and I couldn't get it open. I broke my fingernails on it, then my fingers. I beat on it until the water carried me away."

"The water swallowed you," Charlie said solemnly. "Eden got you."

"She should've," Harry said, his face a mask of shame. "I'd be happier now."

Charlie's eyes focused on him and he charged his brother like he'd done many times with me, wrapping his arms around him in a painful embrace, but Harry took it with a wretched sigh. Tears trickled down his cheeks, and he closed his eyes. "You're alive." The rest of Harry's words turned thick and guttural as his body shook with sobs. "How?" he whimpered. "I missed... you so..." He swallowed and his shoulders shook with wracking cries so that he couldn't get much of anything out. Charlie didn't react, just looked around wildly.

Gordon had turned to stone before my eyes; the only indication he felt anything was the rhythmic grinding of his tight jaw. Maybe it was that his favored son was a broken man now, not the hero he'd always imagined him to be; or was it the guilt of not trying hard enough to find him? Overcome with some enigmatic emotion, Gordon turned his back on his two sons. Charlie noticed and raised his head to stare at his father. Then he shoved past his brother, his shoulder knocking Harry back.

"You killed him!" Charlie shouted at Gordon. The words of madness tumbled from his mouth. "You killed David Payne. He knew how to melt into the rock! And you took it from him. The stick!"

Hunter's eyes narrowed. Brek's hand went to my arm as he pressed it, as the sickness of what Gordon had done overcame me. He'd manipulated the children of the man he'd killed to find this treasure—one that had ended up being completely worthless to him.

"What?" Gordon circled on his raving son, his voice low and

dangerous. "And this is why you stayed away from me? *My perfect boy?* All these years wasted... for what you *thought* you saw?"

"He fell," Charlie said. "He fell. Poor David Payne—his wife was pregnant. They were twins, he told me, a boy and a girl." He came to Brek and me, as if some part of him knew that we were David's offspring. "Poor children without a father. He shot him." Charlie slid off his ring and gave it to me, folding my hand over it and patting my fingers. "The water couldn't wash away all the blood. It was everywhere. Eden released me and I hit my head and ears on the rocks when I melted through the rock. Boom. Boom. And..." he whipped his head over to pin Gordon with a glare. "I saw you in the lake—that mirror of my face looked back at me. You'd never let me go. Harry couldn't help. Poor Harry, he was swallowed up. And Gordon, Gordon... he killed David Payne." It was as if his voice got caught on that like a skip in a record, and he repeated it over and over.

Gordon shouted for him to stop. "Enough! You're insane!"

"Yes!" Charlie growled. "And the rocks came tumbling and David Payne fell. You shot him!" Charlie approached his father as if he faced a memory. "And his wife was pregnant, his blood everywhere."

"Stop! Stop talking this way! He wouldn't work with me. He got what he got!" Gordon's eyes watered with the emotion of a man who'd lost everything, though he still refused to see the full extent of what he'd done. He was to blame for losing everything he most treasured. He held his hand out to Charlie. "Is this why you didn't return? I loved you. You were my son."

But Gordon might as well have been talking to a ghost for all the good it did him; Charlie was not the man he'd been. Tumbling through the rocks after leaving the cave had caused him more damage than it had done to us when we were protected by our vessel. "Gordon..." Charlie said, scratching at his own arm. "He killed David Payne." His voice had grown soft now. "Bad."

Hunter glared at his grandfather with a festering hatred. "All these years, you blamed my father for that? When you did it?" His hand went to his father's arm and he shook it. "It's how he got mom to leave us— she didn't think you'd survive jail. He tried to use it against me too. We all believed that liar."

Harry's reddened face turned a chalky white as the shock settled over him. "You hated me that much?" His lips twisted in revulsion. "Why? All I did was try to win your love. You ruined me."

Gordon turned uneasy and blustered, at a loss for words, before trying to erase it all with a hard look. "Let's just go."

"No!" Harry shouted at him. The vehemence behind it shocked me.

Turning to his mumbling son, Gordon tried to approach him. "Charlie! Come with us. I'll get you the help you need."

Harry stiffened at the threat. The one witness to the murder of my father? Gordon might see it as "mercy" to take Charlie down. I listened to the sound of more helicopters in the distance and prayed that was our backup this time. Harry stepped in front of his brother with a final show of defiance against his father. "You are not taking him anywhere," he said.

"Get in the chopper!" Gordon screamed. "All of you!"

When no one did, he looked over at his men with their guns… then hesitated. This was his family here. Brek and I might not matter, Caitlyn even less, but he couldn't touch us without destroying what he had left. Did he care? He grunted out in frustration then let it all go. "You're fools. You'll get nothing more from me." He put his back to them as he beat a crooked path for the helicopter, a lone man, his broad shoulders stooping the more distance he put between us.

Caitlyn lowered her phone. She had caught Gordon's inadvertent confession, but now she looked sad. Here was a man who had lost everything. Those he had hurt, whose lives had been irreparably damaged, stood like a jury behind him.

As Gordon reached the helicopter, he lurched back as another man emerged from the craft—this newcomer was a rough sort with a hooked nose, slicked back hair, and only the hint of a chin. He reminded me of a rat.

"That's Rooney," Brek said with a grim voice. And Harry had brought him—he didn't look sorry about it. The man's lined face could be cut from marble with the emotion left in it.

The two old tycoons argued at the entrance of the helicopter until Gordon finally gave in, motioning two of his bodyguards to go with him with a sweep of his fingers as he entered the helicopter with Rooney's men—two powerful moguls readying to play chess with their lives; to work together or to defeat the other. Either way, it was out of our hands.

Chapter twenty-one

*E*den's Journal: July 2nd, 1865 — Mountains of the
Deseret

*It hasn't yet been ten years since Lucius deserted me to that trap deep in
that rocky lake bottom. It still seems a distant memory when Adam parted
ways with us at the water's edge while it emptied like a rain puddle in the
desert sun, leaving only a dry husk in its wake. I felt mighty afeared, but I
knowed deep inside I'd done Adam right—else I'd never have chosen another
in his place. As Lucius and I waited to go in, I kept stealing looks at
Lucius, hoping things warn't going to be too bad betwixt us. I needn't
worried. He was so set on that treasure that he'd plum forgot most everything.
Almost—he still rubbed at his chin where Adam knocked him good.*

*We'd done all the Shoshones asked of us, and we knowed when the
time was right to enter them caves, though the fear shook me inside and out
like I was a cold, wet dog. Lucius scoffed and called me all sorts of names to
git me going, so's I'd finally followed him inside and hustled through the
tunnels and pathways with only the light from our torches to see us through.*

*When we come to the place and Lucius saw the treasure in the wall,
there was nothing for it but for him to grapple with it, and what should
happen that his arm got stuck. We tried all sorts of tricks to git him out,
clawing and prying at him until the water near filled the tunnels and there
warn't gonna be any way out if we tarried much longer. I cried and pestered
him to tell me what to do, and even considered cutting his arm loose, but he'd
have none of it, said he warn't gonna go through life a one-armed man.*

*That's when I poked my head up and saw the carving to the side with
the two arms in each hole. I figured maybe that was the way out! But bless
me—that hole was too far away for Lucius to put in his other hand and so*

gritting my teeth and praying I was doing right, I put my hand in the other hole. Lucius was freed with a shout, but I was stuck. He told me, "Sorry, darling, but I ain't gonna risk myself any for you."

And what should he do? He runned off with all my supplies— including my journal and personal effects! I shouted and pled after him, but he didn't slow a whit. And I knelt there, crying and blubbering and feeling as sorry as I could be that I chose Lucius over Adam. Maybe I was bad for Adam, but he was good for me, and there warn't no way he'd have left me down here to die by myself in these black caves, drowning like the rat I'd become. It felt fitting in a way that the whole of my life would end in such a way. I don't know how long I waited for those waters to end me, but it was enough for me to reflect on every wrong, every mistake, every sin I'd made, not only against God, but myself.

Just as I was pleading with God for another chance, I reckon he gave me one, because when the water got in that trap that held me in place, it got all waterlogged and I heard it click and snap and move around and the jaws of it let my hand go. I didn't have the treasure, but I didn't care none, I was free! But for what? The tunnels was all closed off and the water kept raging higher until I was half swimming, half floating. My heavy dress threatened to drag me down and I struggled out of the buttons until I was only in my underclothes. Only then was I light enough for the water to carry me up to the top of the cave where I found a little bit of air to breath.

I supposed then that was the end of me as the water knocked me up against the rock walls, until I heard the ceiling give out a groan as the floods from below pushed me through it—like I was butter leaking through a cheesecloth—and I shot out the other side like a spout. And lo and behold, I was out of that cave and in the lake. But I wasn't past the danger. I bobbed and sunk over the surface, hit up against the rocks, over and over as they scraped over my hands and legs, but I had in me a desperation to live, and so I covered my head from it all and fought myself to the top of the lake again, and got me in a good lung full of air, feeling as if I was one reborn.

My first thought was Lucius, especially as I seen him at the shore creeping around like an old shadow, going through my things like they was his. He'd no care that he'd left me behind to die! He never loved me, and it made me sorry for all the years I'd spent thinking he had. So I scrabbled my way to shore, dripping and moaning and looking a scary sight, but Lucius didn't see me until he was fixin to leave our encampment. And then he turned about with such a look of horror that I knowed he thought I was a ghost. And I couldn't help it none, I laid into him with all his wrongs against me, and I told him, "As long as you and your descendants set your hearts on treasure and none else, you'll never find it!"

And what should you know? That yellow-bellied coward runned off again—with everything I owned. He'd thought I was a ghost until the very end, and even spread word that I come to him and cursed him. That's when I began to see the advantages of dying. Why! I was a wanted woman in these parts—but if I was dead, through the grace of God, I had a chance at a new life, and I found it in the arms of Adam Black. In fact, he accepted me with open arms, told me I was his treasure, held me close and protected me from everything. We married and I took on a new life and a new name—it seemed fitting that Adam should have his Eve. Of course we didn't want to be too noticeable about it, so we settled on Eva, and told everyone I warn't from around these parts. No one guessed a thing. And the good folk of the town? They never let on.

And of course, what better way to find a new life then by burying the old one? It gave the bounty hunters something to go on. Adam and I buried the old Eden in an empty grave near his cottage in the mountains. It was a pretty place and I spent many an evening sitting there and contemplating the old Eden—she warn't all bad. She lived the best she knowed to keep alive, and she'd sacrificed plenty for those she loved, but she didn't spare any of that love for herself. I wondered she didn't know how to do it. No matter, she died in that water and I came out a new person, saved by Providence so'd I knowed I was worth the saving. I was Eden, but now I am Eve. And only God had that power to make such a change. It was fitting that I started my life again. New decisions. New memories. New friends. Children and a husband; almost like my old life didn't exist no more. I remember it sometimes, but more like it happened to someone else in a book from a different time.

My life ain't perfect. How can it? Ain't it always full of hardship? We work hard in these mountains and everything we eat and all our surviving comes from the sweat of our brow. I'd have two children die of pneumonia and my heart felt so swollen at those times I felt I couldn't go on. Adam held me close and learned me about God and how these children warn't lost and it gave me hope to keep on—I'd like to see Lucius ever do such a thing. He'd never!

Adam and I, we dig and plant and see the works of our hands and call it good, though our palms and fingers git rough and blistered. Still, I'd take this hardship over any other because without this life, I'd have no joy—and I have it here with this husband, and I see the immortality of our family in the children who remain with us. The true treasure ain't riches or an abundance of things or even an ease of life that gold can bring. It was living here in these mountains. My Eden.

So why you ask, in heaven's name, did we go after that treasure again if it don't matter to us one way or the other? Truth be told, we went after it because it was ours. We warn't choosing it over love; we warn't choosing it over peace or salvation, but we was fulfilling all we was meant to do. That Spanish priest wanted a man like Adam to find it, and even a girl like Eve. None else.

People say Lucius is cursed and that a ghost named Eden did the deed. Well, if it's a curse, it's one of his own making. He cared for nobody but himself and I pity him and the woman he settles with—I fear they'll both die mournful and lonesome deaths. But should his children turn against his thoughtless and selfish ways, should they take my journal and pass all the tests required by that Spanish priest, then I've left for them my writing as my treasure. I don't know why I done it except maybe someday there would be a girl like me who felt the itch to make something more of her life, to find adventure and love, and everything in between, so here we are. This here's my message to you—that priest left a trap that none except a man like Adam could pass through, but he also left something else in there... a test of love, that would only be overcome when a man loved a woman as deep as Adam loves his Eva, and she him.

The treasure ain't what's important. We go into this life seeking it, and then we leave it all in death—not able to take our riches with us. Yet, that don't matter. Without our treasures, we are far richer than we ever imagined. Someday, my grave will lie next to my husband's. He is my life, though I will die again, this time more at peace. And somewhere to the side will be another grave, and it will run deep and full. A grave meant for Eden Cassidy. And it won't be empty.

—All my love, Eden and Eva

The treasure was buried in Eden's grave—there was no other explanation. And so we stood with our shovels in that graveyard in that sweet little mountain hideaway that Adam had shared with his wife, Eva. I stared at the inscription on the tombstone where they had wrapped the heavy chain around it. "My life," it said. The chain had seemed odd before, but now it seemed symbolic because this was where they had sealed up the treasure.

Caitlyn filmed the whole thing. Bill had even come with Frank and Harlan. We'd gotten Pat through by very difficult means, but he was a hardy fellow and eager to join in the fun, so there was no question of leaving him behind.

The old men had grown up in this town surrounded by the legends of the treasure, and they knew everything about it, especially Bill, who'd had these tales passed down to him through his family. He patted me on the back, his gaze on Hunter. "You've found yourself a good one, girl. Aren't you glad I played matchmaker?"

More than anything. Hunter stood with Brek, waist-deep in the hole that they'd dug into the ground, taking turns shoveling through the hard dirt. Hunter had shoved the short sleeves of his black tee-shirt up his massive biceps. He gave me a wink when he caught me staring. Brek tried hard to ignore our playful back and forth, but finally he flipped some dirt into Hunter's face to get him to pay attention. Caitlyn giggled and Brek smiled up at her—too long, so that this time, Hunter had to push him to get him back to work.

Bill was having the time of his life. "You think I should get those two together?"

I looked over at my best friend and my brother. Why not? It was about time Brek found a girl I could stand. I smiled over at Bill. "Definitely."

Hunter and Brek pushed their shovels through the ground until they hit against something hard. This was it. We all drew to attention. They cleared off the remaining dust from the rotting wood of a coffin as the rest of us leaned over and sat on the edge of the hole to watch as Hunter broke open the lid, then the two men eased it open.

Sure enough, the thing was filled with coins. They were dusty, but when Hunter picked one up and scratched it, he grinned. "It's the real thing!"

Caitlyn let out a shocked cry, and the old men whooped out in delight. We had promised them all an equal share of the find, whatever that was. As for Brekker and I—my debts and mom's new apartment had already been paid off by our YouTube sponsors. My brother was now free of Rooney after Gordon had worked out a deal with the powerful man—he returned the jewels and, to make up for any hurt feelings, gave him a fifty-fifty cut of his next find in the heart of Russia.

Brek had promised me he'd steer clear of them all, which in theory wouldn't be too hard since Gordon was on house arrest for evading taxes on his finds. It was all part of the bargain plea after the raid on his warehouse. Caitlyn had caught everything on her phone about our father, but Gordon had the sleaziest lawyers in existence and we hadn't been able to prove much. Rumor was that Gordon worked deals from his new home base. We didn't know if they involved Angel, though the last we'd heard of her, she was conducting guided white-water tours in Moab. That wouldn't keep her happy for long.

I jumped into the hole, leaning next to Hunter as I reached into Eden's coffin and ran my hand through the coins, liking the feel of them through my fingers, until I finally decided on one and picked it up. It looked exactly like Bill's coin we'd stolen—the Lover's Trap on one side and the missing section of the symbol on the other. "I guess they just had more than they could ever spend," I said.

"Can you imagine the interest that Bill would've had if they had put this in the bank?" Brek said.

Bill laughed. "I'm not greedy. I already own 400,000 acres of this land. Adam bought it back in the day. My parents bought my cousins out, so I'm the sole inheritor."

This was all Bill's? We all froze. I'd known he owned the Grizzly, but… this land was worth a pretty penny. It was just another secret he'd kept from us. We were all silenced by the revelation, except Pat, who toddled closer, mumbling under his breath. I finally could make out what he was saying—he was going off on taxes.

Bill rolled his eyes. "Don't bother me about that! I can see why Adam and Eden finally decided to bury it. They wouldn't want us kids to have it too easy anyway. We turned out all right without it."

"Yeah, I've seen what too much money can do," Hunter said, looking grim before he pushed out of the hole. He gave me his hand and helped me out too.

Pat started going off on inheritance laws. "Yup," Bill said, easily interpreting the old accountant. "No way are we paying most of this out to Federal and State. Keep the camera on, Caitlyn, this is a good teaching moment. The government's going to try to take 47% out because of a finder's tax, but luckily I've got myself a good accountant." He patted Pat's frail shoulders.

Brek finally caught on and beamed. "They can't do that when it already belongs to you."

"Very good," Bill said. "It rightfully belongs to my very great grandmother. And this state goes easy on the inheritance tax. You see, when it comes to finding treasure, it's all about location, location, location."

Pat nodded his head in agreement.

We let the others drone on about taxes as Hunter took my hand and led me through that little cemetery and out of the grove of trees to get to Adam and Eden's cabin. The storm from the morning was lifting. The sun shone through the clouds and gave the mountains and the sparkling stream of water a soft, pastel glow.

We made our way to the porch of the cabin and sat down. Hunter leaned against the wall of logs and I found a post to rest my back against while we watched the lazy clouds in the sky above us. Hunter moved my legs to rest on his lap, and I felt like we were an old couple enjoying each other's company after years of sharing sunsets like this. Maybe Eden had done so with Adam as they'd dreamed of the years to come.

After a moment, I broke the companionable silence with an idea Caitlyn had suggested to me earlier that day. "We have an idea for a new YouTube show," I said.

He groaned and rubbed my legs. "Didn't we learn from the last one?"

"Yes," I admitted, "but this one could be more scientifically based, kind of like something you might find on the Discovery Channel."

"And what are we supposed to do?" Hunter asked. "Live off our glory days from this find?"

"No, we can find new treasure. That's the fun part. Brek does it all the time… and you did too, so you both are experts. It's the adventure, the thrill of the chase—that would be the fun part of this series!"

He smiled. "You are more like your brother than you think."

"I guess I am." I sighed happily and turned back to the horizon. There was a rainbow. If I was superstitious, which I wasn't, I'd say on the other side of it was our treasure; but it wasn't gold or silver, it was being together. I found Hunter's hand and squeezed it.

"I'll do it," he said, "on one condition."

He was talking conditions again. I usually liked his conditions, and so I pulled forward eagerly. "What would that be?"

Before he could tell me, Caitlyn shouted over to us, running through the thicket of trees. Brek was holding something in his hands, and when he came closer, I saw that it was a parchment. He pushed it at me when he reached us. "Look what we found."

My hand brushed over the tattered edge, and I hoped against hope that it was another message from Eden. Those were far better than any of the riches that we'd found so far. But it wasn't that—it was a map. "Brek thinks that's from the Spanish priest Gabriel de Padilla," Caitlyn said. "We found it in Eden's coffin."

Hunter straightened, and we both pushed to our feet to study it— it was an illustration of this entire mountain with shadings for elevation and lakes and rivers. It seemed pretty accurate, with a few slight differences. The priest had coated it with more Spanish symbols. "What's it say?" I asked.

Brek pulled closer to look over my shoulder, and between him and Hunter, they translated it. The map held the record of all the treasure hidden in the mountains—as the Spanish priest had promised. It wasn't just the gold coins. He'd been a busy man, and in turn these treasure hunts would keep us all busy for years. Not that we needed the money, the riches, or the fame anymore.

Brek pulled it away so that Caitlyn could make a big deal over it. "We're going to have to get a lot of permits for this," she said.

He smiled at her. "Most of them from Bill. Your *best friend's* land is a jackpot. Maybe I should just let him go through with his matchmaking schemes."

That pulled a surprised laugh out of her. "Oh? Don't I get a say?"

"No, that's the beauty of matchmaking. You just run out of gas somewhere because someone conveniently cuts the fuel line."

She turned a shy smile on him. "Stop talking and kiss me already."

Hunter took my hand and pulled me away from the two while they flirted. My grin felt out of control. They were moving too fast, even for me. But now that I had Hunter to myself, I wanted to go back to our unfinished business. "What was that condition you were talking about?"

He broke into a reluctant smile. "Only that if this show we're doing is with you, I'm in."

"Deal!" I threw my arms around his neck and pressed my lips against his to complete our little business arrangement.

He pulled away, his eyes probing mine, and I found myself getting lost in those hazel depths. "I'm not talking more episodes of *Poison Ivy and Fortune Hunter*," he said. "I'm thinking more like *Mr. and Mrs. Hunter Gatherer*, the boring married couple that everybody puts the snooze button on. And we'll grow old together just like Adam and Eden."

I beamed. Hunter got me—he was my other half, and I wrapped my arms around him. "I wouldn't have it any other way!" I said.

"Marry me?" he asked and stepped back to pluck a tiny miniature from his pocket. It was far from the diamond ring that I'd expected, but more sentimental. It was a bear charm from the Grizzly. "For your bracelet. It's time you got some of your own adventures on there."

I teared up, and he hugged me tightly. "Yes," I said. "Yes. Let's have lots of adventures together! I *will* marry you!"

Looking over his shoulder, I saw Brek laugh and pick Caitlyn up in a hug and swing her around—they both talked a mile a minute. Now that our hearts weren't set on the treasure, we had everything we needed right here in front of us—a sweet little cabin near the woods, a stream babbling merrily to our side, fresh mountain air, and someone to love.

I squeezed him tighter.

The end

Author bio

Stephanie Fowers loves bringing stories to life, and depending on her latest madcap ideas will do it through written word, song, and/ or film. She absolutely adores Bollywood and bonnet movies; i.e., BBC (which she supposes includes non-bonnet movies Sherlock and Dr. Who). Presently, she lives in Salt Lake where she's living the life of the starving artist.

Latest projects include, a workshop of her musical, "The Raven" in Canada with the talented composer, Hilary Hornberger. She also expects to produce some short films with Triad Film Productions. Stephanie plans to bring more of her novels out to greet the light of day. Be sure to watch for her upcoming books: including books from her Hopeless Romantic Collection, her YA fantasy "Twisted Tales," romantic suspense, an apocalyptic science fiction series, Greek Romance Regencies, Steampunk adventures, and more—many more—romantic comedies. May the adventures begin!

For more information, see: www.fowersbooks.com

For more information on Twisted Tales Series (including faery hunter guide and glossary), see: www.stephanie-fowers.com

For more information on The Raven, a new musical, see: https://www.themusicalhub.com/ho.html

Made in the USA
San Bernardino, CA
02 April 2019